TRUE NORTH

ARIA WYATT

Cover design by Lori Jackson Design
Photographer: Wander Aguiar
Editing by Silvia's Reading Corner and Eve Arroyo Editing
Proofreading by My Brother's Editor, Proofingstyle, Inc., Virginia Tesi Carey, and Amy Briggs
Formatting: Champagne Book Design

Paperback ISBN: 978-1-7359505-0-1

To my husband

This one is for you.
Sorry, but this is as outdoorsy as I'll ever get.
Thank you for supporting my dream and believing in me, and for our beautiful children.
I appreciate you for always making me laugh, keeping me fed, and killing the spiders.
And thanks for looking at me the way Wes looks at Lena.

With all my love,
Your favorite armchair adventurer

TRUE N⊕RTH

CHAPTER 1

LENA HAMILTON

Internal playlist: "Citizen of the Planet" by Alanis Morissette

There is no way in hell this plane is safe to fly. Not only is it too small, but it looks like a fifth grader built it from some cheapo hobby shop kit they found on the clearance table. What gave me the brilliant idea to book a charter flight in the first place? Better yet, what made me think *any* aspect of this trip was wise?

I turn to the freckle-faced kid stuffing my enormous suitcase into the cargo area. "You sure this qualifies as a plane? I mean, is it even made of metal?"

"Yeah." He slams the compartment door shut. "It's aluminum."

I touch the side of the so-called aircraft. "Aluminum *foil?*"

He snorts. "First time in Alaska?"

"What gave you that impression?"

"Let's call it a hunch." He motions to the door. "Hurry up and get in. We've got some shitty weather headed this way, so the pilot's getting antsy."

Oh, great. Miniature plane, bad weather, and an antsy pilot. Sounds like an ominous trifecta of "what the hell am I doing?" Judging by the way my Spidey senses are tingling, something tells me it's a full moon too. And Mercury is in retrograde. Might as well factor in some black cats and broken mirrors for good measure.

What could possibly go wrong?

I know better than to speculate on the possible outcomes; more often than not, the universe responds with a mic drop. As my foot snags in the tiny plane's stupid doorway, sending me airborne, I realize this time's no exception. I shriek and make a feeble attempt to catch myself—wayward limbs flailing like a drunk marionette—but I fail. Miserably.

I land facedown across a pair of jean-clad thighs, knocking the wind out of me. "*Oomph.*"

Mic drop.

"Whoa." A visceral grunt rumbles from the steel lap's owner. His huge palms settle on my lower back, their heat radiating through my sweater. "How the hell did ya manage that?"

Wheezing, I clutch the passenger's shirt. "Oh my God, I'm so sorry."

"No worries." He squeezes my shoulder. "I'll award a nine point eight for style."

The man's sexy accent is *not* one I'd expect to hear this far north of the equator in Fairbanks, Alaska. I roll onto my back.

Wes Emerson.

Forget the mic drop—recognition just throat punched me.

The Australian actor's vivid blue gaze sucks the oxygen from the cabin. My uterus trumpets a fanfare and both ovaries roll out the welcome mat. Meanwhile, my brain short-circuits, spewing thoughts in Morse code.

I'm in Wes Emerson's lap. The Wes Emerson. Oh my God. Get off him, you ass!

I lurch upward, whack my head on the armrest, and tumble to the floor.

"Holy hell!" Wes kneels beside me and grips my shoulders, the contact sending a flare of heat to the South-Central region of my anatomy. "Are you all right?"

I squeak like a seagull with laryngitis.

He's touching me. Oh my God, he's touching me!

He waves a hand in front of my face. "Hello? You okay?"

No, I'm a shitshow, but thanks for asking.

In true hot mess fashion, I laugh. I've always envied those women blessed with girly laughs—the tinkling fairy kind that makes them seem cute. Meanwhile, I'm over here doing a snort-cry-wheeze like an asthmatic Miss Piggy. With Wes Emerson—the hottest dude on the fucking planet—as witness.

His plush lips twitch into a smirk. "Your first landing was better."

Glorious muscles bulge beneath his hunter-green thermal. He's shoved both sleeves to his elbows, exposing corded forearms. A bird tattoo on his left wrist flaps its wings at me. His tawny surfer hair boasts golden highlights courtesy of the Australian sun. Cropped on the sides and back, with the longer top section tousled, it begs to be touched. My gaze slides over his tanned neck and powerful shoulders.

Wes leans over, and his cobalt irises ensnare me from beneath a fringe of dark lashes.

Sweet Jesus, those eyes—

"Seriously, are ya hurt? You clocked your noggin there." He grabs my hand and hauls me up.

Absorbing the enormity of his firm grip, I imagine his hands ravaging my body. I morph from Miss Piggy into a pouty angelfish, my mouth opening and closing with each shallow, attempted breath.

"Did ya hear me?"

I smooth the hair from my face and wipe my eyes. "Uh-huh."

"Then how about answering me?"

"I'm fabulous, and yourself?" I snatch the scattered items that fell out of my purse and shove them back in. "I'm sorry. I don't know what happened there, but if it's any sign of where this vacation's headed, I'm done." I gesture to him. "What are you doing on my charter?"

He cocks his head. "I could ask *you* that same question."

I blink a few times instead of answering. *No way. We can't possibly be staying at the same resort. He's a freaking celebr—*

Wes smirks again. "Questions give ya a bit of stage fright, huh? All right, we'll do statements then. I'll go first." His smirk widens into a megawatt smile. "I'm waiting for my best mates to get their arses on this plane. They're late, as usual. The three of us are flying to the Aurora Borealis resort for a two-week stay. Your turn."

As the universe revs her engine, I play a deer in headlights. This is ludicrous. I'm the kind of woman who can handle her shit. I am *never* speechless. Yet, in a matter of minutes, he's turned me into a goddamn mute, utterly incapable of forming sentences.

He chuckles and rubs his jaw. "Let's try this again." He speaks slowly, like he's worried about my language comprehension skills. "We'll start with your name."

"Lena."

"Oh, good. Your vocal cords *do* work." His grin makes my face heat. "I'm Wes."

"I know."

"What're ya doing on *my* charter, *Lena?*" His resonant Aussie timbre caresses the syllables, throwing gasoline on the bonfire in my nether regions.

The universe skewers some marshmallows and passes them around.

Don't just stare at him. Speak.

I shake my head. "I was browsing travel sites on Thursday afternoon and stumbled across a listing for the Aurora Borealis. It was cheap, so I assumed they had a last-minute opening."

"My brother backed out on Wednesday . . ." He turns his attention to the doorway as another man boards our tiny plane. "It's about bloody time."

My eyes follow, no doubt widening into saucers. *Holy shit. He's friends with Jake Bennett?*

The multi-platinum baritone's chestnut locks are windblown, and he's tucked the ends of a charcoal wool scarf into his gunmetal-gray parka.

Jake's chocolate gaze finds me and flares in surprise. "I see we've got company?" He smiles, and the warmth reaches his eyes. "Hello there. Welcome aboard."

Unlike Wes, Jake's demeanor instantly puts me at ease. While I'm a huge fan of his music, and find him attractive, there's no lightning bolt physical reaction to his presence—my ovaries are too preoccupied with Wes to care.

I return Jake's smile. "Hello and thank you."

"Were you two idiots chasing a root or something?" Wes mutters.

Jake snorts. "Nah, dude. There weren't any women in there. Besides, I'm celibate at this point."

Wes throws his arms up. "Then where the hell ya been?"

"Memphis had to take a leak." Jake glances at me and clears his throat. "I mean, he needed to use the restroom."

Wes points to his watch. "Takes the bloke twenty minutes to piss?"

"Dunno, dude. I left him by the vending machines. He said he needed another snack." Jake leans back and peers out the door. "Relax. He's coming."

Wes eyes me with something resembling annoyance. "What're ya gonna do, stand for the whole flight?"

I slide into the seat behind him and fasten my seat belt. "While your lap was more comfortable, I think I'll park it here."

He swivels toward me and his scowl deepens, making me realize I said it aloud. *Shit.* I peek at my phone as warmth spreads across my face.

Hey, universe, pass me a marshmallow, would you?

"Did y'all try any of this caribou jerky?" The honeyed drawl oozes from the man who boards with a guitar case in tow.

Austin "Memphis" Pines.

No biggie, he's only an international pop superstar I've fangirled for two decades. From the black fedora that conceals his iconic, sandy pompadour, to the unbuttoned blazer he paired with a snug, navy T-shirt and jeans, Austin is the epitome of smooth Memphis soul. My preteen self would have stroked out and died by now. Adult Lena, while still excited to meet him, is busy following my ovaries' lead, sending out pheromones to his buddy from Down Under.

Austin hands his guitar to Wes. "Hold my baby."

"C'mon, mate. I don't wanna bump uglies with your guitar," Wes grumbles, accepting the instrument. "They couldn't fit it underneath?"

"Nah, somebody's big-ass, red suitcase is hoggin' the compartment." Sparkling baby blues meet my gaze. "Mornin', miss." He flashes the smile featured on the posters I once plastered my teenage walls with. "Must be *your* big-ass, red suitcase down there."

I smile. "Guilty as charged."

Austin glances at Wes. "The lodge musta hopped on the chance to sell Reed's room."

Wes twists in his seat and stares at me again. "Yep."

I booked his brother's room, which means I'll spend my entire trip with them. *And it looks like Crocodile Dundee isn't happy about it.*

His gaze burns into me, so I shift in my seat. I know this feeling. Suddenly I'm that nurse who dares to hang out in the physician's lounge at the hospital. Unwelcome and out of my league.

"I know what you're all thinking, 'Some girl's crashing our boys' trip.' Don't worry, I plan to make myself scarce."

"Lena, for the record, that doesn't scratch the surface of what I'm thinking," Wes murmurs, turning his back to me.

What the hell does that mean? "Talk in riddles, much?"

He spins back around. "What's always in front of you but can't be seen?"

I raise a brow. "I'm sorry, what?"

Austin settles beside Wes with a chuckle. "Somethin' tells me it's gonna be a *long* flight."

"You wanted a riddle. Now ya got one." Wes grins, mischief glinting in his eyes. "You gonna give me an answer?"

Courtesy of the maintenance guys at work, I know every corny dad joke—and riddle—in the book. I *know* I've heard this one before, but my memory fails me.

"Uh . . ."

"Tell you what." His gaze drifts to my parted lips and lingers for a beat. "I'll let ya think about it and get back to me." He faces front once more.

Jake smirks and shrugs out of his parka, sliding into the seat next to me. "Ready for an adventure, Lena?"

Is this really happening? The universe gives me a thumbs up, and it dawns on me that Jake asked a question. "Um . . . yeah."

Stupefied beyond belief, I withdraw a novel from my purse. I can't focus on the words, but it makes an excellent shield, and I need to do something besides gawk. With a sharp pinch to my inner thigh, confirming I *am* actually awake and alive, I force a deep inhale and vow to play the part of a grown-ass, professional woman, despite feeling like an oversexed superfan.

The antsy pilot fires up the engines, and before long, we're airborne. I gaze out the window in awe as we fly over immense tundra, glaciers, and gorges. Boreal forests span the horizon, untouched by mankind's destructive hands. Evergreens speckle snowcapped mountains like in a middle schooler's diorama.

Jake taps my shoulder. "Business or pleasure?"

"Excuse me?"

"Are you traveling for business or pleasure?"

"Oh. Um . . . pleasure, I guess."

He cocks his head. "Doesn't sound too convincing."

Actually, it's neither. The impromptu Alaskan odyssey was born from

Garrett Casey's suggestion. My childhood best friend is the steadying force that keeps me grounded, even when it means convincing me to take to the air.

As a Manhattan trauma nurse, days filled with death and chaos are the norm, and I've always had a "take no prisoners" approach. Nurse Lena is the epitome of unflappable, but this week far surpassed the level of pandemonium I'm used to. The unprecedented shitstorm finally broke me and earned me an exile. Worse than the embarrassment of my breakdown, is the weight of my own disappointment. I don't seize up or falter. I'm not supposed to crack under pressure.

But I did.

On my way out the door for the forced leave of absence, my boss's surprise offer of a promotion added torque to my tailspin. At one point in my life, nurse supervisor would have been a dream position, but now I'm not so sure. My uncertainty has me questioning everything that once seemed set in stone. How can Dr. Soteris possibly see me as a qualified candidate for the job when I fell apart in the middle of the ER with all of my colleagues as witness? Now, the very fabric of who I am has a giant hole, and I'm not sure whether to sew it back up, or let it unravel.

"More like solace, self-reflection, and distraction," I mutter.

"Alaska speaks to the soul-searcher." Jake nods his approval. "Where are you from?"

"Upstate New York." Since many people hear "New York" and automatically assume the city, I always try to be specific. "I was born in the Catskills, but I live in Brooklyn now."

He nudges Austin. "Get this, we both live in Brooklyn."

"What do you do for a livin', Lena?" Austin drawls.

While my career is the *last* thing I feel like talking about, Austin seems genuinely interested, and it's not every day one of my teenage idols asks me a question.

"Lena Hamilton's a nurse," Wes announces, before I can even open my mouth.

My head jerks in his direction. "I never told you my last name. How'd—"

"My crystal ball's always ready, and my clairvoyance kicks in at the half-hour mark." Wes glances at his watch and flashes a cocky grin. "I'm ahead of schedule this morning. Must be on top of my game."

You can be on top of my game. Or under it . . . inside it.

I flush at the conjured visuals. "How do you know I'm a nurse?"

He taps his head and winks.

"You'd do a lot more than wink if you could read my mind." The statement leaves my lips before I can stop it.

Me thinks I need a muzzle.

Heat spreads from my cheeks, to my neck, to the cleavage my red V-neck displays. My unflappable hospital persona drains my ability to keep up the no-nonsense demeanor outside of work. In fact, any trace of professional behavior evaporates into thin air the moment I leave through those double doors. Courtesy of my lack of filter, real life Lena rules supreme in the land of flushed skin and blurted statements.

"It's refreshing to meet a woman who speaks her mind, but you didn't intend for that one to slip, did ya?" Wes raises a brow.

This time, I'm too flustered to respond. And that pisses me right off.

"That's all right, we'll skip this question since I already know your answer. You've got your pink cheeks to thank for that. Hell, I could've left my ball in 'Straya."

I've seen many interviews with Wes on TV, and I've always found his pronunciation of Australia incredibly sexy. Turns out, it's even hotter in person. I have half a mind to ask him to repeat himself.

Jake snorts. "No one's interested in any of your balls, bro."

"Are ya sure about that, Bennett?" Wes winks at me.

You smug bastard.

I cock my head and reach for my bag. "Got something in your eye? I have a mirror in my purse." I make a show of rummaging through and discover my hospital badge is missing. I thrust my hand in his face. "Give it to me."

"I've heard that one before." Wes grins and hands over my lanyard. "Cute picture."

I shove the badge in my purse. I'd forgotten about the hospital's decision to update their personnel files. As typical, the universe dealt me a low blow, with the mandatory retake of my employee photo on the day after I called off my engagement to Marc. The hideous picture features my puffy, red-rimmed eyes, dark circles, and a resting bitch face that could freeze lava.

I glare at Wes.

He smirks like the smug bastard he is. "Wow. Your smile's brighter than the sunrise. Bet they call ya *sunshine*."

Jake smacks Wes on the head. "C'mon, man. Stop antagonizing her."

"I'm making an observation, mate. Antagonizing her would be pointing out that's now the *third* time she's blushed in the last ten minutes." Wes flashes a self-satisfied grin and winks *again*.

Never breaking eye contact, I scratch the side of my nose with a not-so-discreet middle finger.

Wes's brows shoot up. He opens his mouth to speak. Then closes it. He pins his gaze to mine, with the hint of a smile playing at his lips.

I flash a sultry wink and watch in amusement as his pupils dilate and his smile widens. Relieved to feel my old sass returning, I settle deeper into my seat.

Take that, Wesley Emerson.

Did I goad Wes with the wink? Absolutely. But I wasn't prepared for his unyielding attention. Now, his gaze becomes a physical weight that freezes my lungs, making it impossible to breathe.

"Got an answer for my riddle yet?"

"No, you told me to think about it and get back to you."

He purses his lips. "Time's up."

"Oh? I wasn't aware of a deadline."

"Well, I'm tired of waitin' for ya."

"Then perhaps you should've made the parameters clear from the start."

"Perhaps." He chuckles. "But where's the fun in that?"

Every time he speaks, my heart speeds up and my brain short-circuits. Then he smiles, and my overworked neurons go on strike. Yep, in a few short minutes, he reduced me to fried synapses and a thundering pulse. I'd feel more comfortable in a room full of surgeons and that dick anesthesiologist from the OR.

My book shield flies back up.

"Must be an interesting story," he says.

Actually, the book sucks, but there's no way in hell I'll admit that he's more interesting.

"It's fascinating," I reply without looking at him.

Wes snatches my romance novel and reads it aloud, "Hands knotting in her hair, his kiss was fire—"

"Give it back." I reach for my shield, but he yanks it away.

"I'd imagine a fiery kiss would burn." Wes cocks his head. "I mean, hot coffee to the lips is bad enough, but flames—"

"You're gonna burn in a minute."

"Is that a promise?"

"Keep pushing me and you'll find out."

"Maybe I'm waiting for ya to say 'please.'"

I clench my jaw. "Give. It. To. Me."

"Now, *that's* even better than please." Wes grins and hands me back my book. "Knew I could make you say it again."

Heat spreads from my cheeks to my neck and lower. The fucking bonfire is out of control and everyone tossed their marshmallows into the flames. I draw a shaky breath and return to my book. But it doesn't matter—it's not like I can focus on the words.

Approximately two hours later, Austin straightens in his seat and points out the window. "Looks like we're approachin' our destination, y'all."

I peer through the glass. A narrow, crystalline lake stretches for miles. As we descend, I focus on the lodge. Set against the backdrop of the rugged Brooks Range, the structure is several stories tall with a steeply sloped roof. A wide balcony extends the length of the building, overlooking Caribou Lake.

We touch down in a small clearing. After the antsy pilot fiddles with his instruments and shuts down the engine, he opens the hatch. Aviator sunglasses in place, Wes hops to the ground and moves aside so the rest of us can exit.

I grip the sides of the doorway, preparing to jump out, when a large hand appears.

"I'd rather not watch you faceplant again."

I accept Wes's hand and gingerly land beside him. "Yeah, Grace is not my middle name." I tuck a strand of hair behind my ear. "Thanks."

He gives me a curt nod before turning his back.

I scan the scenery around me. My experience with Alaska is limited to images on a wall calendar. To see the majestic landscape in person is awe inspiring. Tears prick the backs of my eyes at the tundra's beauty. While shin to knee high vegetation covers much of the land, a small forest cloaks the base of the mountains and plenty of trees surround the lodge.

"I'm assuming this one's yours?" Wes lifts my big-ass suitcase from the compartment and hands it over. "Quite the minimalist, aren't we? Do ya always travel with bricks?"

I know I overpacked, but I like being prepared. It's late summer back home, but here the leaves are already changing color, and it's much colder than Brooklyn. My suitcase is heavier than it appears, loaded with winter clothes and a dozen book boyfriends to keep me warm. Garrett lectured me about packing too many books for a cross-country trip involving charter planes. Yes, he had a point, but I don't care. While I own two different e-readers, I prefer the physicality of a book. I also plan to go on some excursions, so it's not like the wilderness is loaded with electrical outlets to charge the damn battery. Besides, this is my time to unplug.

I peer up into Wes's obscenely blue eyes. "You never know what you might need."

Though I felt varying degrees of warmth from all three men, Wes is the one who most intrigues me, which makes no sense. He almost reminds me of the hotshot doctors at work—the ones whose arrogance turns my stomach. While I'm blessed to have a boss who treats me like an equal, the hospital hierarchy of doctors as gods is pervasive. Nauseating. As a trauma nurse, I spend my days with pompous surgeons who think their shit doesn't stink. Like their white coats are somehow superior to my scrubs. Bastards who take all the credit when I'm the one covered in their patient's blood—exhausted and underappreciated. Nursing is a thankless job, made worse by those who can't see our worth. While I proudly lack the doctors' hubris, I'm tired of being their afterthought. Let's face it; my life's forgotten footnote act is getting old. I deserve better.

I want to dislike Wes, but for whatever reason, I'm drawn to him. Not just physically, but during our flight—when I listened to the guys joke around—he seemed the most thoughtful, the quickest to deflect attention, and generous with his laughter. He's also the one who seems most perturbed by my presence, vacillating from teasingly intrigued to thoughtful to straight up annoyed, then back again. I swear, the dude gave me whiplash on the tiny plane.

Regardless of the tension between us, my attraction to him is undeniable. His face, his eyes, the body, that accent. Wes is resplendent. He has a sly sense of humor and a quick wit that makes me laugh—when I'm not blushing. He's an infuriating combination of cocky and charismatic. And even though he's not on a movie set, it feels like there's a hint of performance, even in his camaraderie with the guys. I wonder who he trusts to share his inner thoughts with. While he may not be thrilled to have me here, I hope to spend more time with him.

My eyes linger on his fine ass. After all, I paid for this view.

Two resort employees roll up in an extended golf cart. They introduce themselves and take over, placing our duffels and suitcases in the back. Thank God I'm finally done hefting my overstuffed luggage around—my old injury is killing me. The porters invite us to ride the short distance to the lodge. The men pile on, making the thing look like a clown car.

"You coming, Lena?" Wes asks, pointing to the empty place beside him. "I don't bite." The wicked gleam in his eyes tells me otherwise, making my lady bits quiver.

"Thanks, but I need to stretch my legs." I adjust the purse on my aching shoulder and smile. While I'd love to sit beside him, I want to give the guys some space, and I need to soak up the peace after the long hours of travel.

He frowns. "You sure?"

"Yep. I'll meet you guys there."

He says something to the porter, who nods and puts the golf cart into gear. I wave at the others as the vehicle ferries them to the main cabin.

Trudging along a gravel path, I take in the lofty, deep-green spruces, which contrast with the golden leaves of the birch trees. Rich crimsons and burnished oranges set the tundra ablaze, and brilliant hues shimmer against a sapphire sky streaked with pinks and purples.

The Hudson Valley doesn't hold a candle to this.

I hum to myself as I walk. This is good. I need some nature in my life. Some of the tension that has clung to me since my hospital ordeal, starts to dissipate.

"Let's go, frontier woman, you're holding us up," Wes calls as I approach. He shifts his weight impatiently. "Some of us are ready to relax."

"You guys didn't need to wait for me. I was taking in the view." I toy with the end of my braid and follow the men inside. *Looks like I'm back in the surgeons' lounge again.*

The concierge greets us in the foyer. Tall and lean, she's tied her straight, black hair in a tidy ponytail. Light brown skin, high cheekbones, and wide, dark eyes serve as evidence of her Inuit heritage.

"Welcome to Aurora Borealis. I hope you had a smooth journey. I'd like to show you around and get you settled into your rooms. The porter will deliver your luggage before you get there. My name's Ellen, and I'm your point-person. Our resort's all-inclusive, with three family-style meals served daily. If you have questions about the menu or any dietary restrictions, our kitchen's located downstairs." Ellen motions toward the staircase. "Besides the kitchen, you'll also find our fitness room . . ."

Fitness room? Images of Wes pumping iron make my heart beat faster. *Thick, bulging muscles covered with a sheen of sweat. Heavy breathing . . . grunts of exertion . . .* I shake my head and try to focus on Ellen's words.

". . . laundry facilities and massage amenities."

Massage? Oh, add that to my list. I shift my weight and rub at my throbbing shoulders. My entire body aches after the long day of travel.

"Your muscles wouldn't hurt if ya packed less," Wes points out.

I meet his gaze. "Minimalism's not my strong suit."

"Good thing you've got others." He winks and follows his friends.

Wait, what?

As we enter the great room, Ellen describes the resort-sponsored activities, which include fishing, canoeing, hiking, and overnight camping excursions.

I listen distractedly and take in the golden rays of sunlight that filter through a wall of floor-to-ceiling windows. A set of French doors opens onto the balcony that overlooks the lake. In the center of the room, a chandelier of intertwined antlers and candles illuminates a mahogany table with seating for twelve. On one end of the room, several armchairs are positioned in front of a stone fireplace with a rustic, wooden mantel. It looks like the perfect spot to curl up with a book.

Or Wes.

I follow as the guys climb the staircase to the second floor. The four guest rooms are located on a loft overlooking the great room.

As Ellen shows us our room assignments, Wes slows his pace to walk beside me. "Did ya forget about my riddle?"

"Nope, but I was kinda hoping you did."

He laughs. "Need a refresher?"

"Uh, sure." *Make that a refreshment. As in, a fucking bottle of wine.*

"What's always in front of you but can't be seen?"

"Okay, you've got me." I pause outside my door, fiddling with my room key. "I'm stumped."

"C'mon, it's an easy one." Wes smiles and my lungs take another sabbatical. "Think about it, Lena." Then he turns and disappears down the hall.

Baffled, I enter my room and close the door behind me. Flopping onto the bed, I reach for my phone and call Garrett. While he may not appreciate Wes's sex appeal, Garrett has a general appreciation for the appeal of sex. Hopefully, I don't interrupt a phone-a-fuck session with one of his women. I'm probably the only female in the Tri-State area who's immune to Garrett's allure. Sure, he's gorgeous and smart and funny, but he's like a brother to me.

He answers on the second ring. "Miss me already, Leens?"

"Gar, you will *not believe* this!"

CHAPTER 2

LENA

Internal playlist: "Drumming Song" by Florence + The Machine

Best friends are worth their weight in gold. Or in this case, attention spans and auditory nerves. Garrett listens to every detail of my celebrity encounter. He's good like that. We talk about everything and that's why I love him so much. While he couldn't care less about a man—or his muscles, accent, gorgeous eyes, and tousled hair—he'll *always* let me talk. Sadly, I have a history of attaching myself to men who don't hear me. Garrett's not like that. He'll listen ad nauseam, but he's not afraid to make his opinion known. Even if it pisses me off.

"He sounds like a cocky fuck."

"Oh, most definitely. Way cockier than Dr. Murray in neurology." I grimace as I think about the physician who always makes me feel like I'm beneath him—and not in a sexy way.

"Then what's the appeal? You hate arrogance."

"I dunno, Gar. He's got a strange mix of flirty, dick-headed charisma that I can't seem to ignore."

"Ignore it, Leens. You deserve better than some asshole who acts like you didn't pay to be there." He clears his throat. "Now that I can picture the exact shade of Emerson's eyes, let's get back to business; have you checked out the fitness center?"

I squeeze my phone and thump my fist on the nightstand a few times. "Ugh."

Garrett chuckles in my ear. "Are you stomping?"

"No, I'm not stomping," I mutter with an eye roll he can't see. "Just beating on the furniture."

"C'mon, Leens, don't get pissed at me. You asked for this, remember?"

"I asked you to keep me focused, not *force* me to exercise."

"I'm not *forcing* you to do anything. You asked me to train you for our run. That means I expect you to hold up your end of the bargain and actually do what I tell you."

"But I'm on vacation," I whine.

"No one's asking you to do the Iditarod. All I said was to get your ass on the treadmill. You went on and on about the all-inclusive meals. Go ahead and eat some fucking muffins, but don't forget, use of the fitness room is also *included*."

He's right; I *did* make him promise to keep me motivated for my fitness goals. I stupidly agreed to run a 10k race with him in the spring. I am *not* a runner. In fact, if someone sees me running, they ought to follow because there's a damn good reason for it—like a wildebeest stampede or something. I *only* agreed to the race because it's for a good cause. One of his favorite employees has lupus and he's raising money for the Lupus Foundation in her name. His secretary, Juliana, is a sweetheart who keeps his office in order—thereby keeping him sane—so the least I can do is push my boundaries a little.

I'm a curvy woman. In truth, I don't mind my curves. I'm not diet-obsessed, nor do I have a poor self-image. All I want is the freedom to eat my desserts and drink my wine without having to buy new clothes. Is that too much to ask?

That being said, I'm way out of shape. If I have any hope of completing this race—or, let's be real, making it past the halfway point—I need to train. I enlisted Garrett's help because he's one of those people who actually enjoys running. I guess I wasn't expecting him to take me so seriously. Then again, this is Garrett. He doesn't half-ass anything.

"You're such a bastard sometimes. I can't believe you're giving me shit from across the country."

He laughs. "Tough love, baby. Besides, I'd give you shit from no matter where I was—Antarctica, Easter Island, you name it. But, in all seriousness, remember why you took this trip in the first place."

I snort. "Wait, *why* was that again?"

"To clear your fucking head. You also need to decide what you're gonna do about your job. Dr. Soteris will expect an answer when you return."

Sure, the promotion offers a higher salary, but my indecision has nothing to do with the money. I currently enjoy financial stability. My loans are paid off, and I inherited a Brooklyn brownstone from my grandmother. Enticed by the currency of time, the crux of the issue is my desire to shed the role of spectator. There is more to life than the hospital—or so I'm told.

The past decade flew by. I was so focused on my career I missed out on everything else. Or at least it feels that way. I crave the opportunity to experience life, free time to pursue my passions. But is it foolish to turn down the promotion? It's what I've been working toward for years. I want this job. *Right?*

That's the problem—the answer is no longer automatic.

A supervisory position would mean separation from direct patient care, which might lessen some of my career's emotional burden, but the reason I became a nurse was to help people. It's a trade-off between status and personal fulfillment.

If there's one life skill I struggle with, it's balance. The scale often tips too far to the emotional side of situations. I need to learn to pull back if I hope to fill Brenda's shoes. I've idolized the retiring nurse manager for years for her ability to navigate the ideals of compassion and self-preservation.

"I don't know what I want to do," I mutter.

Garrett sighs. "Exactly my point, Leens. That's why you're there—to figure it out. Keep your focus and the answer will come to you."

"I know."

"But do yourself a favor," his voice deepens to his signature no-bull-shit tone, "don't let yourself fall for Mr. Dickhead Charisma's charms. He's *not* the kind of distraction you need right now."

I giggle. "Did you just fuck me up with some realness?"

"Damn right, I did." He gives a hearty laugh before his tone sobers again. "I'm serious, Leens. Stay focused."

"No guarantees on that one."

"Had a feeling you'd say that." He chuckles. "I still can't believe you didn't figure out the answer to his riddle."

"And *I* can't believe you know it and won't tell me."

"Seriously? Just look it up on your phone."

"Nope. I refuse to accept defeat. It'll come to me sooner or later."

He snorts. "You're gonna kick yourself when you realize how easy it was."

"Uh, when am I *not* kicking myself for something?"

"True story."

"How are my babies?" I ask, suddenly missing my fur children. I've had the pair of felines since they were kittens.

"Fat and happy. Hermione likes turkey, by the way."

"Gar! I told you not to give them people food. Harry's a diabetic for Christ's sake."

"No kidding. He bit me when I gave him his insulin. Besides, turkey's protein—not carbs."

I roll my eyes. "Whatever. Thanks for watching them for me."

"Anytime. Listen, I gotta run. Have fun, eat your muffins, and flirt if you really have to, but make sure you—"

"I know, I know. Hit up the fitness room."

"I was gonna say, be careful, but yeah, that too. I love you, Leens."

"Love you, too, Gar. Bye."

I hang up and unzip my suitcase, lip curling at the sight of my workout clothes. Stuffing my enormous boobs into a sports bra, I pull on some spandex, lace up my stupid sneakers, and head downstairs.

The light's on, but to my delight, the fitness room is vacant. As I walk in, I snag my shoelace on the barbell some idiot left inside the door. *Who does that?* It's a simple concept—put shit back where you found it. I try to move the thing, but I can't lift it. I make a mental note to mention the weight to Ellen when I go back upstairs. This way, no one will trip and break their face.

I make my way to the center of the room and climb aboard the facility's lone treadmill. Other than the stupid weight bench in front of me, which partially obscures a window, I'd call it a room with a view. If the treadmill had been facing the opposite direction, I would've been staring at a mirrored wall. The only thing I hate more than actual exercise is *watching* myself exercise. At least, here, I won't have to. I shove my earbuds in and select some old-school Salt-N-Pepa to listen to. As the karaoke bars in Brooklyn and Manhattan will attest, nothing gets me going quite like "Shoop." I crank the volume, select a moderate walking speed, and begin my dreaded workout.

As I walk, silently cursing my ineffective bra, I rattle off a few verses of my favorite song. Behind me, a sudden loud crash stops my heart and kills my vibe.

"What the hell?" I shriek, slamming the emergency stop button before I fall on my face. I hop my feet to the sides, away from the moving belt, and peer over my shoulder.

Wes stoops to retrieve the barbell. "Oops." His smirk tells me he dropped it on purpose.

Bastard.

"Oh, so *you're* the moron who left it in the doorway. Nice work. I almost busted my ass. Didn't your mother ever teach you to clean up after yourself?" My eyes narrow on his face. "What's the matter? It suddenly got too heavy for you?"

"What're ya doing in here?"

I gesture to my treadmill. "What does it *look* like I'm doing?"

"Do you really want my answer?"

"I'm exercising, thank you very much."

"Oh, that's what you're gonna call it?" He guzzles some water before setting the bottle aside and raising a brow at me. "Men are your weakness, huh?"

"*Excuse* me?" It suddenly dawns on me that he's referring to a line in "Shoop." Which I was singing *out loud* because I'm a fucking idiot. *Shit.* Before I can formulate a comeback, the universe snickers and drops her mic again.

"If I were you, I'd stick to nursing. Your singing's definitely a weakness."

I curl my lip. "Good thing no one asked for your opinion. Got a reason for interrupting me?"

He straddles the weight bench, directly in front of me, and nods to the mirrored wall. "You're blocking my view."

"I was here first." *Don't stare at his crotch. Don't stare at his crotch. Don't stare at his crotch.* I shake my head to clear it. "And you're ruining mine."

"Funny, I thought I *was* your view." Wes whips off his shirt, lowers himself to his back, and starts bench-pressing, as if to prove his point.

I blink. *Is he seriously that full of himself?* It's not even that. He's one of those men who *knows* he's gorgeous, busts his ass in the gym to *make* himself ripped, yet gets pissed when people notice.

Here's a thought, you arrogant dick, if you're so worried about being seen, don't parade your shirtless body around the resort.

Between lifts, he grunts, "And for the record, I was here before you."

"Room was empty when I got here, Ace." I defiantly resume my walk, selecting a relaxed pace. This way, he won't see my boobs jiggle as much. Let's not forget his view of my ass, courtesy of the mirror behind me.

"Went to get my water."

I shrug. "Sounds like your problem, not mine."

The barbell clanks loudly as he slams it onto the rack above him. He sits up, resting his elbows on his spread knees, and glares at me. "Why're ya here?"

"Uh, because I'm on vacation? That's typically why someone would fly to a remote lodge for two weeks."

"I mean, in *here*. Right *now*."

I point to the treadmill. "Are you dense?"

"I was down here training. Now you're here. Coincidence? I think not."

I stare at him for a second. He actually thinks I'm down here to watch him. Like I truly didn't intend to work out. The realization royally pisses me off. Looks like my promise to Garrett just got easier. Deciding Wes's idiocy doesn't deserve a response, I pop my earbuds back in and return my focus to walking.

His stare doesn't falter, and it occurs to me he's waiting for me to leave. Well, fuck that—this isn't the surgeons' lounge—I paid to be here.

"You're blocking my view," he repeats.

I glance at the timer on the treadmill's display. "I'll be out of your way in twenty-one minutes." *And not a second sooner.* I cock my head. "If you're so intent on looking at yourself, why don't you use those big muscles and slide the bench over a few feet?"

He blinks a few times and runs a hand over his face. "You're *not* going to leave?"

I give him a sweet smile and chirp, "I will in twenty minutes and thirty-seven seconds."

He crosses his huge arms over his chest. "I'll wait."

"Want me to give you a countdown? Or are those numbers a little too high for you?"

The hint of a smirk plays at the corners of his lips as he points to his watch. "No, I'll keep track."

I give him a thumbs-up and crank my music's volume. Katy Perry's "Roar" fills my ears and I grin. I've had these playlists loaded for years, and I've got the thing on shuffle, so the fact that the universe chose *this* moment for the empowering track tells me she isn't always out to fuck me.

Wes sneers. "Are ya happy with yourself?"

"Never better." I snicker inside and consider humming along to my music just to annoy him. But I'm better than that. Instead, I point to the weights. "Go ahead and do your thing. Don't let me stop you."

He rubs his jaw and glowers, watching my every move.

A little voice reminds me I'm starting to sweat, my boobs are showing more bounce than March Madness, and my ass is a bowl of Jell-O, but Katy and the universe cheer me on. He may be *People's* "Sexiest Man on the Planet," but I'm sure as fuck not gonna revolve around him. Garrett would be proud.

Wes leans forward, gaze pinned to mine. "Your form needs work." I pretend not to hear him over my music, so he taps his watch. "Thirteen minutes."

I point to the treadmill's display and give him another thumbs-up. "This may surprise you, but my ability to walk and tell time are *not* mutually exclusive."

"You're unbelievable."

I smile. "Thanks."

"Wasn't a compliment, sunshine."

"Noted. Still don't care." I draw my shoulders back. "Looks like we're on the same page."

The track switches to Christina Aguilera's "Fall in Line" and I know for a fact the universe has my back. Wes Emerson can sulk all he wants, even tell me to leave, but one thing's for damn sure, Lena Hamilton wasn't made to fall in line.

After another few songs beneath his unwavering stare, my tread-mill finally beeps. I press the stop button and step down. Wes's royal blue gaze burns into me as I swig my water and wipe a towel over my face. I stroll over to him, stopping in front of the bench. At six foot five, he's a big man—even seated on the bench, he's nearly eye-level with me. Doesn't matter. I won't let him intimidate me.

Wes leans in close. "Enjoy your workout?"

"Immensely." I gesture out the window. "Since your goal is to avoid sharing a space with me, I'll make it easy and give you a heads-up. I'm gonna rent one of the kayaks, which means I'll be out on the water for a while. If you don't wanna cross paths, I suggest you stay off the lake."

He raises a brow. "Who said that's my goal?"

Here we go again with the "Mary, Mary, quite contrary" bullshit. I narrow my eyes. "You did."

He shakes his head. "Funny, I don't remember saying that. Maybe I enjoyed the view in here after all."

"Maybe *I* didn't."

He blinks, clearly not accustomed to thinking this hard.

I point to the mirror. "You can go ahead now and enjoy bonding with your reflection." I toss my braid over a shoulder. "The view out there is *much* more appealing to me." I feel his eyes glued to my ass as I leave the room. Maybe it's the exercise-induced endorphins fueling my fire—or maybe I'm just a bitch—but I can't help but sway my hips a little.

CHAPTER 3

WES EMERSON

Internal playlist: "I Still Haven't Found What I'm Looking For" by U2

Lena's right, the view on the lake is a better one. I lean against the railing and watch her paddle along the shoreline. The sun glints on her caramel-colored hair. She's a spicy little thing, kinda like those hot cinnamon lollies Reed loves so much. She'd make a good redhead. She's got a snarky mouth on her too. I can't believe the way she stood up to me in the training room. She's got bigger balls than most men.

As Lena crosses the lake with fluid strokes of her paddle, I shudder against the wind and zip my parka to my throat. It was much warmer in the lower forty-eight. Caribou Lake is north of the Arctic Circle, so I can only imagine the water temperature. I focus on the kayak—which doesn't look too sturdy—and wonder how deep the lake is. Hopefully, she knows what she's doing out there. I estimate the time it would take me to row across the lake in the event she runs into trouble. I could probably reach her in five minutes, maybe less.

Then I wonder why I care.

Jake appears at my side and rests his elbows on the railing. "How was your workout?"

"You have no fucking idea, mate."

He cocks his head. "Why? I haven't checked it out yet. Do they have shitty equipment?"

"Equipment's fine." I point to Lena. "But I had company."

He chuckles. "How'd that go?"

"She's a bloody firecracker." I shake my head. "Came down there to use the treadmill and flat-out refused to leave. She claimed *she* was there, first."

"Was she?"

"Maybe in *her* mind. I'd already been down there for a bit, but I ran upstairs to get my water."

"So, you technically weren't there when she arrived?"

"Technically," I mutter. "But that doesn't fucking matter."

Jake raises a brow. "Then why should she leave? She's entitled to use the room."

"You're supposed to be on my side, Bennett."

"I am, but I'm curious why Lena being there was an issue for you. She seems nice enough. Besides, women follow you around all the time."

"That's my point. I'm on fucking holiday in the middle of nowhere and I've still gotta deal with this shit. Had I known ahead of time Reed was canceling, I would've paid them to keep the vacancy. I need a break from people watching my every move and pawing at me. Here, I thought I was finally gonna get a breather, but no, I've got some sassy nurse staring at my dick."

Jake snorts. "Maybe try wearing longer gym shorts."

"Nope, too restrictive." I motion to Lena. "Whaddya think her story is?"

He shrugs. "I dunno, man. Like I said, she seems friendly. When we were on the plane, she mentioned something about self-reflection."

"Yeah, I heard that. I just don't think I believe it. I'm wondering why someone would book a wilderness trip on a whim. She made the reservation on Thursday. Seems bloody ballsy. Maybe she's running from something." I adjust my aviators and nod to where Lena's photographing a moose on the north shore. "Oh, look. She's got a fucking camera too. Big surprise there."

"Yeah, most people bring those on vacation, man." Jake punches my arm. "And I disagree with your fear she's here to stalk you." At my raised brow, he clarifies, "She hasn't asked for an autograph or anything. This is the first time we've even seen a *hint* of a camera. In fact, other than the times *you* have purposefully goaded her, she seemed content to do her own thing."

Damn it, Jake.

He flashes a grin that tells me he's getting ready to bust my balls, so I cut him off at the pass. "What?"

His grin widens. "Been a long time since I've seen you twisted like this. Tell me the truth, she got you squirming?"

"I am *not* squirming."

"Bullshit. You've been on edge since we left Fairbanks. And, from what I can tell, me thinks you tickle her fancy."

Austin appears behind us with a glass of whiskey. "Word on the street is he tickles a lotta fancies."

"Women are interested in Ares, not real-life me. I'm just some bloke with biceps."

I recently finished filming *The Aegean*, the third installment of the *Olympus Fire* franchise. My portrayal of the Greek god of war is, by far, my most successful role to date, but I quickly learned the downside of fame—not everyone has good intentions.

It might be a cliché, but I want a woman interested in *me*, not in Ares or whatever role she imagines me in. I want someone who sees beyond the shit that comes with me—beyond the fame, money, and travel—to the guy who'd be content living in a beach hut. After being burned by a few people inside and out of the industry, I keep it casual. There are a couple of exes I trust enough to have a good time with when we end up in the same location, but it's hard to build something new when I'm always heading off to another shoot. No attachments mean no one gets hurt. The last time I gave my heart, it ended badly. I don't have the time or energy to deal with that shit again. Especially not when I'm supposed to be on fucking holiday.

Jake rolls his eyes. "Keep telling yourself that. I wish I were as pathetic as you and your biceps."

Austin grins. "Bennett's right. You were squirmin' like somebody put your ass in the electric chair."

"Christ," I mutter, returning my attention to Lena.

I love a woman with curves, and she could put an hourglass to shame. As pissed as I was by her intrusion on the plane and again in the gym, she turned me on. Her snug workout clothes put those luscious curves on display, and with each bouncing step and sassy retort, I wanted her more. But when she passed me on her way to the lake, it was the sway of her hips that did me in.

She also didn't seem to give a fuck about Wes Emerson, movie star, whispers a traitorous part of my brain.

Dark sunglasses obscure vibrant eyes the color of frosted emeralds, or the mint juleps my mum loves to drink. The life vest hides Lena's curvy frame. Curves I am suddenly *dying* to trace my hands over, run my mouth along, to see if they are as soft as they look. My cock starts to throb, all too willing to imagine spreading those soft thighs apart and—*Control yourself, Emerson.*

Austin chuckles. "Looks like the god of war has finally met his match."

I shoot him a glare.

Jake laughs. "He's so used to women taking one look at his biceps and throwing themselves at him, he forgot what it feels like to chase one. Now he's lost down here with the rest of us mere mortals. Did the god of war forget how to spar?"

"I've got plenty of fight."

Austin clicks his tongue. "We'll see about that. I got a feelin' Aphrodite out on the lake will give you a run for your money." He jabs a finger in the middle of my chest. "Mark my words . . . she's gonna battle you every step of the way."

Bring it, sunshine. I'll fight you all night long. The thought makes me smirk.

"Here she comes." Jake wags his brows.

Lena paddles up to the dock, climbs out, and secures the kayak. She removes the life vest, unveiling her lush body. As she bends to stow the vest, my gaze locks onto her arse. I shift my weight against the throb in my jeans.

"Hi, Lena," Jake calls out.

She smiles and waves. "Hey, Jake and Austin." Her eyes flick to mine and narrow, but she doesn't greet me. Then she disappears through the lodge's back entrance.

"Oh, shit," Austin murmurs, slapping the railing. "I want ringside seats for this one."

Jake snickers. "I see a TKO in your future, surfer boy."

I cross my arms. "If she's looking for a battle, I'll give it to her."

CHAPTER 4

LENA

Internal playlist: "Eyes on Fire" by Blue Foundation

After several hours of tranquility on Caribou Lake—away from the blue-eyed asshole I can't stop thinking about—I reenter the lodge and approach the office in the lobby. Ellen is seated at a large oak desk.

She looks up from her computer. "Hi, Ms. Hamilton. Can I help you?"

"I want to book a charter for an excursion, please."

Ellen withdraws a brochure from a desk drawer. "Here's a list of our available activities. When you made your reservation, you expressed interest in the camping trip to Gobbler's Knob. Is that still the case?"

"Yes."

Gobbler's Knob is a prime location for viewing the aurora borealis at other times of the year. Late fall in Northern Alaska means the sun only sets for four or five hours, so my chances of seeing the phenomenon are slim. Regardless, I'm eager to spend a couple of nights in the open air.

"All right. Due to a snowstorm in the forecast, management has canceled the Tuesday and Thursday charters. Tomorrow will be the season's final excursion," Ellen explains.

"Well, I'd like to do it, so if tomorrow's the only option, that's fine."

"Excellent." She hands me a printout and smiles. "Here's a list of personal items we recommend our guests pack for camping excursions. Almost all of your necessities will be provided by the lodge, but there is some optional equipment you can rent. On the back page is our travel itinerary. Please meet in the great room at nine."

I thank Ellen and head to my room. Seated on the edge of my bed, I look over the list and make mental notes of what equipment I plan to rent. The resort provides things like tents and sleeping bags, so I just need to worry about clothes, snacks, and cooking equipment. Thankfully, Gobbler's Knob has an established site, so I can grab anything I miss.

After a quick shower, I stuff my thighs into a pair of dark jeans and slide ballet flats onto my feet. I snag a teal, V-neck sweater and shrug it on. I give my reflection a quick once-over and head downstairs.

Oh, good, I'm the first one here.

Since I've reached my cockiness quota for the day, my plan is to grab dinner and scoot out before the guys show up. I snatch a plate and check out the buffet table. The chef prepared a feast of filet mignon, salmon, and roasted vegetables. Helping myself to a small portion of everything, I grab a crescent roll and turn to leave.

"Somethin' smells mighty fine," Austin drawls as he enters the room.

I stiffen.

Jake follows, rubbing his belly. "I'm starving. How was your kayak ride, Lena?"

"Very relaxing, thanks. You guys enjoy your meal. I'm sure I'll see you around—" Turning to leave, I collide with a wall of solid muscle, yet somehow keep my plate from falling.

Wes raises a questioning brow at my plate. "Going somewhere?"

"How about you try 'excuse me'?" I match his raised eyebrow with my own. "That's a typical response when you bump into someone."

"You bumped into me."

I roll my eyes and attempt to sidestep him, but he blocks my path. "Where ya goin'?"

"Upstairs to eat."

"I'd rather ya join us." Wes grabs my plate and carries it to the table. He flashes a cocky smirk and positions it next to where I'm assuming he plans to sit.

Who the fuck does he think he is?

"Oh, suddenly you're fine with me breathing your air?"

"I've always been fine with it, Lena."

In the span of a single day, he's given me more whiplash than a multi-car pileup on the New York State Thruway.

Austin grabs a plate and makes his way over to the food, where he skewers a slab of meat. He looks over his shoulder at me. "Pop a squat, darlin'." He jerks his thumb toward the table. "We insist."

Since I really like Austin and Jake, I decide it's best not to be rude. I walk over and pull out a chair on the opposite side. Before settling, I narrow my eyes on Wes and move my plate across the table, away from him.

He chuckles at my act of defiance and approaches the beverage station. "Lena, would ya like beer or wine?"

"I'd love some wine, thank you." *Make that an entire bottle.*

"Your wish is my command." His gaze lingers on my face. "Red or white?"

My brain misfires at his Jekyll and Hyde performance, and I miss the second half.

"Do you have a preference, or would ya like me to choose?"

"Uh . . ."

"I can see you're having trouble with questions again, so I'll choose." He smirks and picks up a bottle. "Oh, look, they have one from 'Straya. I see what they did there." He reads the label aloud, "Grab your didgeri-doo—" He looks at his friends and laughs. "Are these people serious? Of all the stereotypes to choose from, they pick that? They must think we're all standing there, firing up the barbie and holding our didgeridoos."

You've fired up this Barbie, and I'll gladly hold your didgeridoo.

I flush, silently cursing my traitorous libido and the renegade brain in my skull.

Jake snickers. "They probably followed you around for a while. You've got plenty of mileage there."

"Maybe." Wes laughs and continues reading the label, "Take a trip into the Outback and indulge in this sultry vintage. Prepare for a heady, *full-bodied* experience. Well, Lena, it looks like I'm takin' ya down under."

Oh my God. I press my knees together and beg my lungs to function.

He reaches for a glass, tips the bottle, and fills it halfway. "I hope you like Shiraz because this pairs nicely with," his gaze lands on my breasts, "lots of things."

Holy. Fuck.

Jake hears him and smirks. "Who knew Emerson was a wine connoisseur?"

Wes appears at his side and places the wineglass in front of me. "I like to enjoy the finer things in life, Bennett." He flashes me a wink before settling in his chair.

Feeling flustered and tipsy before I've even had a sip of wine, I turn my focus to the filet, cutting it into strips. After taking a moment to regain my composure, I notice them watching me.

"What?" I arch a brow. "Haven't you ever seen a woman use a knife?"

Wes grins and briefly turns his attention to the salmon on his plate. I flush when our eyes meet once more. He swallows a sip of wine and smirks. "You've got a fiery spirit, Lena. I like it."

"You're cocky as hell." I sip my wine. "And I'm *not* a fan."

Jake chokes on his beer. Austin chuckles and murmurs something under his breath that sounds like, "Round one."

Wes presses his lips in a flat line and stares across the table at me. Ignoring him, I continue eating.

Jake recovers and gives me an approving smirk. "Well, now that we know where everyone stands, how about you tell us a little about yourself, Lena."

"There's not much to tell."

"I don't buy that one, darlin'," Austin drawls.

"Why did ya come to Alaska?" Wes asks.

I cross my arms over my chest. "You writing a book?"

"Maybe."

"Leave that chapter out and make it a mystery."

Wes leans in. "I don't like mysteries."

I smile sweetly. "Too bad."

Austin grins. "Round two."

I grab my book from upstairs while the plates are being cleared. All three men watch me curl up in an armchair near the fire. A window is cracked nearby. Leaves rustling in the autumn breeze and the song of a distant wind chime reaches my ears.

The guys are lounging at the table playing cards. Too distracted by the raw male energy in the room, I stare at the words on the page but can't comprehend them. Every time Wes speaks, his voice caresses my senses.

"Time for another glass of wine," I mutter to myself.

Leaving my book in the chair, I walk over to the beverage station and help myself to more Shiraz. The hairs on my neck prickle. I glance at the table and meet Wes's gaze. His eyes are a deeper blue in the dim light. *Those eyes*—they pierce my soul and leave me breathless.

Red wine spatters on the white tablecloth. I force my focus to the bottle, fill the glass, and resettle in the armchair.

I reach for the novel, even though I know damn well it's a lost cause. I can't catch my breath or think, let alone read. I peer over the top of my book. Wes's heavy-lidded stare persists, so I arch a brow. In response, he flashes a megawatt smile and fries my remaining neurons.

He eyes me like a hungry predator, lounging lazily with a confidence that's born, not bred. I couldn't look away if I wanted to. One thing's for damn sure: if Wes Emerson ever decided to pursue an ordinary girl like me, it would be a short hunt, an easy vanquish. We both know it. He blinks and deliberately licks his lips.

I press my knees together against the heat of arousal between my thighs. If he can excite me with his eyes alone, I can't imagine how it would feel to have him touch me.

"It's your turn, man."

Wes jerks at the sound of Austin's voice and breaks eye contact. "Sorry, mate. Wasn't paying attention." He roughly draws a card from the deck.

"You're a thousand miles away, dude," Jake muses.

Wes swallows a gulp of wine instead of answering.

My fingertips splay against my flushed collarbone as rapid breaths expand my chest. He's brought me to a slow boil without even touching me. I close the book and gulp my remaining wine. I need air, not Wes's brand of mental foreplay.

I set the glass on the end table with more force than necessary, causing their heads to turn. I lurch from the armchair and clutch the book to my chest to hide my hardened nipples.

"Night, guys." I hurry past the table.

"Where ya goin'?" Wes asks.

"Bed." I trip on the first step and drop my book. "Shit."

"Whoa. Are you all right? You coulda clocked your noggin again."

"Yes. Thanks." I snatch the book and continue my retreat, taking the steps two at a time.

"Sleep tight, Lena," Wes calls out.

"She tore outta here like she was bitten by fire ants," Austin jokes.

I pretend not to hear him and slip into my room. Flustered and heated, I flop onto the bed and stare at the headboard.

Forty-seven minutes later, I lie on my side, facing the nightstand. The clock radio's boxy red numbers taunt me. Despite being warm, comfortable, and beyond exhausted, I can't fall asleep. Not that the reason's a mystery.

Wes's lingering stare damn near stopped my heart. No one's ever looked at me that way. Ever. Especially not Marc. He *never* gave me the attention I craved. I could've walked into a room wearing nipple tassels and a headdress, and it wouldn't have mattered.

Throwing the covers off, I climb out of bed. I rummage through my suitcase, in search of my melatonin capsules, and find a package wrapped in brown paper. On it is a scrawled message in Garrett's handwriting.

You're welcome.

"What the hell is this?" I tear it open and burst out laughing. "I'm gonna kill him."

A soft knock turns my focus to the door. Setting my new hot pink vibrator on the nightstand, I sit on my bed and wait, thinking perhaps I imagined it. I hear it again—louder this time, so I pad across the room and open the door.

Wes is standing on the other side, leaning against the frame.

Perhaps, if my brain were functioning to its full potential, I would have asked who it was first. Or hid my vibrator. But, nope. Here I am in all my glory—barefoot, braless, and wearing an oversized T-shirt with zero makeup. *Son of a bitch.*

He smiles down at me. "Hey."

"Hey."

"I didn't look at the time." Peering over the top of my head, his eyes suddenly widen. Along with his smile. "Hope I didn't wake ya . . . or interrupt anything."

Fuck.

"You didn't. I've been staring at the cock. Shit, I mean, *clock.*" I release a heavy sigh. "What do you want?"

Wes pins me with his gaze. "You still haven't told me anything about yourself."

"There's not much to tell." I narrow my eyes. "And why do you care? Looking for a button-pushing opportunity?"

"Always on the lookout for those." Wes holds up my bookmark. "You dropped this on the stairs." Gold inlaid with Connemara marble, it shines in the low lighting from the hall lamps.

"Thank you. My best friend got that for me in Ireland. It's a bookmark." I reach for it, but he pulls his hand away.

"A bookmark, huh?" He turns it from side to side. "Never seen one like this."

"Yeah, well, it's important to me. I'd like it back, please."

"I see a theme here, Lena."

"What are you talking about?"

He shakes his head. "Nothing."

I prop my hands on my hips. "You can't make a statement like that and refuse to elaborate."

Wes holds the bookmark up to my face, his knuckles brushing my cheek. My heart skids to a stop.

He tilts his head to the side and murmurs, "Did ya realize this stone mirrors the color of your eyes?" He traces his fingertips along my jawline, causing a flare of heat in my body. "Exquisitely beautiful, just like its owner."

"Thank you," I whisper, unable to move or think.

He smiles and gently places the bookmark in my hand. "No, thank *you.*"

I clutch it to my heaving chest. *Wes Emerson just called me exquisitely beautiful.* It doesn't seem possible this is the same guy who made me feel like an intruder earlier.

"Sleep well, Lena. I'm sure I'll see you around."

"Good night." My voice is low and husky, making the effect of his touch clear.

He searches my face. "What's always in front of you but can't be seen?" I open and close my mouth a few times, making his smile widen. "Give up?"

"No, I—"

"The future." Wes turns and walks down the hall to his room. I stare after him, frozen in place. Pausing outside his door, he meets my gaze and holds it. "Good night, Lena. I look forward to seeing *much* more of you."

When he disappears into his room, I press the door closed and slide to the floor. I lean against the solid oak and force myself back down to earth. I feel like Cinderella and my bookmark is the missing glass slipper.

Your Prince Charming is a dick, my brain reminds me.

Regardless, I dare to imagine myself riding into the sunset with this charismatic jerk who can bring me to the edge with nothing but a look, a fucking wink. Then there's his riddle, and the way his eyes locked with mine when he revealed the answer.

You still haven't told me anything about yourself. His words echo in my mind. I'm not used to men taking an interest in more than my body. Hell, Marc wasn't even interested in *that.* Cocky Prince Emerson wants to know me? Hardly believable.

Staring at the bookmark in my hand, I recall the feeling of his fingertips on my jaw. The sudden flood of heat between my legs makes me squirm. I release a frustrated breath, glance at my nightstand, and wonder if it's too late for a cold shower.

CHAPTER 5

WES

Internal playlist: "Something Just Like This"
by The Chainsmokers & Coldplay

Alaska is full of surprises. I lift the shade, expecting to see a shimmering, moonlit lake because it's three a.m. after all. Instead, an imminent dawn greets me. The lack of nighttime darkness will take some getting used to. I scrub a hand over my face and yawn. I know I slept, but I don't feel rested. Hell, after those dreams about Lena in that white T-shirt, and what I'd seen on her nightstand, I'm restless as fuck. And if my morning wood's any indication—I'll be hard all day.

Christ, she's beautiful. I can't explain the intensity of my attraction, but Lena's magnetism is undeniable. The way she looked at me last night, when I finally told her the answer to my riddle, *slayed* me. I laid awake for over an hour, just picturing her soulful eyes. Her lips. Those lush curves.

I take a deep breath. The smell of coffee greets my nostrils. Yeah, caffeine sounds like a good plan for my exhausted, horned-up brain.

After a cold shower, I toss on some clothes and head to the great room for a cuppa. I'm impressed with the resort's selection of pastries, but I don't know if I'm in the mood for a muffin or a bagel, so I grab one of each. After pouring a large mug of the Kona blend, I move through the French doors onto the balcony. I get a few steps from the doorway before I stop in my tracks—Lena's already out here.

She leans against the railing. In the brisk autumn air, each rise and fall of her shoulders releases a visible puff of breath, which mingles with the steam from her coffee cup. The great room's soft light illuminates the balcony—and her backside—as she gazes out at the lake. A pale yellow sun kisses the mountains' peaks, casting a subtle glow on the tundra. This is far more beautiful than the sunrises back home. Likely due to Lena's presence.

I contemplate going back inside but decide it would be more fun to push her buttons. I silently approach, stopping about a foot behind her.

"You shouldn't stare directly at the sun."

She jumps and lets out a yelp, dropping her coffee. Hot liquid spatters her ankles. She rounds on me, eyes flashing with fury. "What the hell is wrong with you?"

"Do you want a list?" I stoop to retrieve her mug. "I'm sorry. I didn't mean to scare ya."

She props her hands on her hips. "What did you *think* would happen, sneaking up on me like that?"

"Didn't give it much thought. Hold on, I'll grab some serviettes."

I head back inside, kicking myself for my stupidity. I have a secret love affair with teasing. It all started with my mum and sister. I used to love jumping out of closets and making them scream—especially Isla. My sister's jumpy to begin with, so it didn't take much to get a reaction from her. I still enjoy a good prank. Popping around corners and shit. Maybe there *is* something wrong with me.

I snatch some serviettes and head back outside, still holding Lena's empty mug. I point to her feet. "Did I burn ya?"

"No." She accepts the serviettes and chuckles. "It took me a minute to realize you were talking about napkins." She squats in front of me, wiping off her little black shoes.

I stare at the top of her head and beat back the filthy thoughts surfacing at her position. My traitorous cock twitches, and I clench my hand on her mug.

Refill it, you fuckwit.

"How do ya like it?"

"Excuse me?"

Shit. "Your coffee. How do ya like it?"

Lena peers up at me with red-rimmed, jade eyes, and I notice tearstains on her cheeks. "Oh. Um, no sugar, just a little cream. Kona, if there's any left."

I nod and head for the great room, wondering who or what made her cry. It's none of my business, and I shouldn't care, but that means nothing to the invisible band that tightens around my chest.

I fix her a fresh cuppa and eye the muffins, wondering if she likes blueberry or chockie chip. *She didn't ask for a muffin,* my brain reminds me. I ignore it and grab the chockie chip one because who doesn't love chocolate? Taking a deep breath, I step onto the balcony and approach her.

I hand her the mug. "Here ya go. Again, I'm sorry about that. It was a dick move."

"It's all right. Thanks for the refill."

Remembering the muffin, I hand that over, too. "Wasn't sure if you'd had ya brekkie."

She stares at the muffin for a moment before accepting it. "Thanks."

"It's chockie chip." I say it like I'm imparting some grand morsel of wisdom, and suddenly wonder why anyone allows me to speak.

She smirks. "As long as it's not rabbit shit, I'm good."

"I'd never give ya a shit muffin." *Shut your bloody trap, Wes.*

Lena snorts. "Well, I'd certainly hope not." She sips her coffee. "This is perfect, thank you."

"You're welcome." I join her at the railing, and we stare at the lake in silence. I want to ask her why she was crying, but I bite my tongue. *Don't get involved.* "You're up early," I say instead, after a few moments of arguing with myself.

"So are you."

"Yep. I always rise with the sun. Best time to catch waves and no one's on the beach at this hour." I point to the sunrise. "Beautiful, isn't it?"

"It's breathtaking," she murmurs, tucking a strand of hair behind her ear. "I love sunrises. Dawn gives me hope."

"Whaddya mean?"

"Every morning's a new beginning, a fresh start. It's hard to explain, but it steels me for the daily onslaught of death and tragedy."

I furrow my brow at her morbid words and the catch in her voice. "At your job?"

She squeezes her eyes shut and takes a few breaths before answering.

"Yeah. Every fucking day." She shrugs and sips her coffee. "I grew up in the Catskills, but these mountains dwarf them."

"How'd ya end up in New York City?" I ask, taking her subject change as confirmation that her tears—and break in her voice—are none of my business.

"I moved to Brooklyn when I was in college. My grandmother was determined to live out her days at home, so I transferred my credits from my program upstate and looked after her. She passed after I got a job at New York General."

"I'm sorry to hear that. Were ya close?"

"Extremely. It was a challenging time in my life."

"Is your grandmother the reason you became a nurse?"

"One of them. To be honest, I wanted to be a wildlife photographer. But practicality has always been my strong suit." She releases a wistful sigh. "Enough about me. What got you into acting? Is it your passion?"

"My parents. We didn't have much growing up, but they instilled an early love of theater in my siblings and me. I'm grateful to be able to make a living out of it, but my true passion is the ocean if I'm honest. I'd love nothing more than to spend my days breathing in the salty air and riding the surf. Some of my happiest memories are of my dad teaching my brother and me how to catch waves. Before I got into acting, I thought I'd be a surfing instructor."

"That sounds like a fun job."

"It's still my dream job." I say, thinking back to the carefree days on the beach. "Unfortunately, I don't have as much time to surf now, but I try to channel some of my attention into conservation efforts. I've worked with a dozen environmental groups who protect the oceans because it's an issue that requires worldwide attention."

"I imagine your time is structured during filming?"

"It is, but I try to make the most of my downtime."

"Your family must be ridiculously proud of your success."

"I'd like to think so. They're the reason I keep doing it."

Lena peers up into my eyes. "So, what brings you guys on this grand adventure?"

"We needed a break from reality."

"I can relate," she murmurs, staring at the mountains.

I wait for her to elaborate, but she doesn't. Silence stretches between us as the eerie calls of a loon echo over the lake.

I turn to face her. "I'm curious about something." She looks up at me. "You mentioned that you booked this trip a couple of days ago. It seems ballsy to fly across the country on a wilderness odyssey. Do ya always act on a whim?"

"No. I'm typically a planner."

I rub my jaw. "So, you waited until the last minute to plan a holiday?"

"I wasn't *planning* to take a vacation."

"Then why're ya here?"

"My boss didn't give me a choice."

"Whaddya mean?"

"I don't wanna talk about it."

While the six-word shutdown was made crystal clear by her tone, I still want my answer. What happened at her job? Was she fired? What made her fly all the way out here? *Alone.* More than that, I want to know why she was crying—and what *I* can do to fix it.

I pin my gaze to her face. "Why'd ya come here, Lena?"

She bristles. "For the record, I paid for my trip."

"No one's questioning that. I'm asking *why* you're here."

"That's none of your business."

"Your answer doesn't sit well with me." I cross my arms. "I still wanna know what gotcha so upset that you're hiding out all by yourself in a remote Alaskan lodge."

Lena narrows her eyes on my face. "So, the fact that I told you I don't wanna talk about it means nothing to you?" She shakes her head. "I deal with this shit at work—arrogant dicks who try to push me around, telling me I shouldn't have feelings. I don't owe you, or anyone else, an explanation. It's bad enough I was forced on leave—" She turns away and clenches the railing, digging her nails into the wood. "I *allowed* myself to be talked into this trip, to clear my fucking head, but obviously *that* was a mistake. I didn't plan any of this, and I certainly didn't plan on *you* being here. I'm tired of being treated like a nurse in the surgeons' lounge, having to justify my presence. And I'm done being told to get a handle on my emotions."

She rounds on me, chest heaving, fists clenched at her sides. Eyes welling with tears, she stares up at me without blinking. Like she's determined not to let them fall.

I open and close my mouth a few times. "You think *I'm* an arrogant dick?"

"If the shoe fits . . ." A tear rolls down her cheek. "Thanks for the muffin." Before I can say another word, she retreats to the lodge.

While my mates focus on the baked goods, I plop my gear on the table in the great room and do a quick inventory of all the shit I packed. *Where's my fishing license?* I double-check my pockets and locate the slip of paper.

Ellen enters the room and hands us each a hunting knife. "As soon as Ms. Hamilton comes down, I'll bring everyone out to the bush plane."

"Lena's coming?" Jake asks, flashing a grin in my direction. "You hear that, Memphis?"

Austin's got a mouthful of blueberry muffin, so he gives him a thumbs-up.

Ellen nods. "Yeah, she was the first one to book this excursion." Glancing up to the loft, she lowers her voice. "Truthfully, even though there's a guide at the Gobbler's Knob site, I was shocked she'd be comfortable going alone. I feel better with you guys joining her. I'm sure she does too."

"I wouldn't be so sure of that," I mutter.

"What was that, Mr. Emerson?"

"Nothing." I turn my focus to the knife in my hand.

"All right, I'll be back in a few with your emergency satellite phone."

Jake walks over to me with a stupid smirk on his face. "Looks like you're crashing *her* party this time."

"No shit, mate."

"What's wrong with you? You've been acting weird all morning."

"She thinks I'm an arrogant dick."

"Not for nothing, but have you given her a reason *not* to think that?"

Jake always says, "not for nothing." It's something he picked up from his mum, and for whatever reason, I can't stand it. Probably because he uses it to preface something I don't want to hear, which happens on the regular.

"*Not for nothing*, but I gave her a muffin."

He raises a brow. "A muffin?"

"Yeah, on the deck this morning." I rub at my jaw. "It was a chockie chip one."

"Wow. You're quite the Casanova. What prompted that?" His smirk widens to a grin.

Damn it, Bennett, you intuitive fuck.

I release a heavy sigh. "I startled her, and she spilled coffee all over herself, so I guess it was a peace offering."

"How did she react?" Jake leans against the table.

"Shit went from bad to worse, mate."

His gaze darts to someplace over my shoulder. "Hey, Lena."

"Morning, everyone." Lena staggers into the room with a tackle box, fishing pole, and camera bag. Weighed down by an enormous pack, she looks like a kindergartener on the first day of school. Hunched and off-balance. "Ellen tells me I'll have company on my excursion?"

"Mornin', li'l lady," Austin drawls. "Yeah, we can't resist a campin' trip."

"Well, I thought I'd stay out of your way for a bit," she arches a brow at me, "but it looks like that's not gonna happen."

Ignoring her statement, I point to her pack. "Need some help?"

"I'm good, thanks." She shifts her weight and frowns. "I feel like I'm forgetting something."

I gesture to the fishing pole. "You have your license?"

"Yeah, it's in a pocket somewhere." With both arms full, she purses her lips and blows a strand of hair off her face.

"Are you sure I can't carry something for ya?" I ask a second time because I hate seeing her hunched over.

"Thanks, but I can handle it."

She's sexy, snarky, *and* stubborn. *And she thinks I'm an arrogant dick.*

I shrug. "All right, suit yourself."

Ellen leads us outside to the field where we landed the previous day. We trudge up the path to a waiting bush plane, where resort staff has already loaded the crates with some of our camping supplies. A stout, red-haired bloke with an ample beard stands near the wing smoking a pipe. Ellen introduces him as our pilot, Chuck. He looks like a ginger Santa Claus.

Chuck adjusts his glasses and instructs us to stow our gear in the compartment beneath the plane. He motions to the cockpit. "Who wants to be my copilot?"

Nope. Not happening.

Chuck grins. "C'mon, any takers?"

"I'll ride shotgun, man." Jake steps forward, shakes Chuck's hand, and climbs inside.

Chuck motions to Austin and me. "You fellas climb aboard and help the young lady while I secure the cargo."

Memphis boards the plane with his guitar case—which he's bringing against Ellen's recommendation. He flashes me a wink as he settles, positioning the case so he hogs the two back seats, which will force Lena to sit beside me.

Shaking my head, I remove my pack and hand it to Chuck, who stuffs it in the compartment.

"I'll take your bag, dear." Chuck reaches for Lena's pack, but in her attempt to remove it, she tangles herself in fishing line.

"Ow! Something's pulling my hair." She flails an arm behind her, which only makes it worse.

I confiscate her fishing pole and step around her. "The hook's stuck in your hair. Hold still." Grasping her braid, I try to work it free, but the stubborn woman continues to wiggle. "For Christ's sake, stop moving before ya hook your skin. I've got to take out your braid."

"I'll do it," she insists.

I shake my head and remove her hair tie. "You can't reach."

Silken strands of hair slide through my fingers as I loosen her braid. My heart picks up speed. I swallow tightly and untangle the hook. Clenching my jaw, I drag oxygen and the scent of her vanilla shampoo through my nose. The situation in my jeans gets tighter, and it takes every ounce of my self-control not to tangle my fingers in her hair and kiss her. *Focus, Emerson.*

Her shoulders rise and fall with each breath and goose bumps appear on her neck, telling me she likes my touch. The hook's nearly free, but I stall, fingers tightening on the strands. *I want to kiss every inch of you, sunshine.*

Lena meets my gaze as if she can hear my thoughts. Lips parted, the heat in her eyes mixes with raw vulnerability, and shock—like she's surprised I have the capability of being helpful or demonstrating any non-dick behavior. Jake's words repeat themselves in my mind. *Have you given her a reason not to think that?* Not yet, but I plan to.

The band around my chest squeezes. *You can't do this to yourself. Don't get involved.*

I remove the hook and hold it out. "Here ya go."

"Thank you," she murmurs.

All I can manage is a nod as I climb into the plane.

CHAPTER 6

LENA

Internal playlist: "The First Taste" by Fiona Apple

What in the fresh hell just happened? Dumbfounded, I accept Wes's outstretched hand, and he hauls me into the cramped cabin. My scalp still tingles from his touch. I love when a man plays with my hair. Marc brushed it for me on rare occasions, but it was always short-lived, and he made it seem like a chore. I taught Garrett how to braid it when we were kids, but that's different. Garrett's touch doesn't evoke this feeling inside me. I glance at Wes.

He smiles, and just like the braid, he unravels me.

All morning, my mind has been replaying our conversation on the deck. How Wes seemed genuinely interested in what I had to say. I'm not used to men asking questions about me. Perhaps I was a little defensive, but I didn't want to rehash the work shitstorm with *him*. Last thing I needed was another meltdown. I've been holding back tears for days; it's only a matter of time before that dam breaks.

I squeeze my eyes shut and draw in a slow, deep breath. Wes's clean woodsy scent makes my heart race. My stomach flutters and my palms begin to sweat.

"You all right?" he asks.

"I'm okay. I do better in bigger aircraft."

Tiny plane number two is only the tip of the iceberg—it's the six-foot-five chunk of ice I'm worried about.

"You've got one helluva scowl on your face."

I cock a brow. "Maybe that's my normal face."

"I might buy that if I hadn't already seen you smile."

Knowing he noticed my smile, makes me want to grin. Instead, I force a neutral expression. In my mind, it's cute, but I probably look constipated or something.

We fasten our seat belts and settle in for the flight to Gobbler's Knob. Chuck climbs into the cockpit and tosses us headsets equipped with a communication system. He explains that engine noise from a small plane can damage the ears. The headsets ensure we can hear him and each other during the trip without going deaf.

"All right, kids. Sit back, relax, and enjoy the flight. I'll point out landmarks as we fly over them," he says while firing up the engine.

I grip the armrests. Engine vibrations course up my arms. Closing my eyes, I take a deep breath as Chuck accelerates on the makeshift runway. My stomach flip-flops when we lift off the ground and I clutch the armrests tighter. We ascend to cruising altitude, and the ride feels much smoother now, so I relax my grip.

Chuck's voice crackles through my headset. "We're heading about a hundred-and-fifty-miles due west to Gobbler's Knob. Visibility's great, so you folks can check out the sights." He adjusts his sunglasses. "What brings you all to these parts? Filming a movie?"

Wes speaks up, "Nah, mate. We're taking a holiday. I just finished filming, and those two are working on an album together. We picked Alaska for the isolation factor. We didn't want to hit up some touristy place and be followed around by a bunch of noddies."

"Makes sense. Although, I would've chosen a destination other than Gobbler's Knob," Chuck remarks. "You realize it's near the Dalton Highway, right?"

"What do you mean?" Jake asks.

"Well, it's a prime spot to experience the land of the midnight sun and is a common tourist attraction. I'd say it's slightly off the beaten path, but you'll see other campers, and once word gets out, folks will be pestering you."

"Damn. We'd hoped to avoid that," Jake mutters.

"You searching for solitude, too?" Chuck asks me.

"Isolation's less of a concern for me. I'm hoping to photograph wildlife."

"Now, wait a minute. You fellas want privacy, and the lady wants to see animals. I've got just the place for you," Chuck exclaims. "How about we take a little detour?"

"Whaddya mean, mate?"

"I mean, we change course and head northeast to Gates of the Arctic National Park."

"You can do that, sir?" Austin asks.

"It's my plane, I can do whatever the hell I want. My brother-in-law owns the company, and he's real laid-back. I'll amend the flight plan when I get back to the office and pick you kids up in a few days. But I'll warn you, unlike Gobbler's Knob, this is true wilderness. There won't be supplies available to you like at the commercial camp, so make sure you're comfortable with what you've packed. Also, you'll be on your own. There aren't any guides like they have at the Knob site."

"Lena packed enough for all of us," Wes teases.

I elbow him. "I like being prepared." Grabbing the excursion brochure from my pocket, I skim it once more. "But guys, most of the food was going to be provided at Gobbler's Knob. Do you think we'll have enough?"

"It's only for a few days and we have all those protein bars and jerky," Wes points out. "And I'm pretty sure Memphis brought a whole bag of trail mix."

"Sure did." Austin taps my shoulder. "What's the matter, Lena? You doubtin' my caveman abilities? I'm sure my fishin' skills will keep us fed."

I laugh. "I'd never doubt you, Austin."

Jake speaks up. "I think we can handle a few nights with what we've brought. Everyone on board with that?"

Wes nods. "I'm game."

"Let's do it," Austin agrees.

The men study me expectantly.

"Works for me." I remember reading about the preserve on the flight to Fairbanks. It promises animals galore.

"Then it's decided. We'll be heading about eighty miles north of the lodge. I just can't see you kids wasting your time in some tourist trap and getting mobbed."

"Thanks for your input. We appreciate it," Jake says.

I peer out my window at the mountains, glacial valleys, winding rivers, and clear lakes as we listen to Chuck's narration. We fly over the massive Yukon River and head farther north into the Arctic Circle. Chuck educates us about the history of the park, its rivers, and wildlife. He calls it the last "true wilderness" and explains that there are no roads, trails, or campgrounds.

He plans to drop us off on the bank of the John River, the valley of which dissects the central Brooks Range. The river flows south from Anaktuvuk Pass to the Koyukuk River near the village of Bettles and serves as a primary migratory route for caribou. The chance to photograph the majestic creatures thrills me. I listen as he describes the various ecosystems present in the valley. We pass over Bettles and head deeper into the preserve. The men ask questions and comment on the scenery. Exhilarated by the enormity of what we're about to do, I remain silent. It's been a long time since I've camped, and this is a far cry from your standard campground.

"Cat got your tongue?" Wes's voice makes me jump.

"I guess I'm a little nervous about my outdoorsy skills, but I plan to set up camp on the riverbank, so I have access to water and fish." I chew my lip, mulling the plan over. "I probably won't venture too far from my home base."

"Sounds like a good—"

The violent jostling of the plane cuts him off. I automatically reach for the armrest, clamping my fingers around his wrist.

"Got some turbulence here," Chuck announces as the plane shudders again. "Hang on, it'll pass soon."

I grip Wes tighter and feel his other hand settle on top of mine and squeeze.

"You okay?"

"No," I whisper.

"Just breathe."

Too terrified to release his arm, I focus on filling my lungs.

"All right, kids, this is it. We're gonna start our descent. I see a flat stretch of tundra a few miles ahead that looks like a good spot to land," Chuck calls out. "Sit tight and hold on, 'cause this may be bumpy."

I squeeze my eyes shut, bracing for the aircraft's touchdown. As expected, the bush plane bounces over rocky terrain until it finally comes to a stop. We remove our headsets when Chuck cuts the engines. Frozen in place, I slowly open my eyes.

Wes squeezes my hand. "We're safe now."

"I know. I just need a minute."

"Take your time."

He doesn't move, and it suddenly dawns on me I still have his wrist in a vise grip.

"Shit." I release him. "I didn't realize . . ."

"No worries, Lena." He gestures to the exit. "I'll help ya when you're ready." He climbs from the seat and hops out.

I take a few calming breaths before making my way to the exit. As promised, Wes grips my hand and helps me to the ground.

"No more falls." He flashes a playful wink.

I thank him and take a moment to scan my surroundings.

We landed on the east bank of the river. The rocky expanse of tundra meets the foothills of the Brooks Range. Mosses, lichen, and shrub thickets of birch and alder pepper the valley. A boreal forest of dense spruce and poplar trees cloaks the base of the mountains, becoming sparser as the elevation increases. The snowcapped mountains, with their craggy limestone and granite cliffs, jut toward the heavens. The western bank of the river is a steep outcropping of bedrock, likely carved by a glacier. I listen to the rush of the swift whitewater currents and wonder how cold the water is.

Austin gazes across the horizon. "We ain't in Kansas anymore."

"This is bloody stunning, mate. I'm a little jealous you get to do this for a living," Wes tells Chuck as he marvels at the landscape.

"It ain't half bad." Chuck grins. "Let's unload your gear so you can get settled before nightfall."

Jake, Wes, and Austin help Chuck empty the plane. After donning his backpack, Wes hands me my gear.

"What the hell did ya pack, frontier woman?" He pretends to struggle under the weight. "This is as heavy as your suitcase."

I shrug. "Oh, you know, a few essentials—stilettos, an evening gown, a curling iron, and a blender."

He casts a suggestive glance at my feet. "Tell me more about the stilettos."

"Maybe later."

"Yo, surfer boy. Give me a hand with this fishing stuff," Jake calls, holding his camping gear, tackle box, and all four fishing poles.

"Oh, sorry, mate." Wes grabs the poles.

"So, here's the agenda, kids. Take a look around and commit this spot to memory." Chuck points to the ground. "This is where I'll extract you on Wednesday. Plan to be here by noon with all your gear ready to be stowed. This preserve is 'carry-in and carry-out,' so don't leave any trash. Be vigilant with your campfires. It doesn't take much to spark a wildfire in this brush. In other words, leave no trace. I trust that Ellen got fishing licenses for you?"

"Yes, sir," Austin answers.

"Good. You're likely to hook Arctic grayling, northern pike, Arctic char, and what remains of the chum salmon. All of them are good eats." He strokes his beard. "Be on the lookout for grizzlies. Nasty buggers. Don't eat in your tents and bury any food waste away from your camp. Most of all, have fun." He nods at me. "Take those pictures, dear. Any questions before I head out?"

"You've been very informative, thank you so much," Jake says.

"See you in three days. Remember this spot." Chuck climbs back into the cockpit and fires up the engines, then waves and prepares for takeoff.

The flutter in my belly suddenly surges as I watch the plane disappear into the clouds. My scalp prickles and the humming in my ears isn't from the aircraft. Now that Chuck is well on his way to the flight company's home base in Fairbanks, a restlessness consumes me. I shake my head and force a few shallow breaths to quell my anxiety.

Stay present.

I turn up the collar of my parka. The temperature is probably in the low fifties, but the wind makes it seem much colder. My game plan is to set up my tent and start a fire. Scanning the area, I choose a spot near a cluster of spruce. I figure they'll help break the wind. I adjust my pack and begin navigating the slippery moss-covered rocks.

"Where ya off to?" Wes closes the distance between us in a few long strides.

"I'm going to set up my camp by that group of trees." I point to my chosen spot.

Wes surveys the area, then turns toward me, his gaze focusing on my face. "By yourself?" The question simmers with his smoky, resonant voice.

"That's the plan." I tuck a strand of hair behind my ear.

"Do ya need any help? I can assemble the tent for you. Or start a fire."

"I appreciate your offer, but I'm all right, thanks."

He steps closer, the furrow in his brow deepening. "Are ya sure?"

"Yes, I'm sure." My reply comes out more abrupt than I intended, so I touch his arm. "But thank you."

Wes nods and walks back to where his friends wait. He says something to them, but I can't hear him over the roar of the rapids. Whatever it is, it involves me, because now they're all staring. I give them a friendly wave and start to walk away.

"Lena, wait up." Jake jogs over. "Why are you running off alone? You can hang with us."

"Thanks, Jake. That's sweet of you, but I'm fine. I want you boys to have your guy-time."

"Don't be ridiculous." He rolls his eyes. "You're not bothering us."

"No, really. Thank you, but I'm gonna do my own thing."

Jake cocks his head. "Is the arrogant dick quotient too high for you?"

My brows pop. "He told you what I said?"

"Yep. He's really bothered you called him that."

I snort. "I didn't *call* him an arrogant dick, I simply implied it. If he'd listened to the rest of what I was saying, instead of making it all about him, he'd understand *why* I feel that way." I adjust the pack on my throbbing shoulder. "No offense to you, but in my experience with men, their listening skills are subpar. Wes is clearly no exception."

Jake chuckles. "Yeah, we can be a bunch of fucking idiots—especially Emerson," he glances over his shoulder, "but, for what it's worth, he's more tolerable once you get to know him."

I smile. "I'll take your word for it."

"No, seriously. He has a heart of gold."

I nod and point to my tree cluster. "I'm going to settle in for the night and explore tomorrow. I'll see you guys in a couple of days."

"Okay but be careful. You heard what Chuck said about bears."

"I will. You guys, too." I wave and trudge to my spot.

I unwrap a protein bar and take a swig from my canteen. I have a lot to do and look forward to reading my book in front of the fire. After all, my book boyfriends are *not* arrogant dicks.

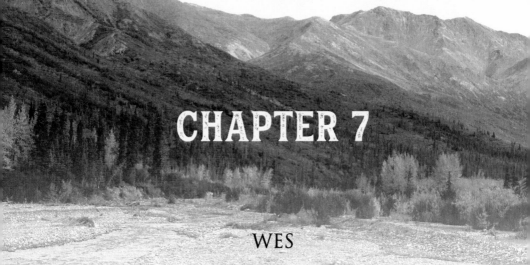

CHAPTER 7

WES

Internal playlist: "Shelter" by Ray LaMontagne

Dragging my feet as I walk, I look over my shoulder to where Lena is assembling her tent. I should be doing that for her. At the very least, I should've made a fire. What if she doesn't know how? It's already cold out, and I hate the idea of her catching a chill when the sun goes down.

"Why the scowl, Emerson?" Jake asks knowingly.

"I've never met anyone so stubborn in all my life."

Austin nudges me. "Other than yourself, you mean?"

"I'm not stubborn. I'm strong-willed. I like getting what I want."

"Well, it looks like you ain't gettin' it right now. Somebody's got other plans."

I grunt. "Tell me about it."

"I don't like it, either." Jake glances in Lena's direction. "I tried to change her mind."

Austin follows our gazes. "Simple solution, fellas. We stay close. Not too close that she can see us or feel like she's under surveillance, but close enough that we can help if she runs into trouble. How about a little beyond the tree line? It's pretty dense, but it's within earshot and we can get a visual every so often."

"Good plan, Memphis." Jake claps him on the back and turns to me. "That work for you?"

I glance over at the fiercely independent woman with an unexpected surge of protectiveness. As the eldest of my siblings, I'm the one who has always looked after everyone. Whether it be defending Reed from childhood bullies, or check ins with Isla while she's away at college, I'm compelled to protect. Though I'm familiar with the feeling, it seems deeper and more primal this time, delving into territory I haven't explored in years.

I sigh. "We can give it a shot, mate."

I don't want to fail Lena; I want to wrap her in my arms and shield her from harm. I shake my head. Where is this coming from? She's not my sister. She's not mine. It's not my job to shelter her. Besides, not only does she have a shitty opinion of me, she wouldn't let me protect her if I tried.

I picture her face on the plane. The fear in her eyes. The way she clung to my wrist. How good it felt to squeeze her hand and tell her it would be all right. She turned to me for safety. No, she's not mine to protect, yet my unease grows with each retreating step.

Don't get involved.

I follow my friends up the mountain and try to focus on my upcoming film. It's a vastly different role from Ares, and I worry about doing it justice. The fast-paced thriller is scheduled to begin filming in the spring. My concern is that audiences will struggle to see me as a character other than Ares, that my appeal is solely in my portrayal of the brooding, muscular god. I want to be remembered as more than some fuckwit with biceps. Hopefully, the role of cutthroat attorney will break that mold for me. My career—and life—needs a new compass.

CHAPTER 8

LENA

Internal playlist: "Utopia" by Alanis Morissette

After a deep, dreamless slumber, I emerge from my tent ready to conquer the day. I need more nights like that—lulled to sleep by rushing rapids instead of horns and sirens. I watch the flames come alive after tossing a log onto the smoldering embers. My stomach grumbles, so I withdraw a protein bar from my stash of food. "Time for your brekkie, Lena," I say, attempting an Australian accent.

I gather my hair into a low ponytail. Although it's less windy than yesterday, that means nothing to the stubborn tendrils swirling around my face.

The bright sun sparkles on the rapids, creating the illusion of a river of diamonds. The pure, unpolluted water is nothing like the murky brown swirls of my native Hudson.

"Oh! Caribou!" I snatch my camera and snap a few dozen pictures, marveling at the creature's impressive antlers and broad, muscular body as he sips at the water's edge. Satisfied, I turn my attention to my camp.

Overnight, pine needles collected atop the tarp I used for an awning. I brush them off and toss them into the fire. They hiss and crackle in the flames, and the scent reminds me of my favorite holiday, Christmas. Well, at least it *was* years back—before Marc ruined it.

Stretching my arms overhead, I arch my body and vow to continue my yoga practice. What I really need is a new yoga studio. I've been avoiding my former one ever since Marc and I split in December. His apartment is a block from that studio. Since I see plenty of him at work, I have no desire for a run-in on my downtime.

Taking in the surrounding wilderness, it occurs to me that I'm truly alone. The rush of rapids and chirps of birds replace the noise and chaos of the city. I draw a deep breath and feel something within me settle. I'm alone, but I don't *feel* alone. There's a difference. Having wasted four years aching for the attention of the one person who should've never made me feel alone, I'll take physical isolation over the pain of an empty relationship any day. At least I didn't marry him.

I met Marc Donnelly in the operating room five years ago. Like me, he wants to heal. He just doesn't know how to heal himself. I wasted four long, loveless years trying to force a connection that wasn't there. Sure, he proposed, but that's what successful surgeons do—they get themselves pretty nurse wives.

But the two-carat diamond couldn't replace his attention, affection, or love. As much as I wanted a husband and a family, I refused to settle for a loveless marriage. I called it quits after another hollow Christmas.

Marc is a machine, and while that behavior was responsible for our split, he impressed me last week with the way he handled the Tall Oaks tragedy. The man was on autopilot. He kept going—surgery after surgery—until he did all he could. His team of orthopedic and reconstructive surgeons repaired broken, mangled limbs like it was as simple as cutting a hangnail. In the span of three double-shifts, I lost track of the number of reattached limbs. Blood-covered and exhausted, Marc didn't eat or sleep until every victim had been treated.

Meanwhile, I fell apart. When the number of casualties surpassed what I could count on my fingers and toes, I broke down. What started as a massive panic attack in the middle of the ER, ended with me collapsing into a blubbering mess in the nurses' lounge. Then Marc had the nerve to tell me I always let my emotions get the better of me. He said I need to grow a thicker skin, like I didn't just watch people take their last breaths, some of them without family by their sides. These people were in pain and *dying*. Alone.

Maybe I didn't need to stay with each patient until the end, but I don't care what anyone says, no one deserves to die alone. If my presence provided even one sliver of comfort, that's enough for me.

A wave of pent-up emotion swells. Unable to suppress it any longer, my eyes blur with tears as it crests and crashes over me. Allowing my despair to pull me under, I stand by the fire and let the rivers run down my cheeks. And now that the dam has finally broken, it feels like I'm drowning in enough sorrow to douse the flames. I wrap my arms around myself in a hug as the sobs rack my body.

A rustling sound captures my attention, and I scan the tundra. A flash of red at the tree line signals Wes's approach.

Fuck.

I quickly wipe at my face and attempt composure.

He waves and trudges toward my campsite. "G'day. I was hoping we could start over." His heavy footfalls crunch on the rocks as he makes his way over to me. "We got off on the wrong—" His gaze fixates on my face. "Are you all right?"

"Yeah," I lie. "I'm fine."

He releases a heavy sigh. "This is now the second time I've come across ya with tears in your eyes. You're not fine. Tell me what's wrong."

"I don't wanna talk about it."

"You made that clear at the lodge. Look, despite whatcha think of me, my goal's not to push you around."

I narrow my eyes. "Then why are you still asking?"

He steps closer to me. "Maybe I don't like seeing you cry."

"Sorry for ruining your view again," I mutter, casting a glance at my feet.

Wes grips my chin and tilts my head up. His cobalt gaze burns into me. "Maybe it bothers me to see tears swimming in your beautiful eyes, Lena. I want to know *why* you're crying," his tone softens, "and what I can do to fix it."

My lip quivers and I feel the tears welling again. "No one can fix it."

"Listen, I'm sorry for the way I've been treating you. I admit, I was pissed that the lodge sold my brother's room. We were mobbed at the airport in L.A. and again in Seattle. By the time we got to Fairbanks, I'd had more than enough. I assumed you'd be like the people we encounter on a regular basis. Essentially, I had a long day and acted like a dick." He tightens his grip on my chin. "But that's not me, Lena. I know I haven't shown it, but I'm a decent bloke at heart. I'm sorry my behavior made you feel like you had to justify your presence—that wasn't my intention. You have every right to be here, and I'm sorry your holiday got off to a rough start because of me."

"Thank you," I whisper, more moved by his mea culpa than I expected. "I'm sorry for being a bitch. I've had a week from hell. My brain's on overload, and my emotions have a hairpin trigger."

He nods. "I'm sorry you lost your job."

"I didn't lose my job; I was placed on a leave of absence. It feels like an exile though. To complicate matters, on my way out the door, my boss offered me a promotion."

Wes smiles. "Congratulations."

"Thanks. I'm still undecided."

"If you don't mind me asking, what's holdin' ya back?"

"I'm not sure I can handle the pressure."

"I dunno about that, Lena. I've already seen evidence to the contrary." I raise a brow and he clarifies, "You don't seem like the type of woman to accept defeat."

"Thanks, Wes, but I *feel* defeated. That's why I'm here."

"Whaddya mean?"

"I work in a level-one trauma center. This week, an apartment building collapsed a few blocks from my hospital. There were fifty-seven casualties." My tone is hollow as I continue, "We tried like hell to save everyone, but it wasn't possible. During my career, I've seen things you can't even imagine, but this . . . this surpassed anything I've ever dealt with. Limbs crushed and broken, some of them missing entirely. When the building collapsed, it caught fire. Our burn unit was at capacity. I'm not exaggerating when I tell you it was hell on earth. Anyway, I worked several doubles and was exhausted. A numbness settled over me, but after the twelfth patient died in my arms, I lost it and completely melted down." I stare across the river and clench my jaw against the welling tears.

"Christ, Lena," Wes breathes. "I'm so sorry you had to go through that. I feel like an arse for complaining about my life."

"Please don't. I totally get it. Sounds like we both need a break from reality."

"I say, fuck reality for a while."

"I'm with you," I murmur, "one hundred percent."

"So, what happened next?"

"My attending swooped in and forced me out the door. He placed me on a mandated medical leave and told me I had to stay away for at least two weeks. But I feel like two weeks won't even scratch the surface . . ." A tear rolls down my cheek. Then another. I don't bother to brush them away because I know there will be more.

Wes places a hand on my shoulder. "Lena, I can't imagine what you're feeling, but I want you to know I'm here to listen."

"Thank you," I whisper. "I'm sorry, I didn't mean to cry."

"Never apologize for showing emotion. You can't keep stuff like that locked inside. It'll destroy you."

"It already has." The tears flow freely. Emotions I've pushed aside for days come roaring back with a vengeance. I know it's strange—pouring my heart out to a stranger—but now that the floodgates have broken, I can't stop. "I barely recognize myself anymore, and I think what bothers me most is how routine it became. I watched the light fade from their eyes and immediately moved to the next one like they meant *nothing*. It was just this conveyor belt of death and I'd become desensitized. That's not *me*, Wes. I've always prided myself on having the gift of empathy, but now, death makes me numb. It's like I'm empty inside until I finally snap. I've lost myself, and I'm afraid I'm losing my humanity." My voice breaks.

"Come here." Wes pulls me into a hug. "You won't lose your humanity. The fact that it concerns you is proof. Numbness is your mind's attempt at self-preservation. It's a natural response to tragedy."

"I don't want to be numb, but I'm tired of watching people die," I whisper into his chest, my arms finding their way around his waist. I close my eyes and melt into the hug I so desperately need.

"You need a new trajectory in life. Change course before ya crash and burn."

"I know." I sigh, tightening my arms around him. "So, I went home that night with no clue what to do with myself. I can't tell you the last time I've had over five days off in a row. We're talking *years*. Anyway, my best friend suggested I get away to clear my head, and here I am. I've got two weeks to decide the future of my career."

"I'm sure you'll find your answer out here," Wes replies. "Just keep an open mind and let the universe guide you."

"I'll try," I whisper.

"Lena, you're a woman of action. Don't try, *do*. Make it happen."

"I know."

"You say that you know, but I can feel your hesitation. What's holding you back?"

"Fear," I confess.

"Fear of what? Failure?"

"That's part of it." I wipe my eyes. "I'm hesitant to be a rookie again. I know what to do when I push through those double doors. I know where everything is, who to call, which treatment protocol applies—it's been my home for a decade. The thought of starting over is terrifying. If I take the position and screw up, everything will change. I'm well-liked and respected in my department."

"Forgive me if this is too forward, but it doesn't sound like you like yourself."

Pulling from his embrace, I cock my head. "What do you mean?"

"I'm sorry. That came out wrong." Wes rubs his jaw. "Let me give you a film analogy. To me, it sounds like you've over-scripted the scene. You've cast yourself as a failure without taking the chance to see what you're capable of. You're playing the part of the actor *and* the director, but they're working against each other. You've slammed the clapperboard and cut the scene before it even started. Does that make sense?"

"It makes perfect sense, and you're absolutely right. I'm afraid of the unknown, of losing control." I cross my arms over my chest, rub at the chill, and hold on to myself.

"I think we all are, Lena. But sometimes we need to let go of control in order to strengthen our grip. Maybe this promotion is the change you need. What does the position entail?"

"It's a nurse supervisory position. I'd be charged with running the emergency department. It would be a separation from direct patient care, but it's heavily administrative, which I have zero experience in. I've always been hands-on. That's what I love about being a nurse."

Wes touches my shoulder. "But it's sucking the life out of you."

"Yes," I meet his gaze, "I'm running on empty. It's been like this for years, but it finally hit me this time. It was too much all at once."

"Take a chance and fill your tank," Wes says with a smile. "Oh, look . . . there's another analogy for ya."

I return his smile. "Thank you."

"Anytime. I've got dozens of them." His gaze focuses on my eyes. "If it makes you smile, I'll give you all of them. I'll just list them, one after another, rapid-fire like a machine gun."

I giggle in response.

"And if it makes ya laugh, I'll unleash my full literary potential and release the bloody Kraken."

I erupt into a fit of laughter, complete with tears. "You may wanna check that one out on *Urban Dictionary*."

"Whaddya mean?" he asks in amusement. "Is there some strange American definition I don't know about?"

"Use your imagination."

"Now, I'm gonna have to look that one up."

I clap his shoulder. "You made my day, thank you."

Wes smirks. "Well, I'm glad to be of service to ya."

We gaze at the river in companionable silence while the morning sun and slight breeze dry the tears on my cheeks.

"Wes?"

He turns to face me.

"Thanks for listening. And for . . . everything."

"Anytime, Lena. I'm happy to help you with *anything*."

I head toward the boisterous laughter coming from the riverbank, fishing gear in tow.

The guys already have their lines in the water. I grin at the good-natured insults they hurl at each other.

"Think I got one." Austin reels in his line. "Nope. False alarm."

Jake snickers. "Yeah, that's the only way he can get *his* line wet."

Wes snorts.

"Y'all can laugh all you want, but last I checked, I was the only one doing *anything* with my pole," Austin retorts.

"Don't remind me," Jake laments. Noticing me, he flushes. "Sorry, Lena. We're being pigs."

"Works for me." I settle on the bank between Wes and Jake. "Let it be known I like my bacon crispy and my sausage in *big* links."

Wes chokes on his granola bar, coughing and sputtering from his spot on the rocks.

I look over at him. "You're supposed to chew that first. You come up for air afterward. It's a coordinated effort." I giggle. "I feel like Jake's a male version of myself. We're kindred spirits, except he lacks a filter."

Jake laughs. "Been told that before. And here I was all worried about offending you."

"Having been a trauma nurse for years, very little offends me." I tie on a lure and cast my line. Wes regains control and stares at me. Feeling the weight of his gaze, I turn. "What?"

"I knew you were sassy, but I didn't realize you were this saucy." He tugs on his line and stretches his legs.

"I'm full of surprises."

He licks his lips and my insides heat. "I bet you are."

"Fish on!" I stand and quickly reel in my line.

"Seriously?" Wes shakes his head. "You've been here for like two minutes."

"What can I say? I've got skills." I struggle to pull my catch from the water. "Damn, he's strong."

Wes stands. "Let me help you."

I wave him off. "I got it." I give the line a hard tug and an enormous salmon breaches the surface.

I stagger backward, colliding with Wes, who snatches the fish and holds it up. "Holy hell, he's huge."

Jake snickers. "That's what she said."

I laugh and reach for the fish. After removing the hook, I realize none of us brought anything to hold our catch. "Thoughts on how we should store this puppy? I didn't think to bring a cooler or cooking vessel."

"We didn't bring a cooler either, but we have a pot and skillet back at camp. We planned on catching and cooking a couple on our own at Gobbler's Knob," Austin says. "Chuck mentioned we shouldn't eat near our tents. Do y'all think we should build a fire here? Then we can cook everything a good distance away."

"Good idea, mate." Wes pulls on his aviators and scans the area. "I'll gather wood since I'm not having any luck with my pole."

"Yeah, I've heard that about you," Jake teases.

I snort.

"You're real funny, Bennett." Wes turns to me. "And what are *you* laughing at? Got a problem with my pole?"

"Nope. You sure you know how to use it?" I smirk as Wes's jaw drops and Jake falls over laughing. I hold up the fish. "I've never seen one this big. He's gotta be almost two feet long. You guys can quit fishing; I'm more than happy to share. I'm gonna grab my fire-starting stuff. Be right back." I head for my camp.

Trudging back to the riverbank with my fire gear and knives, my gaze locks on to Wes's ass as he bends over to pick up a log. I squeeze my knife thinking about digging my fingers into his cheeks while he thrusts. I drop the blade and it clatters to the rocks.

Wes turns toward me. "If you plan to throw knives, let me know when I need to duck."

"Sounds good." It's all I can muster.

I clutch the rescued knife to my chest and rejoin the group where Austin and Jake are lining up stones for a fire pit. I quickly gather grass clumps and birch bark. After a few minutes, Wes returns with an armload of wood. I position the kindling, kneel on the rocks, and shave off some bark.

"Need help?" Wes asks.

"Thanks, but I've got it. I'm a little out of practice, so I wanna give myself a refresher."

I strike the Ferro Rod, and the predictable shower of sparks glitters on the birch dust. This method seems a bit archaic, making me wonder why Bic lighters weren't on the lodge's packing list. Unfortunately, I didn't think to bring one—nor did any of the guys. It just goes to show what inexperienced campers we are. Like, seriously, who forgets something like that?

Then again, maybe the Gobbler's Knob guidepost had them, and we missed out since we chose to rough it. Or perhaps the lodge simply wanted to do their part in preventing forest fires. Who knows? I suppose the reason doesn't matter, because soon enough, the embers grow to a flame. I transfer it to the kindling and turn to discover the three men staring.

I smile as I rise and dust off my hands. "That's how it's done, gentlemen."

Wes eyes me with raised brows. "Clearly, *you're* not here to fuck spiders."

"*What?*"

Jake laughs. "He means you don't fuck around. Seriously, were you a Girl Scout or something?"

"I was until third grade, but I certainly didn't learn any survival skills singing the friendship song or selling cookies."

"Then who taught you?" Wes asks, towering over me.

"My brother taught me the basics when we were kids, and I learned a few other tricks binge-watching survival shows."

Wes smiles in approval. "I'm impressed."

I see my reflection in his aviators and return his smile.

His arms and shoulders bulge in a white thermal, which contrasts with the golden skin of his neck. Dark jeans encase his legs and hug that to-die-for ass. His tousled hair appears much softer without the gel. I ache to knot my fingers in it and pull his lips to mine. And although I can't see it, I know the gorgeous visage hiding beneath those sunglasses. I fight the sudden urge to run my hands over his chest. Instead, I bite my lower lip and force my arms to remain at my sides.

Heart racing, I can barely force the shallow, shaky breaths that expand my chest. My ovaries toss a few logs on the bonfire in my lower belly and my nipples prick the inside of my bra.

It's not fair Wes can do this to me. And the worst part is he knows. I see it in the satisfied smirk that tugs at the corners of his lips, and the way he suddenly stands taller and draws back his shoulders, making his chest seem even broader. He's a peacock on display and those feathers draw me like a moth to a flame. While the universe pours gasoline on my bonfire, at least now I *know* my libido didn't fizzle out and die courtesy of Marc.

He sucked the passion right out of me—I even lacked the desire to take care of my own business. We broke up eight months ago, but it's been well over two years since I had sex—and I've gone even longer without an orgasm. It was always about Marc and his needs over mine. Parched by a dry spell of epic proportions, I endured *years* without pleasure, without passion. But thanks to Wes, my libido has come roaring back to life like a fucking tsunami. I'm *thirsty* and only he can quench it.

The prospect of a fling tempts me, but I'll never go through with it. Deep down, I know I'm not capable of the emotional separation. For me, it's all or nothing, none of this half-assed bullshit. I'd be a fool to hope Wes would give me his all. I know damn well how it would play out. The trip would end, we'd go our separate ways, and I'd simply be an afterthought—again. I refuse to sip from that fountain, but that doesn't mean I can't whet my appetite with the fantasy. Maybe when I get home, I'll wade into the dating pool.

But I'd much rather drown in Wes.

CHAPTER 9

LENA

Internal playlist: "Castle" by Halsey

It's eerie and much darker in the dense boreal forest. I keep stride with Austin as we hike to the men's camp to grab a skillet. They pitched a yellow, six-person tent in a small clearing and stowed all their gear inside.

"Seemed like a lotta work to set up three tents," Austin explains.

"I must not have paid attention to the list of suggested items because I have a running list of things I wish I packed. The first, being an ax. Also, it would've been helpful to have something to cook with. I'm glad you guys brought a skillet, and I appreciate that you invited me to eat with you."

"Like we told you, you're welcome to chill with us anytime." Austin smiles and unzips the tent. "Hang on a minute. I'm gonna get some stuff. You thirsty?"

"Yes, actually. I left my canteen by the river."

He retrieves a bottle of water from someone's pack and tosses it to me. "We brought almost a case of water. Heavy as hell, but worth it. Otherwise, we would've stayed much closer to the river." He pulls out a skillet, a few more bottles of water, and his guitar case.

"Let me carry those." I grab the skillet and water bottles. "I need to make myself useful."

"Well, you already caught a fish and started our fire. That's damn useful." He scans the camp. "I hope I'm not forgettin' anything. Or else, I'll be invitin' you on another field trip up here."

Satisfied with what we picked up, we start our return trek. Austin gushes about his actress girlfriend, Kate Waters, a passionate woman who spends her free time advocating for survivors of domestic violence.

"It's easy to see why you love her. She's like a goddess among us mere mortals."

"Thanks, Lena. She's always been a goddess to me." He stops walking and studies me. "Hey, can you keep a secret?"

"Absolutely. Good God, my entire life is secrets. As a nurse, I know more crazy shit than I care to."

"Okay, so I haven't mentioned this to the guys yet. I don't wanna listen to them raggin' on me the whole trip," he explains. "So, please, don't tell a soul."

"You have my word, Austin." I place my hand across my heart.

"I bought a ring," he whispers, his eyes gleaming with excitement, "and I plan on givin' it to her when I get back from this trip."

I throw my arms around his neck and hug him. "Congratulations. I'm so excited for you!" My fourteen-year-old self would've drowned in sorrow, but thirty-two-year-old me is genuinely ecstatic and honored he chose to confide in me. "Have you planned out an elaborate proposal?"

"Picture this: a private beach house on the French Riviera. We take a moonlit walk along the shore, the salty breeze blowin' through our hair. I pause and sink to one knee—"

"Oh. My. God. That sounds amazing, Austin. You need to teach a class on how to be a romantic man. Most guys are clueless."

"Aw, you just haven't met the right one."

"Like I said, teach that class and send a student my way." I shake my head and think of all the idiots I've encountered. It would be nice if, just once, I met someone I connected with. "Again, thanks for being so cool. I mean, you and Jake have been nothing but warm and welcoming, even though I crashed your boys' trip."

"No worries, girlie. You're much easier to tolerate than those fools." He stops walking and faces me. "I noticed you left someone out. You're not feelin' the warm and fuzzy there?"

I sigh. "Yes and no. He's been kinda Jekyll and Hyde with me. One minute it seems like he's flirting, and the next—"

Austin grins. "He acts like an arrogant dick."

"Jesus, he told you about that *too?*"

"There's very little he *doesn't* tell me."

"For the record, I didn't come right out and call him one."

"Don't worry, he read between the lines," he says with a chuckle. "And you definitely get under his skin." My gaze snaps to his and he adds, "Just not the way you think."

I arch a brow. "Oh?"

"Not as an annoyance, but a fascination." He glances in Wes's direction. "I've known him a long time. He *is* tryin' to flirt, but unlike the women who throw themselves at him, you keep shuttin' him down. He ain't used to that."

"Trust me, Austin, I don't throw myself at *anyone.*"

"That's crystal clear, darlin'." He winks and squeezes my shoulder. "And that's what makes you a source of intrigue."

I roll my eyes. "I'm incredibly intriguing."

"I'm serious," Austin insists. "See, here's the thing about Wes. He's used to runnin' the show and he don't let *nobody* ruffle his feathers. And I mean nobody." A slow grin crosses his features. "But, darlin', you're out here pluckin' him bare. All you gotta do is pay attention."

We rejoin the others, who are bickering about how to cook the fish.

"Y'all are like an old married couple," Austin tells them. "Just quit your bitchin' and cook it."

"God help anyone stuck with surfer boy for all eternity. I'd rather hang from my testicles," Jake says. "He's unbelievable."

"Aw, love you too, mate." Wes catches the water Austin tosses him, chugging the entire bottle in one gulp. "You like our homestead, Lena?"

"Yes. Very cozy." Austin's words echo in my mind as I search for my fish. "Hey, what happened to my catch?"

"The poor bloke was flopping, so I bonked him on the noggin. Skinned him for you too," Wes says.

"Thanks. I dreaded killing him." I shudder. "I'm a lover of all creatures—except for spiders and sharks."

"You wanna pray over his carcass? It's over there. I'll grab it for ya," Wes offers with a grin.

"No, smart-ass. I just don't like killing things." Hands on my hips, I cock a brow. "But at the rate you're going, I may change my mind."

"By that, she means fuck off, surfer boy," Jake translates with a self-satisfied grin.

"Thanks for the colorful translation, Bennett. Wasn't sure what she meant." Wes places the skinned fish fillet in the skillet.

"My translation was less harsh, but thanks, Jake." I scan the area. "What would you like me to do?"

"You just relax, baby girl," Austin drawls.

"Fair enough." I grab my book. While Austin and I hiked, Wes and Jake dragged two large logs near the fireside for seating. I settle, and once again, angle the book to create the illusion of reading.

Wes crouches over the fire and pokes at the fish. "I have no clue how to cook this. It looks done, but I'll let someone else make that call." He motions to Austin. "Memphis, help me out."

Austin inspects the fish. "It's feedin' time, y'all."

We lunch under the Alaskan sun, and I feel surprisingly at ease around them. Austin retrieves his guitar and strums some melodies, his fingers expertly navigating the strings. I recognize the melody to John Denver's "Rocky Mountain High," and it delights me when Jake starts to sing. Never, in a million years, would I have imagined getting a private concert from my two favorite singers. Or garnering Wes Emerson's interest.

It's late evening. Wes kneels at the river's edge and splashes water on his face. He stands and brushes dirt and bark from his clothes before joining Austin on a log. As he dries his face on his shirt, I glimpse the rippling muscles of his abdomen, marred by a surgical scar. I never noticed the mark in any of his movies and wonder about it.

I'm seated beside Jake, skinning and gutting another fish. When I finish, I toss the carcass aside like a vicious alley cat.

Wes points to the pile of guts. "You learn that on TV, too?"

"Sure did. Got a couple of tricks up my sleeve."

"Nice work, Lena-Bean." Jake nods his approval.

"Why, thank you." I smile, but my inner fangirl shrieks. *Jake Bennett gave me a nickname!* I pull my hair into a low bun and use my sunglasses like a headband to contain the wispy tendrils.

Jake eyes me. "Hey, I've been meaning to ask, are those real?"

Wes spits out a mouthful of water and stares at him in shock. Austin gapes beside him, nearly dropping his guitar.

My head jerks to the side. "*Excuse* me?"

"Fuck." Jake buries his face in his hands. "I meant all your earrings. I didn't realize how that sounded until it came out." Redness spreads to his neck and ears.

"You need to work on that filter, mate." Wes laughs. "It's like verbal diarrhea."

"Well, he has a point." Austin gestures to the row of diamonds that climb each of my ears. "Look at all that ice. The lodge musta given you a different packin' list than the one we got."

"Can't help it. I love bling. It's the only jewelry I can wear at work, and I never take them off. And yes, they *are* real." I laugh and mock-punch Jake's shoulder.

"Ah, so *that's* the reason I see nothin' on your neck," Austin says.

I tense at the mention of my neck—I'm definitely not going there with them. "One of many reasons."

"Come to think of it, you have nothin' on your fingers, either." He eyes my left hand. "No special someone in your life?"

"Nope."

"Didn't realize the men in New York were so blind." Austin cocks his head to the side. "Blind, *and* dumb, apparently."

"Yeah." I hope my eyes convey a message of warning.

Austin grins. "I'm shocked, darlin'. I figured a pretty lady like yourself would have them linin' up to put a ring on it."

"Someone did," I mutter. "But I gave the ring back in December." The color drains from Austin's face. "Apparently, I was convenient. He didn't want marriage. He proposed because it was expected of him. All successful surgeons have their little nurse wives," I say bitterly. "I was too stupid to admit our relationship was toxic. That he made me feel more alone with him than I've *ever* felt without him. That was my life for four years until I finally woke the fuck up." I stare at the river and recall last Christmas. "Best decision I ever made."

"I'm so sorry, Lena," Austin murmurs. "I didn't mean to upset you."

"Don't be." I give him a small smile. "I've had plenty of time to reflect on it. See, there comes a point when, no matter how much you may love someone, you realize you can't fight their demons for them."

"Sounds like you're at peace with it," Jake says.

"It was the healthiest thing I could've done. I finally accepted that I couldn't save him. Truth be told, he didn't want saving. It took me four years to figure that out. Four years trying to force something that wasn't there."

"I understand the 'forcing it' thing," Jake mutters, "but sometimes, when I think about getting older and possibly ending up alone, it freaks me out."

"I get it. I'm almost thirty-three. Most of my friends are already married and have started families. That's all I've ever wanted—a family of my own. My reality is so far from what I'd pictured for myself it's almost like a parallel life. If those milestones aren't in the cards for me, then so be it. Maybe I wasn't meant to fit into that mold. Who knows? But one thing's for certain, I'll *never* allow another person to extinguish my sense of self again. I fought too hard to climb from that abyss."

"Sounds like you have it figured out," Jake says.

"It's liberating. I can do whatever I want, whenever I want, and don't have to answer to anyone."

"Do you date at all?" Austin asks.

"Occasionally. I keep my expectations low and, if there's no connection, I move on. I don't have time for bullshit."

"Sounds like ya don't want any connections." Wes meets my gaze through the flames.

I shake my head. "That's not what I said. Don't confuse desire with necessity."

"Care to clarify?"

Not really. Yet Wes's gaze compels my elaboration. "Do I *want* someone to share my life with? Absolutely. Do I *need* another person to dictate my happiness? Hell no." I loosen my bun to combat the developing headache. "All my life, I've lived for others. I'm finally meeting *my* needs. I won't go back. At this point, I'd rather be alone than settle for less than I deserve."

"What *do* you deserve?"

The question's intensity rattles me, but I meet Wes's gaze with ferocity. *If he wants to play this game . . .*

"I deserve to have my world rocked. I want a man to excite me, inspire me to be a better person. I want him to make me laugh and hold me when I cry. I want him to desire me and love me for who I am—not who he thinks I should be." I stiffen. "But most of all, I want to be a priority, *not* a fucking afterthought. Been there, done that."

"Very specific, Lena." Wes rises and walks over to me.

"Like I said, I don't have time for bullshit." I shrug. "But in my experience, that kind of man isn't real; I'm pretty sure he only exists in romance novels." I pick up my book. "Which is why I'm gonna curl up by this nice fire with my book boyfriend."

He smirks. "If it's the one from the plane, he doesn't know what he's doing."

I raise a brow. "Says the man who can't figure out his fishing pole."

"Trust me, I can handle my pole. If you're interested, I'm more than happy to give a demonstration."

"A bit cocky, aren't we?"

Wes squats in front of me, placing both hands on my shoulders. "Tell me, when you read that book, are ya really picturing whatever fuckwit's playing the hero? Or does he happen to look like me?" The heat in his eyes creates an answering throb between my legs. His voice drops to a low rumble that hardens my nipples. "Given the amount of time you've spent pretending to read, I'll bet it's the latter."

I open and close my mouth, unable to answer.

"I've noticed how ya watch me," Wes tightens his grip on my shoulders, "and from what I can tell, you're on the same page as the last time you read."

My jaw drops and my face heats.

A wicked grin spreads across his face. "And your reaction tells me I'm right." He leans in, his nose almost touching mine. "Guess what, sunshine . . ."

My breath comes in little pants. I can't move, can't think.

"I'm better than you could *ever* imagine."

I stare at him, eyes darting between molten cobalt and his full, kissable lips. Wes starts to lean in.

"Let's go, Wes, you've antagonized her enough." Jake's voice bursts the bubble that surrounds us. He gestures to the fire. "Should we pour water on this, or let it burn out?"

Good fucking question, Jake. I draw a ragged breath and try to decide whether I'm grateful or furious.

Wes's gaze lingers on my lips for a moment before meeting mine. Then, he winks and climbs to his feet.

I stare up at him, placing the book in my lap.

"C'mon, Wes," Jake commands. "Night, Lena."

"Sleep well, darlin'," Austin adds.

"Night, guys."

"Sleep tight, Lena." Wes trails behind his friends as they leave, then suddenly stops and turns to face me. Oblivious, the others keep walking.

I stare at the sun-kissed Ares from my position on the log a few feet away. An infuriating smugness laces his heated expression. The air between us is heavy, infused with unspoken words. Fists clenched at his sides, shoulders heaving with his inhalations, his message is clear: he wants me too.

"Guess what, Ace . . ." Stiffening my spine, I cock my head to the side. "I'm as guilty as the day is long." With one hand, I lift the book from my lap and toss it into the flames. The blaze engulfs my romance novel like the inferno of lust raging inside me since the moment we met. Soon, it will be just ash, obliterating my book boyfriend decoy. Kinda like what he's doing to my defenses.

CHAPTER 10

WES

Internal playlist: "Close" by Nick Jonas

Jake sings along while Austin strums a melody on his guitar. They lounge on a log by the fire at our camp, both relaxed. Meanwhile, I'm anything but. I pace the clearing, lost in my thoughts. Lena's driving me crazy. Watching me when she thinks I'm not looking—biting her lip, pressing her knees together. The not-so-subtle clues are damn near burning me alive.

I can't believe how close I came to kissing her. *Fucking cockblock Bennett.* Desperate to taste her lips, I lingered behind my mates. Then she shocked the shit out of me and threw her book in the fire. I intended to call her out, goad her a bit, but I never expected the fiery invitation—and that's exactly what it was. She didn't falter, just stared at me in challenge. I'm not used to being challenged. Lena gives it back as good as she takes it. I like that. Her spirit ignites me. It makes me want to provoke her, just to see her reaction. I can't believe I walked away. What the fuck is wrong with me?

I rake a hand through my hair. I don't want a romantic attachment. *Especially* after everything I went through with Rachel. My life's much simpler this way. Just flings and hookups. No guilt. No jealousy. No ultimatums. Keep it casual and I won't let anyone down. My lifestyle and schedule are too intense for something serious—and it makes the perfect shield to keep women at arm's length.

Staring through the trees toward Lena's camp, I realize I'm venturing into a wilderness of my own. It's been years since I wanted more. After

Rachel, I buried that part deep inside. Yet every time I'm close to Lena, I need her closer. Every time she speaks, I want to listen for hours. Every time she presses my buttons, I want her to push me harder. So much harder.

I can't keep my eyes—or my mind—off her. Sure, she's beautiful. There's no question about it. But it's not just Lena's body that captivates me. It's her mind, her heart, and her soul that draws me in. She provokes me, unnerves me, and entices me in ways I can't describe. Every time our eyes meet, she moves something inside me. And I want to kiss her every time she opens that sassy little mouth.

While Lena's spirit ignites me, her presence soothes the restlessness inside, which is something I thought only the ocean could do. The sea's my drug, but in a few short days, Lena has surpassed that high. She calls out to me like the waves beneath my board, and as she crests and crashes over me, I know I'll quickly become addicted. I know I can't keep her at arm's length, nor do I want to. Lena makes me want to try for something more. Something deeper. I'm ready to lower my shield, hold her close, and let her pull me under.

I replay the scene at the communal fire and repeat Lena's words in my mind. *Don't confuse desire with necessity.* She clearly delineated her wants from her needs. *I'd rather be alone than settle for less than I deserve.* I like a woman who knows what she wants and isn't afraid to make it known. I knot my fingers in my hair. She's not the kind of woman who'd be satisfied with a fling. Hell, she came right out and said it.

While I know damn well that Lena's wants and needs are *not* synonymous, she's giving me the urge to blur that distinction. Having needs puts you in danger of being dependent on people who may not be good for you. She makes me want to be good for her. Even though I shouldn't— and doubt whether I'm *able*—I *need* to be the man she doesn't yet know she wants. I ache to be the man she deserves.

"Please stop pacing and sit. You're giving me anxiety," Jake grumbles.

"I can't."

Austin raises a brow. "Someone got you thinkin'?"

I cross my arms over my chest. "I don't like it."

"Don't like what?" Jake asks with a smirk. "Using your brain?"

"I don't like her down there by herself. It's dangerous. What if something comes after her?"

"Then you're gonna have to go save her, big guy," Austin says.

I withdraw binoculars from my pack and scale a tree.

"What the hell are you doing?" Jake asks.

"Getting a visual."

Jake eyes me in disbelief. "Dude, it's dark out. What are you expecting to see?"

"I dunno, a fire, maybe?" I scan the valley. My mission's a lost cause as the forest is too thick. "I can't see shit," I mutter, descending the tree.

"Why don't you go down there?" Jake suggests.

"She wants to be alone, remember?"

"Yeah, and your point?" He shakes his head. "Not for nothing, but you've antagonized her since you met. Why the sudden concern?"

"Not for nothing, but it's *not* sudden."

Austin points to our tent. "So, tomorrow night, we move our camp closer. Would that make you feel better?"

I nod and settle on a log. I won't feel better until Lena's in my sight. She floats through my mind again. I've never met a woman with so many layers. Sassy, defiant, and brazen: she's a fighter. Compassionate, emotional, and vulnerable—she's a lover, too. I want to peel back those layers and reveal the woman inside. I want to know her. All of her. She stirred my inner alpha, but I shove the thoughts aside.

Don't get involved. Keep your distance.

Deep down, I know it's a lost cause, I'm already involved, and I can't keep my distance. Closing my eyes, I recall our conversation at her camp. How she allowed herself to be vulnerable with me. How her shoulders shook, and tears poured from her beautiful jade eyes. I can't begin to imagine the tragedy she described. Her reluctance to talk about it makes perfect sense, as does her outburst on the deck. I was a dick to push her like that.

I surprised myself when I hugged her. It was an automatic response to her tears, and I expected her to push me away. Instead, she melted into me, her body molding to mine like she was made for me. It shocked me to feel her arms wrap around my waist. The way she whispered into my chest, her tears dampening my shirt, made me want to fix every problem she's ever encountered. Made me want to make everything right in her world. I wanted to stand there all day with my chin resting atop her head, holding her body to mine, absorbing her scent, her softness, and her smile. I remember how she held my arm on the plane, looked to me for comfort. She needed me. *She's mine.*

As much as I shouldn't, I want Lena in my arms. And there's a little voice inside telling me that what I'm looking for isn't temporary. No matter how hard I try to redirect, the needle on my compass keeps pulling toward the snarky spitfire who's hell-bent on pushing me away.

CHAPTER 11

LENA

Internal playlist: "Howl" by Florence + The Machine

I lurch awake to a rustling outside my tent. *What the hell's that?* I silently pull a knife from my pack. I hear it again. It's not the wind; something's in my camp. I contemplate charging from the tent in attack mode, but fear paralyzes me. Instead, I burrow into my sleeping bag and clutch the knife to my chest. If I'm about to be killed, I'm not going down without a fight, but I'm not keen on seeking out my death, either.

I lie frozen in my tent. Ears ringing. Heart pounding. I don't dare move lest I give away my presence. But I know better. Whatever animal it is, it can smell my fear. It most definitely hears me. Even my breath is noisy. I crane my neck and listen. I hear the rustling sound again, but it seems further away. *Maybe it lost interest.* I listen in the darkness for several minutes, maybe hours. Drifting in and out of sleep, I clutch the knife to my body like a security blanket.

The darkness has faded, which means it's nearing dawn. I scuttle to the entryway and unzip the tent a few inches. Cold air wafts in. I peek through the opening and scan the area. No movement.

It looks like I'm up for the day. My head and shoulder throb in tandem, so I massage the tender areas as I dress.

I miss Garrett. I miss Harry and Hermione. I wonder if Garrett found the cat treats I'd hidden. Harry can't have them, but Uncle Garrett would've fed Hermione the whole damn bag in a day. Knowing him, he probably bought more. I can't imagine how spoiled my human children will be. *If* I ever get to have them.

I had a pregnancy scare a few years ago. My period was eight days late, and though I ached for a baby, the prospect paralyzed me. Marc wasn't ready for fatherhood. He couldn't even give me the attention I needed. I didn't want to do it alone. Yet, when my period finally came, I cried my eyes out. I never told Marc. I tried to tell myself it wasn't the right time. But, deep down, I knew he was the wrong person. Too bad it took me so long to act on that realization.

The sun hasn't risen yet, but it's close. Deciding to soak up the peaceful twilight before sunrise, I walk to the river like a woman on a mission.

CHAPTER 12

WES

Internal playlist: "In Your Eyes" by Jeffrey Gaines

Staring at the hypnotic flow of the water as it rushes over rocks and boulders, I listen to the roar of the rapids and think about my brother. I wish Reed were here. This holiday was supposed to be in his honor, a last hoorah before he marries Cora, and a much-needed break for him.

It can't be easy having Cora's mother living with them. It makes sense, though, since their place is near the cancer center where Gwen receives her infusions. After an eight-year remission, her breast cancer metastasized to her lungs and brain. Realistically, she has less than six months to live. Wedding planning has taken the back burner to Gwen's illness. Reed's struggling to help Cora keep it together. I know it breaks my brother's heart to see her that way, and he's already suffered more than his share of heartbreak.

Thanks to me.

Reed had just landed his first lead role, but at nineteen, his bright future was fractured alongside his leg and vertebra. Cora was the only positive to come from the motorcycle accident. As his physical therapist, she helped him relearn how to walk. The tragedy heralded the death of Reed's dream and the birth of my career. After the accident, the producers offered Reed's role to me, but I flat-out refused it. He spent months wearing me down until I reluctantly accepted the part.

I poured my heart and soul into the indie surfing flick. The film received five-star ratings at the Sydney Film Festival that year, garnering the attention of several directors. Thus, began my climb to stardom—on my brother's fucking ladder.

Sure, Reed passed his torch, but I'll never forgive myself for accepting it. Bile rises in my throat and my stomach churns like always. I'm disgusted with my success. I feel like a fraud, undeserving of the life I've stolen. The guilt, like acid in my heart, burns me alive. It resurfaces every time I win an award, every time they offer me a role. It sits on my shoulders like a lead weight during every red-carpet event, every interview, and every star-studded afterparty. Now I'm relaxing on my brother's holiday. He should be here, not me. I rub at the back of my neck.

"What are you doing here?" Lena's voice jolts me from my thoughts. She approaches the log where I'm seated.

I raise a brow. "Do ya own this section of the river?"

She puts her hands on her hips. "Would it make any difference to you?"

I smirk. "Nope."

She settles beside me. "Yeah, I kinda figured."

I gesture to the horizon where a palette of pastel pinks, oranges, and purples gradually illuminates the sky. "Wanted to watch the sunrise."

"You can't see it from your camp?"

"Nope. Too many trees." I study her face. "And you're down here."

Surprise flares in her eyes before her poker face takes over. "What does that have to do with anything?"

I rake a hand through my hair. "Listen, I'm sorry about last night. My mates told me I was being a dick again."

Lena shakes her head. "I'll let you know when you cross a line."

"Please do. I have a few roos loose in the top paddock." Her blank stare tells me the idiom is lost on her. "Allow me to translate. I can be an idiot."

"Ah. I like that one. Unlike the spider fuckery, I thoroughly enjoy the kangaroo reference."

"If roos are your thing, I recommend visiting 'Straya sometime." *Preferably with me.*

"It's on my bucket list." She bites her lower lip. "By the way, I love how you say that."

"Say what?"

"'Straya. You sound so . . . Aussie."

I laugh. "I hope I sound like one. Aside from briefly living in L.A., I've spent my whole life there."

"I admit, I enjoy your accent." She gives me a flirty smirk. "I'm intrigued by your slang and lingo too," her smirk widens to a grin, "especially when you go all outback on me."

I snort. "By outback, do ya mean when I sound like a bloody yobbo?"

She giggles. "I don't know what that is, but yeah. I've also noticed that sometimes your accent is more subtle than others. You fluctuate from almost Crocodile Dundee, to smooth and cultured, then back again."

"That's a product of my speech training for work. Ares is Greek, not Aussie. I can suppress it when I concentrate."

"Well, don't." She toys with the end of her braid. "Like I said, I like it."

I lean closer to her. "Too bad you burned that book."

"Oh? And why's that?" Despite her sassy tone, redness creeps across her cheeks.

"Since ya like the way I talk so much, I coulda read some scenes aloud."

She inhales sharply, and I meet her gaze. Framed by perfectly arched brows, Lena's eyes knock me senseless. Dark lashes fringe the soulful julep orbs. Flecked with gray, the color swirls like the tide pools on the Gold Coast.

"Maybe I'll take you up on that when we get back to the lodge," she murmurs, flashing me a wink. "I brought more than one book."

I blink a few times. *Don't just stare at her. Speak, you drongo.* "Sounds like a plan." My cock twitches, causing me to shift my position. I clear my throat. "So, what's on your agenda for today?"

"I'm either heading upstream along the riverbank or venturing into the woods. I haven't taken nearly enough pictures."

I motion to the mountains in the east. "We're hiking to that summit to look around. You should join us."

"Oh . . . um, that sounds great. Are you sure you don't mind?" She peers up at me with uncertainty.

"Tell me something, if I minded, do ya think I woulda walked all the way down here to invite you?"

"No, probably not."

"You're a fast learner, Lena. I like that about you."

Her lips part and her pink tongue darts out to wet them. *Sweet Christ, those lips. I envision them wrapped around—Stop. Don't be a pig. Focus on something else. Like venomous irukandji jellyfish. Or sharks. Yeah, sharks. Big fucking sharks with sharp teeth. Teeth that bite filthy bastards.* I shake my head to clear it. "Tell me about yourself."

"There's not much to tell."

I shift my body to face her. "Why do you keep saying that?"

She cocks a brow. "Why do *you* keep asking?"

"Because I want to know more about you." Lena's poker face is replaced with an eye roll. I gently elbow her. "Keep doing that and your eyes will get stuck in your head."

Kinda like how you're stuck in mine.

"What do you want to know?" she asks.

"Everything."

She narrows her eyes. "Why?"

Does no one talk to this woman?

"Do I need a reason?" When she doesn't answer, I touch her shoulder. "I wish I could read your mind right now."

Lena's lips twitch into a half-hearted smile. "You leave that clairvoyance of yours back at the lodge?"

I grin. "It wasn't on the list."

She yawns and rubs her eyes. "I'm sorry, I don't mean to be bitchy. I slept like shit. There was some animal rummaging around outside my tent and it freaked me out."

"It was probably Jake."

"I doubt that. It was something between a chipmunk and a grizzly. That's all I can tell you. I came here to warm up and didn't expect to find you here."

"Would ya like me to leave?"

Please say no.

"No," she whispers.

"That's good." I wink. "Because I wasn't planning to."

"Now, *there's* a shocker." She points to the river. "It's peaceful out here. Feels rejuvenating to be away from the chaos of the city. And life."

"I hear ya. It's nice to be out of the spotlight for a bit."

"How do you deal with that? I'd hate having people up in my business."

"Sometimes, I handle it better than others," I mutter. "Case in point, me being a dick to you at the lodge. Again, I'm sorry about that."

"It's fine, Wes. I'm over it. I don't blame you for your initial reaction to me. Of course, I can say that *now*, but at the time, I wanted to slap you."

I chuckle. "I appreciate your willingness to deal with my shit."

"Yeah, well, don't push your luck." She tilts her head. "Seriously, does the fame ever get to you?"

"More often than I'd like to admit." I sigh heavily. "This may sound ungrateful, but sometimes the attention makes me want to scream. I can't go to the grocery store without the headlines reading, 'Wes Emerson buys a loaf of bread at Whole Foods.' Do they really care that I prefer rolled oats over whole wheat? That, and the manufactured stories about my personal life. According to the tabloids, I've been married twice and have three children, which is news to me. Sometimes I read them for a laugh. It's so crazy."

"I guess there's something to be said for anonymity. If the lifestyle overwhelms you, why not step back?"

"I'd love nothing more. But I feel like I can't. At this stage in my career, while I still have the energy and drive, there's tremendous pressure to keep the momentum going."

"Pressure from whom? Your family? Fans?"

"Myself. I can't sustain the physical aspect forever and I'll eventually lose steam. I'm getting older, and I feel like I have nothing to fall back on."

"You do realize your talent goes beyond good looks and muscles, right?" Lena touches my arm. "You don't give yourself enough credit. Your versatility can conquer any role."

Heart pounding in my chest at her touch and kind words, I meet her gaze. "Thank you, Lena."

"I'm serious; you've got staying power that other actors can only dream about."

"I don't want to do this forever."

"Then don't."

"Wish it was that easy, Lena." I return my attention to the river and point to the opposite bank. "What kind of bird is that?"

"It's a loon. I saw him the first day and took some amazing pictures. Have you heard him call out yet?"

"Yes. It's eerily beautiful."

"You like birds."

I cock my head to the side. *Wait, how the hell does she know that?*

"I saw your tattoo," Lena explains as if reading my mind.

"It's a phoenix."

"May I see?" she asks.

I roll up my sleeve and extend my wrist to her.

Her warm, delicate fingers clasp my hand. "This is stunning."

"Thanks. It reminds me of my sister."

Her brows pop. "You've mentioned your brother, but I didn't realize you have a sister."

"Most people don't. I try to keep it that way. She's twelve years younger than me and hates the spotlight. I do my best to shield her."

"What's her name?"

"Isla Rose, but everyone calls her Isla."

"That's a beautiful name. Are you close?"

"Extremely. She's my inspiration."

"I'm sure she looks up to you and your brother."

"She and I are much closer. I'm more patient than Reed. Isla was an adorable child, and I didn't mind her company. I love kids, but Reed, not so much. He couldn't be bothered with her until he was in his early twenties. She's ten years younger than him and was always tagging along and cramping his style. What seventeen-year-old boy wants to play dolls with his little sister?" I say with a chuckle. Even to this day, my siblings share an interesting dynamic. There's a tense undercurrent between them that I'll never fully understand.

"That's probably how my brother felt about me," Lena mutters. "Trevor's idea of playing Barbies was chucking them off the roof or giving them swirlies in the toilet."

"That's harsh."

"It's all right. I got even." She flashes a wicked grin. "When he was a junior in high school, he got the balls to ask this beautiful senior on a date. I staged an elaborate Barbie campground in his bedroom. Imagine his surprise when he brought her home and tried to sneak her up to his room for a kiss."

I laugh. "Well played. That was like Isla and Reed's dynamic. He couldn't stand her. She's funny and smart as a whip—the girl doesn't forget a single thing. In passing, I once made a comment about taking her for her first tattoo. And don't you know it, she called me at five a.m. on her eighteenth birthday and was like, 'When are we getting our tattoos?' and I was like, 'Wait a minute, whaddya mean *our* tattoos?'" I smile and rub my jaw. "Apparently, I'd agreed to get one with her, hence the phoenix. She has a much larger, more colorful one on her back."

"That's awesome." Lena smiles. "Shared sibling symbolism."

My bond with Isla goes far deeper than matching tattoos and eye color.

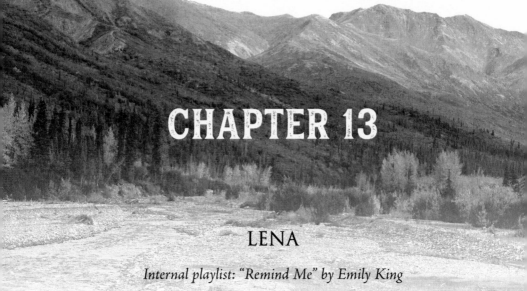

CHAPTER 13

LENA

Internal playlist: "Remind Me" by Emily King

We sit in silence for a few minutes, listening to the rush of the river and the chirps of awakening birds. I'm surprised by the situation's lack of awkwardness. I hate when I feel compelled to fill the silence with empty chatter, but that isn't the case now.

Wes breaks the silence first. "When Isla was twelve, she got really sick. The pediatrician couldn't figure out what was wrong. My parents took her to the children's hospital in Sydney for answers. Turns out, she has an autoimmune disease that attacked her kidneys. By the time they'd diagnosed her, she was in renal failure. The doctors put her on dialysis, which she endured three times a week for a year. They determined she would need a transplant."

His scar.

"You were a match."

"Yes. The only one in our family. Our surgeries were the day after my twenty-fifth birthday." He stares across the river at the loon. "Isla has always been a free spirit, so she wanted a bird tattoo to symbolize her freedom from dialysis, and the freedom to live a healthy life. She has antirejection drugs and a slew of other medications she's gotta take, but other than that, you'd never know it happened most days."

"Most days?"

He shakes his head sadly. "Isla has lupus. Some days she's perfectly fine. But if she overdoes it or happens to be in the middle of a flare, it's downright debilitating. Her ankles swell up and the joint pain gets unbearable. I fucking hate that she has to suffer, and I'd give anything to take the disease away from her."

I touch his arm. "It must be hard to watch."

He clenches his jaw. "It's torture."

"My best friend and I signed up for a 10k race in the spring. The proceeds benefit the Lupus Foundation. That's why I was on the treadmill the other day. I hate running, so I desperately need to train. Now that you've shared your sister's condition with me, I feel better about sweating it out. Isla gives me another person to run for."

He squeezes my knee. "Means a lot, Lena. Thank you."

I'm blown away by this man's love for his family. His sacrifice gave his sister a new life. Wes keeps details about his family private, so it moves me that he chose to confide in me—and it makes me want to know more.

"What are your parents like?" I ask.

"My mum and dad are still very much in love, even after forty years. My mother retired from teaching last year, and now they travel around the country going on day trips and such."

"What did your mom teach?"

"Creative writing courses at the University of Melbourne. I paid everything off for them years ago, but Mum wanted to keep working. Dad's an electrician. He calls himself semiretired and still takes on the occasional job. He hates being idle. I remember he drove Mum crazy when we were kids. He rewired the whole house twice in two years, and she was like, 'Luke, if ya move another outlet, I'm gonna rewire you.'" Wes chuckles. "I swear, he *loves* pushing her buttons."

"Button pushing must be hereditary," I tease. "Between you and your dad, it sounds like she had her share of aggravation."

Wes laughs. "Yep. She calls him her third son."

"What's your mom's name?"

"Rhea." Wes grins. "Dad calls her Raymond when he *really* wants to get her going."

"That's hilarious. Your poor mom. Does Reed share the gift of antagonism?"

"No, not really. He's pretty moody, but he's been through a lot." He sighs heavily. "At nineteen, he was in a serious motorcycle accident that should have left him crippled. The doctors told us he'd never walk again, but Reed had other plans. His recovery was astounding, and he's the most resilient man I know. Mum calls him her pensive one."

"What about Isla? You mentioned she's a free spirit."

"Sometimes, I need to remind myself I'm her brother, not a second father." He shakes his head. "I won't say she's reckless, but she takes free spirit to a new level. I think a lot of it stems from her illness. After being stuck on dialysis, she won't let anything tie her down or hold her back. She's flighty—like a bird or a fairy. Jake started calling her 'Sprite' when she was little." He sighs. "I mean, I understand where she's coming from, but she worries me. Where Reed thinks too much, Isla sometimes acts before thinking."

"Is she in college?"

"Yeah. She's majoring in fashion design. In fact, she's considering an opportunity to do her final year in New York."

"At the Fashion Institute?" I ask.

"I believe so."

"That's awesome." I tuck my hair behind an ear. "Be careful with that overbearing older brother thing. I dealt with that for years. Trevor was stifling—just like our father—and it drove us apart." I shrug. "Not that we were ever close."

"What're your parents' names and what're they like?"

Nothing like yours.

"My mom's name is Adele. She's very warm and sweet. She's selfless to a fault and has spent the entirety of her life pleasing others. By that, I mean being taken advantage of." I shake my head sadly. "She doesn't have a backbone, and my father treats her like shit. When I was a kid, it made me sad. But it angers me now."

"I can understand that you're angry with your dad. I'd feel the same way."

"I'm angry with them both. Roger, the family dictator, aka my father, is an alcoholic. He and I don't have a relationship because he's an oppressive bastard. He's got Mom under his thumb and can be downright nasty, especially when he drinks. I don't understand how she's put up with it for so long. She insists she stayed for us kids, but we're grown, and Mom's done nothing to help her situation. Her passiveness angers me almost as much as my father's behavior."

"It goes back to control," Wes says.

"What do you mean?"

"You're angry because you can't fix it for them. You can't change their dynamic, and it's painful for you to watch."

"You're right. I can't parent my parents, and it's frustrating." I shake my head. "But I swore I'd never be like them. Sometimes, Mom's passiveness creeps up inside me and I force this strong exterior to compensate. Other times, I sense my father's aggression bubbling beneath the surface. I try to stay someplace in the middle."

"I'd say you've accomplished that," Wes declares. "And then some."

I touch his arm. "Thanks, Wes."

"Thanks for telling me about your family, but ya left out the most important person."

I furrow my brow. "Who?"

"You, Lena. I want to know more about *you*."

"You still haven't answered *my* question," I remind him.

"And that was?"

"*Why?*"

"Because I've never met a woman like you." His gaze burns into me, stealing my breath. "And I wanna know you better."

"Oh," I murmur, feeling suddenly flustered. "I guess I'm not used to talking about myself."

"That's quite obvious. How about I give ya prompts?"

You can give me anything you want. "Prompts?"

"Yeah. You don't like questions, so we'll call them prompts." Smiling, he squeezes my knee, and I feel it down to my toes. "Give me three positive personality traits. You know, things you like about yourself."

"I thought you were gonna make this easy." I chuckle and shake my head. "I'll have to ponder that one and get back to you." I always have trouble describing myself in a positive light, but the random question seems ten times more difficult when posed by Wes.

"I find it strange that you have difficulty with that. I could answer in five seconds."

I roll my eyes. "Not everyone's as fabulous and interesting as you."

"Well, I'm happy you think I'm fabulous and interesting, but I'm not talking about me. I'm referring to *your* positive attributes. Give me your list and I'll tell ya what I've come up with."

"Okay, fine. I know you said three, but I've only got two."

"Let's hear them."

"Well, I think my greatest attribute is my level of compassion and concern for others. I strive to make and keep people happy because it really affects me. Like we discussed earlier, my empathy is a strength and weakness. Next, is honesty. By nature, I hold myself to a high standard of integrity and honesty in *all* relationships. I don't have time for deceptive, shady people. I'm straightforward and I don't play games, so I expect the same." I flash him a smile. "And there you have it. Satisfied?"

"Yeah, but I think I have ya beat."

Wes shifts his body to face me, and his knee rubs against mine. I imagine our legs tangled in bed and bite my lower lip.

"And how's that?" My voice is more breathless than I intended.

"Well, I told *you* to come up with three, but *I* have six. I think it's important that we get the chance to see ourselves from an outsider's perspective. I consider myself a strong judge of character and my assessments of others have proven accurate. My ability to read people, weed through the bullshit, and see who they really are, has both protected me and driven my success. I've been burned a few times, but it's strengthened me." His expression is calm, and his eyes focus on mine. "That being said, I want to paint a picture of the woman I've gotten to know thus far. They say first impressions are everything, right? Well, I disagree. I think we learn as our perceptions evolve. It's important to withhold judgment until you have all the facts."

Okay, now I'm nervous.

"Relax and lower that eyebrow. I'll explain." He gives me an encouraging smile. "After the flight to Aurora Borealis, I imagined you as a lost woman seeking refuge. Seemed like you were running from something. I quickly discovered I was wrong. *Now*, I see a fiercely independent woman who's running *toward* something. I just haven't figured out what. And, if my instincts are correct, neither have you."

I stare in disbelief as Wes peels off my cloak, exposing the layers beneath. "You sound like you've got me all figured out."

"Not entirely, but I'm working on it," he replies with a sly grin. "Getting back to your strengths, I'd say your independence counts as number one. I don't mean this to sound sexist, but I admire the fact that you'd take this trip alone. I don't meet too many women who'd willingly trek into the wilderness."

I snort. "It's mostly bravado."

Wes smiles. "Well, I like it. Also, I agree that compassion's one of your strong suits. Sometimes it's easy to turn a blind eye to the suffering in this world. That's not the case for you. It touched me when you became so emotional yesterday. You truly care, and it shows."

"Thank you."

"No need to thank me, Lena. I call it like I see it. Next on my list is integrity. You're an honest, ethical person. There's no question which direction your moral compass points. Again, it's clear in how you carry yourself. So, at this point, we're in one hundred percent agreement, yes?"

"Yes," I murmur.

Is that even my voice?

Suddenly starstruck, a part of me can't believe Wesley Emerson is singing my praises. And not just an "I like your shirt" or "you have a nice smile" compliment. No, these are legit kudos, like the introductory speech before I receive my Oscar. And he's just getting started.

"Number four, your sense of humor. I love your lack of a filter. I never know what will come out of your mouth, and it's refreshing. You have an intelligent, quick wit, yet you're also a perv."

He thinks I'm funny. That's funny.

"You're smirking. Do ya agree or disagree?"

"Glad you appreciate my fusion of pervert and dork."

"I appreciate every fusion you throw my way, which brings me to number five," he pauses, as if reorganizing his thoughts. "Let's see," he meets my gaze, "you've got grit and lots of it. I've never met a woman like you."

"Thanks."

"Wait, I wasn't finished. You're fearless, bordering on brazen, and you don't take any shit. You face a challenger head-on and demand equality. You don't give up on a mission, on other people, or yourself. You're stubborn as hell, stick to your beliefs, and protect whatcha love."

"Holy shit," I whisper. "Wes, I'm at a loss for words."

"Then wait until ya hear number six. Actually, we'll pick this conversation back up later. I feel like makin' you wait."

"Not fair."

"Yo, yo. What's cookin' y'all?" Austin's honeyed voice calls out. "How 'bout we eat somethin'? Who wants more fish?" He picks up a fishing pole. "Did y'all eat?"

Jake follows a few feet behind, his chestnut waves a wild mop.

"I'm not hungry, mate." Wes glances at me. "You need food?"

"I'm all right. I had another protein bar. That should hold me for a couple of hours."

"Who's ready to climb a mountain?" Jake says cheerfully. "Lena, are you coming?"

I smile and gesture to Wes. "Yep. Someone convinced me to come along."

Truth be told, even if Wes and I didn't have our heart-to-heart, I'd still join them. I can't fight his magnetism. Nor do I want to.

CHAPTER 14

WES

Internal playlist: "There's Nothing Holdin' Me Back" by Shawn Mendes

I walk beside Lena as we follow my mates from the river toward the base of the mountain. Replaying our conversation, I rub at the back of my neck. I've never opened up to someone so easily. I don't need my shield with Lena. Now if only she'll lower hers. I hope she believes what I said.

Too bad the cockblockers showed up.

I touch her shoulder. "You won't need to be freaked out tonight because we'll be moving our camp down here later. We figure it'll simplify things for tomorrow morning when we wait for Chuck."

"Good thinking. So, tonight, if I hear an animal outside my tent, I'll assume it's Jake and be done with it."

"Don't assume." I flash a devious grin. "I've been known to trespass."

Her sultry smile hardens my cock. *Jellyfish and sharks. Jellyfish and sharks. Jellyfish and sharks. Jellyfish and sharks—*

"Thanks for the warning, but it's not considered trespassing for a welcome marauder. Certain territories are known to invite a good," her gaze wanders from my lips to my belt buckle, and lower, before snapping back to mine, "plundering."

Holy. Fuck. My mouth drops open. Heat creeps across my face and neck as my cock stands at full attention, no doubt creating an obvious bulge.

Lena smiles. "Oh no, I said that one out loud, didn't I?" Winking, she bites her goddamn lower lip again.

"Yes. Yes, you did." I run a hand through my hair and over my face. "What am I gonna do with you?"

"You sure you want me to answer that?"

She's gonna burn me alive. I force a swallow. "Depends on whether *you* plan to act on your suggestion."

She raises a brow. "Which suggestion? I've made several."

"If I recall, you had a little suggestion for me on the plane." It floored me when she flipped me the bird—no woman's ever done that to me—and I would gladly take Lena up on a little 'fuck-you' action.

She drags her lower lip between her teeth. "What if I said that I do?"

I lean in close. "Then, I'd tell ya you're playing with fire."

"Well, I like it hot."

"If you want heat, I can make that happen. But you'd better think about what you're asking for."

Instead of responding, the sultry little thing flutters her lashes and gives me the finger again.

I pin her with my gaze. "I'll let you in on a little secret, Lena. I'm a man of action, so be very, *very* careful what you wish for."

She smiles up at me. "I'll keep that in mind."

"What's that stupid grin on your face, surfer boy?" Jake's voice slices through the sexual tension like a machete.

Cockblock Bennett strikes again. The thing is, half the time, Jake doesn't even realize he's doing it. The poor bloke's oblivious when it comes to women. He hasn't been with anyone in over two years and wouldn't notice an opportunity if it hit him upside the noggin. He's one of those old-soul types—a hopeless romantic who's equal parts gentleman and perv.

"Asked you a question," Jake says with a shit-eating grin.

"Just allowing my imagination to run wild."

Lena pulls out her ChapStick and brings it to her lips. As she smooths it on, I track the movement, my gaze riveted to her mouth. I envy the minty lip balm, envisioning those lips wrapped around—

"Okay, dude. Have fun with that."

"Oh, I fully fucking intend to, mate."

CHAPTER 15

LENA

Internal playlist: "Starstruck" by Lady GaGa

Jake walks beside me on our way to the summit. Laughing and chatting like old friends, we allow Wes and Austin to lead.

"Let's go, ladies. I've seen toddlers climb a mountain faster." Wes snaps his fingers. "Do I need to trail behind ya with a whip?"

Jake flips him off. "Here's what I think of your whip."

"He'd be wise not to ask me about whips," I mumble. "He might get more than he bargained for."

Jake snorts.

"Said that out loud, didn't I? Shit." I look over at Jake, who chuckles. "I blame you and your lack of filter. It's contagious."

"We're two peas in a pod with that filter issue," Jake muses as we reach the other men.

Wes looks back and forth between us. "What's so funny?" He hooks the aviators on his shirt collar, as it's much darker in the forest. Brilliant eyes sparkle with curiosity.

"Nothing," Jake and I respond in unison.

"Good. Then step up the pace." He motions to Austin. "We're practically running up this mountain, not even breaking a sweat."

Hands settling on my hips, I nod to the sweat on his brow. "What was that, Crocodile Dundee? I suppose that's just the morning dew glistening on your brow?"

"You might wanna rein in your sass, Lena." His deep voice rumbles my name, his eyes, alight with amusement, lock onto mine. "Don't stoke the flames unless you're ready for heat."

"I was born ready. And how many times do I need to tell you I like it hot?" It's over-the-top, but I don't care.

"Oh. My. God. You two with the flirting, heavy panting, and eye-fucking. You're killing me over here." Jake holds his arms up in surrender.

Austin clicks his tongue. "I dunno, I'm findin' it mighty entertainin'."

"That's because *you* have a woman in your life. Some of us suffer from forced celibacy, thank you very much," Jake retorts.

I smirk. "C'mon, Wes, stop making your friends uncomfortable."

Wes glances between Jake and Austin. "What? *She* started it."

"Nope. You've been tryin' to get a rise outta her since the moment you met." Austin wags a finger at him and laughs.

"Funny how he can dish it out but can't take it," I say.

"Actually, Lena, it's a question of whether *you* can take it."

Wes's gaze lingers on my lips, so I lick them and flutter my lashes. "You'd be surprised at how much I can take."

Jake pretends to put his fingers in his ears. "Yeah, still here, guys."

I laugh. "Sorry, Jake. Subtlety isn't my strong suit."

We hike for several hours, occasionally pausing to rest. It's early afternoon by the time we reach the summit. The rugged Brooks Range stretches as far as the eye can see. Jagged peaks reach skyward, and the winding John River cuts a deep canyon in the rock.

I give Austin a brief photography tutorial and let him use my camera for a bit.

Jake peers through a set of binoculars as the wind whips his waves. "This is incredible. Pure, unadulterated wilderness."

Wes stands beside him. "Care if I have a look?" Jake hands over the binoculars, and Wes scans the horizon. "Not even a plume of smoke."

"Makes you wish you were back in L.A., doesn't it?" Jake asks.

"Fuck no, mate. You won't find me in that scene again. Unless I'm filming something, obviously."

"Lena, come with me, darlin'," Austin drawls. "I wanna take some pictures of you with the mountain in the background."

Works for me. My libido could use a breather from the hulking mountain of muscle who's been teasing me non-stop.

CHAPTER 16

WES

Internal playlist: "Tunnel Vision" by Justin Timberlake

"Check that out. *Vogue* over there." Jake points across the clearing.

Lena and Austin laugh while he photographs her against the mountain backdrop. I watch them intently, crossing my arms over my chest.

Somehow Lena's braid has come undone, and the wind blows tendrils of hair around her. I remember when I untangled the fishhook, how it felt like silk and smelled like vanilla. A combination that is now *guaranteed* to make me hard in an instant. I want to run my fingers through it and knot my hands in the strands while I kiss her. Dark sunglasses obscure her eyes, and once again, she's hidden those lush curves beneath a blue parka.

"Breathtaking, right?" Jake says.

I nod. "I've never seen mountains like these."

"I'm not referring to the landscape."

"Yeah, she is."

"She's intoxicating," Jake murmurs. "I feel like we have a connection, and I wanna get to know her better."

"Wait a minute, Bennett." Spinning around, I loom in front of Jake. "I don't think I heard you right."

"You having trouble with English?"

I clench my jaw. "Say it again."

Sure, Lena and Jake have shared laughs, but I didn't pick up on anything more. Unless I've been too preoccupied with my own desire for her. *He knows I want her for fuck's sake!*

"Open your ears, surfer boy. I *said* that Lena and I get along really well. We live in the same city and we have a lot in common. At first, I thought she wanted you, but she's definitely into me." Jake runs a hand through his waves. "I'm *dying* to be alone with her."

I clench both fists at my sides. "You and I need to clear something up."

The muscle in my jaw pulses as I imagine Lena in Jake's arms. Would she smile, laugh, and wink like she's done with me? Would she stare at his lips like she wants to kiss them? Would she melt into his arms and sigh against his chest? Would she bury her hands in his hair and pull him deeper? Would she moan his name? I nearly implode with rage at the thought.

Jake furrows his brow. "You all right, man?"

I remember how she looked a few nights ago at the lodge when I brought her the bookmark. Standing there in the doorway, hair down and soft around her face. That lush body wearing nothing but an oversized T-shirt which revealed as much as it covered and made me want to explore every inch underneath. The thought of anyone other than me touching that soft skin makes my blood boil. I can feel myself morphing into the god of war—only this isn't acting. I step closer to Jake as the caveman in my head snarls, *Mine!*

"You'd better back the fuck up, Bennett."

Jake claps my shoulder. "Relax, dude. I'm just fucking with you. Bet you didn't realize *I* could act." His broad grin is one of self-satisfied glee.

As realization dawns, the tension eases from my body. I stare at Jake in disbelief, reeling from the sheer strength of the rage that gripped me just moments ago.

He cocks his head. "What's wrong with you? What happened to the laid-back surfer dude we all know and love?"

"She's mine."

"I think we've established that." Jake narrows his eyes. "You seriously thought I'd go after her?"

I run both hands over my face. I consider apologizing, but my inner caveman—still stalking around in my brain—deems that a weakness on the claim I just staked.

"I dunno what I thought."

"Yeah, you do. That's exactly what you fucking thought." Jake jabs a finger at my chest. "You're one of my best friends, man. I think you know me better than that." He rests a hand on my shoulder. "I haven't seen you like this since—"

"Don't bring Rachel into it," I growl. "Lena's *nothing* like her."

"I'm not saying that." Jake shakes his head. "I'm talking about *you*. This possessive alpha shit is coming out of nowhere." He gestures across the clearing. "Not for nothing, but *she's* not fling material."

"No shit, Bennett," I snap. "One of these days, I'm gonna not for nothing your face."

Smirking, Jake cocks a brow. "I thought you didn't wanna be attached?"

"I didn't."

"How's that gonna work out? You live in fucking Australia. What about your career? The travel? Paparazzi? Women throwing themselves at you? You think she'll want anything to do with that?"

"I dunno anything right now," I mutter, meeting Jake's gaze, "except that she's mine."

Jake glances over at Lena. "Does she know that?"

"No, but she will."

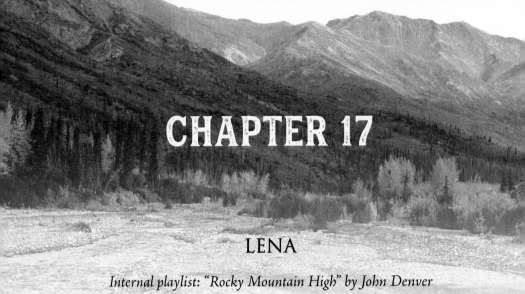

CHAPTER 17

LENA

Internal playlist: "Rocky Mountain High" by John Denver

Feeling like a side street prima donna with busted stilettos and a crooked crown, I laugh as Austin directs me into various ridiculous poses. He snaps dozens of pictures with hysterical running commentary. We pause and scroll through the photos.

"Hey, I look good in these."

"It's all about the angles, darlin'. Katie schooled me on the issue."

"She knows what she's talking about. These are great, Austin. Thanks."

"Email them to me. I'm makin' a scrapbook for Wes."

"Stop it. Don't be ridiculous." I giggle. "Unless he can use it as a coaster or a dartboard, maybe."

I glance across the clearing. Jake and Wes are in a heated discussion, and Wes looks pissed.

What's his problem?

"Like I said yesterday, you've captured his interest. I see how he acts around you."

Instead of addressing that little tidbit, I switch topics. "How did all of you guys become friends? I mean, with Wes growing up an ocean away?"

"Good question. All a matter of chance, really. When I was nine, my mama convinced me to be part of a youth talent competition in Tennessee. I made it to the finals. We competed against qualifiers from other states until there was a group of maybe twenty kids. The competition's coordinator was from Australia. He thought it would be cool to have us be part of their national talent show, so we headed to Melbourne for three weeks. It was an incredible experience. Wes's younger brother is a skilled drummer and was one of the Aussie competitors."

"Reed and I hit it off the first day and were hangin' out twenty-four seven by the end of the first week. They knocked us out of the competition, which was fine because it gave us more time to chill. Naturally, I met his family. Wes was the same age as me. He was busy with a cricket tournament but hung with us when he could. During those three weeks, Wes taught me all about the sport, and we became good friends. I was bummed when it was time to leave. This was back before kids had email and cell phones, you know? Anyway, we agreed to be pen pals and schedule a phone call here and there. I figured I'd never get to see them again. But my amazin' mama made it happen. She was in touch with Wes's parents and they coordinated our family vacations. So, the following year, when we went to Disney, imagine my surprise when I discovered that the guests in the next room were none other than the Emersons."

"Oh my God, that's so awesome. Were they surprised, too?" I ask.

"They had no idea. I literally walked into Reed and Wes in the hotel hallway. We all started screamin' and jumpin' up and down. We've kinda been inseparable ever since. It was easier to get together once we got older."

"How did you meet Jake?"

"I've known Jake since I was twelve. He's two years younger than me. We had the same vocal coach and now we share a record label. We're finally workin' on our collaboration album, but we've done some things in the past. Anyway, when I was seventeen, my mama planned a one-month vacation to Australia. Jake's parents were going through a divorce and he was havin' a rough time, so I asked my mama if he could come."

"That's incredible. So, you brought everyone together and made it all happen?"

"That's what I do, baby girl." Austin laughs. "It was an awesome trip. Me and Jake hung out with Wes and Reed the whole time. Isla was only five, so I think their mama was happy to have a little break from the boys. Wes tried to teach us how to surf." He chuckles. "Key word is *tried*."

"Is he good? I know he mentioned he wanted to be an instructor."

"Wes was born to surf. He's fucking amazing. You should see him out there—he's in his element—kinda like Jake with his piano, or me and my guitar. He rides these huge-ass waves like they're nothin'. I just clung to the damn thing and floated." He snorts. "Meanwhile, Jake built sand-castles with Isla."

"Oh my God, how sweet."

"Yeah, he's got a soft spot for her. Always has."

"What about Reed? Does he surf, too?"

"He did before the accident," Austin explains. "Anyway, I'm the co-ordinator of all our shindigs. I enjoy plannin' shit, so it's cool. Reed was supposed to come on this trip, but his fiancée's mother is real sick. Cora's havin' a hard time with the prospect of losin' her mama. Reed wanted to stay home so he could support and comfort his woman. Smart man in my book. And here you are, darlin', lightin' up our adventure with your daz-zlin' smile." He grins and scrolls through the pictures again before handing the camera back to me.

"You look pleased with yourself," Wes says as he approaches.

"If my next album doesn't sell, I may take up photography," Austin jokes.

Wes turns to me. "I neglected to bring a camera, so I was hoping maybe you could email me some?"

"Absolutely. I tried to capture the beauty of this place, but these shots don't do it justice."

"Mind if I take a look?"

I switch on my camera and hand it over. Wes's hands brush mine as he accepts it, sending a shiver up my spine. "Use this button to scroll left or right, press this one to zoom in and out."

"Thanks."

I turn to Jake. "Austin was just telling me about your sandcastle skills."

Jake laughs. "I don't fuck around, Lena-Bean. I'm the best sandcastle builder north of the equator."

I nudge him. "You don't fuck spiders, either, huh?"

"Fuck no. I hate arachnids."

"Same. So, I take it Isla holds the castle-building record for the south-ern hemisphere?"

A strange expression crosses his features before he clenches his jaw and looks away. "She does."

"Lena, these are amazing." Wes scrolls through my photos.

I lean over to see which ones he's referring to. It shocks me to see my face on the display. "That was all Austin. I can't take credit for those."

"Pretty sure it's the subject," Wes muses, eyes on the screen.

"Thank you."

"Email these as well," he commands. "I want all of them."

Is he serious? What the hell does he want with pictures of me?

"There's that eyebrow again."

"Like I told you, girlie, forget the northern lights, your smile lights up the northern hemisphere." Austin pats himself on the back. "Hell, if you email them to Wes, you can illuminate the southern hemisphere, too."

I flush. "You guys are too much. I'm beyond flattered. Thank you."

"It's not empty flattery, Lena," Wes insists. "I mean the things I say."

"I'll keep that in mind."

We begin our descent since we still need to disassemble the men's camp and relocate it before nightfall. The trip down the mountain is faster, but harder on the knees. We spot the canary yellow tent after a couple of hours. At the men's camp, Jake nearly steps in a large, steaming pile of shit, laden with berries and acorns.

"Whoa! I wonder what kind of animal—"

"Judging by those tracks and the way the bark's been peeled from the trees, I'd say it was a bear. And that looks fresh." I scan the forest. "We need to get out of here."

"Guys, we need to hustle. Lena and I found bear signs over here."

"Help me take down the tent," Wes commands from his place at the other side of camp.

We swiftly empty and dismantle the tent. Aside from the charred wood, it's as if they'd never been there. *Leave no trace,* Chuck told us. I scan the campsite. *Looks good to me.*

"Let's move out." Wes comes up behind me and motions to my arm-load of wood. "I'll carry that. It's heavy."

"It's okay, I've got it."

"Don't be stubborn. You need a free arm in case you trip. I don't want you falling on your face again." His gaze bores into mine. "Give me your wood."

"You gonna return the favor?" Batting my lashes, I unload the sticks into his waiting arms.

Wes's gaze lingers on my lips. "Be careful what ya wish for, sunshine."

CHAPTER 18

LENA

Internal playlist: "Drops of Jupiter" by Train

I'm pretty sure that's the most exercise I've gotten in a decade. It was dusk by the time we reached the base of the mountain, and since I was starving, I headed to the riverbank while the guys set up camp.

I glance over my shoulder at the footsteps approaching me from behind. "That was quick. I figured a tent that big would take longer."

"Like Emerson says, we didn't come here to fuck spiders." Jake joins me with his fishing pole. "Hopefully, we can catch something. Wes is getting hangry, and I don't have the energy for one of his moods."

I wonder what the earlier tension between them was about. Wes chops wood nearby, so I watch his powerful body swing the ax. He slung his parka over a branch and shoved the sleeves of his black thermal to his elbows, once again exposing corded forearms. *Sweet Jesus, those muscles.* I swear he bulges in every piece of clothing he owns. *Wonder what else bulges.*

Squirming, I press my legs together. Wes is my wilderness lumberjack fantasy come to life, and I've got a front row seat.

Jake nudges me. "Why don't you pull out that Canon and snap a few pics?"

Flushing, I turn back toward the river. "Believe me, it's tempting. But he deals with that shit all the time. He deserves an escape from the spotlight. I'll have to rely on my photographic memory." I tap my temples.

"You like him."

"I like *all* of you."

"You know what I mean, Lena-Bean." His warm brown eyes call me on my bullshit.

I peer over my shoulder at Wes. "Is it that obvious?"

He grins. "Only to Austin and me."

"You two may be intuitive, but I'm a realist."

"What do you mean?"

"Let's be honest, this is just an entertaining flirtation for him."

He shakes his head. "You're wrong."

"Me thinks *you're* crazy. I look nothing like the leggy, perky-titted waifs he's used to."

Jake snorts. "Perky-titted waifs?"

"C'mon, Jake. I'm leagues away from the Alainna Bakers of the world."

Wes's *Aegean* costar is easily the most beautiful woman I've ever seen. With her perfect body—curvy yet slender—she's one of those Hollywood model types. She has perfect boobs, a perfect ass with zero jiggle, and a flat stomach. With flowing blonde waves and legs for days, the woman is equal parts ethereal and sultry, and I look *nothing* like her.

"They're just friends." Jake shakes his head. "You're gonna have to trust me on this one."

"Trust you, how?"

"Well, for starters, he—"

Wes approaches with an armload of wood, dropping it on the pile he started. I silently thank Jake for his discretion.

"All right, we have wood for the night. I would kill for a pint right now." He collapses beside me and motions to my pole. "You haven't caught any yet."

I roll my eyes. "Thanks, Sherlock. Here I thought they had invisible salmon in Alaska."

Jake snickers.

"Like I told you before, you keep doing that and your eyes will get stuck." Wes grins and nudges me. "And my pole demonstration offer still stands."

Yes, please.

We relax by the fire, wiped out from the day's activity. Wes divulges some details of Reed's upcoming wedding. He'll be the best man and Cora's sister, Dana, will be the maid-of-honor. I wonder what Dana looks like. A sudden pang of jealousy hits me when I imagine Wes dancing with her at the reception. Squeezing my eyes shut, I shake my head.

I've lost my damn mind. Wake the fuck up, Lena. Get out of your fantasy land.

"Is the smoke bothering your eyes?" Wes asks.

"Just listening."

"You haven't said two words in an hour. You sure you're all right?"

"I'm fine. Just drained from the hike."

He nods. "Me, too. But I'd call it an excellent day with my best mates and a beautiful woman."

I flush and toy with a strand of hair.

"Do you have a best friend, Lena? How'd you meet her?" Jake asks.

Flustered by Wes's compliment, it takes me a moment to respond. "Actually, my best friend is a man. We've been friends since we were seven."

"Really? That's cool. Do y'all stay in touch regularly?" Austin asks.

"Daily. He lives in the apartment downstairs, which is ironic because we started out as neighbors, and here we are as adults, neighbors again."

"Doesn't that complicate things?" Wes asks.

I cock my head. "Not sure what you mean." Garrett's the least complicated part of my life.

"Friendship between a man and a woman—aren't there complications?"

"If you are asking whether we've had sex, the answer is no."

Wes snorts.

"To clarify, have we slept in the same bed? Yes, dozens of times. Have we been intimate? Absolutely not. Garrett is like a brother to me. I love him more than my brother. Does that answer your question, Wes?"

"Yes. But has he seen ya naked?" he asks with a wolfish grin.

"That's none of your business." The answer is yes, but he doesn't need to know that.

"Interesting," his gaze roves over me, "so, how'd ya meet?"

"Long story."

"We're listening," Jake says.

"Sure, why not? We're going back about twenty-five years now.

Garrett grew up as an only child in rural Pennsylvania. His parents struggled to make ends meet and fell on hard times. His father sank into a deep depression and lost his battle with alcoholism."

"My God . . ." Austin murmurs.

"Garrett was seven. I'll spare you the details, but his mom committed suicide about six months after they lost his father. Garrett found her body on the last day of school."

"Jesus Christ," Wes breathes.

"Social services contacted his mother's sister, who agreed to take him in. That summer, he moved in with his aunt, uncle, and their four sons, who were my nearest neighbors. I grew up in the mountains, so we were about a half mile apart.

"I met Garrett at the bus stop on the first day of school. In our district, the kids in elementary school had assigned seats on the buses, so naturally, he was my seat partner. Anyway, I said, 'hello,' but he didn't speak. That became our routine. We stood at the bus stop in silence, rode to school in silence, and he was silent in class. I was too young to understand the whole story, so I just thought he was unfriendly, and I hated having to sit with him.

"On the ride home the day before Christmas break, we had our first conversation. I was excited because my birthday is on Christmas Eve, so the holiday was always a huge deal in our house," I explain.

"A Christmas birthday?" Austin chimes in. "That's awesome."

"It has its advantages. Anyway, I asked Garrett if he was excited for Santa to come, and he told me, 'No.' I couldn't believe it. Who wouldn't be excited for Santa? I asked him why and I'll never forget his response for as long as I live." I look at the ground, lost in memory. "Sorry, it still hits hard when I think about it."

"Hey," Wes murmurs. I meet his compassion-filled gaze, and he raises a brow. "What did I tell ya about apologizing?"

"I know. I'm sorr—" I catch myself this time.

Wes shakes his head. "You don't even realize how often you say it."

I sigh. "After years of being told I'm too emotional, apologizing for it is a hard habit to break."

Wes frowns. "Who the hell told you that?"

"The idiot I was supposed to marry."

"He's a fuckwit," Wes declares with more conviction than I'd expect.

"Yeah." I sip from my canteen and continue. "Anyway, on the bus that day, Garrett said, 'My mom and dad are dead. Santa can't do anything to make me happy.' I remember being stunned. I couldn't even respond. We got off the bus and I ran home to ask my mom if it was true.

"There was a snowstorm on my birthday. After we'd finished with presents, I demanded my mom call Wendy and invite Garrett over. His aunt didn't care either way and dumped him on our doorstep in his boots and snow pants. We played outside for hours." I smile at the memory. "We built a snowman, had a snowball fight, and followed animal footprints through the woods. Eventually, my mom made us come inside, where she had hot cocoa and chicken soup waiting. After lunch, she dug out the container of cookie cutters and we made gingerbread cookies and decorated them with frosting.

"I'll always remember that day. By the end of the afternoon, Garrett was laughing. We hung out the entire Christmas break and have been inseparable ever since. It's funny, to this day, we still make gingerbread cookies every year at Christmas. It's our tradition. He tries to pretend he doesn't want to, but I know he's full of shit. Five years ago, I bought him a Grinch apron." I flash a devious smile and giggle. "You should have seen his face."

"Well, did he wear it?" Wes asks.

"Damn right, he did." I laugh. "Then, I pulled out a reindeer headband, and he was like, 'Leens, you know I love you, but if you take one step closer to me with those antlers, I'm gonna lose my shit.' So, I wore them instead."

The men all laugh.

"I'd bought them to fuck with him, but it was funny to watch him guard his man card so fiercely. He's worn the apron every year since I gave it to him, though. And I wear the antlers like I'm Max and we're on our way to Whoville. Last year, he pretended to be too busy for cookies. I called him on my lunch break and left a voicemail singing, 'You're a Mean One, Mr. Grinch,' except I accidentally called his work number." I snort. "His secretary put the message on speaker for all of his employees to hear.

Anyway, I got home from work and discovered he'd hidden my Christmas tree in the bathroom."

"Was it a big tree?" Jake asks.

"Yes! And it was real, so there was a pine needle trail going down the hall. For a minute, I thought I'd pissed him off and ran downstairs to apologize. I went into his living room and he was lounging on the couch eating nachos. Watching *The Grinch*. He was like, 'Yo, Cindy Lou. Help me eat these chips.'"

"Sounds like he enjoys the tradition as much as you do," Wes says.

"Oh, absolutely. He puts on a front to mess with me, but we've never missed a year. All I need to tell him is that if he doesn't help, he won't get any. Sure enough, every year, he shows up in my kitchen wearing the apron."

Wes lays a warm hand on my arm. "I'm sorry your friend had to endure such tragedy at that young age. It's clear you bring joy to his life. I'm glad he met you."

I stare into the fire. "Garrett said something similar once. He told me I was the beacon of light that had saved him so many times over the years. His teens and early twenties were tough, and he wanted me to know how grateful he was that I'd forced him to come play that Christmas. He gives me too much credit. He's the survivor. I was just along for the ride. The thing is, if you met him today, you'd never know how much shit he's gone through.

"It's like he tapped into that wellspring of sorrow and channeled it in a creative direction. He moved to the city, earned his degree in graphic design, and then got his MBA. He owns a growing design firm, and when he isn't working, he's part of some theater production or other. He's a skilled actor with an incredible voice. The day I booked this trip, he told me about his audition for a new Broadway show coming next year."

A broad smile crosses Jake's face. "He's referring to *Prodigy*. I've seen the script, and it looks like a phenomenal show. When we get back to the lodge, make sure you give me his contact information. I'd like to introduce him to some of my theater people."

Jake is known for paving the way for aspiring actors and musicians. Although his arts foundation focuses on children, he doesn't discriminate when given the opportunity to help.

"That would be amazing. Thank you so much, Jake," I gush. *Garrett's gonna freak!*

"You got it, Lena-Bean."

"Jake, do you think *Prodigy* will be a hit?"

"It has the potential to be phenomenal, but it all depends on the cast. The right people dictate a production's success or failure. That, and whether the audience is ready for it. This one borders on controversial, so it depends on how well it's received. Unfortunately, we don't know that ahead of time."

"Knowing his talent, I'd say it'll be a record breaker."

"Wait, so how did you guys become neighbors again?" Austin asks.

"When I was in nursing school, I moved to Brooklyn to care for my ailing grandmother. I inherited her brownstone when she passed. Although it's paid off, the upkeep was too much for me to handle alone. After Garrett's lease ended in Manhattan, he moved into the bottom two floors of the building. I was uneasy being on the ground floor, so it worked out perfectly. I couldn't ask for a better neighbor. He fixes all the broken stuff, shovels snow, kills spiders, and drives me crazy on the regular. He's currently babysitting my cats, and by that, I mean overfeeding them and buying them toys." I chuckle and motion to Austin and Jake. "I told Wes the other day, but this trip was actually Garrett's idea. My boss made me take time off, and Gar suggested I get away. We found the listing for Aurora Borealis on one of the travel sites, and *no one* does persuasion like Garrett Casey."

"We all owe Garrett thanks. If it weren't for him, you wouldn't be here with us." Wes smiles.

"Thanks for not being dicks when I crashed your boys' trip." I wink at Wes. "Temporary dick behavior is excused."

He gives me a sheepish smile.

"Emerson's still a dick, but me and Memphis are cool," Jake says with a snort.

"Takes one to know one, mate." Wes stands and stretches. "I dunno about all of you, but I could use a shower and a steak."

My face flushes as images of Wes in the shower dance through my mind. Rivulets of water running along that broad, strong body . . . *Stop it,*

Lena. Keep your panties on. He plops on the log and extends his legs. *So long, so muscular—*

"How tall are you?" I ask, even though I already know the answer.

"A bit over six five. The boots I wore for *The Aegean* added another two inches. Gave me quite the vantage point."

"Damn, dude. I didn't realize you had four inches on me," Jake marvels.

"What about Alainna? She must be pretty tall then?" Austin says.

"She comes up to my chin, so my guess is nearly six feet, but I've never asked. I heard she was sensitive about it."

Alainna Baker. A spark of white-hot jealousy singes me as I picture his costar standing so close to him. I think I hate her. The feeling intensifies when I envision the love scenes in his upcoming film. There's no way I'll be able to watch that.

"Lena?" Jake's voice jolts me back to reality.

"Huh?" I turn to face him. "I'm sorry, did you say something?"

"I asked you how tall you are," he repeats.

"Oh, I'm five six."

"Wes, you're like a whole foot taller than her, man," Austin points out.

"Yes, I've noticed." Wes grins. "And I've got her by about fifty kilos."

"I'm sure I'll lessen the gap once we get back to the lodge. I'm ready to eat several pies and some cake."

"Ah, so she bakes her cake and eats it, too," Wes muses.

"Isn't that the only way?" I laugh. "In case you couldn't tell, I *love* sweets. Especially caramel."

"Me, too." Wes nods his approval. "But it sounds like you won't leave anything but crumbs for the rest of us," he adds with a grin.

"Maybe I won't." I playfully punch his arm. "I haven't decided if I wanna share yet."

"Maybe that's a good thing." Wes licks his lips. His gaze wanders over my breasts and lower. "I'm sure we could come up with a *satisfying* solution. You know what they say . . . you are what you eat."

I imagine his lips and tongue on my body and my mind runs away with me again. *I've got an idea, Ace. How about you throw me on a bed somewhere and devour me?*

"A penny for your thoughts?" Wes cocks an inquiring eyebrow.

"Oh, honey, it would take *at least* half a mil for these—"

"Where's my wallet?" He pretends to search his pockets. "Tell ya what, I'll double it for full disclosure."

His gaze burns into me. I wouldn't *dare* tell him what I'm thinking. I can barely handle the heat of it.

Jake squeezes his eyes shut and plugs his ears. "Here we go again with the rampant innuendo and eye fuckery."

Austin clicks his tongue. "Hold on, I'm gonna fry an egg over here. Y'all are burning me up."

"Sorry, guys. Like I said, I've got one helluva sweet tooth." His eyes never leave mine. "When I find something I like, I can't get enough."

Maybe I'm wrong. Maybe I will see more of him at the lodge.

WES

I watch Lena retreat to her tent to sleep. Not that I can help myself. Her jeans show off the curves of her arse to perfection. I want to palm each cheek, pull her close, and bury my face between her thighs. I want to slant my mouth over her and see if she tastes as sweet as I imagine. Luckily, Austin interrupts my thoughts before things get too tight in my jeans.

"You're droolin' again," he points out. "Whatcha thinkin' 'bout, Wes?"

"I'll tell you exactly what he's thinking." Jake leaps to his feet and does a mini-salsa dance. In a mock Australian accent, he adds, "Well, mates, I'd better warm up my didgeridoo. This sassy sheila looks like a screamer."

Austin howls with laughter.

If she's not, she will be when I get ahold of her.

I shake my head. "One of these days, I'm gonna hit ya, Bennett."

"Had the chance earlier, but you fucked that one up, surfer boy." Jake turns to Austin. "Hey, Memphis, let me tell you about an interesting conversation we had at the summit."

CHAPTER 19

LENA

Internal playlist: "Hopeless Wanderer" by Mumford & Sons

There's nothing sexier than three hot guys lounging by a sparkling river, gripping their poles, working hard to catch our food. Wait, that's not true. There's a different kind of hard pole—

"Good morning, Lena-Bean," Jake says, reeling in a salmon. "Nice of you to join us."

"Hey, guys." I unzip my parka to combat the flush creeping over my body.

"You sleep better last night?" Wes asks with a grin.

I'd sleep better with you. "Yes, I was comatose. You?" My libido really needs to chill her tits. I shouldn't sound like a phone sex operator right now.

"Same." He stretches. "So, what's our game plan for the morning? Do we wanna break down the tents now or give it a while?"

"Let's eat and deal with it later. We just need to make sure everything's all set for Chuck's arrival. We don't want to hold him up," Jake says.

Soon, the aroma of fire-roasted salmon fills our nostrils. My stomach growls. Wes must've heard it because he hands me a chunk of fillet.

"Thanks. It's borborygmus." I announce the scientific term for a growling stomach.

Wes furrows his brow. "Come again?"

"You offering?"

Did I really just fucking say that?

He blushes, telling me my question most definitely reached his ears.

That's right, Wes Emerson, Hollywood actor, just blushed at something I said. *Score. Payback's a bitch.* My satisfied smirk gets a chuckle out of Jake.

"Your cheeks are a wee bit rosy there, Wesley," I point out.

"*Your* cheeks will be a wee bit rosy if you keep it up." His gaze travels to my ass. Wanton visuals flood my mind as I imagine myself naked across his lap.

"Promises, promises . . ."

"I said I'm a man of action, didn't I?"

"You talk a big game, Wes, but I've yet to see any action."

His eyes darken. "There will be."

"Uh-huh, whatever you say, Crocodile Dundee." I flash my sultriest smile, then lick my lips. "When do I get number six?"

His lips curve into a smirk. "When I give it to ya."

"Oh? When are you gonna give it to me, Mister Man of Action?"

He grips my chin, his gaze burning into me. "Think about what you're asking for."

Believe me, I have.

I squeeze my thighs together and it doesn't go unnoticed. Swirling pools of blue lava flare with satisfaction.

He has me under his spell. I'm doing all I can to keep my hands off him. And by the looks of it, he's exercising a great deal of restraint.

I can't think straight with him this close. I can barely breathe when I think about what he said yesterday. He seemed so sincere, so genuine. Now, he's morphed into pure sex, incinerating me with words alone. Here it is again, the paradox of Wes Emerson. The man who's currently staring at me like *I'm* Aphrodite.

Taunted by images of his onscreen Aphrodite, I tense. Who am I kidding? I'm closer to one of Aphrodite's servants than the goddess. He's way out of my league. Yes, I consider myself an attractive woman, and yes, I'm smart and kind. But I'm nowhere near the caliber of beauty Wes is accustomed to. I don't have stylists or millions of dollars or a perfect body. I'm just an ordinary girl from upstate New York. I can't get caught up in the fantasy of him truly wanting me. He has an itch to scratch. This is simply an entertaining flirtation for him. I need to accept that reality before I get hurt. I leap to my feet, startling Jake.

"Whoa. Where are you running off to?" he asks as I rush toward my camp.

"I'm breaking down my tent."

"Why the hurry? We've got all morning," Wes calls out.

"Work now, relax later. That's always been my strategy."

Unzipping my tent, I dive in and chug some water while I gather my thoughts. We still have a few hours before Chuck returns. Once at the lodge, I plan to snag a kayak and spend a few hours on the lake. That will give me some distance to clear my mind. Hands shaking, I'm vibrating with nervous energy. What came over me? Amid all that lust, an intense restlessness crept in, and I can't put my finger on why.

I tightly roll and secure my sleeping bag and pack the items in the tent. Emerging, I set my things aside and disassemble my shelter. Once everything is neatly folded and tucked away, I dust off my hands.

Wes approaches my camp. I take a steadying breath and feign normalcy.

"I came to see if you needed help, but it looks like you have it under control."

"Yes, I've got it covered. But thank you." My unsteady tone matches the rest of me.

"Are you all right?" Wes towers over me, his powerful frame blocking out the sun.

A perfect eclipse. He eclipses any man I've *ever* encountered, and I know damn well I'll never meet his match. I peer up at him with a small smile as he searches my face. He's intuitive—I'll give him that. Who am I kidding? I'll give him just about anything.

And that's the problem.

His warm hand settles on my shoulder. "Lena, are you all right?"

"Half left," I deadpan.

A grin spreads across his face. "Shall I rephrase? Are your right and left halves well?"

"Yes. I'm fine, thank you."

"Fine? Why do women always say 'fine'?" He rubs his jaw. "Never mind. Don't answer that. I'll leave ya alone." He turns to walk away.

"Wait," I blurt, gently touching the back of his arm. He stops and turns to face me. "I'm sorry. You didn't do anything, and I appreciate your concern. Truth is, I've never met anyone like you. And having someone, who was a stranger just days ago, read me so well when I can barely read myself is unsettling." I shrug. "I suddenly had all this nervous energy that needed an outlet." I don't need to burden him with my inexplicable anxieties. "I'm sorry if I gave you the impression something was wrong."

"Nothing to be sorry about."

He looks over his shoulder at the sound of Jake and Austin's approach.

"Damn, girl. You don't mess around. You whipped through here like a tornado," Austin marvels. "We should start breakin' down our camp now, whatcha think, fellas?"

"Yeah, let's do it." Wes touches my shoulder and moves to help his friends.

The guys empty and dismantle their tent, stuffing everything into their enormous packs. Austin lugs his guitar and the remaining water. Wes, Jake, and I carry the unused firewood to our riverside fire pit. Chuck is due in a little under two hours, so we settle onto the logs and chat. I feel a tinge of sadness leaving my camp behind. It's so beautiful, wild, and free. Gazing at the river, I try to memorize its rocky curves. What will happen when we return to the lodge? Will I see the guys as much? Or will they do their own thing?

Jake sits beside me on the log, humming to some music of his own while he lines up pebbles by his feet.

Wes glances at his watch. "It's nearing two o'clock. I wonder what's the holdup. He seemed like a punctual bloke."

Chuck told us noon sharp—here he's two hours late. Maybe he tells his passengers an earlier time to ensure he doesn't have to wait on them. I wish we had some way to contact him.

I perk up. "Wait, did Ellen give you guys the satellite phone?"

Austin shakes his head. "No. She said she was gonna grab it, but she never gave it to us. And we didn't think about it till after Chuck left."

"Don't worry; we won't need it," Wes declares.

In my mind's periphery, the universe flails her arms to get my attention. Lips pressed in a grim line, she shakes a finger at Wes.

Ice fills my chest. *Chuck forgot us.* No, there has to be an explanation. Maybe the weather in Fairbanks was shitty. Ellen mentioned a storm in the forecast. *Yeah, that's it. A storm.* I'm starting to wonder if our on-the-fly change of destination was a mistake, since we would've had a guide with us if we'd gone to Gobbler's Knob.

I yawn and pop my bad shoulder.

Jake curls his lip. "Don't do that, it's gross."

"What, this?" I repeat the act.

Jake grimaces, his body shuddering. "It's like nails on a chalkboard."

"Good thing you don't work in the ER. You wouldn't *believe* the crazy shit I've seen."

But somehow, none of that compares to the craziness of this trip.

CHAPTER 20

WES

Internal playlist: "Wheel in the Sky" by Journey

I glance at my watch for the third time this hour. It's nearly four thirty. Still no sign of Chuck. A muscle pulses in my jaw. I've been trying not to clench it, but that's proving harder by the minute. I glance at Lena. She's picking at her nails and gnawing her lower lip. Silence replaces our playful banter as we all think what no one wants to say.

I lurch to my feet. "I don't think Chuck's coming tonight. We should set up camp while there's still plenty of light."

"He's right," Lena says. "My guess is we'll see him tomorrow morning. I doubt he'd fly in the dark." She stands and retrieves her pack. "Back to my cluster of trees, it is."

We grab our gear and follow Lena to her spot. We quickly assemble the two tents, positioning the shelters side by side in the shadow of the Sitka spruce.

Lena unfolds a tarp and holds it up. "Just in case."

I nod and secure the other end to a tree behind our tents. Shelter in place, we trudge to the river and build a fire. Jake and I gather wood while Lena and Austin give it a go with the fishing poles.

An unsettled feeling makes its home in my chest. Its icy fingers wind themselves around my lungs, lacing through my ribs.

What if Chuck doesn't come for us?

I clench my jaw and push the thought aside. There has to be a reasonable explanation, but something deep in my gut tells me otherwise.

Austin tries to keep the mood light, sharing random tales from his months on tour. I silently watch Lena across the fire. Her brow is creased with worry, and she continues to pick at her nails. The wind picks up. She shudders and pulls her zipper up to her throat. I hate the idea of her being cold.

"Would ya put a scarf on?" I grumble.

She meets my gaze. "I don't do scarves."

I gesture to her. "You're making me cold just looking at you."

"I have that effect on men," she deadpans.

There's the sass I love. The spirit that heats me up.

I cock my head. "I'd argue the opposite."

"You'd argue just to argue."

I don't answer because she's one hundred percent correct. I'm in the mood to push her buttons.

If it gets you fired up, I'll argue all night long.

"Okay, boys, I'm done for the night. I'll see you in the morning," Lena mumbles, climbing to her feet.

"Good call." I motion to my mates. "We should all rest."

Everyone heads for camp. My gaze fixates on the swaying hips and arse a few meters ahead, and I envision myself holding on to her hips while I thrust.

Instant hard-on.

Now I get to lie in my fucking tent with blue balls. Not that that's anything new.

CHAPTER 21

LENA

Internal playlist: "You and Me" by Lifehouse

I must have drifted off at some point because I wake with the strong urge to pee. Though I hate the idea of leaving my warm cocoon, pissing the bed isn't an option. Groaning, I crawl out into the crisp night air. I zip the parka to my neck and close the tent flap. I tiptoe past the other tent to the far side of the tree cluster to do my business.

My attention is drawn skyward as I trudge back to the campsite. The northern lights stretch across the Alaskan sky. Greens swirl with purples and subtle pinks join the fray. The beautiful dancing waves of color enchant me. It's my first time witnessing the natural phenomenon, so I retrieve my camera and switch the setting to night mode. I know pictures won't do the aurora borealis justice, but I need to try.

A cracking twig foils my attempt to silently navigate the campsite. *Shit.* I freeze for a few beats, lungs barely expanding with my breaths. There's a rustle in the neighboring tent. The unmistakable sound of a zipper being yanked open. Another zipper, and a head cautiously emerges from the tent. I can't tell who it is until he rises to his full height.

Head darting, Wes is on full alert. Moonlight glints off a metal object—a hatchet.

Time to announce yourself.

"Don't gut me, big guy," I whisper into the silence.

"Christ, Lena! What the hell're you doing? You scared me shitless," Wes exhales in a harsh whisper and closes the distance between us.

"I'm sorry. I was taking some pictures."

"In the middle of the night?" he sputters, clearly rattled.

I remember how freaked out I felt the night I heard something, so I gently tilt his chin skyward. "Look."

"Oh. Wow . . ." He crosses his arms over his chest and stares at the heavens.

We silently admire nature's light show. I never imagined witnessing the aurora with Wes Emerson. I ache to touch him, put my arm around him. Instead, I bask in his warmth, so close, our bodies are nearly touching. I crave his closeness more at this moment than ever before, but I keep my clenched hands in my pockets.

"Wes, what if . . . never mind."

"What if what?" He turns to face me, the moonlight emphasizing the planes of his jaw. His eyes, eerie in the silvery light, meet mine. "Talk to me, Lena."

He can bend me to his will with his voice alone.

"What if Chuck doesn't come for us?" I whisper.

The thought has been tormenting me for hours.

"Try not to think like that. There's got to be an explanation. Ellen said a storm was coming; maybe it wasn't safe to fly." He squeezes my shoulder. "If it's a weather situation, we're better off waiting."

"I know. I guess it's just . . ." I turn my attention to my feet.

He tilts my chin up. "Talk to me, sunshine. I want to know everything that goes on in that beautiful mind of yours."

"Do you ever get a gut feeling? Like, a sense of doom? That unsettled feeling from earlier is back, and I can't shake it. I've been trying to redirect it for hours, but it's not working."

"I know. I feel it, too. But I'm trying to attribute it to being tired and hungry."

"It's like my subconscious is preparing me for the worst-case scenario."

"Let's think positively. Chuck will be here bright and early, and then you can teach me how to kayak when we return to the lodge."

"I'll try," I promise, returning his smile.

He tips my chin to focus back on the marvel that is the sky. I shiver, both from the beauty of the night and the brief touch of his hand on my skin. Wes notices, looping his arm over my shoulders.

I slide a tentative arm around his waist and whisper, "Wes, I'm scared."

He peers down at me. "I know . . . me too."

"What if—"

He presses a finger to my lips. "Shh . . . it's gonna be all right, sunshine."

I need a hug. Swallowing against my hesitation, I turn to face him. I slide my arms around his waist and rest my head on his chest.

Wes pulls me close. "I needed a hug too."

We stay this way for several minutes. I close my eyes and listen to the rush of the river and Wes's breathing. It's a perfect night, if not for the missing Chuck.

CHAPTER 22

WES

Internal playlist: "Kiss Me" by Ed Sheeran

I rest my chin on top of Lena's head and breathe in her warm vanilla scent. She nuzzles her face in my chest and relaxes in my hold.

She was made for me.

I tilt her chin to meet my gaze. The moon reflects in her soulful eyes. All I can do is stare into them. Her lips part slightly, and she licks them, the movement catching my attention. I rivet my gaze to those lush, full lips, wondering if they're as soft as they look. Her jaw trembles and her shoulders rapidly rise and fall.

She's nervous. Kiss her, you coward.

My chest heaves. I've kissed plenty of women in my lifetime. Hell, I've filmed erotic love scenes with less trepidation. But somehow, this surpasses them all. Because I want Lena's kiss more than I want air in my fucking lungs. And she can't decide what she wants from me.

She stands on her tiptoes and brushes her lips across my throat. I feel the goose bumps bloom on my skin.

Sliding a hand to the back of my neck, she pulls my ear to her lips. "Right now, your clairvoyance should be telling you to kiss me." Her whispered breath tickles my ear and hardens my cock. She presses a kiss to my jaw. Then my cheek. Then the corner of my mouth. Her hands weave into my hair, pulling me closer.

"I left it at the lodge, remember?" Bringing my lips to hers, I kiss that sumptuous bottom lip. A soft gasp escapes her, and that sound is my call to action.

LENA

I smile against Wes's lips when he finally kisses me. He grips the sides of my face and deepens the kiss. His tongue sweeps into my mouth, twining with mine. I lightly tug on his hair and a responding groan rumbles in his chest.

His lips are soft and warm. Thumbs stroking my cheeks, his breath comes in pants, and I feel his desire even before I'm aware of the erection pressing into my belly. I moan into the kiss and lightly trail my nails over his scalp. He groans and kisses me harder, his tongue urgently rubbing against mine.

Fire courses through my veins as the bonfire inside me escalates to an inferno. Arousal floods between my thighs, stoking the flames even hotter. No one's ever kissed me like this. No one's ever made me feel this firestorm of lust that obliterates everything in its path.

I'm going to sleep with Wes Emerson.

The thought hits me like a lightning bolt. I break the kiss.

"What's wrong?" he asks, gasping. "Why'd ya stop?"

"Good night, Wes," I breathe out. Without another word, I pull from his embrace and rush to my tent.

CHAPTER 23

LENA

Internal playlist: "Come Here Boy" by Imogen Heap

Heavy footfalls approach, crunching on the rocks. "Are you gonna hide in your tent all day?" Wes grumbles from outside the zippered flap.

I glance at my watch. It's almost noon with still no sign of Chuck. I brushed my hair and dressed in my last clean outfit hours ago, but I can't bring myself to face Wes after last night's earth-shattering kiss.

"Day's not over yet."

He grunts. "I expected a response like that."

"Looks like you didn't need to bring your clairvoyance after all."

"Please come outside."

"I will when I'm ready."

"And when will that be?"

"Dunno, Ace. Haven't figured that out yet."

He sighs. "I cooked some fish for ya. It's by the fire. You should come eat."

I tentatively unzip the flap a few inches and peer at him through the opening. His frame blocks out the sun. *My favorite eclipse.*

"You cooked for me?"

He runs a hand through his hair. "I held them in the flames until the outside was crispy. If that counts as cooking, then yes."

In the four years we were together, Marc never once cooked for me. Hell, he'd pour coffee for himself when my empty cup was right beside his. That's what I was with him . . . an empty cup.

I unzip the flap the rest of the way. "Thank you for thinking of me." *For filling my cup.*

"I've done nothing but think of you since ya landed in my lap. Why should now be any different?" His royal blue gaze softens, and I can't breathe or think. "Then you kissed me." He rubs at the back of his neck. "Now, I'm damn near obsessed."

"You kissed me," I correct him.

His lips curve into a smirk. "You started it."

"Didn't look like you were gonna make a move," I mutter, climbing to my feet. I zip the tent behind me and flash him a smile. "And you know what they say about hesitation . . ."

CHAPTER 24

WES

Internal playlist: "Collide" by Howie Day

I stare after Lena as she walks toward the river. Hips swaying, hair loose around her shoulders, she leaves me in the dust.

Again.

The kiss was incredible. I felt it from my scalp to the tips of my toes. Soft, succulent lips, that little pink tongue. *Right now, your clairvoyance should be telling you to kiss me.* Lena was the best damn kiss of my life. And I don't need clairvoyance or a crystal ball to tell me she enjoyed it. The way she tugged my hair, her nails on my scalp, that little moan. My cock hardens at the memory. *Here we go again.*

But then she pulled away. Retreated to her tent to hide. Stayed in there the whole damn day. Why is she always hiding from me? I paced the riverbank since sunrise. Until I finally had enough and went after her.

As I follow her to the river, it occurs to me that chasing Lena is becoming a theme.

Soon it's late afternoon. Still no sign of Chuck. We grow more restless by the minute as we wait in relative silence.

"This is ridiculous," Jake snaps. "He knows we brought limited supplies and next to nothing in the way of food. Where the fuck is he?" Maybe it's the New Yorker in him, but Jake has never been a patient bloke. When he's anxious, he borders on moody dick territory.

"There's gotta be an explanation. He wouldn't hang us out to dry for no reason," I say somewhat unconvincingly.

"So, what happens if he doesn't show up?" Lena asks, chewing on her lip.

"We hunker here for another night." I whittle a branch with my knife to distract me from the gnawing in my gut.

"No. I mean, what if he *never* comes for us? What if we're stuck out here for days . . . weeks even?"

"Don't let your mind go there. He'll come today," I assure her.

"But what if he doesn't?" she repeats. "What happens when the river freezes over—"

"Jesus Christ, Lena!" I snarl, rounding on her. "Do ya need to list out every worst-case scenario like you're the fucking prophet of doom?"

"Watch your tone with me. I'm putting a realistic scenario on the table. I'd rather prepare for the worst-case and be proven wrong than live in a world of butterflies and cotton candy." Glaring at me, she abruptly climbs to her feet. "There's a very real possibility we could be stuck out here for longer than we bargained for." She waves a finger in my face. "Being a *dick* won't change that reality." She storms back to her tent.

"Wow, man. You handled that well," Jake says.

"Fuck off, Bennett."

"Guys, chill," Austin barks. "Lena makes a good point. We're all tired, hungry, and anxious. We can sit here and stew over it, or we can be productive. If nothin' else, it'll make the time go faster." He rises and points at me. "You broke it, you fix it. You were a real asshole." Snatching a fishing pole, he settles on the bank with his back to me. I glower at him instead of answering because I know he's right. Austin is one of the few people who can get away with calling me on my shit.

Truth is, I didn't mean to bark at Lena. I'm on edge and my answer came out harsher than I intended. I know we're underprepared for an extended stay. And though my instincts tell me Chuck isn't coming, I'm not ready to confront that possibility yet. I scan the tundra and spot her about a hundred yards upstream, venturing inland toward the tree line.

I haul myself to my feet. My entire body aches, and I feel weak. I haven't consumed enough fat or protein to sustain me. I stretch and head in Lena's direction. *Time to face the music.* I know I can be hotheaded and quick to fly off the handle, but I also know when to admit I fucked up.

CHAPTER 25

LENA

Internal playlist: "Breath of Life" by Florence + The Machine

Back at the lodge, I read an article about Alaskan vegetation, so I know the wild blueberries I'm gathering are edible. I also know I don't have the energy to deal with any blue-eyed assholes at the moment, so I ignore Wes's approach and focus on my task.

He trudges to where I'm kneeling. "Hi."

"Hello." My tone is cool in response to his sheepish greeting.

"What're ya up to?"

"Foraging," I answer without looking up.

"What kind of berry is that?"

"A blueberry."

"You sure they're edible?"

"Would I be picking them if they weren't?"

I scrape at a piece of lichen. It looks gross, but they're also edible. Wes shifts his weight. Then he clears his throat. I ignore him and continue to scrape. He stands in silence for a few minutes, watching me. I give him nothing, not even a glance.

I reach for a lichen near his foot and he grunts.

"Christ almighty," he mutters, squatting in front of me. Now I have no choice but to look at him. "Listen, I know you're mad," he begins with a heavy sigh.

"Great deduction, Sherlock. What clued you in?"

"Maybe how ya stomped away from me? Or that you won't look at me? Or the ice in your tone?"

"I didn't stomp."

"Abruptly retreated. However you wanna label it. For what it's worth, I'm sorry you're mad—"

"You're sorry I'm upset? Or you're sorry that you snapped at me for voicing my concerns?"

"Both. You didn't deserve that. I was out of line, and I'm truly sorry."

"Apology accepted." I give him credit for being man enough to admit fault. "I'm not trying to be the prophet of doom. I just have a *terrible* feeling—"

"Me too. But I guess I wasn't ready to admit that. I'm fighting to stay optimistic, but it's becoming more challenging as each hour passes," he confesses. "I'm tired, hungry, and on edge, none of which is your fault. Going forward, I'll be less of a dick."

"Thank you," I murmur. "And I'll try to put a lid on my negativity."

He sticks out his hand. "Truce?"

"Truce," I answer, clasping his palm.

He helps me to my feet. "Walk with me."

As we head upstream, he returns to his jovial, charismatic self. We stop alongside a calmer section of river and sit at the water's edge.

Wes leans over and splashes some water on his face. He straightens and uses his shirt to dry off, exposing his chiseled abdomen. Except *this* time, he catches me looking. I flush and avert my eyes.

He smirks. "You're not as stealthy as ya thought."

I glance at him. "If I can't do subtle, what makes you think I can manage stealth?"

"No need for stealth, Lena," he grins, "or subtlety."

"I'll keep that in mind."

"Also, I'm glad you put me in my place. Never take any of my shit."

"Believe me, I won't," I reply with a chuckle. "I may be a lot of things, but spineless isn't one of them."

We stare at the river in silence for a few minutes. I'm relaxed, despite the concern over Chuck's tardiness.

"Shall we pick up where we left off?"

"Huh?"

Grinning, he pushes up his sleeves. "I suppose I've made you wait long enough for number six."

"I agree."

"Quality number six holds even more validity now that I've kissed you." He licks his lips and meets my gaze. "Lena, you're . . ." he pauses, searching for the right word, "beguiling."

"Uh . . . what?"

"Again, with the eyebrow." He chuckles. "None of this should surprise ya."

"I guess it's not a word I'd choose to describe myself."

"Then *you* don't see what I see." He tilts his head and studies me. "You're a mystery. Just when I think I have you figured out; you surprise me. You're hypnotic and magnetic. You draw me in, push all my buttons, and repeatedly pull the rug out from under me. I'm not used to that. I don't get thrown for loops. And I'm *never* at a loss for words. Yet, on more than one occasion, you've left me speechless."

I smirk. "I'm sure my lack of filter plays a part."

"Sometimes," he agrees, tilting my chin. "But whenever I'm near you, my heart races and I need to remind myself to breathe. You steal my words and my breath with nothing more than a smile. A laugh. A glance in my direction. Whenever you're close to me, I want you closer. When you talk, I want to listen for hours. I wanna know you, Lena. In every way possible." He rubs the back of his neck. "And now that we've kissed, I don't ever wanna stop."

I stare back at him in stunned silence, trying to sort it out in my head. I've known him for less than a week, yet he seems to have an intimate knowledge of my soul. He stripped me bare without laying a finger on me. *There's no hiding from him.* That realization terrifies and exhilarates me.

"You can't do that, Wes," I whisper.

He furrows his brow. "Do what?"

"You can't sit there, looking at me that way, saying things you don't mean—"

"I meant *everything* I said. I already told ya, I don't do empty flattery."

"It's like you're two people—a gentleman and a rogue. I can't decide which one's really you."

He tilts his head. "Why can't I be both?"

"Because you can't. No man's that perfect. I won't let myself believe you're looking for more than a fling." I draw a shaky breath. "I'm not stupid, Wes."

"I just told you what I'm looking for. How much clearer do I need to make myself?"

"How am I supposed to believe—"

"I didn't think you were a coward." He pins me with his gaze.

"Excuse me?" I cock a brow. "A coward?"

"You're afraid to admit whatcha want. You can't even admit it to yourself. You've done your share of flirting too. You're not the type to play games, so you obviously don't realize how goddamn sexy you are." He rakes a hand through his hair. "One minute, you act like you want me, then you run away. You keep hiding from me and it's driving me fucking crazy. Don't pretend with me. You kissed me like your life depended on it. We both know you want to see where this takes us."

"You don't know what I'm looking for."

"I think I do," he insists. "You're just too scared to reach for whatcha want."

I cross my arms over my chest. "Your roos really are loose."

He flashes a cocky grin. "C'mon, Lena, don't get pissy because I called your bluff."

"Says the man I had to *tell* to kiss me." I release a frustrated breath. "If you meant all that, *you* would've done something. You're the one who's bluffing. Before you point a finger at me, I'd suggest you take a look in the mirror, Ace."

"I know you feel it too." He gestures between us. "Don't fool yourself into thinking I won't act on this."

"What are you waiting for?" I whisper.

"Your head and heart are at war. Find a common ground and come see me when you're ready to do something about it. Figure it out and be sure. Because I won't settle for pieces of you, Lena, it won't be enough for me. Mind, body, heart, and soul, I want it all."

"And what happens until then?"

Wes smiles. "We'll keep dancing around until one of us breaks." He climbs to his feet. "I hope ya can tango, sunshine."

CHAPTER 26

LENA

Internal playlist: "Rock Your Body" by Justin Timberlake

Another night in the wilderness is upon us. The breeze picks up, rustling through the tundra. We congregate around the fire pit like the past few nights. I toss some edible ferns into a pot of water and position it over the fire. I see Wes from the corner of my eye. My stomach flip-flops. His words echoed in my mind all afternoon. Afraid to make eye contact, I stir my pot of "fern soup" intently.

It doesn't matter. He hasn't taken his eyes off me. The heat of his gaze warms and unnerves me.

Austin's his usual cheerful self, humming and tapping his feet to whatever song plays in his head. Jake straddles a log and stares across the river. Wes sits beside him and continues to carve his stick into a spear.

"I think it's done," I mutter. "Disclaimer . . . it's probably disgusting."

"It's somethin' other than fish, so I'll take it," Austin says.

I pull the pot from the flames. "I don't know about you guys, but I would kill for a hot shower and some chicken wings."

"Slathered in honey-bourbon sauce," Austin agrees.

The ferns taste better than expected, but a few garlic cloves and some salt would've helped. Jake still hasn't said a word. I squeeze his shoulders as I pass. I know he doesn't want to talk, but it's my way of letting him know I'm here to listen.

"Thanks, Lena," he murmurs. "I'm sorry, guys. My head's in a bad place right now."

"I know. Mine, too." I settle beside Austin. "I'm trying to distract myself, but it's getting harder."

"What are we gonna do?" Jake's desolate gaze meets mine.

"Survive," Wes replies. "That's all we can do. I vote we stay in this spot. We have water, a food source, and shelter. Plus, when they come looking for us, we'll be easily spotted."

"Yes." Austin voices his approval. "We keep our wood supply up and our ears open for planes. When we hear somethin', we toss pine boughs onto the fire to make a smoke signal."

"I wish I brought my mirror," I say.

"You look beautiful, Lena," Wes tells me.

Ignoring his compliment, I explain, "If we had a mirror, we could angle it in the sunlight to signal a plane. It's more effective than signal fires."

Wes stares through the flames, causing my heart to race. Rapid, shaky breaths expand my chest. I shift and pop my shoulder. Jake shoots me a death glare.

"Sorry."

"Is your neck bothering you?" Wes asks. "That sounded painful."

"It's my shoulder. An old work-related injury that flares up sometimes. Sleeping on the ground isn't helping." I massage my collarbone.

"How'd ya hurt it?" Wes asks.

I sigh. "Long story. I'll tell you some other time."

"Why don'tcha tell me now?" he probes.

"Because I said *no*. Not here, not now. Maybe never."

Smirking, Wes points to the salmon. "You should eat something else. You're getting pissy again."

"I'm not pissy." I narrow my eyes. "And you can wipe the smirk off your face."

His smirk morphs into a grin. Then, the bastard winks.

"Wes, you're antagonizing me again. It's infuriating."

"Well, I aim to please."

Jake snickers. "He usually misses."

"Sometimes. But, unlike you, I'm usually within a kilometer of my target."

"Fuck off," Jake mutters.

Wes elbows him. "You're just angry because I'm right."

"Hey, Lena," Jake looks over at me, "how about I hold him down while you wipe the smirk off his face?"

"Nope." Wes shakes his head. "Doesn't work for me. If I let anyone hold me down, it won't be you, Bennett." His heated gaze sweeps over me.

"Keep it up, Wes," I warn, fighting the amusement in my tone.

He wags his brows. "No worries, Lena. I don't have any issues in *that* department."

Jake snorts. "That's because he can't find it in the first place." With a mock Australian accent, he adds, "Where the hell's my bloody didgeridoo?" He pretends to look down his pants. "I can't find that bloke anywhere."

My eyes fill with tears as I succumb to a fit of laughter.

Wes leans forward and watches me through the flames. "If ya think that's so funny, Lena, perhaps you won't mind helping me search."

"I think I'll pass."

Austin laughs. "Damn, she shut you down, man."

Wes pins me with his gaze. "Doesn't have to be a tango, we can waltz if you like."

Jake shakes his head. "Dude, what the fuck are you talking about?"

Wes ignores him. "Tango, waltz, salsa . . . you tell me."

"I don't waltz," I snap. "And you don't wanna tango with me, Ace."

Jake snorts. "What is this? Dancing with the fucking stars?"

Austin raises his hand. "Someone needs to put me on that show. I'll blow all those fuckers outta the water."

I grin. "I'll start a petition for you, Austin. We'll have a vote and get some new contestants on there. All in favor of Memphis burning up the dance floor, say aye."

He does a wolf howl and laughs.

I jerk a thumb toward Wes. "We'll have a disclaimer that states, 'those who can't handle their fishing poles need not apply.'"

Jake and Austin crack up.

Wes leans in and licks his lips. "Trust me, sunshine. I handle my pole even better than I dance. It's a question of whether you're able to keep up. Since you're so spicy, how about the salsa?"

"I don't salsa. I don't samba. I don't foxtrot, and I sure as shit don't flamenco." I level a glare on him.

Wes's heated gaze darkens. "You'll dance with me, sunshine."

CHAPTER 27

LENA

Internal playlist: "I Got You (I Feel Good)" by Jessie J

Now *this* is heaven. I should probably perform a dance thanking the fire gods for the flames that heated this water. I nearly moan at the warmth flowing over my chilled skin.

Wes taps my shoulder. "What the hell're ya doing?"

I jump, spilling water on my shirt. I had just gotten dressed after a dip in the river to bathe. Now I'm attempting to wash my hair. I didn't hear his approach over the current.

"Why the hell are *you* sneaking up on me?"

"I said 'Good mornin' when I saw you," he insists, standing over me. "No, really, what're ya doing?"

"What does it look like I'm doing?" I peer at him through a curtain of wet hair.

He shrugs. "Kneeling half-naked at the river. I dunno, a baptism?"

"I'm washing my hair, you idiot." I squeeze the excess water from my locks before dramatically flinging my head back.

Wes frowns at the sprayed water droplets.

Serves him right for sneaking up on me. I towel off with a sweatshirt before wrapping it around my head. I must look ridiculous. *Whatever. I'm clean.* I got up at dawn and successfully washed my body in the frigid water. It was a two-part plan. After getting dressed and warming up by the fire, I used a bar of soap and some heated water to wash my hair.

"Aren't ya cold?" Wes rubs his arms.

Sitting back on my heels, I arch a brow. "What do *you* think?"

He stares down at me with a roguish grin. "I'll go with a *hard* yes on that one."

I glance at myself. *Fuck.* I forgot my stupid bra in the tent and removed my flannel to keep it dry. My nipples are hard, and my damp white tank leaves little to the imagination.

"Whoa. Am I interrupting something?" Jake approaches cautiously.

"No, mate. Just taking in the view."

"Have fun with that." Jake picks up the ax. "I'm gonna head upstream and look for kindling."

"I'll help ya in a bit," Wes calls out. "I'm a little . . . busy at the moment."

Rolling my eyes, I snatch the flannel and shove my arms into the sleeves, cold fingers fumbling the buttons.

"What's the hurry?" Wes's gaze fixates on my chest.

My shoulders rise and fall with each rapid breath, drawing more attention to my breasts. Pupils dilated, his gaze travels to my face and locks onto mine, nearly incinerating me.

"Need any help?" His voice drops an octave. "I'm more than happy to assist."

"No, I've got everything under control, thank you." I arch a brow. "You enjoying the show, Wes?"

I feel both exposed and exhilarated. As much as I want to hide, the part of me that wants him to look is taking over, leaving a brazen goddess in its wake.

"More than you know."

My gaze travels from his broad shoulders and chest, over his washboard abs, and lingers on the bulge in his jeans. *Oh, I bet he's huge. Thick and hard, just like the rest of him.* The thought makes my insides heat. It's been too long since someone touched me, kissed me, thrust inside me. I arch my back and give him a look that tells him *exactly* what I'm thinking.

It's his turn for a sharp inhale. His mouth drops open, but no sound comes out.

I rise in front of him. Our bodies inches apart, heat radiates from him. I peer from beneath my lashes and trail my fingertips down his chest.

"Speechless?" I press my body to him, his erection hard against my belly. "The rest of you is saying plenty, Wesley."

"Lena . . ." Chest heaving, fists clenched at his sides, he growls the warning, "You're playing with fire."

"We've been over this, Wes." I bite my lower lip and slowly drag my tongue over it. "I can handle the heat." I stand on my tiptoes, deliberately rubbing him, and Wes looks like he might implode with lust. "The question is . . . can you?"

At that, I turn on my heel and make my way to the fire. I settle on a log and remove the sweatshirt from my head. Damp locks cascade down my back. I peek over my shoulder.

Wes hasn't moved or taken his eyes off me. The heat in his gaze reaches inferno level. I bite my lower lip and wink, goading him because I rather enjoy doing it.

He stalks to the fire, pausing directly behind me. "Keep dancing, sunshine." He grips my shoulders, bringing his lips to my ear. "We both know where you'll be when the music stops." The heated whisper sends chills down my spine. Moisture pools in my nether region.

"And where's that?"

His teeth graze the outer shell of my ear. "Naked beneath me."

Every nerve ending flares to life. I press my knees together to quell the throbbing ache between my legs. Still standing over me, he notices, of course.

"Keep pressing those legs together . . . the song's almost over."

"Good thing I'm tone-deaf, Ace."

We spend the day fishing, gathering wood, foraging, and lounging by the fire. No one addresses it directly, but we begin to accept the reality that Chuck isn't coming.

We're all tired, hungry, and on edge. *Especially* Wes. Lust and frustration radiate from him. With every sultry smile, lip bite, and flutter of eyelashes, I push him further. I can't help myself. The inability to control my response to him melds with my desire to make *him* squirm.

And squirm, he does.

It's not in my nature to play games, but the thought of dying in the Alaskan wilderness reduces me to a product of my body's chemistry.

He said he won't make his move until I sort myself out, but I know better. Wes is holding on by a thread. My mind replays his words from earlier. *I won't settle for pieces of you. Mind, body, heart, and soul, I want it all.*

It's been years since I felt wanted. Years. Wes wants my body—that much I know for certain—erections don't lie. As I watch him through the flames, I imagine myself in his arms. I long to feel the heavy weight of his body moving on top of mine, the thick length of him inside me. I reflexively press my legs together again. Not that it matters, I've been aroused since the moment I laid eyes on him.

But Wes is right; I *am* at war with myself.

I don't do casual sex. My body is a package deal that can only be unwrapped when my heart feels secure. I want more than a fling with Wes. *Much more.* But I'm not convinced he feels the same. As much as I want him, I know I shouldn't go there. I need to safeguard my heart before it winds up in a pile with the bow and crumpled tissue paper.

It would be easier if his gaze didn't feel like a physical touch. Or if he hadn't already listened more intently than any man I ever met. Or if he hadn't held me when I cried. Or if he didn't infuriate me and make me laugh in the same breath. Maybe then I'd have a chance at resisting him. *We'll keep dancing around until one of us breaks.*

I've never met anyone like Wes, and I know damn well I'll never meet his match. Either way, he'll break me, so why not fuck him? Let him curl my toes and make me scream. I deserve that much. I should give myself one night to feel desired, one night to feel something. Let him indulge me. Eat that fucking cake for once . . . and the goddamn frosting.

CHAPTER 28

GARRETT CASEY, BROOKLYN, NEW YORK

Internal playlist: "Unsteady" by X Ambassadors

My cell rings, startling me awake. Still stretched out on the couch, I've been dozing since my ass hit the cushions around nine. I scrub a fist over my face and glance at the clock. It's already after eleven. I smile at the script lying on my chest. I can't wait to tell Lena I got the part in *Prodigy*.

My phone rings again. *Right.* I lurch upward and reach for it, nearly toppling the glass of water on my end table.

"Fuck." I catch it in time.

It rings a third time. Snatching it, I furrow my brow at the unfamiliar area code. *Who the hell's calling this late?*

"Hello?" I answer gruffly.

"Good evening, I'm looking for Mr. Garrett Casey." The male voice at the other end of the receiver crackles in my ear.

"This is Garrett."

"Mr. Casey, this is Officer Dan Mayfield of the Alaska State Troopers. We have you listed as the emergency contact for Lena Hamilton. Is that correct?"

"Is she okay? What happened?" Scalp prickling, I clutch the phone. A sick feeling washes over me, erasing all traces of slumber.

"Sir, we regret to inform you that Ms. Hamilton has been reported missing."

"*What!* What do you mean, missing?" My ears ring as I try to process the man's words.

"The Aurora Borealis resort contacted us. Ms. Hamilton and three male guests chartered a private plane for a camping excursion."

Emerson and his crew.

"When they didn't return as scheduled, the resort contacted the flight company and learned that the plane and pilot are also missing."

"No. No … no, this can't be happening. You have to find her," I stammer.

"Sir, we're doing everything we can to locate Ms. Hamilton, the other campers, and the pilot."

"Do more," I snarl, pacing the living room. The buzzing in my ears grows louder. "How does a plane go missing? Track down its satellite signal. Do something!"

"This is a small bush plane, Mr. Casey, it doesn't work like that. There's no satellite signal. The last contact with the pilot was his distress call, which wasn't reported to us until after we began our investigation. We've scoured the Gobbler's Knob region. There's no sign of the plane."

"Why the fuck didn't they report a distress call?"

"That's our question, too. Turns out, the company has some licensing issues and was operating under an expired permit. Not wanting to expose the illegal operation, they attempted to locate the plane themselves, but failed."

"I can't believe this."

This is my fault. I encouraged Lena to take that trip. Now she's lost in the wilderness, maybe even dead. I sink to the couch. *This can't be happening. Not Lena. Not the one person who cares about me.*

"… there's a full investigation underway, and we've deployed search and rescue teams throughout the region. We'll keep you informed as new information arises. Are you able to contact Ms. Hamilton's family?"

"I'll take care of it."

"I'm sorry, Mr. Casey, I know this is difficult. We're doing everything we can."

"Thank you," I say weakly, ending the call.

It feels like my heart's been ripped from my chest. Lena's my best friend. My sister. I'd do anything for her, even give up my life. I can't fucking breathe. I'm across the country sitting on a couch, what can I possibly do to help her now?

I stare at the phone in my hand. I know I need to make the call, but I can't bring myself to dial.

I finish my remaining water in one swallow and reach for the remote. I need some background noise before the deafening silence suffocates me. I'll call in a few minutes. I'm the only one who knows she's there; I need time to process before I open *that* can of worms.

I stare at the weather forecast, stock market update, and sports segments. *What am I gonna do?* A report on the celebrities' disappearance is the kick in the ass I need. *Call before her name is on the fucking news.* Taking a steadying breath, I dial my phone.

"Hello?" A woman's voice picks up after the second ring.

"Adele, it's Garrett."

"Garrett, honey, it's late. Is everything all right?" Lena's mother asks.

"No . . . no, Adele, it's not . . . It's about Lena."

CHAPTER 29

LENA

Internal playlist: "River" by Bishop Briggs

Austin stands and stretches. "All right, y'all. I'm gonna hit the sack. I've had enough sittin' around for one day."

"I'm with you." Jake rises and turns to Wes. "You coming?"

"No."

Jake shrugs. "Night, Lena-Bean."

Standing, I dust bark bits off my jeans. "Wait up, I'll walk with you." I step over the log and move to follow Jake.

"Lena, I need to talk to you," Wes announces from across the fire.

"I'm exhausted. We can talk in the morning."

"This will only take a minute."

I glance at Jake and Austin. "Night, guys." They head for the tents. I fiddle with my canteen's lid and turn to Wes. "What's up?"

"Come here."

I raise an eyebrow. "Excuse me?"

"You heard me. I said, come here."

Who the fuck does he think he is? "Make me."

"Make you what?"

"Make me come." I realize what he did as the words leave my lips. "If you think you can."

"I *know* I can."

I roll my eyes. "What do you want, Wes?"

"I've already answered that."

"I mean, right now."

"The time or place doesn't change my answer."

"You wanted to talk?" I say, quickly losing patience with his domineering attitude.

"Come here," he repeats. "*Please.*"

"I can hear you just fine from over here. What's up?"

"You tell me." His tone hardens my nipples.

"I dunno, Ace, you're the one who wanted to talk." Hands on my hips, I wait.

"You baited me this morning."

"Ever consider a career change? You'd make one helluva detective."

"I think it proved we're done dancing, Lena. I know I'm done. And I think you are, too."

I snort. "Find your crystal ball today? You seem to have me all figured out."

"Do I?" He climbs to his feet.

My insides heat and flutter, but I give him a lackadaisical shrug. "Maybe."

Wes takes a step closer. "What do you want, Lena?"

"I want you to quit your act."

Brows knitting themselves together, he tilts his head. "My act?"

"Either you want a hookup, or you want more. I *know* it's not both. Pick one and be clear about your intentions because I don't have the energy for games."

"I don't play games, Lena. I see what I want, and I go after it. I want everything about you." With his gaze pinned to mine, he prowls around the fire and looms over me. "I think you're just scared of how much *you* want me. I don't understand why you're trying to lie to us both."

I stare, shaking my head in disbelief. "You seriously have a roo loose in the top paddock."

Wes steps closer, clamping his hands on my waist. "What're ya scared of, Lena? Afraid I'll put all your book boyfriends to shame? Might need to burn the others, too."

"Bite me." I pull from his grasp and stalk toward the tents.

"Don't think I won't." He blocks my path. "So that's it? You're just gonna stomp away again? Run and hide from your feelings?"

"Fuck off, Wes." I step around him.

"You talk the talk, but can't walk the walk," he growls. "Then ya have the balls to accuse *me* of acting."

Who the fuck does he think he is?

I want to slap him. Eyes welling, I spin around. "I spent four *years* with a man who couldn't be bothered to look up from his phone when I walked into a room; four years talking to someone whose idea of listening was waiting for his turn to speak. Four years being told I'm too emotional. Four years as a fucking afterthought." I clench my jaw and narrow my eyes. "I left him eight months ago, but it's been over two *years* since anyone's touched me. And I can't remember the last time someone made me come."

Wes's eyes flare in shock, then darken and sweep over my body. "That's unacceptable. I'd be happy to chan—"

"So, forgive me if I have a hard time believing Wes Emerson wants anything to do with *me*. I see the women you surround yourself with—like Alainna Baker. Really? You expect me to believe I come close to *her*? I'm a nurse from upstate New York. I'm an *ordinary* woman, Wes. Not the Aphrodite goddess model types you're used to."

Blinking back tears, I throw my arms out to the sides. "Look around! I'm the only woman for miles and we may die out here. *You've* got nothing to lose. I know how hard I could fall for you, how fast you could take my heart. You're already headed there. I want you, but I won't let you destroy me when you leave." I squeeze my eyes shut, and a single tear rolls down my cheek, but I don't bother to brush it away. At this point, I don't care if he sees me cry. "You don't want my heart, Wes. Don't pretend to be sincere. Don't act like you wanna keep me when you're just gonna sink your teeth into me and rip me apart. I won't let someone reduce me to scraps again."

He grips my shoulders. "This is *not* a fucking act."

"Bullshit. You—"

"It's not my *teeth* I wanna sink into you," he growls, nose touching mine, eyes bringing the heat of a blowtorch. "And I want more than your body. What's it gonna take for you to believe I wanna make you mine *and* keep you?" He tightens his grip. "Every. Part. Of. You."

Holy. Fuck. The canteen slips from my grasp.

Wes glances at the fallen vessel. "Don't," he warns, voice unrecognizable.

"Don't, what?" Ripping from his hold, I defiantly sink to my knees. Shoulders back, spine stiffened, I snatch the canteen and stare up at him.

Wes tenses. Chest heaving, fists clenched, the muscle in his jaw pulses. But it's his eyes that stop my heart. Like a savage beast about to strike, unfettered lust fills his gaze.

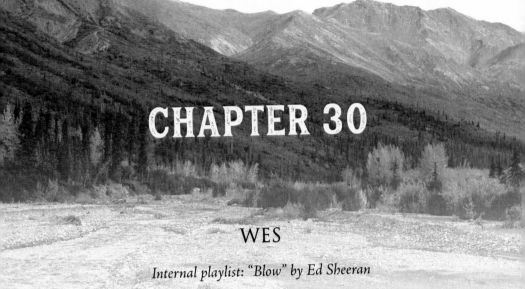

CHAPTER 30

WES

Internal playlist: "Blow" by Ed Sheeran

I stare down at the mutinous woman on her knees and feel the last tethers of my self-control unraveling. I'm seconds from squashing Lena's little rebellion.

My inner caveman cracks his knuckles, tightening his grip on the club he carries. He's joined by a pacing beast who licks its chops in anticipation. The beast roars and gnashes his teeth. The pair have grown tired of my hesitation and wait for the opportunity to strike.

Lena's parted lips are glossy from the tongue that just licked them. Furious gaze scorching me, the sultry hellion rises to her full height. She twists the cap off the canteen, lifts it to her mouth, and boldly stares from beneath her lashes. Wrapping her lips around the mouth of the canteen, she takes a slow, deliberate sip.

I clench my jaw tighter. I can't breathe, can't think. No one's ever stood up to me like this. Ever. Not only did she ignore my command, but she blatantly defied it. I'm used to getting what I want, used to people asking, "How high?" when I tell them to jump. Not Lena—she called my bluff *and* rubbed my nose in it.

Defiant. Stubborn. Sexy as hell. She's a wild card. She doesn't fall at my feet or hang on my every word. She refuses to allow me the upper hand and won't take my shit. I dish it out, she gives it back harder. I laid out all my cards . . . and she flipped the fucking table.

Sure, she started this little game of roulette, but I'm not gonna let her win. I'm about four seconds from fucking the fight right out of her.

She takes a daring step closer, and I shake my head in warning. *Don't do it.*

She narrows her eyes and lifts the canteen to her mouth. Lips parting, she pauses. Watching. Waiting to play her ace.

Go ahead, sunshine, pull the trigger.

She cocks an emboldened brow at my unspoken message. Then, her tongue darts out and licks the canteen's rim.

Mine! My caveman swings, the beast lunges, and I fucking lose it.

"Fuck this." Nostrils flaring, I snatch the canteen and heave it behind me. It clatters on the rocks. "Song's over, sunshine."

Her eyes widen.

I seize her shoulders and crush her body against me. "You're *mine.*"

I swallow her surprised gasp in a plundering kiss. My tongue surges into her mouth, tasting her, *claiming her.* Channeling my lust and frustration, I thrust my tongue the way I want my cock inside her—fast, hard, and deep.

Lena stiffens, fisting my shirt like she wants to pull away. I knot a hand in her hair and kiss her harder. I know she relents when the tension leaves her body. She clutches my shoulders and slides a hand to the back of my neck. Deepening the kiss, she moves her mouth in rhythm with mine. I clamp her hip and pull her closer.

That's it, sunshine, feel me. Every rock-hard inch.

Lena moans against my lips, weaving her hands into my hair. She tugs the strands. I groan as my primal, animalistic instinct roars to life. My blood burns with lust. I'm going to bury myself so deep in that hot body, neither of us will know where one stops and the other starts. I'm gonna fuck her. *Right now.*

I pull Lena closer and slide my hands to her arse. Grabbing a fistful of each cheek, I lift her, and she wraps her legs around me. I lower us to the ground and settle on top of her without breaking our kiss. I grind my hips, and a moan escapes her chest. *Let me hear you, sunshine. I'll have you screaming my name in no time.*

Breaking the kiss, I yank the zipper on her parka. I stare into her eyes as I unbutton her flannel, revealing the tank top beneath. *That little white shirt.* It's been driving me insane since I saw her at the river's edge. I push the material to her armpits, eyeing her lacy black bra. She'd retreated to her tent to put one on after our riverside encounter.

I roughly tug her bra cups down. "You should've left this off."

Lena gasps when the arctic air meets her exposed skin, causing her nipples to harden into mouthwatering peaks. "I was feeling fancy, Ace."

Interlacing our fingers, I pin her hands to the ground. I take a moment to admire the full, lush breasts that rise and fall with each breath, before lowering my mouth to a nipple. Her hips flex upward as I flick and swirl my tongue. My cock begs for entrance, so I rub it against her and give her a few hip thrusts. *Mine!*

"Oh, God, Wes . . ."

I swirl my tongue again, releasing one of her hands. It weaves into my hair. Mirroring my tongue, I drag my free thumb over her other nipple. Lena moans when I give her a hard suck. Her eyes flutter closed. She pulls my head closer, and I smile against her soft skin.

I release her hand and lift my head. "You like that?"

"Yes," she gasps.

"What was that, Lena?" I thrust my cock against her. "Didn't catch that."

"*Yes.*"

I unbutton her jeans. Yanking the zipper, I shove the denim over her hips to her ankles and fight the urge to shred her little pink panties with my teeth.

"Now would be a good time to tell me to stop," I growl, running my hands up her goose-bumped thighs to the waistband.

I slip a hand inside. She gasps when I drag it from her clit to her body's entrance, gathering the moisture.

"Look at me."

She opens her eyes.

I stare into the wintergreen pools. "Do ya want me to stop?"

"No."

Circling my thumb over her clit, I slide a finger inside. Her eyes flutter closed as I stroke her.

"You're so wet," I groan, massaging her clit with the pad of my thumb. I add a second finger, and she moans loudly.

She's so fucking responsive . . . and tight. *It's been over two years since anyone's touched me.*

Chest heaving, I lean forward and kiss her. Her urgent tongue meets mine, hands fisting my hair. She clenches around my fingers as I thrust them harder and faster.

It doesn't take long to bring her to the edge. Lena bucks against my hand, unable to stifle her moans. Then, my third finger meets with resistance and I pull back.

Slow the fuck down before you hurt her.

Lena breaks the kiss. "Don't you dare stop."

"I'm just getting started, love." I meet her gaze, rubbing her G-spot with curved fingers.

"Wes . . ." She digs her nails into my scalp.

"Let me hear you, sunshine," I growl, quickening the pace.

Lena's legs tremble and her back arches off the ground. I rub her clit, and she comes apart in my hands.

"Oh, fuck," she moans. "Oh, *Wes.*"

Eyes locked on hers, I ride the waves of her release. Lena's orgasm is the most beautiful thing I've ever witnessed. Lips parted, breasts heaving, body clenching my fingers, she's a fucking goddess. I see nothing but her. Hear nothing but her gasps and moans as she climaxes. Feel nothing but my cock straining to fuck her.

Lena. The woman who, in a few short days, turned my world upside down. She draws me in with her soulful jade eyes and succulent lips. That soft hair and lush body pulls me closer. But it's her laugh that brings a smile to my face, her sass that ignites me, and her mind that holds me captive. But what I want most, is her heart. I feel it calling out to me, begging for solace, affection, and attention. Aching for love, craving the warmth and shelter of a partner who sees her worth. She keeps it locked behind the walls she built. Walls that will take time and persistence to climb.

Yes, Lena's body awakened the animal inside me, but it's her heart that brings the man to his knees. I want, no, *need* her more than I've ever desired anyone in my life. But her body's not ready for me, and I can't trust myself not to lose control. She deserves better than a hard fuck on the cold ground.

She reaches for my zipper and tugs.

I grip her wrist. "We've gotta slow down."

"Please, don't stop."

"I won't fuck you on the ground like some animal."

"Wes, I need you."

"I don't wanna hurt ya, love."

I'm acutely aware of my considerable size. Previous lovers struggled to accommodate me. I could never let go out of fear of hurting them. Sure, I have a pleasurable love life, but it's one of restraint. I'm a caged beast who's yet to reach his full potential.

I know it will be different with Lena. She pushes me further, harder, than I ever thought possible. The beast inside me wants to claim her. Mark her as its own. Dark, primal need surges through my veins, saturating every muscle, every cell. *She deserves better.* She rattled my cage, but Lena isn't ready for my beast. Not yet, anyway.

"You won't hurt me," she insists. "Don't stop."

I bring my lips to her ear. "Don't worry, sunshine, I'll make you come so many times, you'll beg me to stop. Because if I can do this with my hand, wait until you feel my tongue."

"Oh, God, Wes," she hisses.

I kiss her in a sensuous dance of lips and tongues. Lena's hips move in rhythm with my fingers. I sense another climax building. Ignoring the pressure in my cock—and the caveman who demands I take her—I keep my pace agonizingly slow.

She clings to me, and the urgency in her kiss escalates. Vibrating with desperation, she thrusts her pussy onto my fingers, but I keep my movements tender. *The woman's putty in my hands.* Her second climax crests, and she moans loudly.

"Shh. The guys will hear us."

Lena lifts her head. "I don't give a flying fuck *who* hears us."

I chuckle and withdraw my fingers.

She grips my face and stares into my eyes. "Fuck me, Wes. Right here, right now."

I shake my head. "You deserve better than that. I can and *will* give you better than that."

"Don't you want me?" she whispers against my lips. The vulnerability in her gaze is a knife to my chest.

As if there's any fucking question.

I press her hand to my jean-covered cock. "I know you feel that. Lena, I want you more than I wanna breathe, more than the blood in my fucking veins." I growl. "But not like this, love. You mean too much to me." I kiss her again. "You're *mine*, sunshine. Even if you don't quite believe it yet."

CHAPTER 31

LENA

Internal playlist: "Feelin' Love" by Paula Cole

On my back near the fire, with Wes between my legs, I see the flames reflected in deep blue. His reverent gaze makes me feel like a goddess. No one's ever looked at me like this. No one has *ever* kissed or touched me like this. I just experienced the ecstasy of two orgasms in under ten minutes, with minimal effort on his part. It makes me realize just how selfish Marc was.

Wes kisses me again and my eyes flutter closed. I absorb the warm weight of his body, the pressure between my thighs, and the brush of his thumbs against my cheeks. He's so strong, authoritative, and primal. But at the same time, he's tender, caring, and protective. I want both sides of him. I want the man and the beast. I want him to make love to me *and* fuck me senseless.

Wrapping my arms around his waist, I pull him closer. We lie on the ground, kissing for a while.

The wind picks up, making me shudder. Wes presses himself to his knees and fixes my bra. He smooths the tank top, and I rebutton the flannel.

"Better?" He tugs my panties and jeans up over my hips.

"Yes, thank you." I nod to his bulge. "What about you?"

He raises a brow. "What about me?"

"I don't wanna leave you hanging."

"I don't work that way. Clearly, your ex made ya believe otherwise, but some of us can give without taking. I'd pleasure you all night long, but it's too fucking cold out." He fastens the zipper on my parka.

"Oh," I murmur. "Won't you be uncomfortable?"

Wes chuckles. "Trust me, I'll live. I've been hard since you landed in my lap that first day. Why should now be any different?" He stands, pulling me to my feet. "Looks like we're getting that storm Ellen mentioned."

The wind swirls snowflakes around us. I shudder again, and Wes pulls me close.

"Thank you," I murmur, hugging him.

"For what?"

"All of it." My lips curve into a smirk. "Especially the action, Mister Man of Action."

"I aim to please." His smile fades and his eyes focus on mine. "I know you don't believe what I said—"

"Wes, stop—"

He touches my cheek. "Let me finish. You don't believe me, and I can understand why. But I want you to know I mean the things I say. Actions speak louder than words, and I plan to *show* you I'm being sincere. Just gimme a chance."

"I'll try," I whisper.

We walk toward the tents. The snow comes down harder, mixing with sleet. We navigate the slippery rocks and nearly reach the cluster of trees when Wes stops me.

"For the record, I've wanted you since the moment you first stumbled into my life. Even when I was a dick, I still wanted you. I swear, I nearly kissed ya when you hopped off that treadmill and got sassy with me." He chuckles. "But when I brought your bookmark to your room and you looked at me with those lust-filled eyes, I knew I had to have you." He runs a hand through his hair. "You stared at my lips like you wanted to kiss them, and I felt like the luckiest man alive."

I open my mouth to speak, but Wes holds a finger to my lips.

"After we spoke on the deck, and again at your camp, I wanted to learn everything about you. And when you looked across that fire into my eyes and told me the kind of man you deserved, I wanted to *be* that man. It's only grown from there. So, the fact that you're the only woman for miles means nothing to me. It just makes it harder for you to resist my advances—"

I silence him with a kiss. Standing on my tiptoes, I weave my arms around his neck and kiss him fiercely, showing him how deeply his confession affects me. Wes wraps his arms around my waist and pulls me closer. We stand like this for several minutes, in the freezing cold, the snow and sleet dusting our hair and eyelashes while we kiss.

Wes pulls back, gripping my chin. "Lena, you *are* a goddess. I want to worship every fucking inch of you. I don't care whether you believe me. I'll prove it in time." He lowers his voice. "But if I hear you call yourself 'ordinary' again, there will be consequences."

"Oh?" My insides heat up once more. "What kind of consequences?"

"You'll see," he says, eyes filled with heat.

"I'll keep that in mind. How about you let me know what *else* a girl needs to do to get herself a good spanking around here?" I purr as I brush past him and hurry to my tent. Unzipping it, I peek over my shoulder at him.

Wes gapes. His priceless expression is one of lust-filled shock.

I wink dramatically, scratch my nose with a middle finger, and lunge into my tent. Zipping the flap behind me, I grin and crawl to my sleeping bag. I hear his footsteps on the rocks outside.

"Sunshine, be careful what you wish for."

The heated warning sends chills down my spine. *Oh, God, yes.* I imagine him taking me over his knee and nearly moan aloud.

CHAPTER 32

WES

Internal playlist: "The Warmth" by Incubus

I jolt awake, rubbing a gloved fist over my eyes. I reach for a flashlight and shine the beam at my watch. *Midnight.* We still have several hours until sunrise. The wind howls, violently flapping the fabric walls. Teeth chattering, I look over at my mates, who are both burrowed deep within their sleeping bags. I instinctively move closer to Jake, but that doesn't help. Even with the body heat of three blokes, the air in the tent is frigid. I'm so cold I can barely move.

Lena.

The thought sucker punches me. I yank open my sleeping bag and shove boots onto my feet.

Austin stirs. "What's up, man?"

"I'm gonna check on Lena. If I'm this cold with you two in here, I can't imagine how she feels." I unzip the tent.

An icy wind gusts through the opening. I climb out and quickly close the flap. Shielding my eyes from the bite of the wind, I peer through the snow squall. I locate Lena's tent and trudge through several inches of snow.

Yes, it's late August, but this is Alaska. And we're in the Arctic Circle.

"Lena?" I call out. "Are you all right?"

No response.

"Lena?" When she doesn't answer the second time, panic fills my chest. "I'm coming in." I yank the zipper.

It's pitch-black in Lena's tent. Like a fuckwit, I left the flashlight with my mates. I crawl to where she huddles in her sleeping bag. Teeth chattering, her entire body trembles.

"Are you all right, love?" I ask, unzipping her bag.

She looks at me but doesn't speak.

"Lena, answer me."

"C-C-Cold . . ." Her voice is little more than a whisper.

I shove my arms beneath her and lift. "I'm takin' ya with me." I scoot toward the tent flap and climb outside.

Shuddering, Lena burrows her face into my chest.

"Let's getcha warmed up." I charge through the snow. "Austin! Jake! Open the flap!"

Jake's face appears. "Memphis, grab blankets!"

He moves aside so I can enter with Lena, zipping the flap behind us. Austin flicks on a lantern. Lena seems unaware of her surroundings.

I place her in my sleeping bag and remove my parka. "Her fucking lips are blue. We need to warm her up before she freezes to death." I wrap the parka around her.

"You gotta do skin-to-skin, man," Austin insists. "Blankets won't do shit at this point."

"Whaddya mean?"

"I mean, you gotta take off your shirt *and* hers. Use your body heat to warm her up. I'll try to get a fire started so we can heat some water, and I'll grab her sleeping bag while I'm out there." Austin pulls on his boots and points to me. "You're gonna have to let Jake help."

Jake meets my gaze, his eyes widening.

"You heard him. Take off your shirt." I frantically work the buttons on my flannel. I remove it and pull off the thermal beneath.

Jake follows suit, whirling layers off and placing them in a pile on his sleeping bag. He frowns. "This isn't gonna work—we can't all fit in one bag. We need to zip ours together."

"Good call." I lean over Lena. "Listen to me, love."

She looks up at me while Jake works on connecting our bags.

"I'm not being fresh, but I need to take off your shirt. Jake and I are gonna huddle close and use our body heat to warm ya up, okay?"

She nods.

I remove her parka and unbutton the flannel. I pull it off and toss it aside, along with the white tank top. I climb into our new double sleeping bag and pull her against my bare chest. Her skin is ice. Reaching around, I unhook her bra and remove it.

"Get in, Bennett."

Jake climbs into the sleeping bag behind Lena and presses his chest to her back. "Holy shit, she's freezing."

I clench my jaw and stare at his face. Fear and urgency war with my possessive instinct. Sure, Jake clarified he's not a threat during our confrontation at the summit, but that means nothing to the caveman inside me. All *he* can see is the male too close to his half-naked woman. But if we don't get Lena warmed up, things could get terrible fast. As much as I hate it, I need his help. I know my unspoken message is received when Jake gives a small nod, as if he hears my conflicted thoughts.

Austin layers blankets and parkas on top of us. "You," he points at me, "cut the alpha shit. I saw that death glare you shot him. Man the fuck up and deal. This is survival."

"I know," I growl, pulling Lena closer. "Doesn't mean I have to like it."

"I'll be back." Austin snatches a lantern and unzips the tent.

"Be careful, Memphis," Jake says.

"Y'all just try not to kill each other," he warns, glancing from me to Jake.

"Got it, Memphis," I grunt, briskly rubbing my hand over Lena's arm and shoulder. "We're gonna stay like this for a while, love."

She nods and burrows into me.

I'm furious with myself. I should've checked on her sooner. No, I should've made her sleep in our tent. Or I should've gone to hers and kept her warm. How could I leave her alone out there? She could've frozen to death. I glance at Jake and clench my jaw. Now, I need another man's help to do what I should've done. *Way to stake a claim, fuckwit.*

Sandwiched between us, Lena's trembling slows, and the color begins to return to her cheeks.

After what feels like an hour, Austin returns with a canteen full of warm water. "How is she?"

"Not shaking as much," Jake replies.

"She needs to sip this." He crawls over to us. "Baby girl, I brought you somethin' to drink."

Austin hands me the canteen.

"Sit up a little," I instruct Lena. Careful to keep her breasts hidden, I hold the canteen to her mouth while she drinks a few sips.

"Thank you," she whispers.

"Drink more," I insist.

She obeys and then eases back down.

Jake touches her shoulder. "You feel a little warmer, so I'm gonna give you some space, Lena-Bean." He scoots over and resettles closer to Austin.

Austin pulls his sleeping bag behind Jake and climbs inside. "Don't tell nobody I was spoonin' Bennett."

"Moving forward, she sleeps in here with us," I announce.

Jake nods. "We need to build a better wind shield."

"Or reposition the tents closer to the trees," Austin adds.

"Yeah," Jake agrees. "We've been fine, but the wind came from the other direction with this storm."

"What happens when the river freezes over?" Lena asks in a small voice.

"Don't think like that, love. They'll come for us. They know we're out here."

"I don't wanna die," she whispers, tears welling in her eyes. "I'm so scared."

"I know you're scared." I tighten my arms around her. "I'm scared too."

"We all are," Jake chimes in. "But we have to stay positive. It's gonna be all right, Lena-Bean."

Lena's body shakes as she cries, her breath catching in her throat. I stroke her hair and share a look with Austin.

"Don't cry, baby girl," Austin says. "We ain't gonna let Mother Nature win. We've got each other and, like Wes said, they'll come for us. We just gotta stay strong till then."

"I'm sorry," Lena whimpers. "I don't mean to be negative."

"Lena, I hope I didn't just hear you apologize. You have *nothing* to be sorry about. *I'm* the fuckwit who didn't check on you sooner."

I clench my jaw and make eye contact with Jake. Compassion fills his gaze, and for once, the bastard doesn't seize an opportunity to fuck with me. It speaks volumes about the gravity of our situation.

"Don't beat yourself up, man. You *did* check on her, and now she's safe. That's all that matters," Jake says.

We huddle together for hours, listening to the howling wind. Lena falls asleep in my arms. Tormented by images of her frozen in her tent—and the caveman and beast who sneer at my carelessness—I cling to her. I stare at her face and picture us together, remembering how good it felt to hold her. Kiss her. Pleasure her. *She's mine.* There's no question in my mind. But I need to prove it to her. Actions speak louder than words. And I left her to freeze to death. *Nice move, dick.*

I must've drifted off at some point because I awake to the sound of the tent zipper.

Austin climbs in and pulls off his snow-caked boots. He crawls to his sleeping bag and glances at me. "Still snowin'. Got about four inches, I think."

"Did the fire go out?" I whisper.

"Didn't check. Had to piss," he explains. "Don't eat the yellow snow."

I smirk. "Thanks for the tip."

"That's what *she* said."

"Now ya sound like Bennett."

Jake rests on his back, softly snoring. Since we confiscated his sleeping bag to make our double, he moved into Lena's empty bag once she warmed up enough to not need his body heat.

"She asleep?" Austin asks.

I nod.

"Good. She needs to rest." He rolls to his side with his back to us.

My arms reflexively tighten around Lena. I need to keep her safe. The rest will come later. But that may be a challenge. I need to warm her up before I even *think* about giving her more than the tip. My cock stirs. *Not now, you stupid fuck.*

Lena moves closer to me. She's beautiful when she sleeps. Eyes hidden beneath her lids, long lashes brushing her cheeks, lips parted. She looks serene. No, she looks like a goddess. My goddess.

I stroke the exposed soft skin of her back. Her full, beautiful breasts are pressed to my chest. I pull her closer. My traitorous cock gives me a smug salute and stands at attention. *Son of a bitch.*

Her eyes flutter open, and she peers up at me. "Hey."

"Hi, sunshine." I smile and kiss her forehead. "Warm enough?"

"Yes. Thank you." She nuzzles into me, then lifts her head and smirks. "What?"

"Are you happy to see me?" she whispers with a coy flutter of lashes.

I bring my lips to her ear. "You should consider a career change. *You* can be Sherlock. I'll be your sidekick."

Lena shakes her head in amusement. "Yeah, I like it better with you as the sidekick, Ace."

"I'll be anything you want me to be." I nip her earlobe. "Santa Claus . . . the Easter Bunny . . . Willy Wonka."

She grins. "Just be *you*, Wes. That's who I want."

Her declaration steals my breath. She wants *me*. Not Ares, not any other role I've played, just me. This goddess wants the real Wes, and that makes me want to worship her even more. I cup her face and kiss her, pouring the entirety of my soul into the act. Lena weaves her hands into my hair and kisses me slow and deep. I roll her onto her back and climb on top of her. Bracing myself on my elbows, I indulge in her kiss for several minutes before forcing myself to stop.

I meet her gaze. "I'm sorry I didn't come for you sooner. You should've been with me—not left alone to freeze."

She strokes my cheek. "Thanks for caring enough to check on me."

I glance at my watch. It's nearly eight. Lena dozed off again, but my mates are awake.

Jake sits up and pulls on his shirt. He scrubs a fist over his face and looks at me. "Is she all right?"

I nod.

"Good." Jake buttons his flannel. "I'm starving. I'm gonna put a line in. Where's the canteen? I'll heat more water."

I hand it to him and clamp a hand on his wrist. "Thanks for your help last night. I'm sorry I was a dick."

"No worries, man. I know you'd do the same for me."

Austin sits up. "If y'all are comparing dick sizes, you're gonna get punched."

"We're not."

"There's no comparison anyhow," I joke.

Jake leans toward Austin. "That's because he can't find his." With a broad grin, he adds, "His didgeridoo ran off with his balls."

"Bennett, one of these days I'm gonna punch that smirk off your face."

"You tell me when and where, big guy."

"The testosterone in here is enough to choke an elephant," Lena mumbles. "Women don't sit around and compare cup sizes."

"They should." Jake snorts. "Someone, please invite me when that becomes a thing."

Lena giggles. "Watch some porn, Jake."

I point to Jake. "He already does relentlessly. Got a cabinet full of DVDs."

"Are we going there, surfer boy?" He retorts in amusement. "Shall I run down your list of vices?"

Lena arches her brow at me. "Do you have a 'red room of pain' somewhere?"

"Maybe. Perhaps you should take a trip Down Under and find out."

"I was referring to his doll collection," Jake teases.

"My mum moved Isla's Barbie shit into my old room," I explain. "Jake likes to come over and play with them. You know, position them inappropriately and such."

"So, you're saying I need to get Jake some Barbie dolls for Christmas?" Lena snorts. "You should see *my* Barbie collection. It's like an entire civilization. My mom called recently and asked when I was getting them out of her attic. I'll just give her Jake's address."

"Don't judge. I have killer Barbie game." Jake nods to me. "Tell Sprite she's not getting Malibu Stacy back."

Lena giggles. "You seriously have her?"

"Sure do. Isla gave her to me when she was ten."

"That's adorable," Lena says.

"What can I say? I'm gracious as fuck." Jake gestures to himself. "When a little girl gives you a gift, you keep it."

"*I* never got any gifts from her," Austin points out.

Jake grins. "Sucks to be you."

Austin laughs and turns to Lena. "How are you feelin', baby girl? You scared us last night."

"Much better, thank you. I appreciate you guys taking care of me."

"That's what friends are for, darlin'."

I hand Lena her bra and watch her put it on. Watching her dress is almost as sexy as pulling her clothes off. *Almost.* As she fixes her tank and dons the flannel, I notice scarring on her collarbone and shoulder and make a mental note to ask her about it in private.

"How much snow did we get?" she asks.

"I'd say about three or four inches," Austin replies.

Jake holds his hands a few inches apart. "Much longer than Emerson's didgeridoo."

Lena snorts a laugh. "You don't miss an opportunity to fuck with him, do you?"

"I try not to," Jake replies with a chuckle.

I hold up both middle fingers and wave them in front of Jake, who blows me a kiss. Turning to Lena, I say, "I swear to Christ, he's like the little brother I never wanted."

Austin shakes his head. "Y'all are nuts." He shrugs on his parka. "Let's catch us some fish."

I reach for my hat, scarf, and gloves. Lena already put her hat and gloves on but doesn't have a scarf. I can't stomach the thought of her being cold again. I reach out and loop my scarf around her.

Lena shrieks and yanks it from her neck. Eyes wide with terror, she scrambles away from me.

"Lena! What's the matter, love?"

"Don't touch me!" She gasps, cowering behind Austin. Her entire body trembles and tears pour from her eyes.

I stare in horror. "Lena, take it easy, love. I was just trying to put a scarf on you."

Flinching, she clutches at a shocked Austin.

"It's the scarf, man," Jake snaps. "Get it the fuck out of here."

I yank the flap and heave the length of fleece into the snow. I crawl toward Lena, who hides her face. It stops me in my tracks.

Austin gathers his wits and places a hand on her shoulder. "You're all right, baby girl. No one's gonna hurt you."

I can't move or breathe. I meet Jake's gaze in bewilderment. "I-I . . . was just," I stammer, unable to form the words. "Lena, I wasn't trying to hurt you."

She curls into a ball, and I want to die. It's like a switch flipped inside her. My brazen goddess—the woman who never backs down from anyone or anything—retreated.

She's hiding from me.

The agony of the realization makes my eyes burn. I clench my jaw and blink rapidly. *I don't do scarves.* She said it more than once, but I didn't realize there was a reason behind it. I think about Reed's behavior after the accident. My brother dealt with PTSD for years—nightmares, flashbacks, panic attacks.

It's definitely a panic attack. Probably PTSD. *And I'm making it worse.*

I back toward the tent flap and climb out. I stand outside and knot my hands in my hair. What the fuck happened to her?

I hear Austin's voice. "Calm down, girlie. You're all right. Nobody's gonna hurt you. Just breathe now."

"Take it easy, Lena-Bean. You're safe. The scarf's gone. He went outside."

Not only are other men comforting my woman, but they're telling her she's safe from *me.* My chest tightens. I trudge to the riverbank and settle on a log, a sick feeling churning in my gut.

Someone traumatized her.

Logic tells me to figure out the reason behind it so I can make sure it never happens again. But exhaustion, frustration, and remorse have other plans. I haven't cried in years—not since I learned Isla needed dialysis—but, right now, I don't have the energy to fight it. I hold my head in my hands as tears drip onto my knees, seeping through my jeans.

CHAPTER 33

LENA

Internal playlist: "Head Above Water" by Avril Lavigne

Lungs burning, I hear my gasps. I've been down this road before, so I know it's a panic attack. I try to pull away from the terror that squeezes my chest. *Calm down. Breathe. You're safe.* I repeat the words in my mind until I slowly believe the mantra.

I meet Austin's gaze. "I'm sorry."

"No need to apologize."

"Where's Wes?"

"Outside," Austin replies. "You know he'd never hurt you, right? He'd *never* hurt any woman."

"I know," I whisper. "It wasn't him."

"What happened?" Jake asks.

Fresh tears fall from my eyes. "Just a flashback. I'm sorry. Didn't mean to freak out."

"The scarf triggered something?" Jake probes.

"Not the scarf. Just when he put it around my neck. I'm sorry . . . I don't wanna talk about it. I should've warned you guys sooner. Never touch my neck," I stammer through my tears.

"We won't," Jake swears. "Ever. You don't have to tell us anything, but you need to talk to Wes."

"I know. I'll explain everything to him once I calm down. I just need to be alone for a few minutes, please."

"You got it, baby girl," Austin says. "Holler if you need us."

The men exit the tent. I hold my head in my hands and cry. Like acid rain, the tears come in sweeping torrents, burning my cheeks as they fall. I cry without making a sound, releasing a deluge of pent-up emotion and frustration. The pain of the apartment building tragedy mixes with the fear that courses through my veins. Remorse over my reaction to Wes joins the fray. *I need to make this right.*

I trudge to the fire. Jake sits at the water's edge with a fishing pole. Nearby, Austin's seated on a log beside Wes, arm draped over his shoulder. Wes hangs his head, holding his face in his hands.

I stop in front of Wes. He lifts his head and meets my gaze with red-rimmed eyes and tear-stained cheeks. His expression of self-loathing breaks my heart.

"I want to talk to you."

He nods and climbs to his feet. We walk to my tent in silence. He zips the flap behind us and looks at me.

"I'm so sorry," he whispers.

I hold a hand up. "Stop. I'm gonna explain. But first, know it had *nothing* to do with you."

"You had a panic attack?"

I nod. "I should've warned you sooner, but I didn't wanna talk about it." I take a deep breath and reach for his hand. "Something traumatic happened to me years ago. I think the cold, hunger, and the stress we've been dealing with just amplified things. I *know* you wouldn't hurt me, and I'm so sorry my reaction gave you that impression."

"Who hurt you?"

"By law, I can't tell you *who*, but I'll explain *what* happened. I'd just graduated from nursing school and my first position at the hospital was overnights in a lock-down psych unit. It was me and my dear friend Rita. Why they stuck two women alone on that floor is beyond me. Thankfully, they've stopped." I shift and squeeze his hand like a lifeline.

"It was nearing the end of my shift. I was exhausted and eager to get home. It was Garrett's birthday, and he was leaving later that day for a month-long trip to Ireland. I wanted to see him before he left.

"We still had to pass the six a.m. meds and brief the incoming staff. The unit was horseshoe-shaped, with the nurses' station in the center and the locked med-room behind the counter. Anyway, the patients who received morning meds lined up at the counter, and Rita and I gave everyone what they needed. There was one patient who didn't show up. We'll call him 'Steve.' The docs were still trying to figure out what combination of meds worked for him. Again, I was in a hurry to leave, so I stupidly put all his meds in a paper cup and went looking for him. His room was at the far end of the hall." I wipe at my tears.

"Steve was a big man, nearly as tall as you. The door to his room was open. He stood staring out the window. I called his name as I came up behind him. He must not have heard me the first time, so I said it again and touched his arm." I squeeze my eyes shut.

Wes lifts my hand to his lips and kisses my knuckles. "You don't have to continue if it's too hard for ya."

"No. I need to make sure you understand why I reacted that way," I insist, taking a deep breath. "I came up behind Steve and touched his arm, which was a stupid move. He spun around and charged at me. He grabbed my throat, dragged me into the hallway, and body-slammed me against one of the housekeeping carts. The corner struck my collarbone, causing a compound fracture and dislocating my shoulder." I prod my clavicle. "Steve lunged on top of me and squeezed my neck with both hands. I couldn't breathe and lost consciousness. He fractured part of my windpipe. Three male patients pulled him off me and restrained him while Rita screamed for security over the loudspeaker. That was my last shift in psych."

I glance at Wes through my tears. His face is frozen in a mask of shocked fury.

"Did you press charges?" he growls.

"No. Steve was sick. I was the idiot who approached him from behind. They transferred him to a different hospital," I explain. "I was out of work for six months. Went through two surgeries and eighteen months of physical therapy. I should still do the exercises."

Wes's eyes are glued to my neck.

"It was a long road, but I'm better now. The physical healing was the easy part. Mentally, not so much. I was in a dark place for a while. Every so often, it creeps to the surface."

"That's why you don't wear a scarf," Wes mumbles. "Makes perfect sense now."

I nod. "I can't have *anything* touch my neck: no scarves, necklaces, shirt collars, nothing. You'll notice I only wear V-neck shirts and, trust me, it's not about flaunting my cleavage. I honestly don't know how I'm tolerating this parka or the flannels I've been wearing. And I won't allow *anyone* to touch my neck. I should've told you."

"It's all right, love. I understand."

I shudder and fresh tears stream down my cheeks. "I'll never forget the suffocating pain I felt that day and for months afterward. And I'll *never* forget the look in his eyes."

Dr. Turner insisted that talking about the incident was part of the healing process. I feel safe with Wes. A closeness that compels me to continue despite the dredged-up vulnerability.

"The hospital mandated I go to therapy, which I would've done regardless. Since the incident, I've suffered from PTSD and panic attacks, but with all the treatment, it's gotten much better. Or so I thought." I wipe my cheeks and continue, "Garrett was my rock. He got me through the worst of it. He refused to let me hide in the apartment. He'd make me eat, make me talk, make me care. He was such a bastard." I give a watery laugh. "He'd drag me to the bathroom, strip me, and shove me into the shower. He brought me to the zoo, the library, hiking, the grocery store, wherever he could, just to get me out of the house. Doctors' appointments, therapy, he was there. He'd hear me scream when I had nightmares . . ." I cling to Wes as memories hit me. He squeezes my other hand.

"He has a key, so he'd let himself in, climb into my bed, and hold me until it stopped. I'd either wake up or stop screaming and drift back to sleep. Sometimes I wouldn't even know he'd been there if it wasn't for the already-brewed pot of coffee. I lost count of how many times it happened. I don't know where I'd be without him—probably still hiding out somewhere. And Rita too. She was an angel. She came to check on me every day, forced me out of the house on weekends. Rita and Garrett sorta tag-teamed me," I add with a tight smile.

"I'm glad you had them."

"Me too. For a long time, I was afraid to be alone with any man who wasn't Garrett. I was afraid to date, afraid to walk down the street at night. I'm much better now, mental health-wise. I just have to deal with the residual pain and a few hideous scars."

"Show me."

"What?"

"Your scars." He squeezes my hands. "Let me see them. Show me the stuff you keep hidden from everyone else."

"Why?" I whisper.

"I want more than your light, sunshine."

Wes's presence is a sanctuary from my fears. I draw a shaky breath, unzip my parka, and slide out of it. Under his watch, I remove my flannel. I pull the tank top and bra straps aside, exposing my collarbone and shoulder. I point to the scarring on my shoulder.

"These are from my surgeries." I slide my fingertips along my clavicle and pause at another scar. "This is where I struck the cart and part of my bone broke through the skin."

The scars serve as a constant reminder of the trauma. I'm extremely self-conscious about the one on my collarbone. No creams or lotions helped it fade. Wes traces his fingertips along the length of my clavicle to my shoulder, then slides my bra strap in place and fixes my shirt. He hands me the flannel and watches my shaking hands attempt to button it.

Wes reaches out and takes over. "Tell me where to stop."

I point to the skin above my cleavage. He buttons to the place I indicate.

"Thank you for telling me." He takes both of my hands in his. "I don't want you to hide from me."

"It's so hard to let people see my weaknesses. I try to act strong—"

"You *are* strong," he insists. "No one's immune to vulnerability. It's normal for some of that to seep through the cracks when shit gets rough."

"Cracks under pressure," I mutter. "Yep, that's me."

"Everyone cracks. Everyone breaks down, and we all fall apart now and then. You're perfectly human, love."

"I wish I was better at holding it together."

"I think you hold it together too well." He shakes his head. "I wish you could see what I see."

I look up at him and force a smile. "You may need your eyes checked."

"I have near-perfect vision." He smirks. "What I mean is that you don't see your own strength. Your fierceness. Sure, a few cracks popped up, but it's not an empty shell. You have so much beauty inside you. All that pain, fear, and pressure has formed you into a gem. You don't see the diamond I see. You just focus on the rough."

"How do you always know the right words to say?"

"Well, on the rare occasions when you don't have me too flustered to speak, they come easily. It's not hard to describe what's in front of your eyes." He shakes his head. "But I'm off to one helluva start in the action department."

"What do you mean?"

"I feel like I've already screwed things up. I told ya I'd prove myself to you, and so far, I left you to freeze to death *and* traumatized you. All I want to do is shelter and protect you, but I keep hurting you."

"You haven't hurt me." I climb into his lap and wrap my arms around his neck. "I'm not afraid of you, Wes," I whisper. "I feel safer in your arms than I've ever felt in my life. Please understand this wasn't you."

Wes kisses my forehead and pulls me close. "I understand, love. And you *are* safe with me. I'll do everything in my power to get us out of here. But please don't ever hide from me again."

I kiss his cheeks and run my fingers through his hair. "I want all of you, Wes. I want to know what goes on inside that head of yours too."

He smirks. "No, you don't. It's a fucking zoo up there."

"I'm a lover of all creatures—let me in."

"So, you can rattle my cages and climb into the enclosures?"

I grin. "Baby, I wanna rattle *all* your cages *and* feed the beasts inside."

His gaze heats and sweeps over me. "Then you'd better plan on tossing me more than scraps. I want the whole damn gazelle. Flesh, bones, antlers, and hooves—bring it *all*."

"Quite the glutton, aren't we?" I laugh.

"Waste not, want not."

"Also, gazelles have *horns*." I playfully punch his arm.

He wags his brows. "I'll give ya a horn."

"Please do," I purr. "Immediately, if not sooner."

"Haste makes waste."

"Look at you, throwing idioms now," I tease. "Here, I thought you were limited to analogies and metaphors."

Wes grins wickedly. "Then you'll love it when I release my kraken."

I laugh. "You looked it up?"

"No, I asked Bennett. He educated me on the two different meanings." Wes snorts a laugh. "The one I'm referring to doesn't involve a toilet."

"Baby, I *know* what you're referring to." I allow my gaze to roam over his broad shoulders and chest. "I hope I can handle your kraken."

CHAPTER 34

LENA

Internal playlist: "One and Only" by Adele

Wes and I stroll along the tree line, gathering tinder and berries. We laugh and chat like we've known each other for years. The tent incident brought us closer, but I want more.

"So, I've told you all my secrets," I begin. "Tell me yours."

He smiles and touches my cheek. "What would ya like to know?"

"How is it that a woman hasn't already snatched you up?" I ask. "I mean, other than the two wives you didn't know about."

"I haven't made myself snatchable in a *very* long time." He leans against a tree trunk. "It didn't end well the last time."

"Was she an actress?"

"No. Rachel was a girl from home. Cora's cousin, actually. We dated throughout high school and several years after. She knew me *way* before I started acting."

"What made you guys break up?"

"Jealousy." He rubs his jaw. "She couldn't handle all the female attention I get."

"Some of that's understandable, right?" I tilt my head. "Don't you *want* a woman to be fierce about you?"

"Absolutely. But it would've been different if her ferocity came from a place of love." He sighs heavily. "In a very short time, I went from being a nobody to a life in the spotlight. I didn't expect it to be easy for Rachel, but I tried to do my best to reassure her. She knew the attention came with the territory, but no matter how much I expressed my commitment, it was never enough."

"She didn't trust you."

"Right. And I'd never given her a reason not to. She tried saying it was the other women she didn't trust, but I was the one she took it out on."

"What do you mean?"

"Rachel was extremely insecure. It didn't matter that I thought she was beautiful or only had eyes for her. My actions, *my* reassurance, meant nothing. Instead, she focused on what other people were doing. For example, when we'd go out for dinner, she'd give me a hard time if someone even looked in my direction. Like I could control what other people did. Meanwhile, I was looking at *her*. Her jealousy became possessiveness. She didn't want to *be* with me; she wanted to *have* me."

"I take it she wasn't supportive of your career?"

"No, not at all. She tried to talk me out of auditions, insisted I not accept certain roles. So much was happening at once, you know? Reed had his motorcycle accident and nearly died, Isla got sick, I had my surgery . . . I needed her support. Instead, I got bitching, guilt trips, unreasonable demands, and ultimatums. She became a whole different person from the woman I'd fallen in love with. I put up with it for years."

"Why?"

"Because I loved her. When I'd envisioned my future, I thought it would be with her. We'd been together forever, she knew my family, she knew everything about me. I hoped she'd realize that, for me, nothing had changed. I had it all planned in my head—us getting married and having a family. But it finally got to be too much for me."

"What was your breaking point if you don't mind me asking?

"Rachel was at my place when I got home. I was excited because I'd just been offered the role of Ares. *Olympus Fire* was a three-movie deal. The producers were renowned, and I just *knew* it would be a turning point for my career. This was my chance, my big break, you know? If I successfully played that part, I could pay off my parents' home, deal with Isla's lingering hospital bills, and provide for Rachel." He sighs and stares across the tundra. "I hadn't told anyone yet because I wanted her to be the first to know. That's the thing—I would've done anything for her. But it became obvious she wouldn't do the same. Instead of pushing me forward, she was determined to hold me back. You know what she said to me that day?" He meets my gaze. "She looked me in the eye and said, 'I'll leave you if you accept that role.' It felt like a fucking knife to my chest."

I squeeze his hand.

"So, I walked across the kitchen and held the front door open. The look of shock on her face was something. It's like she couldn't believe I chose my career over her. But it wasn't the career I was choosing, it was a chance to help my family and feel like I was worth something. She stared at me for a while. Then, she started to cry. But I didn't move. She finally grabbed her purse and walked out." He shakes his head. "I broke her heart. And I felt terrible about it. But you know what? She broke mine long before that."

"I'm sorry, Wes," I murmur.

"You live, you learn, right?" He forces a laugh. "With my career, it's been difficult to have any meaningful relationships. Women look at me but don't see me. They want everything that comes with me. They try to hide it behind a pretty face and pretend to be in love, but the truth always comes out. I've kept it casual for years because I don't wanna get burned, nor do I wanna hurt anyone."

"So, just flings?"

"Yeah, but I'm not some man-slut. I've been very selective with whom I trust. And with filming *The Aegean*, it's been close to a year since I've seen anyone. No one has made me want more." Wes grins at me. "Until ya threw yourself into my lap on the plane."

My jaw drops. "I did not throw—"

Our heads turn at the sound of Austin's shout. He holds something up and flails it around.

Wes shields his eyes and squints. "What the hell's he doing?"

"I don't know. What's in his hand?"

We trudge through melting snow to the fire and discover that Austin's holding a huge dead squirrel.

"Whatcha got there, cowboy?" I ask.

"This here's a tundra marmot. Wild, vicious creatures feared by many. Commonly known as a squirrel. We got meat, y'all."

Wes claps Austin's shoulder. "How the hell did ya catch that?"

"He threw a boulder at it," Jake reveals.

"Wasn't a boulder," Austin corrects him. "Just a small rock. Saw him in that tree eatin' a nut. Figured I'd test my aim."

"I'm impressed, Memphis. We've got our own Davey Crockett." Wes laughs.

"Yeah, I'll use fishing line to sew the tail onto your hat," I offer.

"Y'all can laugh all you want, but you know damn well if anyone can rock a squirrel-tail hat, it's gonna be me." Austin snorts. "Wes, gimme that knife."

Austin skins and guts the animal. Before long, it's time to eat skewered chunks of squirrel meat. Wes hands the guys and me generous portions.

I arch a brow. "You're not eating?"

"I'm fine, love. You eat." He presses a kiss to my forehead. "I'll have the salmon."

Austin waves his hand at us. "I see y'all made amends."

Smiling, Wes wraps his arm around me. "We weren't fighting to begin with."

"It was a misunderstanding," I add. "Sorry you had to witness that."

"No worries, girlie. We're just glad to see you smilin' again."

"Thanks for being understanding."

"That's what friends do, Lena-Bean," Jake says.

I return his smile and scoot closer to Wes, so our thighs are touching. His warmth radiates into me as he tightens his arm around my shoulders. I love being close to him.

I tear off a piece of squirrel meat. "Open up," I command, placing it in his mouth. I flush when his lips brush my fingertips.

"Thank you." Wes's eyes fill with reverence.

"Sharing is caring."

He kisses my forehead. "Thank you for caring."

"You two went from one extreme to the other," Jake says with a snort. "But I'll take the lovey-dovey shit over the eye-fucking any day."

"Don't worry, mate. There's still plenty of that."

I laugh and brush hair out of my face. "Where the hell's my hair tie?" I check my wrists. "Ugh. I'm gonna run to my tent and grab one." I hand Wes the squirrel. "Hold my meat, please."

"I'd rather ya hold mine."

"And back to the fuckery." Jake laughs.

CHAPTER 35

WES

Internal playlist: "I Want You" by Third Eye Blind

Warmth spreads through my veins and I smile to myself. She fed me. It's a simple gesture, yet it means so much. In the short time I've known her, Lena feeds much more than my belly. She fills my heart and soul too. I want to shelter her. Take care of her. Make love to her. The more she feeds me, the deeper my hunger. I know that once I get a taste of her, it'll never be enough.

Privacy will be an issue—and tents aren't soundproof. I consider sending my mates on a hike so I can have my way with her. But that would be too obvious, and I don't want to make Lena uncomfortable. *I don't care who's around—I'm used to filming erotic love scenes.* Then again, the more I think about it, the less I like the idea of my mates being nearby. For one, I don't need those fuckers hearing her moans of pleasure. Her sounds are for my ears only. But beyond that, I don't want to risk them glimpsing her body when I thrust inside her.

Also, I didn't bring any frangers, so I'll need to ask my mates for some. *And have an adult conversation with the woman about sexual health and birth control, you fucking Neanderthal.*

I lean forward and address Jake and Austin in a low tone, "Do either of you have any frangers?"

"What the fuck's a franger?" Jake asks.

"You know . . . condoms," I clarify.

"So, we're moving beyond eye-fucking now. Great."

"Why in the hell would I pack condoms for a campin' trip when Katie's back home?"

"I dunno, mate. I'm just asking."

"Besides, even if I did, they ain't gonna fit you, dino dick," Austin says on a chuckle.

Jake climbs to his feet. "I have a whole box in my pack."

I perk up. "Really?"

"You ain't been laid in years. Why the fuck are *you* carryin' condoms?" Austin laughs harder.

"I stole a box of finger cots from the first aid kit at the lodge. They should fit his didgeridoo." Jake snickers.

"I hate you both. Now, shut the fuck up, she's coming."

"She *will* be . . . later tonight." Jake shakes his hips in a mini salsa.

Lena approaches with a baffled expression. "Are we having a dance-off now?"

Austin and Jake howl with laughter.

"Okay, lemme guess. You two are laughing, and Crocodile Dundee's over here with a scowl." She points to the tents. "Should I grab a tape measure so we can settle it once and for all?" She laughs and waggles her brows.

"Don't bother, love." I chuckle. "I don't wanna embarrass them."

"How'd you know?" Jake asks Lena in amusement. "I swear, it's like you're part dude or something."

"I can assure you I'm all woman." Lena laughs. "Need I remind you I have a male best friend?" She points at Jake. "You two would get along. Garrett's a sick bastard just like you."

"Thank God you're not all prim and proper. That would suck," Jake says.

"I'm far from prim and proper. Call it exposure therapy." She chuckles. "Between the guys I work with and the lunatic downstairs, I've seen and heard it all."

"Garrett's as pervy as you?" I ask, elbowing her.

LENA

"Garrett is much, much pervier than me. And it's funny because when people meet him, they're like, 'Is he the same Garrett you talked about?' He puts up a good front, you know, acting all debonair, like he's Mister Smooth and Sophisticated. Don't get me wrong, he's smart and has an impressive vocabulary. But don't be fooled by the suave exterior. His favorite word always has been—and always will be—fuck."

Jake laughs. "Yeah, we'd get along well."

"He's a smart-ass and a prankster too," I add. "You wouldn't believe the shit he's masterminded. He goes out of his way to trick me."

"Like how?" Wes asks.

"There are so many examples." I laugh. "Okay, here's a more recent one. Gar has a couple of female *friends* that come over."

"Fuck buddies?" Jake grins.

"Yep." I shake my head. "I always tell him, 'I don't care what you do. Just watch out for the crazies and I'm not ready to be Auntie Lena.' Anyway, there's this one chick who comes over, and I cringe when I see her walk up the stoop."

"Why?" Wes asks.

"She's loud . . . like really loud." I grimace. "I came home from work one night and settled on my couch with a glass of wine. All I wanted to do was relax and watch reruns of *Everybody Loves Raymond*. Next thing I knew, he had Yowling Yolanda down there, rearranging furniture and swinging from light fixtures."

"Is her name really Yolanda?" Jake asks with a laugh.

"No, that's just what I call her. Anyway, I got up and banged a broom on the floor. It was unnerving, so I ended up going to bed. The next morning, after I saw her leave, I went downstairs and confronted him. I was like, 'Your ass will pay for the electrician when she pulls the fan off the ceiling.' He apologized and that was it. Or so I thought." I shake my head and laugh. "He's such a bastard. So that night, I got home from work and was back on the couch with my wine. Suddenly, there was a fucking orgy happening behind me. I jumped up, spilling the wine everywhere. Garrett had hidden a Bluetooth speaker behind the couch and was streaming hardcore porn audio into my living room." The men erupt in laughter and I continue, "I marched downstairs, flung open his door, ready to kill him. He was sitting on the couch with his phone, acting all nonchalant, like he didn't know why I was there. Except, he wouldn't look at me. And I could see him fighting back a smirk. So, I was like, 'Garrett Liam Casey, do I need to leave another voicemail at your office?' Then, he just burst out laughing. We laughed so hard that both of us had tears coming out."

"Did you leave an embarrassin' message for him?" Austin asks.

I grin. "I took it one step further. I subscribed him to a porno magazine and had it delivered to his office."

Wes barks a laugh. "That's fucking brilliant."

I pat myself on the back. "Yeah, I thought so too . . . until one fell out of my work locker for all of my coworkers to see."

"Oh, he's good," Jake marvels. "Did you get him back?"

"No, he's way out of my league. Nobody does payback like Garrett. I sent him a text that read, 'you win.' He was out on the stoop when I got home, gloating like the smug bastard he is."

"Wow, you've got your hands full with him," Jake says with a chuckle.

I smile. "Yeah, but I wouldn't have it any other way."

"That reminds me of some of the shit Reed's done to the flight risk," Austin points out.

"What's a flight risk?" I ask.

Wes snorts. "My sister. Austin calls her 'Flight-Risk Isla' because she's always in motion, flitting from place to place. Reed calls her 'Bird Brain,' which is pretty fucked-up, but that's their dynamic, I guess."

"Is it wanderlust or lack of focus?" I ask.

"Not wanderlust, really. Her biggest issue's indecision," Wes explains. "She's somewhat scattered and changes her mind frequently."

"Didn't Reed make a calendar of all the boyfriends she's had?" Austin asks.

Jake stiffens and stares at the fire, his lips pressed in a grim line. Jaw clenched, brow furrowed, he's now completely silent.

Wes nods. "Yeah, last year."

I snort. "Why? Are they hot?"

Wes shakes his head. "He made it because she just doesn't keep any of them around for more than a couple of months. Every Christmas it's a different guy. Gives me whiplash."

"Maybe she's looking for the right one," I say.

Wes sighs. "She doesn't know what she's looking for."

CHAPTER 36

LENA

Internal playlist: "Lights Down Low" by MAX

The sun takes the warmth with it as it dips below the horizon. We lounge on the logs by the fire for hours, sharing stories and memories. Wes still hasn't removed his arm from my shoulder. The wind picks up and I reflexively move closer to him.

"Don't worry, love," he tightens his embrace, "I'll keep ya warm."

"It's crazy how fast the temperature drops when the sun finally goes down."

"This *is* the Arctic, sunshine."

From across the fire, Austin pipes up, "I'm thinkin' we should get outta this wind soon." He rubs his hands over his arms. "Hopefully, we don't get any more snow tonight."

"I'm surprised how much melted," Jake says. "I still think we need to build some kind of wind break tomorrow. Maybe some of the wood will dry out by then."

"How will we keep it together without a hammer and nails?" Wes asks. "I mean, we've got rope, but I don't like the idea of cutting it into pieces."

"What about saplings?" I suggest. "Like skinny, bendy branches? Maybe we can use them to tie the pieces together. Or we can weave sticks around each other." I shake my head. "I'm trying to remember what they did on one episode—"

"What if we move our tents into the forest?" Jake asks.

"That would help with the wind, but we'd lose the visibility advantage," Wes replies. "Now, we're in a prime spot if someone were to fly over."

Austin gestures to our group. "Looks like we're gonna have to snuggle, y'all. I don't think it would be smart to move our camp just yet. Not unless we have to."

"I agree," Jake says. "C'mon, Memphis. Let's go spoon."

Austin stands. "So we're clear, you're gonna be the little spoon, Bennett. I don't need you gettin' all handsy with me."

"Don't worry, mate. He's too busy getting handsy with himself. Having a wank and whatnot."

"Nah, it's too cold for Bennett Jr.," Jake says. "That fucker's in hibernation."

Austin snorts. "Except he ain't seen a *cave* in months."

"Years," Wes corrects him.

Jake climbs to his feet and gives his friends the middle finger. He gestures to Wes and me. "You two coming? Or are you gonna canoodle under the stars?"

"Option B," Wes says. "We'll be in later. Go warm up my spot."

Jake nods, stepping over the log. "Night."

Wes grins. "Sleep tight, spelunkers."

Jake smirks at me. "Poor guy has to use big words to compensate for smaller things." Pointing to Wes, he teases, "You don't even know what that means."

Wes gives him the finger. Jake blows him a kiss and follows Austin to the tent. Anticipation flutters in my belly as they disappear from sight. I turn back to Wes.

He's staring.

"What?"

"I'm looking at ya," he murmurs.

Blushing, my heart picks up speed. "How do you do it?"

"Do what?"

I stare at the flames. "Make a glance feel like a physical touch."

Wes touches my chin, turning my gaze to him. "It comes naturally when you're the one I'm looking at, sunshine."

"You look at me like I'm—"

"A goddess?" he offers. "Because that's what I'm thinking."

"No one's ever looked at me like that."

"Then the rest of them are blind."

I meet his gaze again. "No one's ever spoken to me the way you do or listened like you have."

"You're easy to open up to, and I already told ya, I wanna know everything about you." Wes tucks a strand of hair behind my ear.

My eyes water, so I squeeze them shut.

"What's wrong, love?"

"I didn't expect to fall for you this easily."

"I didn't expect the woman of my dreams to fall into my lap," he wipes the tear that escapes from beneath my lashes, "but you did."

"How can *I* be the woman of your dreams?"

"How can you *not* be?" He brushes his knuckles over my cheeks. "Open your eyes and look at me." I obey, and he continues, "I don't know why we ended up out here, but we were supposed to meet. This isn't some crazy coincidence or chance encounter—it goes beyond that. There's a reason for all of this. I feel it in my gut and my heart." He squeezes my hands. "Lena, you hit me like a lightning bolt. You're unlike any woman I've ever met, and I've *never* felt so alive. Look at us—we're lost in the fucking wilderness. We're freezing our arses off, and we're tired, hungry, and scared."

"I know," I whisper.

"But for whatever reason, I don't *feel* lost." He kisses my forehead. "Maybe our stars aligned, or whatever Memphis always says. I can't explain it. But one thing's for certain; we were destined to spark and catch fire."

"I don't want to get burned."

"Neither do I," he insists. "I have no intention of burnin' ya, sunshine. I just wanna heat you up and keep you warm."

I cup his face and kiss him. With a rough exhale, he pulls me close and kisses me slowly, allowing his tongue to glide against mine. He tightens his embrace and pulls me into his lap. I shift my body to straddle him, heat blooming in response to the hardened length pressed between my legs.

Wes breaks the kiss and studies my face. "You blow my mind, love."

"Likewise." I bite my lip and release a shaky breath. "No one's *ever* kissed me like you do." Flushing, I shyly add, "Or touched me."

"It's the way you deserve to be kissed and touched. And when I make love to you, I'll show you the way your body deserves to be worshiped."

I tremble at the thought.

"Listen, I wanna be up-front with you," he begins. "I didn't bring any protection, and I don't know where you stand with that. But I will tell ya that I've never *not* used it, and I'm clean."

"I trust you, Wes. It's been over two years for me, and I've *always* been a 'no glove, no love' kind of girl."

He nods. "You on the pill?"

"I have an IUD, so I won't need to worry about that for another year."

"That's convenient."

"Tell me about it. I can't even fathom the alternative." If I got my period in the wilderness with these three, it would send me over the edge. I'm one of the lucky women whose periods stopped altogether after insertion of the hormone-releasing device. But I'm not about to discuss *that* with him.

"Huh?"

"Never mind." I shake my head.

"I don't wanna hurt you," he whispers. "In all seriousness, I'm well above average and it's been a long time for you. I could feel it when I touched you."

"Then you're just gonna have to warm me up," I murmur.

"I've been dying to warm you up." He flashes a devilish grin. "Did you pack the suspicious object I noticed on your nightstand?"

Heat floods my face at his mention of the hot pink vibrator. "No, I didn't."

"Too bad." He nips my earlobe. "We could've had fun with that."

"For the record, *I* didn't pack it to begin with."

He smirks. "Whatever you say, sunshine." Brushing his lips over my ear, he adds, "But the better question is whether you've used it on this trip?"

I feel my cheeks grow hotter. "No comment."

Heat and amusement flare in his gaze. "Don't worry, I've got other ways to warm you up."

"I'm sure you do."

"Tell me, do you taste as sweet as you look?"

I suck in a sharp breath. "While the thought is beyond enticing, there's no way I'm letting you do *that*."

Wes cocks his head. "Why not?"

"I feel disgusting. I've only had sponge baths, my legs are hairy, and that's too intimate for my comfort level. Trust me, I'd be far too self-conscious to enjoy it."

"I beg to differ."

"I'm serious, Wes. That's off-limits," I insist.

"How the hell am I supposed to warm you up?"

"Hold me, kiss me, and touch me. And when the time comes, go slowly."

"I don't wanna hurt you," he repeats.

"I'll tell you to stop if it hurts."

"You promise?"

"Yes, I promise."

He weaves his hands into my hair and pulls my lips to his. I clutch his shoulders, meeting his urgency with desperate strokes of my lips and tongue. I need more from him; I need him inside me. I roll my hips, grinding in his lap.

Wes releases my hair and his hands travel over my breasts to my hips. Gripping them, he pulls me closer. "I want you."

Meeting his gaze, I gyrate in his lap, rubbing the entire length of him. Hips flexing upward, he tightens his hold on my hips.

"Keep rolling those hips, love," he whispers. "We won't even make it to the tent."

"What?" I purr. "You mean, *this*?" Watching his face in the bright moonlight, I swivel my hips in an invisible hula hoop.

Wes slides his hands to my ass and squeezes both cheeks, tugging me deeper into his lap. Arching my back, I squeeze his hips between my thighs. His cock jerks in response.

I flash him a sultry smile. "Oh, are you happy to see me?"

"You have no idea what I wanna do to you."

"I love it when you get all growly." I lick my lips. "It turns me on." Leaning forward, I kiss the triangle of skin beneath his ear. Goose bumps appear on his neck. "It makes me want to hear you roar." Kissing my way to his earlobe, I let my teeth graze it before whispering, "How long are you gonna make me wait?"

His hands clench my ass. "I'm about three seconds from ripping your fucking clothes off."

I give him a slow smile. "Should I start the countdown?" Reaching down, I rub his cock through his jeans. "Three . . . two . . . one."

Wes lurches to his feet, lifting me with him. I wrap my legs around his waist. Squeezing my ass, he carries me to my tent. He sets me down, unzips the flap, and nudges me inside, yanking the zipper behind him.

In a flurry of movement, parkas and boots are shed.

"Jeans off," Wes commands. "You can leave your shirt but get rid of the bra."

I flutter my lashes. "Aren't *you* going to undress me?"

"Sunshine, if *I* undress ya, there won't be anything left of those clothes. So, unless you want scraps of fabric, I suggest you do what I ask."

"And what happens if I don't?" I give a sultry lip bite. "Will there be consequences?"

"I'm holding on by a thread, love." Chest heaving, fists clenched at his sides, he kneels beside the sleeping bag and waits.

The raw heat in his eyes make my insides quiver and clench. My lower abdomen heats, and my nipples prick the inside of my bra.

Wes raises a brow. I make no move to undress. Instead, I toss my hair over a shoulder and boldly place my hands on my hips.

"You hear me?" The low rumble of his voice makes me even wetter.

"Heard you just fine, Ace."

His gaze darkens. Like a bomb about to detonate, lust and fury roll off him in waves. Raw, untamed, and ready to conquer, Ares materializes before me.

"Clothes," he growls, "now."

Fuck the roar, I want his battle cry. My veins pulse with the desire to push him over the edge. I crave his intensity, his loss of control. It's been so long since I've felt something. With Wes, *everything* feels more intense, so why should that stop with sex? Sure, the other guys are in the next tent, but I don't care. In this moment, I'd invite the Pope to pull up a chair and watch. I've got no use for restraint or tenderness. I don't want some muted, scaled-back version of Wes; I want him full fucking throttle. He can make love to me some other time, but right now, I need him to fuck me.

I arch a defiant brow. "Make me."

CHAPTER 37

WES

Internal playlist: "Earned It" by The Weeknd

ine!

I lunge, knocking Lena off-balance. Pressing her onto her back, I straddle her hips and fist her flannel, meeting her heated gaze. Equal parts resistance and surrender, the lust in her eyes scorches me, begging me to take her. A coy smile curves her lips and satisfaction diffuses her features.

"What did you say?"

She bites her lip. "You heard me."

"I wanna hear ya say it again." I start unbuttoning her shirt.

"I said, make me," she repeats in a husky whisper. Her gaze sweeps over me, lingering on my cock. "If you can."

I yank her shirt open, sending buttons everywhere. Tugging it over her shoulders, I snatch her arms. I pull the flannel from beneath her and hold it up.

"You like this shirt?"

"Yes," she breathes.

"Too bad," I growl, ripping it in half. Lena gasps as I toss it aside and grip her tank top. "What about this one?" I tug the straps. "You like this, too?"

"Yes," she says more loudly.

The lust in her eyes is volcanic. And the sultry flutter of lashes unhinges me. I tear the tank down the center, yanking the material away from her. I chuck it in the corner by the torn flannel.

"Well, sunshine, it looks like you'll be needing another." Reaching around her back, I unhook her bra. I whip it off and fling it across the tent.

Lena's mouth falls open in shock. Her breasts rise and fall with each panting breath and her nipples beg to be licked. Dipping my head, I drag my tongue along her rib cage and over the lower curve of each breast. When my teeth graze a nipple, she gasps and clutches the sleeping bag.

"You like that?" Without waiting for her reply, I repeat the act with her other nipple.

"Yes . . ." she hisses.

"You gonna keep pushing me?" I whisper against her flesh.

"Damn right, I am."

"Good." Rearing up, I lick my lips. "Push harder." I cup both breasts and drag my thumbs over her nipples. "I like it. I'll give you everything I've got and more, sunshine." Reaching for the button on her jeans, I pop it open and lower the zipper.

"I'm already *waiting* for you to give me everything you've got."

Clenching my fingers in the denim, I yank the jeans over her hips. I move aside and tug them to her ankles, then toss them behind me. I stare at Lena's nearly naked body. All that remains are little purple panties low on her hips. I trail my fingers over the fabric, and she presses into my touch. *Damp little purple panties.* My cock twitches, begging to be inside her.

"Maybe I'm waiting to hear you beg, love." I circle my thumb over her cotton-covered clit. "You wanted to play—"

Lena moans and jerks her hips.

I feather my fingertips across her breasts, down her sides to her waist. I stroke and tickle her thighs, behind her knees, the curve of her arse. My fingertips barely skim her clit. I move closer, then pull back, and resume my touch elsewhere.

"Please touch me," she begs.

"I *am* touchin' ya, sunshine."

"You know what I mean."

"Do I?" Pressing her thighs apart, I kneel between them and continue to tease her.

"Stop fucking with me." Lena's hips flex upward. "Just fuck me."

Sliding my hands up her thighs and over her pussy, I meet her gaze. "Make me."

Lena's eyes narrow. "Don't be a bastard."

"Why? What are you gonna do about it?"

"If *you* don't do something soon, I'll just have to touch myself. Oh, but don't worry, I'll let you *watch*, Mister Man of Action."

My cock throbs at the thought of Lena stroking herself. I envision her fingers dipping inside her wet heat and can almost hear her moans.

Lena continues in a husky whisper, "We can make it a competition and see who makes me come first. I wonder, will it be me or you?" She eyes my cock. "I bet *I* could do it faster."

Gripping the waistband of her panties, I tug them off, balling them in my fist. "You don't want me tastin' ya, but I'm sure as fuck keeping these." I toss them over to my parka. "Now, back to that theory about who's faster—"

"I dunno, Ace. How about you remove a few layers first?" She motions to me. "I'm in here freezing and you're still fully clothed."

I smirk and lift the shirt up over my head. She's right. It's freezing. Lena's gaze travels from my shoulders, to my chest, down my abs. Her lips parting, her breaths come faster.

"Like whatcha see?"

"Show me more," she commands. "Lemme see what I'm working with."

I unbuckle my belt and slide it from the loops. Next, I unbutton my jeans and pull them off. With only the fabric of my boxer briefs restraining me, my cock juts proudly. I smirk and give her a few pelvic thrusts for effect.

"Ready for my kraken, sunshine?"

Lena's gaze focuses on my bulge. "Give it to me."

"Been waiting a long time to hear you say that again."

Her impatience wins out. She tugs my boxers down, frees my cock, and gasps. Her jaw drops.

Cringing, I squeeze my eyes shut. *Here we go.*

"You're huge," she breathes.

"You understand why I stopped us last night?"

"Yes."

"Having second thoughts now?"

"No," she insists, taking me into both hands. She strokes me from base to tip, eyes fixated on my cock.

"Look at me."

Lena hesitates. When she finally makes eye contact, I notice the heat in hers cooled off a few degrees. I raise a brow, sighing heavily.

"I hope I can handle you," she whispers.

Me too.

The trepidation in her voice resonates with my thoughts. I've learned over the years that bigger isn't always better. In fact, I expect the sharp inhales and widened eyes that accompany the first glimpse of me in the nuddy. I hoped it would be different with Lena, but my size alarms her. It doesn't help that she's so tight. I vowed to go slow, but still, we've got no lube, which may be a deal breaker. I know from experience it's a necessity. And Lena won't let me warm her up properly. Her reasons for refusing to let me taste her are ridiculous, but I'm not gonna push the issue. I'll just need to rely on my hands.

Cupping Lena's cheek, I brush my thumb over her lower lip. "You will, love. I'll make sure your body's ready to take me."

She nods and continues stroking me. I squeeze my eyes shut and savor her touch. But *I'm* not the one who needs warming up.

I lean forward and kiss her. "Let me take care of you, sunshine. I wanna make you blaze."

Lena wraps her legs around my waist and pulls me close. My cock glides through the hot slickness between her thighs.

"You're so wet," I groan, circling my hips.

"I want you, Wes." She reaches down and guides me to her body's entrance. "Take me," she whispers.

"I need to warm you up first," I say, pulling back. "I don't wanna hurt ya."

She cups my face, flexing her hips toward me. "I'll be fine. Just go slowly."

I kiss her, tongue spearing into her mouth. I know I need to touch her first, but her whispered pleas and viselike thighs beg me not to wait. I find her hands and interlace them with mine. Pinning them at her shoulders, I meet her gaze. "Tell me to stop and I will. No questions asked."

Lena nods, clenching my hands in hers. "I trust you."

I slowly press my hips forward, the head of my cock nudging her entrance. Lena gasps and squeezes my hands. I push farther, maybe an inch or two. Yes, she's drenched, but she's tight.

"Lift your hips," I command. She obeys, and I advance a little farther. Every time I press forward, she tenses. "Relax and let me in."

"I'm trying," she gasps.

She's too tight. I'm hurting her. I'm not even a quarter of the way inside. *Change positions.*

"Let's try something else." Releasing Lena's hands, I roll onto my back and pull her on top. "You do it. Work your way down onto me. You're in control, go as slowly as you need to. We'll worry about the rest once you're comfortable with me inside you."

Lena lowers herself, taking the head inside. She lifts and takes me a little farther the second time. Holding on to her hips, I massage her hipbones with my thumbs. She lifts and slides down a third time, taking me even deeper. She gasps and clutches my shoulders.

"Just like that, sunshine," I groan. "You feel so fucking good."

She lifts and slides farther down. *Almost there. Help her.* I release one of her hips and circle her clit with my thumb. She moans, hips jerking. I add a little pressure and massage her. Her inner muscles rhythmically clench and release—and relax. I increase the pace.

"Oh, Wes . . ." Her hips flex and roll with the strokes on her clit, and I don't falter. "You're gonna make me come."

"Let yourself go, love. Come for me."

I increase the speed and pressure, and Lena orgasms. Hips rocking, pussy spasming around me, she takes me to the hilt and whimpers.

Everything feels more intense without a franger. She's so fucking wet; I swear I'll die from pleasure. I've *never* buried myself so deeply inside a woman. Never felt a pussy grip my cock so tightly.

"Oh, fuck, Lena," I groan, clamping my hands on her hips. "Your body was made for me." I roll my hips, and she cries out. "That's it, love. Let me hear ya. Move yourself in a circle."

Clenching my jaw, I watch the goddess on top of me arch her back and rotate her hips. Lena clutches my shoulders and lifts slightly. Then, she slides back down, causing us both to moan.

"Wes," she breathes. "I need—"

"I have you, love." Lifting her hips until she's halfway free of me, I pull her back down.

"Wes . . ."

"Shh," I warn in amusement, lifting her again.

"Oh, *Wes*," she groans when I pull her down.

I repeat the motion—harder this time. She moans even louder. Nothing compares to Lena. Nothing. I love the way she says my name. I want to drive my cock inside her until the screams rip from her throat. Instead, I clench her hips. Lifting, then lowering. The pace is agonizingly slow, but I feel her relax around me.

"You all right?"

"Yes," she gasps. "But I don't want to be on top anymore. Hold me."

"We can do that."

I roll us over without pulling out. I press her thighs open and draw back until just the head of me is still inside. "You're so fucking perfect." I stare into her gorgeous eyes. "You don't know what you do to me—"

Lena clasps the back of my neck and pulls my lips to hers. Breaking the kiss, she whispers, "Make love to me, Wes."

CHAPTER 38

LENA

Internal playlist: "God Is A Woman" by Ariana Grande

I cling to Wes's shoulders as he eases into me. The thick, hard length of him stretches and fills me. He pulls back again and enters more deeply. My body parts for him, accepting him. With each stroke, he goes deeper.

He draws his hips back and whispers, "Are you ready for me?"

"Yes." I clutch his shoulders.

Wes surges forward. I wail his name, nails digging into his flesh, and take him deeper than I thought possible.

"You're a goddess," he whispers, rolling his hips. "Oh, fuck, Lena . . ." He pulls back and thrusts into me again. His strokes are a mixture of pain and pleasure so intense all I can do is cling to him. His powerful thigh muscles contract as he slowly makes love to me.

The clench of his jaw, and how he squeezes his eyes shut and fists the sleeping bag, tells me he's holding back. He maintains a tightly leashed pace, his hips moving like pistons in a well-oiled machine. Except, I don't want Wes restrained, caged, or controlled. *Fuck restraint. Lose control with me.*

I tighten my legs around him and grip his back. Each thrust brings more ecstasy than the last. My hips move in rhythm with his. Wes groans, quickening the pace. He interlaces our fingers and presses my hands into the ground at my shoulders.

"God, Lena, you're killing me."

Spurred by his desire for me, I meet him thrust for thrust. I squeeze my thighs and dig my heels into his ass. The delicious friction strokes nerve endings I never knew existed. An orgasm builds deep inside. As Wes stretches and fills me, his enormous cock rubs the long-neglected tender places within. Toes curling, back arching, I buck beneath him, begging him not to stop. Wes grunts something incoherent and keeps moving.

My pleasure crests in a wave of ecstasy so intense, I wail his name. I never imagined sex could feel like this. I never knew my body could experience an orgasm that simultaneously feels like a lightning bolt of sensation and sensory obliteration.

He's a man. An animal. And a fucking god. The god of sex.

WES

Lena's moans and gasps of pleasure fill my head as I power into her wet heat. She takes me to the hilt, her body surrounding me perfectly.

She is fire. Earth. Air and water. Light and sound. Chaos and serenity. Nirvana. Valhalla. Heaven. The fucking Garden of Eden.

I slam into her, triggering her second climax. Her nails dig into the flesh of my knuckles. Legs clamped on my thighs, she pulls me deeper.

"Don't hold back. Gimme everything you've got." She moans amid her body's spasms. "I need you to take me."

The beast inside me takes over. Sweat pours from my brow as I pump my hips. Her moans consume me. Her body annihilates me. Lena's next climax brings forth my own. Moaning her name, I lose myself in her and come harder than ever in my life. The spasms of her body intensify my release, and it seems to go on forever.

I let go of her hands. She wraps her arms around me. With heaving chests, we tangle in one another's embrace. I crush her body to mine, holding on to her for dear life. The air inside the tent is warm, filled with gasps and sighs of pleasure. I'm still inside her, pulsing with the aftershocks of my orgasm. For several minutes, neither of us moves or says a word.

Lena possesses me. Consumes me. I'm so deep inside her, she saturates every cell in my body.

"Are you all right?" she asks.

"No," I gasp. "Not even in the same galaxy as all right." Pressing myself onto my elbows, I stare down at her in wonder. Wide julep eyes peer back at me. Lips swollen from my kisses. Cheeks reddened by the scrape of my stubble. "Never, in my life . . ." I begin. "There aren't words . . ." I shake my head to clear it. "You have no idea."

I give up and kiss her, pouring my unspoken emotions into the act. With the slow, deep tango of my tongue, I show her what I'm unable to say.

CHAPTER 39

LENA

Internal playlist: "Let It Be Me" by Ray LaMontagne

I awaken to raindrops pattering my tent. Wes sleeps, his body curved around mine. I press into his shelter and sigh. I stay in this position for God knows how long, savoring his embrace. I soak in his warmth. Memorize the lines on his hands. I trace a fingertip over his palm, noting the size and feel of it. Thick, strong, and muscular, just like the rest of him.

My eyes flutter closed. Heat blooms in my lower belly and I reflexively press my knees together. The sex was beyond anything I've ever experienced. To call Wes well-endowed is an understatement.

Once I got over the initial bite of pain, full-body ecstasy replaced it. Wes stimulated areas inside me that no one has ever touched. From my toes to the top of my head, I felt him. In fact, I can still feel him inside, hours after we finished. Grimacing, I make a mental note to bring an extra shirt to sit on by the fire.

Except, thanks to Wes, I don't have any extra shirts. No one has *ever* ripped off my clothes and shredded them, but I loved pushing him to the point of frenzy. It was beyond hot when he morphed into a primal sex machine, and I found it just as sexy when he switched gears back to a lover. *Ignite, then smolder.* I've lost count of the ways he heats me up—from wildfire to crackling hearth, embers to inferno, he scorches me. Wes's constant interplay of sweet and savage tops my list of things I love about him.

Love.

Wes detours that train of thought. "Good morning, sunshine."

I roll to face him and slide my arm around his waist. Burying my face in his chest, I listen to his heartbeat. "Morning, Ace."

"How'd you sleep, love?"

"I slept well." I feather my fingertips across his back. "You?"

"Well, my woman was a greedy little thing last night. She wore me out, and I slept like a log." I hear the smile in his voice. Lifting my head, I peer up at him with a smirk. Brilliant azure eyes look back at me, filled with tenderness and satisfaction. "But waking up with her in my arms is a great start to the day." He tightens his embrace. "It's where you belong, and I'm never lettin' ya go."

"The feeling's mutual." I press a kiss to the center of his chest. "You've made me fall for you."

"It only makes sense, since you *fell* into my lap." He grins. "I still maintain that you threw yourself, but—"

"I did not throw myself," I insist with a chuckle. "I fell."

"But *I* caught ya."

"Yes, you did." I touch his cheek. "In every way possible."

He dips his head, brushing his lips over my forehead. "Same here, love."

"Please hold on to me," I whisper.

Wes rolls me onto my back and climbs on top of me, supporting his weight on his elbows.

"Look at me."

Our gazes meet and I lose my breath.

"Since you lack my gift of clairvoyance, I'll spell it out for ya," he begins. "I'm not going anywhere. I can tell you don't realize it yet, but I'm yours. Completely." He kisses my bottom lip. "I know it's fast, but I've fallen just as hard for you. I've never felt anything like this. And I'm terrified, but there's no going back for me." He grips my chin. "Last night solidified that."

"I was nervous I'd disappoint you," I whisper. "I wasn't sure I could live up to your expectations—"

"It was the highlight of my life. I need you to add the statement about disappointing me to the same category as calling yourself ordinary. Both are off-limits. You were so . . . I mean, when we . . . I just can't . . ." He shakes his head. "I'm speechless, Lena." Running a hand over his face, he adds,

"You blew my fucking mind. I've never . . . And it was like, you . . ." He squeezes his eyes shut. "See what you do to me? I hope you like your men mute because I can't do words."

"You're the kind of man I like, Wes." I kiss him. "*You* are the man I want, the man I need, whether you're mute or wooing me with analogies. I want your words and your actions. When you're sweet *and* even when you're moody. I want the calm and the chaos, the man, and the beast. I want you to give it all to me. Every side, every angle, every sharp line, and rough edge. I just want *you*, Wes." I run my fingers through his hair. "You blew my mind too. Please never stop."

He slides a hand to my hip. "Are you all right?"

"Yes. I'm more than all right."

"You sure I didn't hurt you?"

"There were moments when it hurt, yes. But they were just that— moments. The pleasure far surpassed any pain I felt." I flush. "That was the first time I've ever orgasmed from inside."

"Seriously?"

"Yes. It's never happened before. Then you get in there and rewrite my entire sexual history."

"I plan to rewrite your sexual future, too."

"Please do."

"You let me know when you're ready for round two."

"I will," I say, flushing. "I need a little rest down yonder. I'm thinking tomorrow?"

"You sure you're all right, love?"

"Yes, I'm fine. You made sure I was comfortable." I stroke his cheek. "Thank you for that."

"May I kiss you?"

"Never stop kissing me."

The rain tapers to a cold drizzle by mid-afternoon. We emerge from the tent like bears coming out of hibernation. Rubbing my hands together, I try to rid the damp chill from my body.

"I'd give a large sum of money for a cup of coffee or tea, or just about anything hot."

Wes smirks. "I've got something hot for ya."

"You demonstrated that, Ace."

We trudge over to the fire, which, thanks to Jake and Austin, is still burning. The guys are seated at the river's edge with fishing poles.

"Anything biting, mates?"

"Nope," Austin mutters. "Been sittin' here an hour."

"Go warm up by the fire. I'll take over for a bit." Wes reaches for the pole.

Austin hands it over and trudges to the fire. "Hey, darlin'."

"Hey, Austin." I turn to Jake. "You go sit with him. We've been lounging. It's your turn to relax."

"I'm all right, Lena-Bean, but thanks."

I shrug. "Okay, well, let me know if you change your mind."

"Will do."

I make my way over to the fire, smiling at Austin as I approach.

"Pop a squat, baby girl."

Furrowing my brow, I stand over the log. I forgot my cushion in the tent. I settle without it and wince.

Austin smirks knowingly.

Well, fuck. They definitely heard us. Heat spreads from my ears to my cheeks and neck. Refusing to be embarrassed, I arch a brow. "Got something to say?"

"Nope," Austin replies with a grin. "Just glad Double-D done ya right."

"Double-D?"

"Ask him about that one later." Austin snorts. "That way I don't get punched."

"Will do." I look up as Jake approaches with a turbulent expression. "You okay, Jake?"

"Yeah, I'm fine," he mutters. "Just can't get out of my head today." Running a hand through his waves, he settles across from me. "What day is it?"

"Sunday, I think," Austin answers, standing. "Be right back. Gotta piss."

Jake watches him leave before discretely pulling a prescription vial from his pack. He quickly pops a colorful capsule and two tablets into his mouth before chugging some water. He shoves the empty bottle in his pocket.

I'm not denying I'm nosy, but I'm also a nurse, so the fact that Jake just took the last of whatever medication he needs, concerns me.

"What was that?" I ask.

He flushes, scanning for his friends. "Nothing."

"I'm not trying to be in your business, but if you have diabetes or high blood pressure, I'd like to know so I can keep an eye on you."

"No, it's nothing like that." He sighs and rubs his temples before standing. He walks over and resettles beside me. "I don't like talking about it."

"That's fine, Jake. I'm not pressuring you to. Like I said, the nurse in me wants to know if it's something serious." I peer at his face. "The friend in me is concerned that your container's now empty."

"Me fucking too," he mutters, casting a furtive glance behind him. "I don't want the guys to know."

"Unless your health is in jeopardy, I won't say a word to them."

He rests his elbows on his knees. "Although, soon it won't matter."

"What do you mean?"

"I mean, they'll figure it out when I start to fucking unravel."

"Like withdrawal?" I murmur.

"Yeah." He lowers his voice. "I deal with crippling anxiety. Normally, I can keep it at bay with therapy and meds. Look at me now, my doctor's in Manhattan and I'm stranded in the fucking Arctic without meds. I knew I should've brought the whole months' worth, but I only packed enough for the excursion plus a few extra days, you know, *just in case*." He squeezes his eyes shut. "I apologize in advance for the shitshow I'm about to become."

I nod and touch his shoulder. "No apologies necessary. While I don't have a degree in psychology, believe me when I tell you, I have extensive experience with anxiety and depression. If you need to talk, need a hug, whatever it may be, I'm here for you."

Jake pats my knee. "Thanks, Lena-Bean. That means a lot to me."

"Anytime, Jake."

It amazes me how celebrities manage their façades. Over the years, I've seen Jake on TV performing, giving interviews, hosting, and presenting at award shows. I've seen him numerous times in concert. Thanks to Garrett and the shit I've dealt with, I consider myself attuned to mental health issues, but I never had the slightest clue about Jake. How challenging it must be to suffer in silence while leading a life in the public eye. More than that, I'm struck by the fact that he hides it from his best friends.

Garrett and I don't have secrets. Never have, never will. I wish Jake felt that same comfort with Wes and Austin. If nothing else, I'll make sure he feels it with me.

CHAPTER 40

LENA (FIVE DAYS LATER)

Internal playlist: "Immigrant Song" by Led Zeppelin

I kneel at the river's edge and splash cool water onto my face. It's not the same as coffee, but it helps.

A crisp gust of wind chills my damp skin. I walk over to the fire and add more wood. I plop on a log and examine my dry, cracked hands, wishing I packed lotion. Movement along the riverbank catches my eye. I peer across the flames to the area upstream and my blood runs cold.

An enormous bear lumbers in my direction. I know it's a grizzly by its sheer size and brown-tipped coat. Slowly rising from the log, I back away. The bear noses its way around the gut pile, emitting chuffing sounds.

I sprint for the men's tent. Yanking the flap open, I dive on Wes, roughly shaking him by the shoulders.

"Get up! Bear! Hurry!" I shriek.

After tugging their boots on, the men rush out of the tent.

"Let's go." Wes grabs my arm and pulls me toward the tree line.

The bear meanders through our riverside spot, sniffing at the logs by the fire. We run into the forest.

"Grizzlies have trouble climbing. We need a tree." I gasp.

"This way." Wes points to an enormous balsam poplar. "Climb as high as you can."

Austin scales the tree with ease. Jake follows suit, settling onto a high branch. Wes climbs a little way and waits for me. Lacking the upper body strength, I rely on my legs. Wrapping them around the trunk, I squeeze my thighs and drag myself up, making it about five feet off the ground before I lose my footing. My jeans catch on a sharp section of bark and tear along the inner thigh, ripping my skin in the process. I slide down the trunk and land on my ass. Leaping to my feet, I make a second attempt. A quick glance over my shoulder freezes my blood. The bear lumbers to-ward the tents.

Wes is behind me in an instant. "I'm gonna lift her up. You guys grab her."

Bending forward, he grabs my thighs and lifts me to his shoulders. "Hold on to a branch and pull. I'll push your feet up."

I reach for a thick branch overhead and pull to where I can stand on Wes's shoulders. Fabric shreds as the bear ransacks my tent. Wes holds my ankles in a vise grip. With a grunt, he straightens his arms, heaving me upward. Austin snatches me around the leg, hauling me onto the branch he straddles. With everyone else safe, Wes swiftly climbs the tree and settles on a branch facing Austin and me, his face drawn in panic.

"Thank you," I whisper.

He nods, craning his neck toward the camp. My tent collapses as the animal pulls the stakes out of the ground. The bear rips the fabric with its front paws. My body begins to tremble.

Austin squeezes the back of my knee where he holds on to me. "I won't let you fall, darlin'. Just breathe. We're safe up here."

"That was close. Too close." Wes's tone is hollow. "If you hadn't woken us up, we would've been right there." His terror-filled eyes meet mine. "We can't stay here. He's identified a food source. He'll be back. What if we're asleep or someone's alone? We were idiots not to bury the fish guts."

"Where should we go? Do we follow the river and head south?" Jake asks from behind me. "At this point, I think it's safe to say they aren't coming for us. What about Bettles? We flew over it on our way up here."

"We definitely gotta stay near the river. I agree with Jake; we oughta head south," Austin says.

"Then it's decided. We wait for the bear to leave, pack our shit, salvage what we can of Lena's, and move the fuck out." Wes swipes the sweat from his brow. "Lena, you good with that?"

"Yes," I whisper. "Oh, God, it's coming."

The grizzly lumbers across the tundra to the tree line. Austin's grip on my leg tightens. No one dares to speak or even breathe. I bite my lower lip and stare at Wes's face. His jaw's tightly clenched, the muscles pulsing violently. He white knuckles the branch, digging his nails into the bark. The bear tramples through low-lying brush and shrubbery. A huffing sound comes from its throat as it lifts its broad snout and sniffs the air. I can feel the blood running down my leg. *Can he smell it? Am I luring it to us?*

The bear emits a low growl. Closer and closer it prowls. Austin's fingers dig into my leg. It sniffs the base of the tree and rubs against the trunk. Stretching its front paws upward, clawing the bark, it rises onto its hind legs and stares at us. No one moves or makes a sound. Deadly three-inch claws dig into the tree. Air rushes over my face as it swipes a massive paw. The tree shakes. We cling to it for dear life. Long, razor-sharp, yellowed canines protrude from its mouth. I stare into the eyes of the beast, willing it to leave. *Please, please leave us alone. Please don't hurt us.*

After a few harrowing minutes, the bear loses interest and drops to all fours. It makes a chuffing noise and rubs the tree again. By the grace of God and all that is holy, the animal retreats toward the river, pausing every few feet to look over its shoulder. It heads upstream, back in the direction it came from. We release a collective exhale. Austin stops cutting off the circulation in my leg.

"Pretty sure I just shit my pants," Jake says.

"I lost six years off my bloody life," Wes sputters. "Let's wait a little longer and make sure he's gone before we climb down."

We give it another twenty minutes or so before we carefully descend from our perch. Blood soaks the fabric surrounding my thigh wound. Wes catches sight of it as we walk toward the tents.

"What the hell happened to your leg?"

"It snagged on the bark when I fell. It's fine. I'm gonna change into different jeans. Hopefully, my clothes aren't all ruined."

We stop in front of what's left of my tangerine tent. One pole sticks straight up in the air. I must've had a granola bar in the pocket of one of my hoodies, because remnants of it lay several feet from the tent.

I bend over and pick up a piece of the wrapper. "I tried to be so careful. I didn't know this was in there."

"We need to move quickly. It doesn't look like he bothered with our tent. I'll help Lena get her stuff together," Wes tells Austin and Jake, who are already dismantling the men's shelter. He turns to me. "Let's salvage what we can. Fold up the poles and grab the stakes. We may find a use for them."

We sift through my belongings, gathering everything that isn't damaged. Fortunately, the only casualties are the sweatshirt and the tent itself. I shove items into my pack and roll up my sleeping bag. Stripping out of my ripped jeans, I bandage my leg with a piece of the sweatshirt. I pull on fresh jeans, hook my camera over my shoulder, and scan the area.

Austin removes his beloved guitar from its case, strokes the wood, and places it atop the ruined tent, next to my bloody pants. He fills the case with kindling and the ax. He hasn't said a word since we were in the tree. Our eyes meet as he slings the case across his back. A deep-seated pain threatens to consume him. I see it in the raw vulnerability on his face and the hard set of his jaw. I quickly wrap the gleaming instrument in what remains of my tent, and he nods his thanks.

From the riverbank, we retrieve the fishing gear, our cooking vessels, several knives, and Wes's "spear." Once we gather all we can carry, we head downstream. We still have several hours of daylight ahead of us but no idea where we're going or whether we'll find civilization.

For several hours, we trek south along the meandering bank of the mighty John River. The tundra flood plains morph into a rockier wooded terrain, nearly as dense as the forest by the camp. Austin and I walk side by side behind Jake and Wes, who warn us of loose rocks, slippery moss, and gnarled roots. Every so often, I glance over my shoulder to make sure we aren't being followed. My empty stomach churns as a reminder I haven't eaten yet.

"Thoughts on setting up camp soon? None of us have eaten or had anything to drink. Why don't we call it a day and move at dawn?" I suggest.

"Sounds good," Jake agrees. "Let's stop at the next clearing and get our lines wet."

We select a flat spot some twenty yards from the riverbank. Jake and I grab fishing poles and settle on the bank while Wes and Austin assemble the tent.

"How are you holding up?" I ask.

"I'm surviving, Lena-Bean." He reels in his line. "That's all I can do. Do I seem off to you?"

"Not at all, which makes me wonder how much you're suppressing."

"It's the obsessive thoughts that are killing me. I can't get a handle on them. I can control most of my compulsions—especially since there's nothing for me to clean out here," he says with a snort.

"So, it's straight up OCD?"

"No, it's a delightful trifecta of OCD, generalized anxiety, and depression." He gestures over his shoulder. "Do you think they can tell something's up?"

I shake my head. "I think everyone's too preoccupied with our situation. I mean, Wes is clearly anxious, since he paces every time we stop for a rest, Austin hasn't said a word in hours, but no one is talking about it."

Jake nods. "What about you? How are you doing?"

"I'm scared, but I'm trying not to be a prophet of doom. Let me ask you something."

"What's up?"

"How come you keep your anxiety hidden from the guys? They're your best friends."

He sighs. "I dunno. I guess part of me is ashamed. I mean, I don't judge anyone else or buy into any stigmas—"

"Except when it comes to yourself," I say, squeezing his arm. "You remind me a lot of Garrett."

"He doesn't talk about stuff?"

"No, he *only* talks to me about stuff—not his cousin or any of his guy friends."

"You're easy to talk to, Lena-Bean."

"Thanks. And like I said, I'm here if you need someone."

"I appreciate that more than you know."

"You good with double-fisting it? I'm going to try to get a fire started." I hand him my pole.

"Good call." He positions both poles.

I help Wes clear an area for the fire pit and lay down a bed of kindling. He layers branches and brush over the top and I use the Ferro Rod to ignite it.

Jake already caught and cleaned a salmon, which he brings over to the fire to cook. Austin silently gathers loose brush. Wes chops a few more logs while I duck into the tent and lay out the sleeping bags. The sun is going down, taking with it what little warmth remains, so I dig through my pack and layer on another flannel. I emerge, fill everyone's canteens, and plop between Wes and Austin. Jake divvies up the salmon, and we eat ravenously.

"I'm bloody knackered," Wes says between bites. "How far do ya think we hiked?"

"Maybe three or four miles," Jake says. "The terrain slowed us down."

"The forest will shelter us better if we get shitty weather, but it definitely limits visibility," I add. "I'm hoping it thins out as we head farther south."

Austin silently stares across the river as he eats his portion of fish.

"Memphis, you all right, mate?" Wes reaches across me and pats Austin's knee.

"No," he mutters without looking at Wes.

Austin studies his hands and inhales slowly. A tear appears from beneath his lashes. He bends his head, holding his face in his hands. Tears silently stream down his cheeks. I wrap my arm around his shoulders. His body shakes as he cries, so I hug him tighter.

"She's pregnant. Katie's carrying my baby," he whispers on a sob. "I'm gonna be a daddy, and I may not live to see it."

The fear and anguish pour out of him as the day's events take their toll. I glance at Wes and Jake. Both wear the same open-mouthed expression. Blinking rapidly, neither one moves.

I squeeze one of Austin's hands. "How far along is she?"

"She's ten weeks at this point. I promised I'd be with her every step of the way." He sobs. "She was so fuckin' scared when we found out, and I swore I'd be there at every appointment, every ultrasound. Now, I'm gonna die out here and leave her alone—" The rest of what he's trying to say is lost in his anguish.

Wes shakes his head, finally coming to his senses, and squats in front of Austin. He places his hands on his shoulders. "Memphis, listen to me. We're not gonna let that happen. We'll find a way out of here, we have to. We've gotta be strong and keep pushing forward. Somehow, we'll be rescued. Either they'll find us, or we'll find them. We're not gonna die out here."

"I hope you're right, man." Austin looks up from his hands with reddened eyes and tear-stained cheeks. "I'm scared I'll leave her to raise our baby without a daddy. I don't wanna orphan my child."

"Like Wes said, we won't let that happen." I gently squeeze Austin's hand.

Jake comes to his side. "Don't torture yourself with those kinds of thoughts. Shit got real today. We've gotta be realistic about the danger we're in, but we can't give up hope. We have some tools at our disposal, natural resources everywhere, and most importantly, we have each other. As long as we stick together and look out for one another, I think we have a fighting chance."

"Thank you. I love you guys," Austin whispers.

"We love you too." Wes straightens. "We all need to get some rest. We have a lot of distance to cover tomorrow."

Jake claps Austin's shoulder. "Are you ready for me, big spoon?" His comment successfully forces a crooked smirk from Austin.

"Big daddy's always ready." Austin climbs to his feet. "Even when I'm not."

CHAPTER 41

LENA

Internal playlist: "We Can Make Love" by SoMo

Hours later, I crawl to the tent flap and freeze at the sudden grip on my ankle. *Looks like not everyone's asleep.*

"Where ya goin'?" Wes whispers harshly.

"I've gotta pee, if you must know." I've already lain here for twenty minutes thinking about it.

"I don't want you going out there alone."

"Thanks for your concern, Ace, but you're not coming."

"Fine. But don't sneak out at night. Let me know where you're going. Then, if you're gone too long, I can check on you."

"But you need sleep."

He tightens his grip. "Don't argue. I don't have the energy for it. Please do what I ask for once."

"Fine. I'll wake you up. But tomorrow, I want the spot closest to the flap."

Satisfied for the time being, Wes releases my ankle.

Smirking, I find a distant tree to squat behind. *Now I need to ask his permission to pee.* I love when he takes a bossy tone because it gives me a chance to push his buttons.

I gaze at the clear night sky for a few minutes. The full moon casts an eerie, silvery glow over the forest, making it feel enchanted. Shrouded in sterling, spruce and birch trees tower over the frosted rocks and roots below. I return my attention to the heavens. Without the city's light pollution, many of my favorite constellations are visible. I locate the North

Star, which appears brighter than ever before. Given our proximity to the North Pole, it makes perfect sense. In my eyes, this *is* true north.

My head turns at the sound of a zipper. Wes emerges, scanning the area. He locates me and marches over, heavy footfalls crunching on rocks and brush.

"Shh," I hiss, "you're stomping like a friggin' sasquatch. You'll wake the dead."

He looms before me in silence, the moon lending a silvery glow to his cobalt glare.

"What's *your* problem?" I whisper.

"Thought I made it clear that I don't want ya wandering the forest alone," he grumbles. "But you're out here counting stars and talking to the moon."

"I'm not wandering the forest." I point to the ground. "Standing still, right here. Didn't realize my bathroom breaks had a time limit. Next time I'll ask for a hall pass."

His tone softens. "Keep up that sass and you'll find yourself in detention, young lady."

"I'll keep that in mind." I trail my fingertips down his chest. "Still working on that spanking we discussed."

"Does right now work for ya, sunshine?" Wes growls. "I have a pair of knees I'd love to bend you over."

"Let's pencil it in for another time, shall we?"

"How do you do it?" he asks in disbelief.

"Do what?"

"Infuriate me one minute, then turn around and make me wanna fuck you the next?"

"I dunno, Ace." I grin. "But if you wanna fuck me, I must be doing *something* right."

"Lena," my name leaves his lips in warning, "if I had my way, I'd be inside ya from dawn till fucking dusk." He steps closer, tracing the curve of my breast. "And all night long."

I run a hand down his chest. "Too bad we only have one tent now, huh?"

"You think that's gonna stop me?" Wes grips my forearm and leads me farther from the tent.

"Where are we going? It's a little dark for a hike."

"You've earned yourself a quickie under the stars. Think you can keep quiet this time?"

Oh my God.

He doesn't wait for my reply. Instead, he presses my back to a tree trunk and seizes my lips. This isn't a slow dance of tongues—it's a claiming. Fisting his hands in my hair, he grinds his hips as he kisses me. I clutch his shoulders and surrender to him.

Wes lifts me by the thighs, carrying me to a different tree. This one's partially fallen, creating the perfect perch. He sets me down and roughly unbuttons my jeans. In one smooth motion, he grips the waistbands of my jeans *and* panties and shoves them down; I gasp at the urgency as I step out of them.

Wes removes his parka, draping it over the tree trunk. "We wouldn't want any splinters in that sweet arse of yours, now would we, sunshine?"

He lifts me onto the tree. Higher than a kitchen counter, it's the perfect height for him. He presses my thighs apart and steps between them. He drops his jeans to midthigh, springing his massive erection.

I'm not ready.

"Wait."

Wes stills, meeting my gaze. "What's wrong?"

"Nothing's wrong." I hop to the ground. "I've wanted to do this for days." I slowly sink to my knees in front of him. "Can *you* keep quiet?" Gripping his cock, I brush my lips over the head and push his thighs back toward the tree.

"Not fair, you won't let me—"

I flick my tongue and suck the head of his cock into my mouth, causing him to groan. Swirling my tongue, I suck him deeper and stroke my hand in tandem. His hips jerk and a gasp leaves his chest. I slide my other hand down to touch myself.

"Oh, fuck," Wes groans. "You're gonna kill me."

Smiling, I pull back slightly. Then I surge forward, taking him to the back of my throat.

"*Fuck.*" He weaves his hands into my hair, tugging the strands.

With one hand gripping his cock, I flick, swirl, and rub my tongue on the underside of his shaft. Below, my other hand readies myself for him. Spurred by his gasps, feral groans, and moans, my fingertips massage my clit and ease inside. With trembling legs, Wes clenches my hair and moves his hips in rhythm with me.

"You gotta stop," he gasps, "or I won't last another minute."

I reluctantly pull back and peer up at him. His lust-filled expression is priceless. He bends forward and hauls me onto the tree. I wrap my legs around him, his cock nudging my entrance. I tilt my hips, giving him easier access.

Wes snatches the hand I used to pleasure myself and sucks my fingers into his mouth. "Mmm, as sweet as I imagined."

My mouth drops open. Though it shocks me, the erotic act makes me even wetter.

Wes eases his cock inside me. I cling to his shoulders, feeling every thick inch stretch and fill me. Once fully seated, he clamps his hands on my hips and slowly begins to move, drawing back and pressing forward again. Our bodies join like a lock and key, the connection so primitive. So raw. So perfect.

"You all right?" he asks.

"Yes. Doesn't hurt this time. Go a little faster."

Wes nods, picking up the pace. I close my eyes and absorb the feeling of him moving inside me—stroking nerve endings, rubbing my G-spot, and every spot imaginable.

"You feel so good inside me." I gasp. "Oh, God, Wes . . ."

"You're *mine*, sunshine." He growls. "Every part of you." He reaches down and rubs my clit with his thumb. "Especially here."

I moan, spreading my legs wider. "Give it to me."

He increases the pace and intensity while slowly circling his thumb. I fist his ass cheeks and pull him deeper.

"Oh, fuck . . . Lena . . ."

I can almost taste my impending orgasm. "Harder." He slams into me. "Oh, Wes," I moan.

"You like that?" He gasps.

"Yes! Just like that."

Wes stops rubbing my clit and clutches my hips. Eyes locked on mine, he thrusts in a powerful, driving rhythm. Hips slamming, flesh slapping, he fucks me like his life depends on it.

"Lena, fuck," he groans through a clenched jaw. "Come for me."

My body acts on his command, fracturing into an orgasm. The moans come freely as I spasm around him. He increases the intensity of his thrusts.

He's close. I squeeze his ass. "Let yourself go, baby."

Wes climaxes with a groan. Gasping my name, thrusting until he's given me everything he's got. His cock pulses inside me. I squeeze my muscles around him, holding him close in every possible way. He wraps me in his arms and pulls me closer, shaking his head in disbelief.

Our bodies still joined; we hold each other in silence. I close my eyes and bury my face in his neck. His pulse throbs against my lips as I kiss him.

"Lena, you're a supernova, love. I swear to Christ, I'm never letting you go."

"I won't let go, either," I whisper. "You're mine."

CHAPTER 42

LENA

Internal playlist: "More of You" by Josh Groban

"G'day, sunshine." Wes greets me as I emerge from the tent. "Ready to cover some distance?" He cups my cheek, pressing a sweet kiss to my lips. Other than a cheek or forehead peck, it's the first time he's kissed me in front of his friends, a fact that warms me better than the parka I'm wearing.

"Morning, Wes." I wrap my arms around his waist. "As ready as I'm gonna get."

He kisses me again, deeper this time, weaving his hands into my hair.

Jake clears his throat. "You gonna suck her face off or hike?"

Wes laughs. "I'd much rather suck her face off, but you're probably right." He swats my ass. "Let's get moving."

We hike the treacherous terrain for several hours. An unforgiving wind burns my cheeks and makes my eyes tear.

Break time.

"Guys, can we stop for a breather?" Chest heaving, I lean against a tree. "Everything burns—my legs, my lower back, my shoulder, all of it." I hate whining, but my churning stomach is digesting itself and the guys are all too macho to suggest a break. "We should really eat something."

Wes nods, allowing his pack to slide to the ground. He carries the heaviest load on his back, and despite those glorious muscles, his pace has slowed with exhaustion.

He wipes his brow and sips from a canteen. "How about we give it a go with the fish?"

We all grab our poles and settle on the bank. Wes reels in a large salmon and quickly skins and guts it.

"Anyone up for sushi?" Jake asks. "I can't see us wasting time and energy to build a fire when we wanna cover more ground."

"Agreed." Austin slices off a hunk of fish. "I like sushi."

I finish my portion of raw salmon and stretch into a back bend. My aching muscles warn me to stop neglecting them. I pop my bad shoulder and wince.

"Gross," Jake mutters, shaking his head. "I hate that sound."

"Sorry. Had to do it. My shoulder felt misaligned. I'll warn you next time." Placing my hands on my hips, I twist from side to side. Then do a few sun salutations. If I live through this trip, I really need to get my ass back into the yoga studio.

"Walk with me, Lena." Wes motions for me to follow.

I trail behind him. "What's up?" We have a lot of ground to cover, so it doesn't make sense to go for a stroll.

"I wanted to make sure you were okay. I hope I didn't hurt you last night."

"You didn't. My shoulder's just outta whack." I stand on my tiptoes and kiss him. "Last night was amazing. You can fuck me under the stars any time you like," I add with a wink.

He grins. "Don't you worry, sunshine, I fully intend to."

I glance to where Wes is seated on a log. He carves another stick, sending curls of bark to the ground. After his little remark, he passionately kissed me up against a tree. My lips still tingle from the scrape of his stubble. I will never get tired of kissing him.

He meets my gaze, glances skyward, and winks.

I flash him a sultry smile and point to my watch.

He grins and perks up as something on the ground catches his attention. "Whoa. Look at this bloke. He's a beaut." He prods a giant brown spider.

"Damn, he's a biggun'," Austin marvels. "Reminds me of the wolf spiders back home."

The spider crawls along Wes's stick.

"I'm telling you right now, man," Jake points at Wes, "you better keep that fucker away from me."

"What, no love for arachnids?" Wes's face lights up with a devilish grin. "How about you, Lena?"

He climbs to his feet with the stick. The spider approaches his hand, so he switches his grip to the other end.

"Wesley Emerson, come any closer to me with that spider and I'll beat you," I warn, my skin crawling and the hairs on the back of my neck standing on end.

"What if I *want* you to beat me?"

The wicked gleam in his eye and diabolical expression tells me this is payback for last night's little spanking remark. He continues to approach.

"Wes, I'm warning you—don't take another step." I force an even tone when what I really want to do is scream like a banshee. Give me snakes, scorpions, mice, bats . . . anything else. Just not spiders.

"Don't you wanna pet him?" He steps closer. "Look, he's kinda cute." He rapidly extends his arm, sending the spider flying in my direction.

I shriek. My legs take off running before I know what to do with them. My left foot snags on a gnarled root and I tumble to the ground. Pushing myself up, I glare at him.

"Fuck!" Wes rushes to my side. "Are you all right?"

I roll up my pant legs and wipe at my bloodied knees. "You're on my shit list, Ace."

"I'm so fucking sorry, love." Wes knots a hand in his hair. "Let me help you up." He hauls me to my feet.

I point a finger in his face. "Don't *ever* come after me with a fucking spider again!"

He holds his hands up in surrender. "I swear, it won't happen again. I'm sorry."

"You crossed a fucking line."

WES

I'm a fucking idiot. I meant to tease Lena; spark the fire I love so much in her. Instead, I caused her pain—and pissed her off. *What the fuck is wrong with me?*

I think back to our heart-to-heart in the tent when she told me about the attack at her job. How I saw fear and vulnerability in her eyes. She didn't want to talk about it, but she did. She placed her trust in me, allowing me to strip away her defenses. I want to shelter her; be the safety she craves.

I ache to share my secrets with her. Her gaze unlocks me, coaxes me from my shell. I want to tell her everything. Every fear. Every hope. Every regret. I've kept it all inside for years, hidden behind a façade of strength. I'm tired of being the fortress. I want to seek shelter in her.

But I keep hurting her instead.

I want to find that Steve and beat him. I'd like to punch her ex in the face too. More than that, I want to beat myself. First, I leave her to freeze to death. Chivalry at its finest. Why not up the ante and trigger some PTSD, too? And if that's not bad enough, I chase her with a spider. Then, she falls and cuts her knees. *Way to put the icing on the cake, you fuckwit.*

Why do I always hurt the people I love?

CHAPTER 43

GARRETT (MANHATTAN, NEW YORK)

Internal playlist: "Make it Rain" by Ed Sheeran

My phone vibrates in my coat pocket as I cross Bryant Park. Glancing at the screen, I stop breathing when I see the 9-0-7 area code.

"Hello?" I choke out the greeting.

"Mr. Casey, Trooper Mayfield here. I know you're meeting with the NYPD tomorrow, but I'd promised to keep you informed."

I struggle to breathe. *Please, God . . .*

"We located the plane."

"Oh, God," I whisper, plopping onto a park bench.

"It crashed seventy miles northwest of Fairbanks—an area nowhere near the path indicated by the flight plan. The pilot's body was found in the cockpit. We're awaiting autopsy results, but my gut says that the guy had a heart attack and lost control of the aircraft after dropping the passengers off."

"How can you tell?"

"All cargo areas were empty, and the blood was localized to the cockpit. Given the mangled state of the aircraft, fatalities or serious injuries would've been sustained. The main hatch and emergency exits were sealed, meaning no one had entered or exited the plane since takeoff. Ms. Hamilton was not on that plane when it went down."

"Oh, thank God. Then where the hell is she?"

"That's what we're trying to figure out. The chartered destination was Gobbler's Knob, which is due west of Fairbanks. The plane was headed southeast from the Brooks Range when it went down. Again, this is no-where near Gobbler's Knob. We're working with local agencies and the Alaska Fish and Game to revise our rescue efforts. We're shifting our focus north and expanding the boundaries of our search. The flight company informed us that this particular pilot had a tendency to change course without notice. They're compiling a list of his favored coordinates."

"How can I help?"

"We're trying to figure out the reason for the change in course. Gobbler's Knob isn't exactly an adventure spot, so it would make sense if the pilot redirected them to the wilderness. What was Ms. Hamilton doing in Alaska?"

"Lena wanted solitude. She brought her camera and hoped to photograph some animals."

"Hmm . . . There are several untouched wildlife refuges in the Arctic. That gives us something to think about. Thank you, Mr. Casey, you've been very helpful."

"Thanks for keeping me in the loop. I suppose it's to her benefit she's lost in the woods with a trio of celebrities."

"We'd search just as hard, Mr. Casey. We'll find your girlfriend."

"Thank you."

I don't bother correcting him. The man wouldn't understand the depth or complexity of our relationship. I end the call and stare at my phone for a few minutes.

Could Lena still be alive?

CHAPTER 44

LENA

Internal playlist: "Weight of the World" by Evanescence

"Did you guys hear the wolves last night?" I ask, as we awaken the next morning.

Wes shakes his head. "Wolves?"

"Yeah, they were howling in the distance." I stretch and pop my shoulder. "Was going to wake you—"

"Why didn't you?" He rubs his temples. "That's a damn good reason to wake someone."

I shake my head. "I didn't see the point. What were we gonna do? Run through the dark forest?"

Austin speaks up. "We need weapons other than the ax and our knives."

"Let's scout the area," Jake suggests, opening the zippered flap. "Maybe we can find something useful."

We leave the tent as the sun begins its arc across the sky. I scan the forest while the guys break down camp. Soon everything's packed, and Wes hands each man a stout walking stick that can be used as a club if need be. Austin gathers an armload of wood and wraps it in a tarp. We hike south along the meandering riverbank, heading for the base of a mountain, through which the winding river carved a canyon. Rock outcroppings jut over whitewater rapids. We move inland, away from the slippery riverside cliffs.

Resting in the shadow of the Brooks Range, we face a new dilemma. Either we climb the mountain or go around it, and given the mountain's rocky slope, neither are pleasant options.

"Terrain may be easier if we go around, but who knows how far inland that would take us. We'd risk losing sight of the river," Wes points out. "We have no choice but to climb."

"How the hell will we manage that one? It's a vertical climb," Jake laments.

"We lighten our load," Austin suggests. "Sift through our gear and only keep the essentials."

"It's all essential out here," I say.

"We keep some kindling but leave behind the guitar case of wood. Keep one cooking vessel, lose some clothes," Wes says.

I gnaw my lip. "But it's only getting colder. Without layers, we'll freeze to death."

Wes lets his pack slide to the ground. "We'll have fire and each other. We have no choice." He kneels and riffles through his belongings. "Jake, do ya have any rock-climbing experience?"

"None whatsoever."

Austin squeezes Jake's shoulder. "I'm a decent climber. You hang with me."

I turn to Wes. "How are we gonna do this?"

"You stay with me. I'll get us up that mountain. We take it slow and steady and rest as often as you need. From what I can tell, it's not a sheer cliff, just really steep. Don't worry, love. We'll make it happen."

The late afternoon sun filters through scattered spruce trees. The mountainside starts off as a steep, rocky incline before switching to almost sheer rock face near the summit. After the guys spend a few moments discussing the best strategy, we decide to climb diagonally toward the left, where there appears to be a wide ledge. We figure we can rest on the ledge before tackling the remainder. Jake and Austin get a head start. The goal is for them to reach the ledge first and send down a length of rope to help Wes and me.

I clench my jaw and watch the men begin their ascent. Austin uses his experience to assist Jake as they scale the incline in tandem. I glance at Wes. His shoulders carry a lighter burden, and he appears to stand taller.

He smiles. "Ready to do it?"

I nod.

"Stay in front of me. Take your time, love. We can—" He's cut off by a howl that echoes through the canyon.

My blood runs cold. *We're being stalked.*

"Move!" Wes pushes me ahead.

Raw, unadulterated terror consumes me as I frantically crawl over rocks and boulders. The scabs on my knees and thigh reopen, soaking the front of my jeans with blood. Wes presses me forward as he scrambles behind me.

The wolf's howl is closer, and others join in. Jake and Austin can see the animals from their vantage point.

"Hurry! There're three of them and they're headin' this way!" Austin bellows.

He and Jake have nearly reached the safety of the ledge. Wes and I are only about three-quarters of the way up when the snarling animals breach the tree line.

"Oh my God," I whimper, clawing my way over jagged rocks, hands and knees burning. Weakened by exhaustion, I climb to the best of my ability.

"Don't think. Just move," Wes orders. "You can do this."

CHAPTER 45

WES

Internal playlist: "Aerials" by System of a Down

F ear gripping me, I look overhead to the ledge where my mates are waiting. *Another four meters.*

The wolves struggle against the incline as they clamber over rocks and boulders. I put every ounce of my energy into pushing Lena forward. If we reach the end of that rope, it'll be too steep for the animals.

Mercifully, the rope is finally within reach. Holding Lena against me, I send the gear up to my mates. We've got another two meters until we reach the guys. The wolves stop just beneath us where the terrain morphs from steep to nearly vertical. Our bodies hug the rockface, and although Lena clings to me for dear life, she appears to be in a trance, completely paralyzed with fear.

"You ready?"

She stares at the wolves and doesn't answer. I wrap the rope around my right arm, looping the other arm around Lena's waist. My plan is to do a walk/climb and hold on to Lena while the guys pull the rope.

"Hold on to me. They're gonna help pull us up."

She rivets her focus on the snarling beasts. One of the wolves is particularly aggressive. Larger than the others, with a thick, black coat and muscular build, the alpha male's gold eyes lock on to Lena as if claiming her.

"Lena, are ya with me? Snap out of it." Though she slowly turns her head toward me, her eyes never leave the wolves. "Hold on to me. I won't let you go. Lena, look at me."

I need to get her attention away from the wolves.

Tightening my grip on her waist, I drop my voice to the low growl that usually gets a response from her. "Look at *me*."

Lena's gaze snaps to mine, giving me a thread of relief.

"Focus on me, love."

The guys begin pulling us up. With the rope as leverage, I stretch my right leg upward into a lunge of sorts and wedge my foot into a crack. Using the strength of my thighs as a boost, I help lift us while the guys pull. Back in the game now, Lena follows suit, mirroring my lunge.

Suddenly, a section of rock cleaves off beneath her feet. She screams as she slips from my grasp and starts to fall. I catch her by the forearm.

The momentum slams the back of my head against the rocks. The throbbing pain is joined by the warm trickle of blood down my neck. Her fingers tighten around my forearm, but her other hand hangs at her side.

"Grab on to my arm." She doesn't move—just dangles like a piece of fucking sirloin. "Lena! Grab my arm! Use your other hand."

She stares up at me with haunted eyes. "Just let go, Wes. You can't hold us both. Let me fall. You climb to safety."

Ice fills my chest. "*What?*"

"I said, let me fall," she repeats in a hollow tone, "before we both do." Defeat replaces her earlier terror. Now she's on the verge of shutting down.

"Cut your shit and grab my arm," I bark the order, but she makes no effort to move. "Lena, what the fuck? Grab on to me!"

"I can't do this. Climb to safety, Wes." Her voice is eerily calm, as if resigned to her fate. "I need you safe."

"No!"

Icy claws of panic steal my ability to breathe. Arms stretched in opposite directions, one hand clings to the rope, fibers digging into my flesh. My other hand is clamped on her arm. Sweat threatens the integrity of my grip and she slides lower, so now I've got her by the wrist. Her fingertips weakly encircle my wrist.

"Let go, Wes, before we both fall," she murmurs. "I don't think I can fight anymore." Her fingers begin to relax around me.

Wild with terror, I squeeze her wrist. "Don't you fucking dare let go!" I roar, a beast in my own right. "Lena, so help me God—"

CHAPTER 46

LENA

Internal playlist: "Heavy In Your Arms" by Florence + The Machine

I flinch at Wes's tortured, inhuman scream. Staring up at him, the raw, agonizing terror in his eyes slaps my face.

"Please hold on to me. Don't do this. *Lena*," his voice breaks on my name, "don't give up on me."

Desperation fills those gorgeous eyes and spills over, tears sliding down his cheeks.

I shake my head and grab on to him with both hands. Arm straining, he grits his teeth and slowly curls his arm to lift me. His neck veins bulge with the effort. I regain my footing. Wes clings to my waist, nose touching mine. I can't look away from the pain and fury in his eyes.

"Hold on to me. If you fall, I'm fucking falling with you. That whatcha want?"

"No." My voice is barely a whisper.

He clenches his jaw. "Then put your goddamn arms around me."

I weave my arms around his neck. Austin and Jake pull the rope from above, and Wes uses his legs to propel us.

Finally, we clear the ledge. Austin grips Wes's belt and drags him over. Jake grabs on to me and pulls me up.

"Holy shit. You guys scared us," Austin stammers.

Wes lies facedown, resting on his forearms. His forehead presses into the earth and tears drip from his eyes onto the dirt. His chest heaves with each ragged breath. He must've hit his head at some point because rivulets of blood trickle from his crimson-stained hair, down his neck.

The rope shredded his palm. Dirt, sweat, and rope fibers mix with his blood.

I lie on my side. Shame replaces the terror that took over my body and logical thought. *I almost got us both killed.*

After a few beats of silence, Wes turns his head in my direction. I dare a hesitant glance at his face.

The fury in his gaze burns me. Outrage replaces tears and desperation. Without breaking eye contact, he slowly pushes to his knees. A muscle pulses in his clenched jaw. His nostrils flare with each inhale.

"Wes, I—"

"*Don't,*" he snarls the word. "Don't say another word to me." He climbs to his feet. "Are you that fucking selfish?"

"Take it easy, man." Austin steps between us. "Watch how you speak to her."

"Fuck off. This is between her and me."

Jake appears at Austin's side and places his hand on Wes's shoulder. "Emerson, calm down."

"Don't fucking touch me," Wes snarls, vibrating with fury. "And get the fuck out of my face."

Jake removes his hand, but neither he nor Austin budge.

"Take a walk, man," Austin commands softly. "This isn't you."

Pressing myself up, I attempt to kneel. Wes's head jerks in my direction. The volatility in his gaze paralyzes me. Eyes narrowed, nostrils flaring, he seethes with rage. I can't breathe or think, nor can I escape his attention.

Jake shifts, blocking his line of sight. "What the fuck is going on?"

"None of your fucking business."

"You're scaring her," Jake growls. "Can't you see that?"

"Walk away, man," Austin commands. "*Now.*"

"What?" Wes snaps.

"I said you need to take a walk," Austin repeats calmly. "Walk away. Get some air."

The ledge is actually a large clearing where the slope levels out. A perfect place to set up camp. Wes stalks across the clearing, releasing a rage-filled scream at the sky. It reverberates through the canyon.

Flinching, I hug my knees to my body. Tears stream in rivers down my cheeks.

Once Wes is a safe distance away, Jake assembles the tent and builds a fire.

Austin settles beside me with a damp cloth. "Gimme your hands." He wipes the blood from my palms. "What was that about?"

"I pissed him off," I whisper.

"No kidding." Austin gestures to Wes, who has his back to us. He's holding his head, resting his elbows on his knees. "This is outta character for him. He can be hotheaded, but I've never seen him lose his shit like that."

"I'm sorry," I repeat without looking at him.

"No need to be sorry for me." Austin tilts my chin to face him. "But you're gonna tell me why he's livid."

"I was so scared I froze."

It's a half-truth. As I dangled, bloody hand slipping and wolves inches from my feet, exhaustion and terror convinced my brain I was going to die. Suddenly, what happened to me didn't matter. Only Wes mattered. At that moment, his safety came before mine, and the only thing that made sense was to let go. Except letting go—or trying to—had put him in even greater danger.

Austin shakes his head. "I'm not buyin' it. He wouldn't be mad at you for that."

Wes marches over to us. Still enraged, he stops directly in front of me, making me cower behind Austin.

He glares at me for a minute. "You pull a stunt like that again—" He rakes a hand through his bloodied hair. "I don't understand why you would—" Swallowing hard, he tries again. "Do you have *any* idea—" He throws his arms in the air and stomps away, settling in a spot across the clearing with his back to us.

Austin eyes me. "You scared him."

"I know," I whisper, averting my gaze once more. "I need to lie down." I slowly climb to my feet and trudge to the tent. Jake shoots me a questioning look, but I simply shake my head and retreat behind the safety of the fabric.

I burrow into my sleeping bag and stare at the tent ceiling. In my misguided effort to save him, I damaged my relationship with Wes. Bitter tears of regret well in my eyes.

WES

I look over my shoulder at Austin's approach. "If you came to lecture me, save your breath."

He sits beside me. "I didn't."

"I'm sorry I yelled at ya."

"No big deal, man. I can handle it. But I don't like how you spoke to Lena."

"Makes two of us." I sigh. "I'll talk to her when I cool down."

"She said you were mad at her for being scared?"

I shake my head in disbelief. "She thinks *that's* why I'm angry?"

"What's your reason, then?"

"She said, 'Let me go.'" I meet Austin's confused gaze. "She told me to let her go. Let her fall."

"Jesus Christ," Austin breathes. "She wasn't serious?"

"She wouldn't grab on to my arm, Memphis." I hold up my thumb and forefinger. "This. Fucking. Close. I almost lost her, and I don't know why."

"What the hell came over her?"

"She kept telling me to get to safety."

Austin touches my shoulder. "Putting your safety before her own—sound familiar?"

"I should be protecting her, not the other way around."

"Listen, I get that you're angry, man. But you gotta cool down. Last thing you want is her afraid of you, and that's where you're headin'." Rising, he pats my shoulder. "Go easy on her. She knows she fucked up."

I nod, staring at my shaking hands. My right palm is marred with a deep gash where the rope tore my flesh. I can still feel Lena's grip on my left wrist. I don't know how I lifted her with one arm. My body's running on empty. The ordeal eviscerated me, depleted every ounce of my strength.

I almost lost her.

The thought alone is enough to destroy me. I squeeze my eyes shut and draw a ragged breath. My stomach turns, picturing that black wolf shredding her porcelain flesh. I would've gone after her. I would've kicked, clawed, punched, and bitten my way through those wolves. I would've done whatever it took to save her—even given up my own life.

At this moment, I realize that I'll stop at nothing for Lena. If it ensures her safety, I'll endure any pain, face any danger. I'll die for her, even kill for her if it comes down to it. The primal desire to protect her surges through my veins with a ferocity that surpasses anything I've ever felt. I thought I loved Rachel . . . and maybe I did in some capacity. But this goes beyond that. My previous understanding of love and affection doesn't scratch the surface of what I feel for Lena. *I need her.*

No, I wasn't looking for love, but I found it. Lena holds my heart captive, and as the cliff ordeal just proved, she has the power to break it.

CHAPTER 47

LENA

Internal playlist: "Lost" by Dermot Kennedy

I lie in the tent, replaying the events of the past twenty-four hours. *What the fuck was I thinking?* How could I freeze like that? And how could I have expected Wes to let me fall? I nearly got him killed.

"Lena, can I have a word?" Wes is right outside the tent.

What can I say? He has every right to be angry. Hell, I'm angry with myself. I lie motionless in my sleeping bag, a heavy numbness in my chest.

He sighs. "Fuck this. I'm coming in." He unzips the flap and climbs inside, consuming all of the air.

I nervously slide deeper into the sleeping bag, so my entire face is hidden. We sit in silence for several minutes.

"Since you're hiding, I'll take that to mean you don't wanna talk. That's fine—I don't care what you want right now—I'll do the talking. You don't get to make any more decisions today." He sighs again. "I'm just trying to understand why. What were you thinking? I need to know what was going through your head. Because I don't understand, and it's driving me fucking insane."

I don't make a sound.

"You're so goddamn stubborn." Wes unzips the sleeping bag and peels back my shield. "Don't hide from me." He tilts my chin. "Look at me. Tell me why."

The pain in his gaze rips me apart. "I'm sorry," I whisper. "I'm so sorry."

"I'm sorry I screamed at ya," he murmurs. "You didn't deserve that."

"Yes, I did. I was just trying to . . ." A fresh wave of tears floods my eyes, and I swipe them with a fist. "I didn't mean to put you in worse danger."

"I need to understand what happened."

"You were trying to hold me. Your hand was slipping . . . I-I didn't want you to fall . . . I wanted you safe."

"And you think I would've let you go?" he asks in disbelief.

"No . . . I dunno, but I wanted you to." I take a breath. "I didn't *want* to fall. But I thought we were both going down, and I didn't have the energy to fight anymore." I squeeze my eyes shut. "Right now, it sounds crazy, but at that moment, it felt like the only way."

"It seemed more logical than holding on to me like I asked?"

I meet his gaze. "All I cared about was you, Wes. I didn't care what happened to me." My body shakes on a sob. "I just wanted to save you."

"What would've happened if you fell? You think I would've stood back and watched them rip ya apart?"

"No," I whisper.

"I would've gone after you and we'd both be dead."

"I didn't want you to die trying to save me."

"So, you were willing to sacrifice yourself so I could escape?"

"Wes, I would've done *anything*."

"But why?"

I wipe my cheeks. "I guess I'll spell it out for you. Austin has a baby on the way. He's going to be someone's *father*. The three of you have *millions* of people who would be devastated to lose you. Despite what you may think, it would have a global impact. But me . . . I'm just an ordinary girl."

Wes's eyes darken. "Lena—"

"Let me finish. My scope of influence is limited," I explain. "I'm jus—"

"No! I don't want to hear another word of that shit. Let me tell you something about scope of influence. Yes, Austin and Jake are talented singers with millions of fans, I'll give ya that, but I'm just a man who makes a living by pretending. We're entertainers. In the grand scheme of life, what we do is meaningless. I'm a glorified fraud—"

"Don't say that about yourself. You make people happy."

"And *you* save people's lives. Heal the sick, comfort the dying. *That's* the kind of shit that matters. Think about Garrett. How would he feel if he knew you'd given up like that? You didn't let *him* give up, did ya? You told us he said he wouldn't be here if it weren't for you. Sounds influential to me. So, don't sit there and feed me some bullshit about limited scope of influence. Don't you *dare* discredit yourself. I'm fucking tired of it." He shakes his head.

"Lena, I realize your ex gave you the impression you don't matter, but I'm here to tell you how wrong he was. Losing you would destroy the people who know you. It would destroy *me*."

"I'm so scared."

"I'm scared, too. And in all my life, I've *never* felt the fear I felt today. Not with the grizzly, not the wolves, none of it. Nothing compares to what I felt when you almost slipped through my fingers. *Nothing*." He runs his hands over his face. "You scared me more today than I have *ever* been in my life. My *fighter* threw in the towel. You can't do that to me." His eyes flash fire. "You can't give up on me like that. Lena, I swear to God, it would've killed me."

"It won't happen again. I'm sorry. I just wanted to protect you. Wes, I . . ."

He pulls me across his lap and wraps me in his arms. My body shakes with sobs, so he draws me closer. Burying my face in his chest, I melt into his embrace and cling to him, his strength, his warmth. In this moment, we are the only two people in the world.

"I *need* you, sunshine," Wes whispers. "More than ya know."

Wes holds me for over an hour. We don't speak, just sit in comfortable silence. I squeeze his hand, lift it to my lips, and kiss his mangled knuckles.

My inner nurse finally gets her shit together, and I examine the wound on his palm. "I need to bandage this." He allows me to cleanse his hand with water from a canteen and wrap it in a strip of cloth from someone's shirt. "Let me ask you something."

"Anything."

"Why do you call yourself a fraud?"

"Because I'm living a stolen life," he mutters, looking at his hands. "I don't deserve my success."

"Um, yes, you most certainly do. The awards speak for themselves."

"Fuck the awards. They don't belong to me."

His self-degradation doesn't make sense. I've seen his films. Wes doesn't act the part; he becomes the part. His authenticity and versatility are astounding.

I raise a brow. "Sorry, but I call bullshit there."

"Acting was Reed's dream, his true passion. I wanted to teach surfing, you know, real lofty beach bum aspirations." He shifts uneasily. "But Reed lived and breathed theater, acting in plays since age five. Everything changed after the accident. I'm living the life he dreamed of. I robbed him of his future, and now he gets to watch me succeed. It just feels wrong." He stares at the tent ceiling. "This is one instance where I'm happy to take his place. I keep thanking God Reed backed out of this trip. He's been through enough. If he were lost out here . . ." Wes squeezes his eyes shut.

His self-disgust is palpable, pouring off him in waves.

"You didn't steal his life, Wes."

"Yes, I did. It's my fault. All of it."

Austin calls out to us, "Hey, y'all, I don't mean to interrupt, but I caught us another squirrel. You both need to eat somethin'."

Wes crawls to the tent flap. "He's right. Come outside with me. I want you to eat."

"Wait." I grasp his wrist. "Wes, I'm sorry—"

"I know. I'm sorry, too. Let's put it behind us." He gently grips my chin. "But I want you to promise me something. No matter what happens, whether we live or die out here, we do it together. That means no one is going rogue or sacrificing themselves to the gods. I don't know what brought us together—or why we ended up out here—but I'm not lettin' ya go. Don't you dare give up on me. Promise to hold on to me."

"I promise," I say, pressing a kiss to his knuckles. The oath comes from my heart.

CHAPTER 48

WES

Internal playlist: "Bent" by Matchbox 20

The John River winds its way south, becoming increasingly treacherous. Rocky cliffs line turbulent whitewater rapids for what appears to be miles. The opposite bank of the river boasts friendlier terrain.

I lower my binoculars. "Looks like we're gonna have to cross," I yell from my position in a tree on the summit. "This side's nothing but mountains. The river narrows a bit up ahead, so we may be able to cross there."

"Any sign of civilization?" Jake shouts.

I climb a little higher. "Actually, I think I see a plume of smoke in the distance. I'm guessing a trapper's shack." I slowly descend the tree, hop to the ground, and return the binoculars to my pack.

"Oh my God, humanity," Lena gushes.

"Don't get too excited. It's a long way off and we still have to cross the river. From what I could see, it looks like at least class-three rapids." I rub my jaw. "I dunno how we'll do it."

"Let's build a raft," Lena suggests.

I shake my head. "The current's too strong. But like I said, it narrows a bit up there, so maybe we can figure something out."

"Ain't nothin' to it but to do it," Austin says. "Let's roll, y'all."

Carefully navigating gnarled roots and slippery mossy rocks, we make our agonizing descent. We finally reach the base of the mountain at dusk. We set up camp and steel ourselves for another night in the wilderness.

I drop a load of firewood behind Lena and toss on a large hunk of birch. *She looks cold.* I retrieve a fleece and drape it over her shoulders.

"Thanks, Wes."

I sit beside her, so our thighs are touching. She leans her head on my shoulder, melting into my warmth like always. If I can keep concentrating on this moment, facing the next battles might not be so bad.

Jake paces the clearing with careful, measured steps. Brow deeply furrowed, eyes fixated on the ground, his mouth moves, but no sound comes out. I make an unsuccessful attempt to read his lips.

Is he counting?

He abruptly kneels over a pile of kindling and taps his index finger three times on every single piece. Then he rearranges the wood, lining the sticks up in size order—smallest to largest. He does the same with the rocks for the fire pit. He moves to our pile of logs and unstacks it. Then he neatly restacks it, so all the logs face the same direction—bark up. After that, he straightens the four fishing poles, carefully tucking the hooks on the line guide loops. He reaches for a tackle box, flips it open, and sorts the lures.

Enough with the rearranging.

I scratch my head. "What the hell're ya doin'?"

Jake meets my gaze. "I dunno."

"Are you all right?" I ask.

"No." Knotting his hands in his hair, he glances at Lena and settles beside her. "No, I'm not all right."

Austin leans over. "What's goin' on, man?"

"I'm losing my fucking mind."

Lena squeezes Jake's knee. "Now would be a good time to talk to your friends about it, don't you think?" Her tone confuses me, making me wonder if she knows something I don't.

Jake stares at her face for a minute, like they're sharing some unspoken message, then sighs heavily. "My anxiety is out of control. I took the last of my meds a week ago and they're not something I'm supposed to stop abruptly. On top of what I usually deal with, I'm still going through withdrawal."

"You take an anti-depressant?" Austin asks.

"Yeah," Jake mutters. "I'm on a few, but one's more specific for the type of anxiety I deal with."

"What kind of anxiety?" I study Jake. "How long have ya been dealing with this?"

And why is this the first I'm hearing about it?

"I've got major OCD, general anxiety, and depression. It's been this way—with the rituals, organizing, obsessive thoughts—for longer than I can remember. The meds keep it at bay, but right now, I feel like I'm fucking short-circuiting."

"I never knew that, mate."

"My mom and Jesse are the only ones who know." Jesse is his childhood best mate, so it makes sense Jake would tell him, but I'm a little hurt he kept me in the dark. "Mom forced me to get help years ago. I've been on meds since after my parents' divorce." He glances at Lena, then back at his hands. "Lena knows too. I told her last week when she saw me finish what was left of my meds."

"How come you never told us?" Austin asks. "Here I thought you liked shit clean and organized because you're anal. I never knew there was a reason behind it."

"I wish you'd said something." I lean in. "I know I've fucked with ya over the years. I'm sorry for being insensitive—"

"It's cool, man. You didn't know." Jake shakes his head. "I dunno, I guess I'm a suffer in silence type."

"Cut that shit out, man," Austin says. "We love you no matter what."

"We're your best mates. Don't keep shit like that from us. Like Memphis said, we love ya regardless."

"Thanks. Just bear with me; I'm anxious as fuck."

I feel like a dick for not noticing any of this before. Jake was there for me through the hardest times in my life, and all these years I've been oblivious to his pain. It bothers me that he seems ashamed of his condition, especially around Memphis and me. I study Lena's face. She never let on that she knew. While I'm slightly jealous of their bond, I appreciate that Jake can talk to her—everyone needs a sounding board and confidante. I ache to share my secrets with Lena, but I worry about what she'd think of me.

"Jake, who's your therapist?" Lena asks.

"Dr. Lola Ortiz in Manhattan. She's phenomenal."

"You're in good hands." She wraps an arm over his shoulder. "She's the doctor who saved Garrett's life."

Jake looks up at Lena. "She gave mine back to me."

CHAPTER 49

LENA

Internal playlist: "Making Love on the Mountain (Sexy Mix)"
by The Woodlands

It takes us three days to reach where the river bottlenecks. It's not as narrow as we hoped, and given the current, my raft idea is an impossibility.

It's dusk. We set up camp in a clearing near the bank.

I've lost track of the number of days we've been out here, but it must be common knowledge that I'm among the missing. A pang of guilt assails me at the thought of my mother getting this news. I never even told her I was leaving.

I worry about where Garrett's head might be. I pray I survive this mess, not just for my sake, but for his. He needs me to help keep the darkness at bay.

The men return with wood and fish and collectively collapse by the fireside. I study Wes's face. The stubble is gone. Now he's in beard territory. His face is thinner and his bronzed skin paler. He hands me a generous portion of our catch, leaving little for himself. The gesture means the world to me, but as the strongest of the group, he requires more sustenance. *This is the first thing we've eaten all day.* My stomach churns at the thought.

"Please eat more, Wes."

"I'm good. You eat."

I divide my portion in half and tilt his chin. "I don't have the energy to argue. Now, open up."

Parting his lips, he accepts the bite and squeezes my knee. "Thank you."

The only sound is the crackling of the fire, as we're all too exhausted to speak. But the desperation on our faces speaks volumes.

When everyone is fed, we retreat to our tent. Austin and Jake enter first. Wes leans over and kisses me before settling in the spot closest to the flap.

The men are all asleep in minutes, their slow, deep breathing a testament to their exhaustion. I toss and turn for several hours. We chose a shitty location for the tent, and I can't get comfortable. I move closer to Wes. He's always so warm. Shuddering, I burrow against him.

A racing mind keeps me from sleep.

What will we eat when the river freezes?

Will it hurt to freeze to death?

How will we get out of here?

We need a signal fire.

I shudder again, both from my thoughts and the temperature.

Fabric rustles and a warm arm encircles my torso. Wes is right behind me. We've been zipping our bags together ever since my hypothermia incident. Closing my eyes, I allow my body to relax and press into his warmth.

His breathing is still slow and rhythmic. I savor the weight of his arm, feel the nearness of his hand to my rib cage. I stroke my thumb in circles on the inside of his wrist and feather over the veins and tendons of his forearm.

His arm flexes and pulls me closer, his hand resting at my navel. His mouth finds my ear. "Restless, much?"

"A little." I'm lying on my side with my back to him, head cushioned by his bicep. I listen to the rush of the rapids and savor his embrace, burrowing closer.

He flattens his palm against my lower belly and pulls my hips flush, his erection pressing into my back. "Keep wiggling that arse, love." The harsh whisper tickles my ear as he trails his fingertips over my breasts.

I press my hips back and hear his sharp inhale, so I wiggle again.

Wes unzips my jeans and shoves the denim over my hips. Next comes my panties. His fingertips brush my ass as he lowers his zipper. He pushes his jeans and boxers down, and I feel his warm length against my back.

I shimmy my hips invitingly. Wes reaches between my legs, stroking a hand through the moisture.

"You're so wet for me," he whispers, lining himself up.

I press my hips back and feel the broad head of his cock slide in. "Oh, yes . . ." I whisper.

Wes grips my hips and rocks his way inside, silently taking me from behind. "Bend forward." He tightens his grip and strokes even deeper.

We both gasp. The angle of penetration curls my toes, each thrust forcing the air from my lungs.

It's pitch-black in the tent, and the guys are sleeping a few feet away. The sex feels forbidden, which turns me on even more. I know I need to be quiet, but I want to moan out my pleasure. Instead, I wrap an arm around my head and bury my face in the crook of my elbow.

Wes rolls me onto my stomach and shoves a wadded-up parka beneath my hips. It lifts them slightly, allowing him better access. I bite my arm to stifle a moan. He moves his hips in a steady rhythm, his thrusts cushioned by my ass.

Flexing my hips back, I relish the ragged breaths that leave his chest. Wes spreads my legs wider apart and changes his pace to slow, grinding thrusts.

"Oh, fuck, Lena." His lips are at my ear. "You're so wet and tight that I wanna come right now."

I fist the sleeping bag, meeting his fluid thrusts. *I'm so close. He's holding on by a thread.* Pressing my face into the ground, I tighten and relax my inner muscles. A few more thrusts bring me over the edge, my body spasming around him. I forcefully press my hips back, feeling him orgasm inside me. Harsh breaths and whispers of my name gust my ear as he rides the waves of release.

With each thrust, he embeds himself deeper in my soul. As I lie in his arms gasping, I mouth the words I wish I could say aloud.

Still tucked against Wes, nestled in our sleeping bag, my eyes flutter open when Austin climbs over my feet.

Waggling his brows, he makes a heart shape with his hands, winks, and exits the tent.

Eventually, Jake leaves too.

As the zipper closes, Wes grabs a fistful of my ass. I shiver in anticipation and roll to face him. Sliding my hands beneath his shirt, I stroke his back. Slowly. Tentatively. The way I'd pet a lion. Then, I lightly trail my nails down his spine.

Next thing I know, I'm on my back beneath him. A muscular leg wedges between mine, spreading them apart. Wes shackles my wrists, pinning my arms overhead.

"Playing with fire."

"That was the plan, Ace."

He rears up, his breathing erratic. Rocking his hips, he rubs his cock at the juncture of my thighs and watches my response. My sharp inhale makes him repeat the motion. A wicked grin comes with the third flex of his pelvis.

He releases my hands, and then his lips are on the triangle of skin below my ear. I tense.

I wait a few beats for the panic to set in, but, for the first time in nearly a decade, it doesn't. I want him to touch and kiss my neck, trust him to break that barrier.

"Stay with me, love." His whispered words soothe me. "It's just us, here in this moment. Let yourself relax. Don't think, just feel. Let me show ya how good it can feel."

My head falls back as he kisses the side of my neck. The warm wetness of his mouth contrasts with his stubble as it brushes against my collarbone.

He gently sucks and nibbles the curve of my shoulder. It's been years since I let *anyone* touch my neck. Wes unravels me, tongue gliding over the sensitive skin, fingertips stroking the column of my throat.

His lips find my neck once again. I lift my chin, allowing him access. I'm open, completely exposed to him. Trust replaces vulnerability, and fear surrenders to pleasure as he caresses my neck and throat.

I fist his hair, silently urging him on. His lips move to my collarbone. He kisses, sucks, and strokes his tongue outward to my shoulder, pausing at my scar, giving it sweet, tender kisses. He repeats this on my other side, then comes back to the center and kisses the area beneath my jaw.

"You okay, sunshine?" His breath tickles my throat.

I tilt my chin to give him more access. "Yes."

"This is mine now too. I love kissin' ya here." He swirls his tongue over my throat. "Only me?"

"Only you, Wes." I feel his smile as he licks me. "Oh, God, please don't stop."

One hand grips my shoulder. The other traces the outer curve of my breast and slides down to my hip. He lifts and presses my lower body against him, lips never leaving my jawline.

I surrender to him. Wes can do anything he wants to me. I grind my hips against him. He's enormous and rock hard. I slide my hands down his back and squeeze his ass.

Wes groans into my neck and bites my earlobe. He sucks on it while rubbing his cock against me. I nearly orgasm from him kissing the long-forgotten erogenous zones of my neck.

Cloaked in Wes's warmth, I listen to his harsh breaths and almost forget we're lost in the wilderness.

I've fallen for him.

I didn't want to, but it happened on its own. It began as a fantasy starring a stunningly gorgeous man. The fantasy hasn't faded but morphed into an affection so deep, so raw, it steals my breath. I crave his strength and direction. I'm drawn to his warmth, his humor. Thoughtful and intuitive, Wes is a haven for me to share my fears, vulnerabilities, and secrets.

He gives me strength, gives me the will to push forward. He makes me feel alive. He makes me feel safe. I gave him the most vulnerable part of my body—my neck. And when he held me close and kissed me so tenderly, giving nothing but pleasure, he broke through my remaining defenses.

I love him, completely and irrevocably.

He kisses my throat, jaw, collarbone, and shoulders, teeth grazing my skin.

"Oh, God, Wes," I hiss. My lower body surrenders to the weight of his hips and pelvis. Even through the layers of clothes, his heat ignites me. "Make love to me."

"Bossy this morning, aren't we?" he murmurs in amusement.

"Wes, I need you." I yank his zipper open and tug his jeans and boxers over his hips. My jeans and panties follow.

With our clothes shoved to the bottom of the sleeping bag, Wes presses my thighs open and moves between them.

"I need to warm you up first," he insists, sliding a finger inside me.

"No." I dig my heels in his ass. "I need you."

"Well, I'm more than happy to meet my woman's needs." Wes withdraws his finger and sucks it into his mouth. "When are ya gonna let me go down on you?"

"Not until I have a shower."

His eyes darken. "When we finally get out of here, you'd better be ready for me." He slowly eases his cock inside me, rocking his hips until he's fully seated. "I'm gonna devour ya, sunshine. You just *wait*."

He pins my hands at my shoulders and kisses beneath my left ear, swirling his tongue on my skin, stubble scraping my jaw. He thrusts in a slow, steady rhythm. *I need him deeper. I need it harder.* I writhe beneath him, hips flexing up to meet him. I tighten my legs, pulling him closer. Wes kisses my neck in a slow, sensual tease.

"Oh, God, Wes . . ."

His lips brush my ear. "Let me hear ya, sunshine."

"Please don't stop kissing me."

"You mean here?" He trails kisses down my neck.

"Yes," I lift my chin, "it feels so good."

I feel my climax building deep inside, as the thick, hot length of him strokes me, so I tighten my inner muscles.

"I love when ya squeeze me. Don't stop."

Clenching around him, I feel myself getting closer. He's so hard, he fills me so completely, the pleasure is indescribable. I rhythmically relax and tighten, my thighs pulling him deeper.

"Give it to me," I moan, jerking my hips to meet him.

Wes picks up the pace, thrusting harder and faster as his hands tighten around my wrists.

"You're paradise, Lena. I love being inside ya."

I shatter into a climax.

He seizes my mouth, lips on mine, tongue in my mouth, absorbing my moan. The orgasm goes on forever, intensified by the passion of his kiss. He doesn't stop moving. The power of his hips and the depth of his kiss bring me over the edge a second time. He releases my hands. I knot them in his hair and kiss him with everything I've got.

Hips slamming, he powers into me. "Oh, fuck . . . I'm coming." He climaxes with a feral groan, his thrusts driving me into the ground. He buries his face at my neck and moans my name, his cock pulsing as he releases inside me.

He kisses me tenderly, his fingertips stroking the sides of my face. We stay like this for a while. Hearts racing, chests heaving, bodies still joined.

"Lena, I'm crazy about you."

"I'm crazy about you too, Wes."

CHAPTER 50

LENA

Internal playlist: "Without Fear" by Dermot Kennedy

We're about to pack up camp when a strange expression crosses Jake's features. He rubs his temples and slowly sinks to a log.

"What's wrong?" I ask.

He squeezes his eyes shut. "Got tunnel vision . . . think I'm getting a migraine. Can't hike right now. I'm sorry."

I hold up my hand. "Stop apologizing."

"Between you and Lena, I'm sorry'd out, mate. Let's start strong tomorrow." Wes runs a hand through his hair. "We've gotta figure out these traps anyway. Memphis, can ya show me?"

"We need a bunch of saplings." Austin picks up the ax. "C'mon."

Wes follows Austin into the forest.

I press a hand to Jake's pale, clammy forehead. "Do you often get migraines? If so, what are your triggers?"

"A few a month." Jake sighs. "Being tired and hungry."

I pick up a canteen. "I can almost guarantee you're dehydrated. When's the last time you peed?"

"I don't remember . . ." he confesses. "Before bed?"

"You haven't gone since you woke up?"

He shakes his head.

I thrust the canteen at him. "Drink."

He takes a sip, then presses the heel of his palm against his eye socket. "This sucks."

"I know. Can I get you anything? Do you want some blueberries?"

"No thanks. If I eat anything, I'll hurl."

I gesture to the tent. "You should go nap."

"I will when they get back. I don't wanna leave you out here alone."

I smile and touch his shoulder. "Always the gentleman."

Jake snorts. "I wouldn't classify myself as a gentleman, but thanks."

"But you are. Beneath the wisecracks and sick fuckery, of course."

He bumps fists with me. "Perverts unite."

I laugh. "I'll have Garrett make us a logo—we can get bedazzled denim jackets."

"I'm down. But you've gotta put lots of sequins on mine and rhinestone it the fuck up."

"Will do. On the back, we'll have big-ass gold hearts." At his raised brow, I explain, "Hearts of gold."

He chuckles. "Yeah, a heart of gold's gotten me real far in love."

"What do you mean?"

"I mean nice guys finish last," he mutters. "At least, that's been the case for me."

"Many women don't finish at all, so it's thoughtful of you to hold off."

Jake laughs. "You're one of a kind, Lena-Bean."

We stare at the river for a few minutes. I picture the Russian model he dated for several years. "Have you seen anyone since Nadia Korchevsky?"

His lip curls. "You mean the ice queen?"

"Why? Was she bitchy?"

"Nadia had one priority—herself. She came around when it suited her, or when *she* had something to gain. She wasn't there when it mattered, and I got tired of feeling disposable."

"Yeah, you deserve better than that."

He nods. "The real kicker was when my dad died, she didn't come to his funeral—she was too busy on some runway in Paris. And no, there hasn't been anyone since."

"I'm sure you'll find a sweet girl who will be there when it counts."

"I'm starting to lose hope, Lena-Bean."

I squeeze his arm. "Don't lose hope. She's out there somewhere."

"Yeah." Clenching his jaw, Jake stares at his hands. "I know she is."

"Then what are you waiting for? Go get her."

He shakes his head. "I'm not one of those alpha types who sees what he wants and goes after it. It doesn't work like that for me. It's . . . complicated." He sips from his canteen.

"Does Wes know you're in love with his sister?"

Jake spits out his water. His widened gaze snaps to mine and redness creeps across his cheeks, spreading to his ears and neck. He opens and closes his mouth, but no sound comes out.

"Ah, I thought so." Smiling, I gently elbow his ribs. "You're not the only intuitive one out here."

He squeezes his eyes shut, releasing a heavy sigh. "No, he doesn't. And I'd like to keep it that way."

I place a hand over my heart. "Your secret's safe with me."

"Thanks."

"Does *she* know?"

"Nope," he says, popping the p.

"Well, I wouldn't be so sure of that. I think you've made yourself quite clear."

Jake tilts his head. "I'm not sure what you mean."

I flash him a giant grin. "You wrote 'Desert Rose' about her, didn't you?"

It's my favorite track from his last album. Haunting, poetic imagery infused with emotion. The song brought tears to my eyes the first time I listened to it.

"Please tell me it's not that obvious."

"Only if you're paying attention." I chuckle, patting his shoulder. "I mean, a flower blooming in adversity, a phoenix spreading her wings, those are pretty telling lines. It all makes sense now that I've seen how you react when her name comes up."

"And how's that?"

"With the body language of a lovelorn man."

He runs a hand through his chestnut waves. "I try so fucking hard not to react, but *clearly*, I'm a shitty actor."

"There are others, am I right?"

He furrows his brow. "Others?"

"Other songs about her." I wag my brows. "Like maybe an extremely sensual hidden track on *Shades?*"

He hides his face in his hands. "Fuck me."

"Well? Is it about her?"

He meets my gaze. "Yes, 'Crave' is about her. There are several songs on that album—I'm sure you've figured them out at this point, which means I'm royally fucked."

"I think I know which ones. How about the upcoming album?"

"There are at least three." He rubs his jaw. "Maybe four if I get the balls to release one of them."

"Do any of your friends know?"

"Yeah, Memphis figured it out years ago, but I think he likes having me alive, so he hasn't told Wes. The only other person who knows is Jesse, my best friend from elementary school. He's met Wes many times, but they aren't tight." He rubs his jaw, his chocolate gaze finding mine. "And now you."

"Well, you don't have to worry about me, but like I said before, what the hell are you waiting for? Go after her."

Jake eyes me in disbelief. "No fucking way."

"Why not?"

"Do you want a list?"

"Jake, you're a sweetheart. Any woman would be lucky to have you, Isla included. Why not give it a chance?"

"Uh, have you met her brothers?"

I snort. "Just the cocky, hotheaded one."

"He would feed me my balls. Oh, and need I remind you of the age difference?"

"She's twenty-three. That's grown-ass woman territory in my book." I nudge him. "You make it sound like you're in your fifties. Ten years is nothing."

"She *just* turned twenty-three, so it's nearly eleven years," he corrects me. "We're at different stages in our lives and I need *much* more than she'd be capable of giving."

"How can you be so certain of what she's capable of?"

"Because I am," he mutters, rubbing his temples. "Besides, she lives on the other side of the planet."

"Pretty sure you can afford plane tickets, Jake Bennett."

He sighs. "She's off-limits, forbidden fruit, however you want to classify her. I have too much respect for Wes and Reed."

"I think Wes would want to see his best friend happy and his sister with a man who'd treat her like a queen."

"I'm not crossing that line, Lena-Bean."

"Fair enough." I can tell he's getting flustered, so I drop it.

After what feels like an hour, Wes and Austin return with armloads of saplings. Wes drops the hatchet near a log, squeezing Jake's shoulders as he passes him.

Austin stops in front of Jake. "How are you feelin', man?"

"Like shit," Jake mutters. "Head's throbbing and I'm nauseous."

"Good thing we've got our own personal nurse out here, mate." Wes smiles at me.

"Well, *someone* needs to play the caretaker role." I chuckle. "Who knew my role-playing abilities were so awesome?"

Wes settles beside me, resting a hand on my knee. "What other roles have you played?"

"Been Garrett's wife a time or two." Thinking back to *Karaoke Kamikaze*, I shudder.

"This I'd love to hear," Wes murmurs darkly.

Austin snickers. "Oh, shit. Here comes Double-D, the caveman."

"What? I'm curious," Wes insists.

I wave them off. "It's a long, ridiculous story."

"Aw, c'mon, Lena," Austin drawls. "Let us in on the fun."

"Let's just say there's a particular karaoke bar in Manhattan I'm banned from."

"*You're* banned from an establishment?" Jake breathes. "I'm shocked, Lena-Bean."

"Not one of my finest moments."

"Now you *have* to tell us," Wes teases.

"Okay, fine." I point at them. "But no judging." I perk up and flash a wicked grin. "And first, you need to tell me what Double-D stands for."

Wes barks a laugh. "These fuckers are jealous of my anatomy, so they started calling me Dino Dick years ago."

I giggle. "I'd say it's a fitting nickname."

Jake makes a pretend barfing gesture. "Enough about Emerson's manhood. We wanna know about *your* illegal activities." He rubs his hands together in excitement.

"All right. So, I'd just dumped my cheating boyfriend. This was the guy before Marc," I explain with an eye roll. "Anyway, the hospital was having some big party in Manhattan. I didn't wanna fly solo, so I made Garrett come. The event was boring, so a bunch of us headed to a karaoke bar to get drunk and sing."

"Sounds like a top night to me," Jake says. "Which bar? I'm dying to know."

I flash a devious grin. "I'll never tell. Anyway, Gar's always on board when it comes to karaoke. So, we get there, and by this point, I'd already had a few drinks. You know, drowning my sorrows and whatnot. Garrett doesn't drink, so he was busy mingling. He ran into some clients and got sucked into small talk. Meanwhile, I hit up the bar and knocked back a few kamikaze shots. Then, my drunk ass got onstage and started belting out Mariah Carey's 'Fantasy.'"

The guys all laugh.

"I got all flirty with some guy while singing." I notice Wes's gaze darken. "I finished the song and he started to chat me up."

"Where was Garrett?" Wes asks.

"He'd gone to the men's room. I was drunk, and I stupidly followed the guy outside to the back alley." I shake my head. "The asshole started getting handsy . . . and uh, wouldn't stop. He went to kiss me, but I deflected it. When I tried to get away, he grabbed my arm and dragged me down the alleyway." I gnaw my lip. "I was so fucking stupid, you know?"

Wes touches my knee. "How did you get away?"

"Garrett couldn't find me, and a coworker told him some guy had brought me outside. He charged through the door and bolted after us. The guy heard him coming and stopped. But he didn't let go of my arm. Gar said, 'You have one second to get your fucking hands off my wife.' The guy still didn't let go. *Then*, he had the balls to take a swing. Now, if you hit Garrett, you'd better make it count—he's an avid boxer with MMA training. If he gets up, you're fucked." I sip from my canteen. "The guy's fist grazed Gar's shoulder. By that point, I'd pulled free. Garrett yanked me behind him just as the asshole took another swing. This time, the punch hit the middle of his chest. Well, Gar went *nuts* on the guy. Punched him in the face and literally threw him in a dumpster."

Jake's mouth falls open. "Holy shit. He doesn't fuck around."

"You have no idea. Meanwhile, someone had called the cops—"

"Oh, snap," Austin murmurs.

"Next thing I know, Garrett and I are sitting in the back of a cop car."

Wes cocks his head. "Why were *you* in the cop car?"

"Well, I might've hit some chick with a beer bottle. Apparently, dumpster guy was her boyfriend. She went after Garrett. Naturally, I had to kick her ass."

"Sunshine, you surprise me every day," Wes muses. "You guys get locked up?"

"Surprisingly, no. There were plenty of witnesses. Garrett acted in my defense and I reciprocated. We were banned from the bar, but that was it."

"I'm glad Garrett was there, darlin'," Austin says.

"Damn right," Wes agrees, squeezing my knee.

"Me too. He'll never let me live it down, though. And I'm not allowed to do kamikazes . . . like, ever again." I snort a laugh. "He calls that night *Karaoke Kamikaze*. And, to this day, anytime he hears that Mariah Carey song, he makes it a point to fuck with me."

"Kinda how Bennett fucks with Wes," Austin points out.

"Somewhat," I say, nodding. "But with Gar, it's more of a 'remember I always have your back' type of thing. When I think about how reckless I was and what could've happened, I'm so grateful for him. He keeps me in line."

"I have Wes's back, too," Jake insists. "I just love pissing him off."

I wink. "I never would've guessed that."

CHAPTER 51

LENA

Internal playlist: "Seven Devils" by Florence + The Machine

The following morning, Austin taps on the tent fabric. "Wake up, y'all. We caught us a rabbit."

"We'll be right out." I nudge Wes awake. "Morning, sunshine."

I kiss him sweetly. "We caught a rabbit. Let's go see."

Wes sits up and stretches. Then, he flashes a devious smile in my direction. "The rabbit's not going anywhere, poor bloke's already dead."

"Not now, Ace." Lowering my voice to a whisper, I add, "The guys are right outside."

Wes cocks a brow. "You think that bothers me?"

"Clearly, it doesn't. But we need to eat and get moving. Plus, I want to check on Jake."

"Was worth a try."

We climb from the tent and approach the fire. Austin holds a dead rabbit in one hand and a knife in the other.

"Wow, mate. He's huge." Wes marvels at the creature.

"Our traps were successful. We caught this fella in the deadfall."

"What the hell's a deadfall?" I ask.

"Basically, you cut notches in some sticks and prop up a big rock. The animal grabs the bait, knocks the sticks outta whack, and down comes the rock," Austin explains with corresponding hand gestures.

I pat his shoulder. "I'm impressed."

Austin grins. "I'm gettin' the hang of this trappin' thang."

I turn to Jake. "How are you feeling?"

"Much better." He gives me a small smile, his gaze locking with mine. "Thank you . . ." His eyes finish the sentence for him.

"Anytime."

Our heart-to-heart brought us closer, and while I've never been in his situation, I understand Jake's need for a confidante, even if *he* doesn't realize he needs one. From his eyes, to his posture, to the tone of his voice—Jake changes at the mention of Isla. I wonder how Wes hasn't noticed. Or maybe he knows and chooses to ignore it. Doubtful. From what Jake told me, Wes would lose his shit if he knew. Poor Jake. Talk about a rock and a hard place.

Glancing at the sweet little bunny, I gnaw my lip.

WES

"It's survival, Lena," I murmur, tipping her chin.

"What? I didn't say anything."

"It's all over your face."

She sighs. "He's just a cute bunny, that's all."

I grip her shoulders. "Come with me. You're not gonna watch Austin skin him. Let's get more kindling." I steer her away from the dead rabbit.

"I'm heading downstream to snag a couple of fish." Jake gestures to where the river bottlenecks.

I point to a downed tree in the distance. "Let's check out that tree. Bark looks dry."

It's an uphill climb. Lena and I carefully step over rocks, logs, and tangles of roots that protrude from the soil. The tree fell toward the cliff-like riverbank, and the top branches dangle over the edge. We have to yell to hear each other over the deafening roar of the rapids.

Prodding the tree trunk, I peel off a layer of bark. "I'm gonna break off some branches," I shout.

Lena gives me a thumbs-up and stoops to grab a clump of dry grass.

I make my way along the length of the tree, stopping about a meter from the edge. As I snap off some dead limbs, my parka snags on a branch. I give it a tug, but it won't budge. *Shit.* I forcefully yank it free, sending me off-balance. I throw my arms out to catch myself but slide on a patch of wet moss and lose my footing.

A startled shout escapes me as I fall.

CHAPTER 52

LENA

*Internal playlist: *SCREAMING**

Wes yells, and I look up in time to see him slam his head on a rock and plummet into the river.

"Wes! *No!*" An inhuman scream rips from my throat as I rush to the edge.

I watch in horror as the current pulls his limp body beneath the surface. My legs move without command. Screaming for Jake and Austin, I race down the embankment toward our camp. I catch sight of Jake downriver and flail my arms, motioning to the rapids.

"Lena! What's wrong?" Jake bellows.

"Wes fell in the river! He hit his head—" Tripping on a root, I tumble headlong to the ground. Pain blooms across my face. I struggle to my feet and stagger forward, blinded by the blood and tears running into my eyes.

Oh God, please help us save him.

The guys intercept Wes, pulling his body from the water. I burst through the brush and dive to the ground beside him, noticing his skin's sickening blue pallor.

"He's not breathing." I morph into nurse mode, shouting commands, "Get the wet clothes off him. We need to bring his temp up!"

Jake and Austin strip Wes of his boots, pants, and coat. I wrap my parka around his lower body. Pressing my ear to his chest, I feel his neck for a pulse. *Nothing.*

"Fuck." I yank open his flannel. "His heart's not beating!" I tear his T-shirt down the center and shove the fabric aside.

I position my hands on his bare chest and lock my arms. Counting aloud, I perform thirty chest compressions. With a head tilt and chin-lift, I open Wes's airway. Pinching his nostrils closed, I seal my mouth over his, breathing into his lungs. I watch his rib cage rise and repeat with a second breath.

"Please come back to me."

I reposition myself for the next cycle. Again, I count to thirty and assess his breathing. Still nothing.

Two more rescue breaths.

More compressions.

"What can we do, Lena?" Austin knots his hands in his hair.

"Breathe for me. I'll tell you when. Tip his head back, tilt his chin up, and pinch his nose. Breathe steadily for one second. Watch for his chest to rise," I gasp between compressions. "Twenty-nine and thirty. Now!"

Austin provides two breaths.

I feel for a pulse. "Goddammit, Wes, don't you fucking do this to me." I continue the compressions, tears spilling from my eyes.

"Breathe!" I shriek, knowing damn well that CPR has low success rates outside of a hospital setting. Smoke from the campfire fills my nostrils, burning my eyes. As I stare down at the man I love, images of the apartment victims fill my mind. Limp, lifeless souls, their bodies bleeding. Mangled. Bones broken. Limbs crushed. I held on to them as the light faded from their eyes. I performed CPR, breathed into their lungs—just like I'm doing now—and still, I lost them.

I can't lose him. I can't let him die.

Two more breaths.

My arms burn. A muscle in my neck seizes up. I don't stop.

I won't stop.

A strangled sob escapes me. "Wes, *please . . .*"

Please don't take him from me.

CHAPTER 53

LENA

Internal playlist: *PRAYING*

My body shakes on a sob as I begin another cycle. I can't see through my tears or hear over the buzzing in my head.

"Wes, please . . ." My arms give out and I collapse forward. "Austin, take over," I gasp.

He jumps in and finishes out the cycle.

I seal my mouth over Wes's and breathe.

Come back to me. Please, don't leave me.

Jake places his hand on my shoulder. I press two fingertips against Wes's neck and freeze.

Oh, God, please . . .

I snatch his wrist. A *pulse!* Faint, but it's there.

"Lena, what's going on?" Jake whispers through his tears.

"His heart's beating! Quick, help me roll him onto his left side."

Jake and Austin turn Wes to his side. He coughs. Water trickles from his mouth. He coughs again. More water. His chest lurches in a gasp and he coughs again.

I turn my attention to the gash on his head. "Jake, give me your scarf." He hands it over, and I wrap it around Wes's head in a makeshift bandage. "He can't afford to lose more blood. We need to bring his body temp up and you two need dry clothes. Let's bring him to camp. Watch his left shoulder. I think it's dislocated."

The guys carry Wes to the sleeping bag I placed by the fire. They dress him in dry socks, boxers, and jeans.

"Don't bother with a shirt. I'll have to take it off when I put his shoulder back into place. Someone, please boil some water. I need to clean his wounds."

Jake lurches to his feet with a canteen.

I turn my focus to Wes's breathing. He still hasn't come to. It's better this way—his body's protecting him from the pain.

Now that his heart is beating, his lungs are working, and the bleeding is under control, I need to assess his injuries. I know I'm dealing with multiple rib fractures as I felt one break when I performed CPR. It's a common, albeit unfortunate, side effect of the chest compressions. His feet and legs are fine—I took note of that before they dressed him. The waist up is a mess.

"Austin, I need something to prop his arm up so I can stabilize his shoulder."

He retreats to the tent, returning with a folded blanket. I position it under Wes's upper arm and shoulder.

"Fortunately, I can treat a shoulder dislocation. The problem is that without x-rays, I have no way of knowing if there are underlying fractures or tears. Then again, there's nothing I could do anyway."

The muscles of his shoulder and upper arm begin to spasm.

"I'd prefer for him to be awake for this, but that's not an option." I look up at Austin and Jake grimly. "There's already a good deal of inflammation. His muscles are spasming. I have to do it before any more damage is done."

"What do you need to do, and how can we help?" Austin asks.

"I wanna check out the rest of his torso, and I'll need you both to assist. Sorry, Jake, you're not gonna like this one, but I need you."

"Whatever you need. You're in charge here," Jake says.

"As I suspected, he has several fractured ribs." I slide my hands over his torso. I palpate his right side and count. "Jesus Christ. I think I can feel four. My hospital has a three-rib threshold, meaning if a patient has three or more fractured ribs, we admit them. They're given oxygen and a morphine drip. We keep them for a few days and monitor them. I'm flying blind out here. I have no diagnostic tools and nothing to give him for pain."

"Can't we use something to bind them? Won't the pressure help?" Austin asks. He's clearly watched enough hospital dramas in his lifetime to know the usual treatments.

"We don't do that anymore because it prevents the person from inhaling deeply or coughing. If they only take shallow breaths and don't cough to clear secretions, there's an increased risk of pneumonia. With the amount of water he aspirated, his risk is already through the roof. And when he wakes up, he'll be in so much pain that there's no way he'll be able to inhale deeply." I press my ear to his chest. "And if he has a punctured or collapsed lung, there's nothing I can do."

Closing my eyes, I listen to the breath fill his chest. It sounds normal, but without my stethoscope, I can't tell for certain. A punctured lung would be a death sentence in this environment, and we fought so hard to save him.

"Okay, here's what's going to happen. I need you guys to sit him up. Jake, get behind him and hold him steady. Austin, you'll apply traction to his arm, and I'll manipulate his shoulder blade until it pops back into place. This isn't my favorite technique, but given that we don't have a gurney, I have no choice."

The men lift and support Wes's torso while I grasp his wrist. I guide his arm, holding it parallel to the ground.

"Austin, kneel in front of him. With your right hand, pull his arm straight forward. Your left hand will rest on his collarbone and push the shoulder back. You'll be pushing and pulling in opposite directions at the same time. Make sense?"

He nods, moving into position.

"Okay, Austin, start gently. I want firm, continuous pressure, not jerky movements." I take my place at Wes's side. "I'm going to rotate his scapula until the joint pops in." Placing my hands on his shoulder blade, I slowly manipulate the bone, guiding it to its proper position. "A little firmer, Austin. Rotate his arm outward. Slide your right hand farther up his arm. Perfect. Keep the pressure steady. Just a little further." The audible clunk of the glenoid fossa returning to its home is a welcome sound. "Bingo. Nice work, guys."

Jake looks like he's going to hurl.

"You all right, Bennett?" Austin asks.

"Just gimme a minute," he mutters. "Lena, I don't know how you do what you do."

"You fix a lotta shoulders?" Austin asks as we slowly lower Wes to his back.

"Yes. My hospital's a level-one trauma center, so unfortunately, I see a lot of dislocations and fractures. Usually, I'm the one in your spot, assisting the physician with joint relocation. But I told you my ex is an orthopedic surgeon, right?"

They nod.

"When he's not in the OR, Marc spends a lot of time seeing patients in the emergency department, which is where I usually am. Like most hospitals, we're over-budget and understaffed. We have three orthopedists, though we could really use double that. The physicians rely heavily on nurses for assistance. He taught me several relocation techniques. Even after we split, if I'm working, he requests me for the assist."

"Is it hard to work with him?" Jake hands me the pot of steaming water, which still needs to cool a bit before I can use it.

"Oddly enough, no. Marc's a brilliant surgeon. Professionally, we make an excellent team. I respect him. But he was a terrible partner. The trouble with Marc is that there's no off switch. It's not healthy to be in job-mode twenty-four seven. That leaves nothing for himself or anyone else. I needed so much more than he was able to give. You know, like time and attention."

"I've seen many breakups in the entertainment industry where the couple can't even be around one another. That's good that you can still work together, and it doesn't make you uncomfortable," Jake says.

"It really doesn't. I hope he finds someone who can draw him out of the darkness." I turn my focus to the unconscious man in front of me. "Okay, Mr. Emerson, you have a heartbeat, you're breathing, the bleeding's stopped, and your shoulder's in place. So far, so good. I can't do anything about your ribs or your pain level." I run through the checklist aloud, more for my own benefit than anyone else's.

"You knew exactly what to do . . . and how to do it." Austin has a catch in his voice.

"That's triage, baby. Tackle each problem in order of severity until your patient is stable and good to go. Unfortunately, we aren't out of the woods yet. God, I wish I only meant that figuratively." I pull my hair into a bun. *I'm a mess.* Dirty. Covered in both of our blood. Clothes torn. And that's just my appearance. I gently probe the wound at my temple. It stopped bleeding but throbs like a bitch.

"Our major issues are pain control and pneumonia prevention. We can only do so much, so that means we keep him comfortable. We make sure he's warm, rested, and hydrated. And when he's ready, we feed him. We're gonna have to hang in this location for a while because there's no way he'll be ready to hike anytime soon."

I retrieve a tank top I washed yesterday, dip it in the warm water, then wring out the excess.

"Let's clean you up before we move you into the tent," I murmur, gently dabbing the cloth on Wes's forehead. I wipe away dirt and dried blood, pausing to rewet the cloth.

"You saved his life." Austin's voice is barely above a whisper. "I'll never be able to thank you enough for what you did today."

Our eyes meet. His baby blues are bloodshot and weary.

"You and Jake were as much a part of this. I wouldn't have been able to pull him from those rapids. I just did what I've been trained to do."

"So, the fact that you care for him means nothing?" Jake levels me with a hard stare.

"Listen, I've been a nurse for nearly a decade. During my career, I've performed CPR dozens of times. Sometimes successfully, sometimes not. But it's always been in a controlled environment, never out in the middle of nowhere. There have always been other medical professionals, defibrillators, oxygen, epinephrine—all the tools I'm accustomed to having at my disposal. And I've been fortunate to never have to do it on someone I know. This was the first time I had to rely solely on my hands. This was the first time I had to fight to save someone whom I . . ."

Eyes welling, I clench my jaw. I inhale deeply, forcing back the wave of emotion that threatens to pull me under. *I can't go there right now.* Jake rests his hand on my shoulder. I glance at him. Compassion fills his warm, brown eyes. *He knows.* The look on Austin's face tells me they both do.

Our heads all turn at Wes's anguished moan. Fists clenched, his head thrashes from side to side.

"Is he all right?" Austin kneels at his right side.

"He's hurting. He's in what they call an agitated semi-conscious state. Basically, he's aware of his pain on a subconscious level. When he comes out of it, he's going to be very disoriented. The only thing he'll understand is pain. Be prepared for that." I sigh deeply. "I wish I could make it easier for him. I'd give anything for a vial of morphine."

I wring the cloth out and dab at the dried blood on his ear. Wes moans again, both legs twitching. I stroke his cheek, wiping the remaining blood from his face. I use a different shirt to dry his hair. I lift one of his clenched fists and gently massage the back of his hand until his fingers relax.

Wes mumbles something incoherent. His teeth grind. His eyes flutter open. Vivid orbs stare straight ahead, unable to focus. Hissing in pain, he squeezes them shut. A vein in his neck bulges.

It's hard to watch, but just like that, he drifts out of consciousness.

"Why don't we get him into the tent now? We can settle him before he resists moving," I suggest.

"Jake, you get his legs." Austin carefully slides his arms under Wes's torso and lifts.

I hold the tent flap open. They lay him down, and I zip Wes into a sleeping bag. I fold a sweatshirt and place it under his head as a makeshift pillow. A different shirt cushions his shoulder. Fairly confident his lungs are intact; I sit beside him and monitor his breathing.

Austin sits on his other side, arms hugging his bent knees.

"I'll cook that rabbit. We're all fried, and we need to keep up our strength if we're going to help him," Jake says. "Lena, do you need me to heat more water?"

"Yes, please."

Austin flicks on one of the lanterns. We sit in silence, listening to Wes breathe.

"This whole nightmare has opened my eyes," he says after a few minutes. "All my life, I've taken so much for granted. Worried about dumb shit. Always waitin' for the next big thing. Like, if I sell X-number of albums or win this award or tour X-number of cities, I'll be happy. But it's never enough. I swear to God, if we live through this, I'm gonna make damn sure I'm more present. If I get to meet my child, I'm gonna savor every waking moment. This life's a gift. I see it so clearly now."

"Me, too. I want to actually participate in my life, not just watch the years fly by. I've been out of school a decade, but it feels like I graduated yesterday. All those years are a blur." I shake my head sadly. "And I'm going to start telling people how I feel about them, not assume they know. If I ever see my mom, Garrett, or my friend Rita again, I'll never take another minute with them for granted. I'll make sure they know how I feel."

"What about Wes? You gonna tell him how you feel?" He meets my gaze intently.

I glance at Wes before returning my focus to Austin. "I'm not sure that matters."

"What the hell do you mean?"

"You know how I feel." I stare back at him. "But I'm an ordinary girl, no matter what Wes thinks. I want him, Austin. I want all of him— good, bad, or indifferent. Sometimes I see it so clearly. Then I remember I wanted the same things with my ex. I know Wes isn't Marc; God, they're worlds apart. But there's still a part of me that feels like I'm not good enough for anyone, let alone Wes."

"I wouldn't be so sure of that. There's a lot you don't know about him. He puts on a good front, but he's an ordinary guy."

"He's far from ordinary."

"And so are you." He shakes his head. "I wish you'd open your eyes."

We sit in silence for a few minutes. I remember something Wes mentioned that I've been meaning to ask about.

"Can I ask you something, Austin?"

"Sure, girlie."

"What happened to Reed?"

Austin tilts his head. "Why do you ask?"

"Wes said something the other day that bothered me. I'm trying to understand where he's coming from. We were discussing Reed's accident and he started to elaborate, but then you called us outside to eat."

"Reed lost a lot of blood, and the doctors didn't think he was gonna make it. He damaged his spinal cord and busted up his leg. The surgeons told his parents that if he survived, he'd never walk again."

"Oh my God."

"But Reed's a fighter. He pulled through and proved those suckers wrong. He did his physical therapy and relearned how to walk. He's got a limp now, but he gets around okay. It was a rough time for their family. Then a few years later, his little sister got sick."

"Wes told me about Isla's transplant."

"Did he? I'm surprised. He's very private about his family."

"So, I gather Reed doesn't act anymore. What does he do now?"

"He's Wes's manager. Keeps track of everything like contracts, schedule, and finances. The business aspect suits him," Austin answers. "He's also the admin for all of the social media accounts—Wes hates that shit."

"Do you think he resents Wes?"

"I think Reed's happy to be alive. He's never expressed any bad feelings toward Wes."

"Then why does Wes feel like he stole his brother's life?" I ask.

"He told you that?" Austin breathes.

"Yes. He said he was a fraud and that everything was his fault. Like I said, he started to elaborate, but we were cut off."

"Lena, the fact that you know anything about the accident speaks volumes. Wes doesn't talk about that night with anyone, not even me. All my information came from Reed. Wes doesn't normally talk about his feelings. Before this trip, I'd only seen him cry once, and that was when he learned Isla needed dialysis."

"But he's cried a few times now."

"And each time it had something to do with you, darlin'. Don't mean to make you feel bad, but I'm tryin' to prove my point. Remember what I told you when we first got here? He's different with you."

"Then tell me why he feels this way."

Austin sighs. "Reed scored the lead in a surfin' flick, but the accident forced him to surrender the part. The producers offered Wes the role instead." He rubs his jaw. "Wes wanted nothing to do with it. Didn't wanna steal his brother's thunder. Reed convinced him to take it though."

"So, he took Reed's place in the film and got noticed?"

"Exactly. Wes won't talk about it, but I can sense his guilt. He rose to fame while Reed was sidelined."

"I guess I can understand why he'd feel guilty," I concede. "But what I don't get is why he holds himself responsible for Reed's misfortune. He kept saying it was his fault—"

"Reed wasn't supposed to go out that night. He'd had a long week and wanted to hang at home. Wes had planned to go joyridin' with the guys but backed out when his jealous girlfriend gave him hell. Rachel was always hittin' him with guilt and ultimatums, even before the fame. Anyway, he convinced Reed to go in his place, told him he needed a night out." He meets my gaze. "Reed was ridin' Wes's motorcycle when a drunk driver ran a red light and T-boned him."

"Oh my God," I whisper in shock.

His guilt, his self-disgust, all makes sense. Burdened by his own success, Wes has carried the weight of Reed's accident on his shoulders for years.

Wes groans, shuffling his legs and fisting the sleeping bag. Torso arching off the ground, a pained moan escapes his throat. I stroke his hair. Panic-stricken eyes shoot open, darting wildly.

"You're all right, Wes," I murmur, leaning over him.

He lurches upward, backing away from us.

"Take it easy, man. It's us," Austin says.

I crawl toward him. "Baby, you're all ri—"

Wes's fist connects with my shoulder. I try to get out of his way, but I'm not fast enough. His second swing hits me square in the mouth. I scream and fall backward.

Austin lunges on top of him, pinning his arms to his sides. "Stop!"

Wes bucks beneath him, bellowing incoherently.

I cower in the corner. I taste the blood that pours from my split lower lip. Wes kicks and flails like a wild beast, dangerously unaware and extremely strong.

Jake charges into the tent. "What the fuck just happened?"

"Wes, enough!" Austin roars. "Stop!"

He finally breaks through. The fight leaves Wes's body and he slumps against the ground. Panting, with sweat pouring from his brow, he stares at Austin in bewilderment. He tries to sit up, but Austin holds him in place.

"Take it easy, man. You're hurt real bad. Stop fightin' me."

Jake grabs my arm, pulling me from the tent.

CHAPTER 54

WES

*Internal playlist: * SOMEONE PLEASE FUCKING KILL ME NOW*

"What happened?" I ask on a moan. Every breath is agony. My head throbs, and my left shoulder is on fire. "It . . . hurts . . . to breathe . . ."

Austin releases me, sitting back on his heels. "What do you remember?"

"I was with Lena. Nothing . . . makes sense. There was a tree. We were . . . gathering bark. My coat got stuck . . . I fell." I remember slipping, and then everything went black. "Where's Lena?"

"Outside with Jake." Austin takes a deep breath. "I didn't see it go down, but according to Lena, you lost your balance, hit your head, and tumbled into the river."

It hurts to talk, but I need to understand my pain. "Jesus Christ . . . how'd I get out?"

"Lena screamed for us. Jake and I intercepted you downstream. We dragged you outta the river. She took over and started CPR."

I stare at Austin in shock.

"You weren't breathing, man. You had no pulse . . . nothing. Your skin was blue. You were . . . gone." His eyes fill with tears. "I watched that woman bring you back from the dead. She breathed into your lungs, forced your heart to beat with her bare hands until her fucking arms gave out. She felt a pulse just as I took over."

Unable to speak, I just stare.

"You were gushin' blood from where you hit your head. She bandaged that. We dressed you in dry clothes and moved you by the fire. Your left shoulder was completely out of its socket. We helped her put it back in. You have at least four broken ribs. She cleaned the blood and dirt off your face." He takes a steadying breath. "She hasn't left your side, man. Not until a few minutes ago."

"That's why I can't fucking . . . breathe," I groan.

Austin looks up as Jake unzips the tent and climbs in.

"Hey, man, welcome back." Jake squeezes my hand. "I've been sent to find a dry shirt." He scans the tent and reaches for Lena's bag.

"How is she?" Austin asks, raising a brow.

"What's wrong with Lena?"

AUSTIN

Avoiding Wes's gaze, I watch Jake intently.

"Physically, she's coming around, but the adrenaline's worn off." Jake runs a hand through his hair. "She fell apart. Completely broke down. Been sobbing for the past ten minutes. I need new shirts for both of us."

"Why's there blood on your shirt?" Wes asks.

"I dunno. It's probably yours," he answers Wes, but his eyes remain locked on mine.

"I wanna see her," Wes whispers.

I raise a brow.

Jake shakes his head and slowly backs out of the tent. "Not right now, man. She needs some time."

"Why can't I see her? Why ya acting strange?" Wes lifts his head and stares at me.

I sigh. "Listen, man, I don't wanna upset you—"

"Tell me."

"You've been driftin' in and out of consciousness. You're in a lotta pain. You're disoriented."

"No, I'm not."

"Maybe not right now, but minutes ago, you were a rabid animal."

"What're ya getting at, Memphis?"

"What I'm tryin' to say is, you hurt her."

"The fuck you mean, I hurt her?" Wes growls.

"You came out swingin' and you hit her. You were out of it. We know you didn't mean to, she just happened to be in the line of fire—"

"I hit her?" he whispers.

"You," I swallow tightly, "aw, fuck, man, I'm sorry." I pinch the bridge of my nose. "You punched her . . . twice. I dove on you and Jake dragged her to safety."

He stares in horror.

"I'm not tryin' to upset you, but you should be prepared so it isn't a shock when you see her." I meet his tortured gaze. "You split her lip. The blood on Jake's shirt is hers."

I knew it wasn't going to be a well-received message, but I had to tell him. It guts me to watch as desolate tears slide down his cheeks into his ears. They keep coming. He doesn't make a sound, just stares at the top of the tent, his face twisted in a mask of torment.

"She's not upset with you, none of us are. Like I said, man, you weren't even conscious. No one blames you."

He doesn't answer.

I rest a hand on his shoulder. "It's all right, man."

"No," Wes grinds out, "it's *not* all right. She saves my life and I assault her? I'm a fucking monster." He turns to face me. "I need to talk to her. I need to fix it."

"What you need to do is relax. You just had the ever-lovin' shit beat out of you by that river. You need to sleep so you can heal. Rest now and you can talk to her in the morning." I move to leave the tent.

"Austin, please . . ." His anguished whisper freezes me in place.

"I'll see if she's up to it," I murmur, leaving him alone with his thoughts.

CHAPTER 55

LENA

Internal playlist: "Meaning of Life" by Kelly Clarkson

I'm raw. My throat hurts from crying, and I feel stupid for underestimating Wes's strength. I knew he could awaken in an agitated state, but in my desire to be close to him, I ignored the signs.

Jake hands me more rabbit meat. "Eat."

I take a small bite and thank him. He hauled me from that tent, gave me a cold compress for my lip, and comforted me when I sobbed uncontrollably. Once the adrenaline wore off, I could barely hold myself up.

Wes had been, by all medical standards, dead. My colleagues would've stopped CPR, would've accepted the inevitable, but I couldn't let go. Refusing to state a time of death for the man I love, I kept going until my body wouldn't let me. And by some miracle, some act of God, he pulled through.

Another wave of emotion threatens to consume me. A sob rips from my throat, and Jake pulls me close.

"He was gone, Jake. I was moments away from calling it."

"I know," he whispers, resting his chin atop my head.

Wrapping my arms around him, I weep into his chest, soaking his shirt. "I almost let him go."

"But you didn't. And we love you for that."

"I love him, Jake. So fucking much."

"Make sure he knows that. I dunno if Memphis told him what happened yet, but when he does, it will destroy him."

A few minutes later, Austin approaches and settles beside me. He gently pats my knee and tilts my chin to face him.

His eyes widen. "You all right, darlin'?"

"Physically, it hurts, but I'll be fine. Lord knows, it's not the first time a patient's hit me. I feel like an idiot. I should've seen it coming. All the signs were there. Had it been anyone else and had I been at work, he would've been stabbed in the ass with a sedative." I sniff and force a weak smile. "He sleeping?"

"No, he's awake," Austin answers, "and he's requestin' your company."

I lurch to my feet.

He grabs my wrist. "Easy there, cowgirl. He's not goin' anywhere. Listen, I told him everything that happened—"

"How'd he take it?" Jake asks.

"Not good, man." Austin squeezes his eyes shut. "He's fuckin' devastated."

"I'm fine," I insist.

"Lena, he punched you. Twice. He's disgusted with himself. I've never seen him this upset. He's in there cryin' his eyes out."

"But it wasn't his fault."

Austin rubs the back of his neck. "Try tellin' him that."

"I'm sure I look like shit, but I'll be back to normal in a week or so." I probe the wound on my temple again. The bruising on my cheekbone is tender to the touch and my split lower lip feels huge. "I'll go set him straight. He was hurting and scared. I got in the way of his fight or flight. That's it, plain and simple."

"Good luck," Austin whispers as I walk away.

CHAPTER 56

WES

Internal playlist: "Power Over Me" by Dermot Kennedy

I lie in total darkness, wondering if Lena will come to me. The fact that I hit her—not once, but *twice* sickens me to my core.

"Knock, knock." Lena's voice breaks the silence. "I'm coming in." She unzips the flap and climbs inside. "What happened to the lantern?"

"Turned it off," I reply in a strained voice.

"Oh, okay. How are you feeling?"

"Like shit."

"You thirsty? I can bring you some water."

"No, thank you."

"Well, sooner or later, you're gonna have to eat and drink something. I have no qualms about force-feeding you, just so you know." She kneels by my feet.

Silence stretches between us.

"Austin said you wanted to talk to me, but I don't hear you talking."

"I'm sorry," I whisper. "Lena, I am so—" My breath catches in my throat. "Sorry."

"I know." She rests her hand on my ankle. "I'm not upset with you. You were scared and in pain."

"It's no excuse."

She crawls to my side and runs her hand through my hair and down my cheek. "Wes, stop. I'm fine." Cupping my face in her hands, she softly kisses my forehead.

I flick on the lantern. She pulls away, hiding her face in the shadows.

"Come here. Let me see what I did."

As expected, she ignores my command, so I grip her wrist and pull her. My breath catches at the sight of her face.

"See? I'm fine. Moving along."

"Jesus Christ," I whisper. "I'm so fucking sorry." My voice breaks, and more tears slide down my cheeks. Reaching up, I brush the hair off her forehead. "Fuck."

"Stop. You can't hold yourself accountable for something that happened in semi-consciousness. Your eyes were open, but you weren't seeing what was in front of you. You backed away like a cornered raccoon. I'm the idiot who went after you. I was perceived as a threat. It's science, Ace."

"I'm the threat," I say in disgust.

"Okay, you know what? You're starting to piss me off with this self-degradation. This is a pattern with you, and it needs to stop. Bad things happen, Wes. You can't keep everyone safe, and you can't blame yourself for life's every tragedy. It isn't your responsibility to carry the weight of the world on your shoulders."

"Except when it's my fault."

She grips my chin, forcing me to meet her gaze. "You did *not* cause Reed's accident. *You* weren't the drunk who got behind the wheel that night. Survivor's guilt serves no one. What happened was horrendous, but it wasn't your fault. Remember that Reed survived. He loves you, and, though I don't know him, I'm willing to bet my life he doesn't blame you, either. You need to forgive yourself, Wes."

Lena reaches for my uninjured hand, interlaces our fingers, and squeezes. I stare at the tent ceiling as the tears slide down. She wipes my cheeks and continues, "You've gotta let go of what happened." Lifting my hand to her swollen mouth, she presses a kiss to my knuckles. "Stop torturing yourself and move forward."

"But I hurt you." *I keep hurting people I love.*

"You still don't get it, but so help me God, I'm gonna get through to you." She takes a deep breath. "You nearly died. Correction, you *were* dead. The trauma sustained by your body is unimaginable, and that's coming from a trauma nurse. Your job now is to rest. I need you to breathe deeply and cough when you feel the urge, no matter how much it hurts. You aspirated a lot of water, and you need to clear it from your lungs. Your risk of pneumonia is real, and it's not something I can treat out here." She squeezes my hand.

"Your ribs will heal in a few months, but it's not gonna be a fun ride. When you're sitting up, I'll make a sling to stabilize your shoulder. You *will* listen to me. You will eat and drink when I tell you. I don't care how stubborn you are, know that I'm even more stubborn. I'm the medical professional here; I know what's best for you. Agonizing over something you couldn't control is not in your best interest. You need to channel that energy into your lungs.

"You see my face and it upsets you. I get it. But I'm all right with it, and I'm going to tell you why." She meets and holds my gaze. "Does it hurt? Yes, it hurts like hell. But you know what? That right hook to my shoulder means your heart's beating. That uppercut to my mouth means your lungs are working. The pain I feel is welcome because it means you are *alive*." The word leaves her lips in a growl. "And *that* is what I would've bargained my fucking soul for."

She points to her face. "This swelling will go down; my lip will heal; the bruises will fade. But if we'd lost you . . ." A tear slides down her cheek. "Ugh. I promised Jake I was finished crying." She quickly wipes it away. "Wes, I don't think you realize this, but you were gone."

"Memphis told me."

"I'll never forget what it felt like to hold your wrist and feel no pulse." She wipes her eyes. "I didn't think I could bring you back," she whispers. "It almost didn't happen."

"I know."

Lena peers into my eyes and strokes her fingers down the side of my face, wiping my tears. "I love you, Wes."

"Lena, I—"

She strokes a finger over my lips. "Hush. I realize it's only been weeks, but I feel like you know me better than I know myself. You listen *and* hear me, not just what I say, but what I keep hidden. No one's ever taken the time to figure me out. You look at me and kiss me like I'm the most beautiful woman in the world," she whispers, swiping at tears. "You ask me questions, not because you have to, but because my answers matter to you. You make me feel like *I* matter to you. I've never had that before." She clenches her jaw. "When you hold me, I feel like I belong in your arms. *You* feel like home to me, and that scares me more than you can imagine. But I had to tell you because I can't hide from you anymore. You need to know how much you're loved. That holds true, not only for me, but for your friends as well. You didn't see the desperation on their faces or the terror we all felt. So, I don't want to hear another goddamn word about it. Understood?"

I stare at her in awe. "Yes."

Beautiful, even in her battered state, she's a force to be reckoned with. I owe my life to her.

And this goddess loves me.

I open my mouth to speak but close it as the tent zipper is yanked open and Austin pops his head in.

"What did I miss?"

"Memphis, you have shitty timing."

"Sorry." He hands Lena a canteen.

She places a hand behind my neck, gently lifting my head. "Drink."

I swallow a generous sip.

"You warm enough?" she asks.

"Yeah."

"How about your feet, ankles, and legs? Any pain there?"

"No. They just feel like lead."

"Okay, I'm going to palpate your belly to feel for swelling in your organs." She unzips the sleeping bag and gently presses on my abdomen, her hand feathering over my surgical scar. "Does that hurt?"

"No."

"Good. How about your right arm and shoulder? Lift it and bend at the elbow. Other than general fatigue, does anything feel off?"

"No."

"Moving to your left side. Obviously, this one's gonna hurt, but I need to check your range of motion. Lift your arm so it's perpendicular to your body."

I obey and wince.

"Move your wrist in circles. Is any part of your hand numb?"

"No."

"Good. Then I didn't pinch any nerves putting your shoulder back in. Now, lower your arm and stretch it out to the side. Does anything click in your shoulder?"

"No."

"Okay, moving to your ribs. On a scale of one to ten, with ten being the worst, rate your pain."

"Twenty-three," I groan.

"I'm sorry, but I need to check them. I wish I could give you something. I'll be as gentle as possible." Rubbing her hands to warm them, she places them on my bruised skin. Starting at my collarbone, she works her way down, sliding her fingers along the length of each rib. I flinch and grit my teeth when she's midway down my rib cage. She completes her examination, fixes the blanket, and zips the sleeping bag.

"I think you have four broken ribs. I can't tell for certain without an x-ray, but going by feel alone, that's my estimate. I felt one break when I was doing chest compressions. Sorry." She smirks. "I break your bones; you punch me in the face. Guess we're even."

"Not funny, love."

"Wasn't meant to be, Ace. Do you want to try and sit up? Austin can help you."

"Yeah, man, anything you need, I'm here," Austin says.

"Not yet," I gasp. "I need to lie here for a bit."

"That's fine. We'll work on that tomorrow. You must have one helluva pain tolerance. I've seen people in agony with two rib fractures."

"The agony's there, just trying to keep my manly image for you. Wanna curl into a ball and cry. Feels like I'm being stabbed."

"No acting with me." She runs her fingers through my hair. "Let your shoulders relax into the ground and draw the breath from your belly. Pull it from a place deeper inside than your lungs." She places a gentle hand on my abdomen. "You need to eat something. Jake cooked Austin's rabbit."

"Don't have the energy to chew," I grunt.

"Like I said, I'm not opposed to force-feeding you. Don't think I won't pre-chew your food like a mama bird."

I chuckle and clutch my side. "Don't make me laugh. It hurts."

"I'll be back in a few minutes. And you *will* eat." Lena waves her finger at me and leaves the tent.

"She'll definitely force-feed you," Austin says.

"Yeah, I know she will."

"Come to think of it, there's little she wouldn't do for you."

"I know."

"Do you?"

I meet Austin's gaze. "Yes, I do."

"I sure hope so, man. You should've seen her. I've never seen anything like it."

Lena returns after a few minutes with a generous portion of rabbit meat and a canteen full of fresh water. She kneels beside me and hands me a chunk of meat. "You have two choices. We can do it the easy way or the hard way, which do you prefer?"

Without breaking eye contact, I accept the rabbit and take a large bite.

"That's what I thought," she says smugly. "I'm not trying to give you a hard time." She folds a blanket and positions it beneath my elbow.

"I know, sunshine." I grip her hand and gently squeeze it. "Thank you." I sip from the canteen and finish the rest of the meat.

LENA

I doze intermittently throughout the night. I wake, check Wes's breathing, and then fade back under. My mind keeps me just beneath the surface of wakefulness, in the crossroads of dreams and rational thought.

At some point, my worries take over and sleep becomes impossible. While the men doze, my fingertips memorize every contour of Wes's body. As I trace them along the scar from his surgery, my inner nurse takes over. I flick on the lantern to make sure blood hasn't soaked through the bandage on his head wound. Thankfully, the bleeding is under control, so I spend a few minutes just watching him sleep. Every line, every freckle, and every hair imprint in my mind. He looks much younger in his slumber, especially in the way his lashes rest on his cheeks and his plush lips are slightly parted.

Without the intensity of those gorgeous eyes, he almost seems innocent. I imagine what he looked like as a child. Probably blonder with sparkling blue eyes and tanned skin. I envision him learning to surf with his father, laughing and splashing in the waves.

I love kids, especially babies, though I haven't held one since my friend Rita's twins were born a few years ago. I love their smell, their softness, and their innocence. Nothing gives me more joy than the sound of a baby's laughter. I ache for a child of my own, a little being to nurture and love unconditionally. I decided to give it another five years—either it will happen on its own or I'll adopt. One way or another, I'll make my dream of motherhood a reality.

Wes said he loves kids. I wonder if he wants children and what kind of father he'd be. Would he be present? Would he be loving, playful, encouraging—all the things my father wasn't? Would he be there for his children, to pick them up when they fell, to wipe their tears and tell them it would be all right? Would he be there, cheering them on, celebrating their accomplishments, and accepting them for who they were, not who he wanted them to be?

Deep down, I know he'd be all those things. And deep down, I dare to envision myself sharing a life with him, raising children, and growing old together. I cling to that flicker of hope as I drift off to sleep.

CHAPTER 57

WES

Internal playlist: *STATIC*

I'm suffocating.

I need to cough but can't fill my lungs. I try to roll onto my side, but excruciating pain blooms in my shoulder. Unable to move or catch my breath, I clutch the sleeping bag in panic.

Lena sits up. "What's the matter?" She hovers near my face. "Talk to me."

"Can't . . . breathe," I gasp, my lungs gurgling.

"I'm gonna help you sit up. You have to cough for me."

The pain in my ribs is so intense, I can't lift myself. Lena struggles to help me and nudges Austin, who scoots from his sleeping bag to assist. Jake stirs and props someone's pack behind me.

Lena hands me a folded-up parka. "Hold this against your chest and try to cough. Hug it like a pillow and use the counter-pressure to help you."

Lena and Austin brace me as I cough—deep, wet, and gurgling. Beads of sweat coat my brow with the effort, and I feel lightheaded from the pain.

"Keep going as much as you can tolerate," she coaxes. "I know it hurts, but you have to get the fluid out."

"I can't," I groan through a clenched jaw.

Lena turns my chin, forcing me to meet her gaze. I focus on her and everything around me blurs. All I can see is the frosted emerald of her eyes. Like a beacon in the fog, drawing me to shore. "Wes, you have to."

Her voice washes over me in a soothing wave. "You can do this, honey." She helps press the parka to my chest, and I struggle through a few more coughs. "Okay, take a break now." She addresses Austin and Jake, "New plan. He can't lie flat on his back anymore." She rubs my back. "Every hour you're gonna try to cough. I don't like how your lungs sound."

I nod. I can breathe better sitting up, and as much as it hurt, the coughing helped marginally. I've never felt so helpless in my life. No amount of physical training could've prepared me for this. Reduced to a limp lump of meat, I don't know how I'll survive the agony. Every breath is a knife to my chest. My back. My sides. Each moment feels like an hour.

"I can't take it . . ." I gasp, strangled by the agony.

How many times can I be stabbed before I die from the pain?

CHAPTER 58

LENA

Internal playlist: "Remedy" by Adele

I kneel by the river, splashing water on my face. Five agonizing days have passed since Wes's ordeal. Pneumonia is imminent. I developed a routine for his recovery, which includes scheduled cough sessions. While his shoulder hurts, the excruciating rib pain is worse. Nothing could've prepared me to watch him suffer.

I glance over my shoulder. Wes stands outside the tent.

"Um, excuse me, but did I give you the all-clear to walk around on your own?" I climb to my feet. "Pretty sure I said to wait until after I looked you over."

"Can't lie there like a slab of rotting meat. I'm going crazy."

"Honey, you're the world's sexiest slab of rotting meat."

"Must be your head injury talking."

"Someone's grumpy." I twist my hair into a bun. "Good thing I know how to handle it."

Wes wears a blanket like a cape, pulling it tightly around him. "Could someone please help me with a shirt?"

"Sure, man." Austin hops to his feet and heads for the tent.

"Had a different someone in mind," he mutters under his breath.

Austin returns a few minutes later with a flannel and hands it to Wes. "I can't find any of yours. This one's mine, it should fit you."

"Thanks." Wes attempts to put it on.

"Oh, shit, man. I'm sorry. When you said help me with a shirt, you meant put it on you. My bad. I'm not awake yet." Austin shakes his head and helps guide Wes's arms into the sleeves. He pulls it up over his shoulders and furrows his brow. "It's a little snug in the arms. Want me to look for a different one?"

"No, this is fine. Thanks, mate."

"No problem. Just don't flex and rip the seams open," Austin teases.

"I can hardly lift my arm. There won't be any flexing."

"Gimme a minute and I'll make you a sling," I call out. "Where are those scarves I washed yesterday?"

Jake points. "On that branch over there, Lena-Bean."

I retrieve a dry scarf and approach Wes. "Take off your belt."

He hesitates, glancing to where his friends are seated. "Here?"

"I'm not trying to get into your pants, I need it for the sling."

"Oh." He removes his belt and hands it over. "Hopefully, my pants don't fall off."

"Yes, that would be a shame, wouldn't it?" I loop the scarf over his shoulder. I brace his arm and tie the scarf, using the belt for added stability.

Once the sling is in place, we join the others by the fire. Jake cooked some fish. Wes watches me intently as I eat.

Thinking of my bruised face, I suddenly feel shy. *I still can't believe I told him I love him. I wonder what he would've said if Austin hadn't interrupted us.*

I tense and study my hands. We've been alone since then—he's had multiple opportunities to tell me how he feels. I know he cares for me, but maybe it doesn't go as deep as love. If that's the case, it's better he didn't say it back. I'd rather have silence than empty words.

The hairs on the back of my neck stand on end and I freeze.

What was that sound?

Something high-pitched echoes in the distance. I look at the others. No one seems to have noticed anything.

There it is again.

I slowly climb to my feet, scanning the forest.

"What's up, Lena?" Austin asks.

"Thought I heard something." I crane my neck and listen. The high-pitched sound comes again, followed by a different sound. "You guys don't hear that?"

"Hear what?" Wes asks.

"It sounds like . . ." I hear it once more and my blood runs cold. "Wolves."

The men lurch to their feet. Jake gathers our walking stick clubs. The sound comes again—we all hear it this time. Austin retrieves the ax and distributes everyone's knives.

I clutch my knife in one hand and the stick in the other. I stand close to Wes. If we're going to be mauled by a pack of wolves, I'll protect him with my life.

We hear the high-pitched sound again.

They're coming closer.

My heart races and my stomach twists into sickening knots. I know I promised Wes I wouldn't be a martyr, but I lied. If his life is at stake, I'll throw myself to the wolves without hesitation. If this is the end for us, I want my final moments to happen by his side.

"Austin, Jake, I need you guys to do something for me," Wes says calmly.

"What do you need?" Jake asks.

"Take Lena and run. Get her to safety. I don't have the strength to fight off wolves either way, and I'd rather die knowing you're all safe."

Austin rounds on him. "Shut the fuck up, Wes! Not a chance in hell!" His voice is a snarl unlike anything I've heard from him.

Jake shakes his head. "We're staying with you."

"I won't leave you." I slide my arm around his waist. "Remember what you said in the tent at the summit? Whether we live or die, we stick together. I nearly lost you once; I won't go through it again."

Wes cups my face and stares deep into my eyes. "Lena, I want you to know that I love you too." He kisses my battered lips and murmurs, "More than words, love."

CHAPTER 59

LENA

Internal playlist: "I Won't Give Up" by Jason Mraz

The wolves are even closer now. Close enough that I can tell there are several.

But somehow, they sound . . . different. *What the hell's that weird, high-pitched sound?* I think I hear something else, too, like a shout. I look up at Wes. *He heard it too.*

"Guys," I say cautiously, "I don't think those are wolves."

We hold our breath and wait for the next sound to reach our ears. A stretch of silence. And then, there it is. A long, high-pitched whistle followed by a shout in the distance.

"Someone's blowing a whistle. Those aren't wolves, they're dogs." I clutch Wes's arm. "We're being rescued!"

"Oh my God." Jake cups his hands to his mouth and shouts, "Help! We're by the river!"

The other people call out to us, telling us to stay put.

WES

I don't have the lung power to yell. I suddenly don't have the energy to stand, either. Overcome with relief, I sink to a nearby log. I don't even know how long we've been lost, but it's finally over.

We're being rescued.

I watch as Austin, Jake, and Lena coalesce into a group embrace. Jake wraps her in his arms, lifts, and spins her around like they're a pair of Olympic figure skaters. I want it to be me. I want to clutch her precious body to my chest and rejoice with her, but I can't even summon the strength to speak.

I turn my head in the direction of the barking dogs and watch as a team of six uniformed men crest the hill. Eight dogs charge forward with their tails wagging excitedly. As the animals burst into the clearing, Lena sinks to her knees. I watch the tears of joy slide down her cheeks as my vision blurs with tears. A gorgeous russet husky excitedly licks her face. Peals of laughter ring out as she wraps her arms around the dog and kisses his snout. Jake and Austin pet the dogs and shake the hands of the men who introduce themselves as state troopers and fish and game officers.

Lena makes her way over to me. She grips my face and passionately kisses me before turning her attention to the troopers.

A black and white husky with one blue eye and one brown eye bounds over and rests its snout on my knee. I stroke the dog's head and shake the paw he offers.

"I see you've met Jaxson." A kind-faced man smiles at me. "You're Wes Emerson?"

"Yeah."

The man extends his hand. "Brendan Grady, Alaska Fish and Game." We shake hands and he continues, "How badly are you injured?"

"Got a few broken ribs and a dislocated shoulder." I nod to Lena. "She fixed the shoulder, but thinks I'm getting pneumonia."

"Hey, Dan, we're gonna need a team of medics down here," Officer Grady calls out to another man, who appears to be in charge.

The one in charge approaches, introduces himself, and withdraws his satellite phone. "Trooper Dan Mayfield here. We've located all four missing persons and they are alive and well. I repeat, the missing parties have been located. I need a medical team here for extraction as multiple injuries have been sustained." He gives the coordinates and returns the phone to his pocket.

Another fish and game officer approaches and hands me a bottle of water, several granola bars, and a baggie of caribou jerky. Clenching the baggie with shaking hands, I thank him and devour the snacks.

Trooper Mayfield addresses Lena, "Ms. Hamilton, how did you sustain your facial injuries?"

"I hit my face on a rock when I tried to run," she lies. "Wes fell in the river and I wanted to get to him. I wasn't paying attention to my footing."

Trooper Mayfield nods and scrawls in his notepad. Lena makes eye contact with me and flashes a look of warning.

Why'd she lie? She must have her reasons. I subtly nod and keep my mouth shut.

God, I love her. I grit my teeth against a surge of emotion. No, I more than love her, I cherish her, adore her. My sun rises and sets with her smile. Her eyes outshine the stars, and her heart brings me to my knees. I ache to crush Lena's body to mine and pour my heart and soul into her. I can't believe we're finally being rescued.

"Anyone else injured?" Trooper Mayfield asks her. "Why did we find a pair of your bloodied jeans? Were you attacked by a grizzly?"

"No. He came after us, but we climbed a tree. I ripped my leg open on a branch when I tried to climb it," she explains.

"Smart move leaving them behind. Gave the dogs something to work with other than your clean clothes from the resort."

"I honestly didn't even think about it. We were in such a rush to get out of there before the bear came back. I just threw a different pair on and left them. It didn't make sense to bring them," she explains between bites of jerky. "Hey, what the hell happened to Chuck? Why didn't he come for us?"

"Charles MacGregor is deceased. It seems he went into cardiac arrest after leaving you. We located the plane some ninety miles southwest of here," Trooper Mayfield answers.

"How the hell did you find us?" Jake asks.

"It wasn't easy. We received a call from Ellen at Aurora Borealis when you didn't return as scheduled. Upon contacting the flight company, we discovered the plane and pilot were missing as well, which they'd failed to report. We checked in with the staff at Gobbler's Knob who told us you never arrived, so we did a search of the vicinity and came up empty. The flight company informed us this particular pilot often changed flight plans. We broadened our search and brought in more teams." Trooper Mayfield shakes his head. "It's a miracle we found you. And even more amazing that you survived out here for nearly three weeks. We partnered with the NYPD to gather information about Ms. Hamilton and Mr. Bennett to find some clue as to where you may have been rerouted. Something Ms. Hamilton's boyfriend said about wildlife photography made us expand our search to wildlife refuges and preserves."

"He's my best friend, not my boyfriend," Lena interjects.

"He's been completely torn apart by your disappearance. I assumed you were together. I suggest you contact him once we reach the clinic."

"I will."

"Thanks to Mr. Casey's input and information from the flight company, we redirected our search efforts. Trooper Mulaney and I spotted your orange tent when flying south along the John River." He points to the officer that just handed over Austin's beloved guitar. Austin's grin stretches ear to ear as he thanks the man and caresses the water-damaged instrument. "We found your jeans and the guitar and called in reinforcements. You guys covered a lot of ground. We had to hustle to catch up."

"We stayed in this location for a few days so Wes could recuperate," Jake explains. "Lena saved his life. This woman's a hero."

"I had help," Lena says. "They pulled him from the river and helped move him. I didn't do it all alone. But I'm very concerned about him. He aspirated a lot of water and is in tremendous pain. I'm worried he's developing pneumonia."

"All of you will get checked out when we head up to Anaktuvuk Pass. There's a health facility there," Trooper Mayfield tells us.

Lena walks over and settles beside me. I stare into the forest, distractedly stroking Jaxson's ears.

"You all right?" she murmurs.

"I can't believe we're finally being rescued. I honestly thought I'd die out here." I look into her eyes, trailing my fingertips along her jaw. "I love you, Lena."

She leans in and kisses me. "I love you too, Wes," she whispers. "With all my heart."

I crane my neck at the hum of an approaching helicopter. Shielding my eyes with a hand, I squint through the clouds in the direction of the whirring rotors. The dark speck gradually increases in size and volume until it hovers overhead. The troopers shout instructions as the medics aboard the chopper send down a stretcher, followed by a swaying rope ladder.

"I can climb, you know," I insist.

Lena cocks a brow. "Journey's not over, Ace. You'll do what's best for you, remember?"

"Of course, love." I smile, touching my fingertips to her lips. "At least we're out of the woods."

The breeze picks up and gusts through my hair, burning my cheeks and stinging my eyes. As the wind whistles through the pines, I swear I hear it whisper, "*Wilderness can take on many forms.*"

The journey continues . . . Stay tuned for *NORTH STAR*

PLAYLIST FOR TRUE NORTH

"Citizen of the Planet" by Alanis Morissette

"Drumming Song" by Florence + The Machine

"Shoop" by Salt N Pepa

"Roar" by Katy Perry

"Fall in Line" by Christina Aguilera

"I Still Haven't Found What I'm Looking For" by U2

"Eyes on Fire" by Blue Foundation

"Something Just Like This" by The Chainsmokers & Coldplay

"The First Taste" by Fiona Apple

"Shelter" by Ray LaMontagne

"Utopia" by Alanis Morissette

"Castle" by Halsey

"Close" by Nick Jonas

"Howl" by Florence + The Machine

"In Your Eyes" by Jeffrey Gaines

"Remind Me" by Emily King

"There's Nothing Holdin' Me Back" by Shawn Mendes

"Starstruck" by Lady GaGa

"Tunnel Vision" by Justin Timberlake

"You and Me" by Lifehouse

"Kiss Me" by Ed Sheeran

"Come Here Boy" by Imogen Heap

"Collide" by Howie Day

"Breath of Life" by Florence + The Machine

"Rock Your Body" by Justin Timberlake

"River" by Bishop Briggs

"Blow" by Ed Sheeran

"The Warmth" by Incubus

"Head Above Water" by Avril Lavigne

"One and Only" by Adele

"I Want You" by Third Eye Blind

"Earned It" by The Weeknd

"God Is A Woman" by Ariana Grande

"Let It Be Me" by Ray LaMontagne

"Immigrant Song" by Led Zeppelin

"We Can Make Love" by SoMo

"More of You" by Josh Groban

"Weight of the World" by Evanescence

"Heavy in Your Arms" by Florence + The Machine

"Lost" by Dermot Kennedy

"Making Love on the Mountain (Sexy Mix)" by The Woodlands

"Meaning of Life" by Kelly Clarkson

"Power Over Me" by Dermot Kennedy

"Remedy" by Adele

"I Won't Give Up" by Jason Mraz

Thanks so much for reading my words! It means the world to me. If you enjoyed True North, please leave me a review.
Up next: *North Star*

Website: www.ariawyatt.com

Facebook: www.facebook.com/AriaWyattAuthor

Join my readers' group on Facebook: Aria Wyatt's Speakeasy

Instagram: www.instagram.com/ariawyatt_author

TikTok: www.tiktok.com/@ariawyattauthor

Twitter: www.twitter.com/AriaWyattAuthor

OTHER BOOKS

Compass Series:
True North
North Star
Horizon
Symphony (forthcoming)
Title TBD (forthcoming)

Busy Bean Standalone:
Afterglow

Prodigy Series
Masquerade
Prodigy (forthcoming)
Supernova (forthcoming)

CHAPTER 1

LENA HAMILTON

Internal playlist: "Awake" by Josh Groban

I press my forehead to the cool window of the hovering chopper. The swaying rope ladder was a bitch to climb, but I made it. On the tundra beneath me, Alaska State Troopers strap the man I love to a stretcher. Broken, battered, and on the fast-track to pneumonia, Wes Emerson is lucky to be alive. We *all* are.

Alaska's Far North, with its raw beauty and untouched wilderness, was a brutal hostess. For three weeks, Mother Nature walloped us with unforgiving terrain, harsh elements, and deadly predators, but—by some miracle—we survived.

I glance at Wes's two best friends. Austin Pines is leaning against his headrest with his eyes closed, lashes resting on tear-stained cheeks. He clutches the edge of his seat as his lips move in a silent prayer. Beside him, a windblown Jake Bennett stares out a different window. With his gaze riveted to the scene below, he gnaws a hunk of caribou jerky, chewing in the way a distracted llama might.

The troopers signal to the medics on board.

"Okay, let's get him up here," a stocky, redhaired man says, gesturing to another medic. "He's got broken ribs, so we need to take it slow and steady."

"Please don't drop him," I blurt.

"Don't worry, Ms. Hamilton, we won't."

At six foot five, Wes is a mountain of chiseled muscle, and I know damn well how hard it is to move him. I hold my breath as the pair uses a rope harness to hoist the stretcher into the chopper. After what feels like an hour, it clears the entrance, and the medics close the door.

Wes grins. "I could've climbed the ladder, ya know."

I roll my eyes. "Now's not the time for your tough-guy act."

"It's not an act."

He's right—it's not an act. "Tough-guy" doesn't scratch the surface of his strength and will to live. Even the god of war, Wes's most renowned role, would've accepted defeat when thrown against jagged rocks and dragged beneath the John River's icy rapids. I still can't fathom how he endured the trauma. It wasn't Ares who survived—it was Wes. The *real* man who breached the walls I'd built around my heart.

Wes juts his chin at Austin. "Memphis, you all right, mate? You look like you're at a funeral."

"I'm still tryin' to wrap my mind 'round it, that's all." Austin slowly shakes his head. "I thought we were gonna die out there . . ."

Jake pats Austin's shoulder. "Me too, man."

The rotor blades spin faster, and the chopper lifts. Lost in the helicopter's deafening drone, I watch as the troopers shrink beneath us. The medics tend to Wes as the pilot flies north to Anaktuvuk Pass, a remote village in the Gates of the Arctic National Park.

I relax my head against the headrest and take a slow, deep breath. *It's over.* We've finally been rescued, but that doesn't mask the desolate feeling that grips my chest. These men have become my friends. Correction, they are like *family.* But now, our tight foursome will soon be split up. One question has been circling my mind since our rescuers found us.

What will happen with Wes and me?

The Anaktuvuk Pass hospital is a one-story building—much smaller than the emergency department in New York General, where I work as a trauma nurse. Jake, Austin, and I disembark on the hospital's helipad. A blonde nurse waits with a gurney for Wes, and I peek at her name badge. Grace. A fitting moniker for the circumstances. If the doctor's name is Faith or Hope, I'm going back to church.

The medics transfer Wes from the stretcher onto the gurney and help wheel him in.

Grace touches my shoulder. "Don't worry, we'll take good care of him."

I nod my thanks and follow the group inside. It's a sterile, yet cozy facility. A handsome doctor is speaking with Wes in the hallway. He smiles and nods as I pass.

"That's Dr. Jacobs, he runs this facility," Grace explains. "He'll see you soon. So, as you can see, Ms. Hamilton, we're a small facility. We service the Anaktuvuk Pass community and the occasional traveler who passes through. We have only three inpatient rooms, one of which is occupied. We'll need to room you with one of your companions. Do you have a preference?"

"Please put me with Wes." That's a given. He's the embodiment of certainty. Shelter and safety. He's my harbor. My haven. Ironically though, our future together is the most uncertain part of my life.

"We can do that. On the right is the ladies' room. I'm sure you'd like to get out of your dirty clothes and have a nice hot shower."

"Oh, God, yes!" After nearly three weeks in the wilderness, a shower is more enticing than a winning lottery ticket. Even though we all took daily bird baths in fire-heated river water, I've never felt more repulsive.

"I laid out a hospital gown, slippers, and toiletries. Toss your dirty clothes in the bin and we'll wash everything for you. There are extra towels in the closet, along with lotion, disposable razors, and a blow-dryer if you're interested. You get freshened up while I deal with your friends."

"Excellent, thanks."

"You're so welcome, honey. After you get cleaned up, we'll work on getting everyone fed. Fortunately for you kids, we just had a supply delivery this morning, so we have fresh fruit and veggies to offer you." Grace smiles warmly.

I quickly latch the door, strip out of my filthy clothes, and toss them into the labeled bin. As I pass in front of a full-length mirror, I freeze at the sight of my battered face. My lower lip is lacerated and swollen like I'd undergone a botched lip-filler procedure. There is also extensive bruising on my cheek and forehead. Sections of my caramel-colored hair are matted to my scalp with dried blood, and the rest of it's a filthy, stringy mess. While I still have my hourglass-shaped figure, my breasts are smaller and my hips and thighs have slimmed down. I've always been soft around the middle, but even that's flatter. I can't wipe the shocked look from my face at my transformation.

I grab some toiletries, turn on the faucet, and step inside.

I close my eyes and lean into the powerful stream of hot water. As it flows through my hair, saturating my skin and cascading down my body, I decide this is the most luxurious moment of my entire life. While I lather my body, the heat and steam relax my tired, achy muscles and melt away the tension that accumulated during the recent, merciless weeks. I shampoo my hair, my head falling forward as I rinse. Like a butterfly bursting free from her chrysalis, my metamorphosis from dirty to clean feels soul deep.

Through the thick steam, I watch as blood-tinged water flows down my legs before it circles the drain. The small crimson cyclone funnels down, washing away most of the physical evidence of the ordeal. Too bad the cuts and bruises won't go quietly into the night as well. I condition my hair and loosen any remaining knots and tangles, then get down to business with the razor.

Once satisfied, I dry off and dress in a hospital gown. I stare at my reflection as I floss and brush my teeth.

I'm a new woman—and not just physically. My impromptu Alaskan odyssey was supposed to be an escape from the chaos of New York, or, more importantly, a reprieve from my stressful job at the hospital. And, in some ways, it was. But the universe had other plans when my treacherous journey to self-discovery culminated with falling in love.

I don't wear my heart on my sleeve for a reason. My history has proven that love is a fusion of bliss and uncertainty. As someone who operates on the anxious end of the spectrum, my mind is quick to bolster my fears and give life to my insecurities, all while trivializing any reassurances. It's something I've been working on for years, but no matter what I do, I can't seem to get a handle on it. The unknown is my nemesis. If there's one thing I know beyond a shadow of a doubt, it's that I don't know shit about shit.

I slide on the hospital-issued slippers before exiting into the hallway. Grace stands outside a patient room and waves me over. "Feel better?"

"There aren't even words."

"Good thing, since I'm pretty sure ya used up all the water north of the Arctic Circle," Wes calls from inside the room.

"Quiet, you." I wave him off and turn to Grace. "Where do you want me?"

"In here with Mr. Emerson, honey." She motions to the empty bed closest to the window.

His gaze sparkling, a lounging Wes sips from a glass of cranberry juice. He flashes his megawatt smile—the one that makes my knees weak every time. "G'day, roomie."

"Howdy, Ace." I kiss his cheek before flopping onto my bed. "Oh my God, a mattress." My head instantly sinks into the soft comfort of a pillow.

Wes gestures to my hospital gown. "Cute dress."

"Thanks. I scored the modeling contract with my greasy-haired, un-fed appearance."

He snorts. "I'm not allowed to shower until they check out the gash on my noggin, so you're stuck with a smelly Aussie."

"Spent the past few weeks in a tent with you. I think I'll survive." I point to the phone on our shared nightstand. "Did you call your family?"

"Yeah. I spoke with Mum, Dad, and Isla. I forgot about the time difference and woke them up—Melbourne's like twenty hours ahead."

"I think hearing you are alive is an acceptable trade-off for sleep, wouldn't you agree?"

ABOUT THE AUTHOR

Aria Wyatt is a pharmacist mom who spends the inhumane predawn hours with a cup of coffee and her laptop, gleefully indulging in her passion for romance. Her novels range in heat from steamy to scorching, and she doesn't shy away from writing flawed characters with real life issues.

She resides with her husband and two children in New York's picturesque Hudson Valley, near the Catskills and iconic Woodstock. The avid reader balances marriage, motherhood, her pharmacist career, and her romance author dream. When not writing, she dabbles in photography, using the natural beauty of the region to her advantage. She's a self-proclaimed cat lady who cannot live without coffee, chocolate, music, and books.

Author of True North and the Compass Series, Aria has a soft spot for those who are searching, yearning, and ultimately, finding. Whether on a mission to find themselves, find love, find forgiveness or solace, she believes the answer is out there somewhere.

"Journey to Love."

ACKNOWLEDGEMENTS

True North was my first book—my book baby—and to be perfectly honest, I never imagined I'd be able to write a novel, much less publish one. People always say it takes a village to raise a child, but I've discovered the same goes for writing a book. There are a ton of folks who've supported me along this journey, so bear with me while I attempt to express my gratitude.

First and foremost, **Dana Fisher**, thank you for the proverbial ass-kickery that jump started this. I will never forget your "find your fire" speech. Those are truly words to live by—as are *all* of your "manifest and call it in" monologues. Thanks for listening to countless stories over the years and for encouraging me to bring *True North* to life. Thanks for being my best friend and for asking me to play jump rope way back in first grade. I adore you. Thirty years and counting, baby.

Krista Villielm, thank you for your friendship and for being the first one to read this book in its entirety. Your enthusiasm gave me confidence and your feedback along the way was invaluable. *You* are a treasure.

Amanda Madsen, you are the goddess of blunt and I love you for it. Thanks for being my sounding board and for putting me in my place when I tried to make my characters do dumb shit. You were right, by the way… (about all of it, you biotch!) You're an amazing beta and a cherished friend. *True North* wouldn't be what it is without you.

Dana Kragh-Swingle, as always, thank you for your constructive feedback. You helped me get all my NYC/Brooklyn details straight and your input about the original start of the book was spot-on. You've always been supportive of me and my writing. I adore you, Donna Krog.

Jen Liese, thank you for your cheerleader pep talks. You are one of the kindest, most badass women I've ever met. Thanks for being my friend and believing in me with such ferocity. I love you.

Kevin Nordstrom, thanks for being the first dude to read my book.

Your manly insights are much appreciated. You're a brilliant artist (and screenwriter) and I'm lucky to have you as a friend. We still need to co-author that rom com.

Kristie Wolf, my writing/birthday sister, I am beyond grateful for your friendship. You're a phenomenal author and I'm so happy to have you in my life. You've taught me tons about craft and resilience. Thanks for massacring my darlings (Even though I may have kept a few anyway…) and yelling about passive voice. I love you and feel like I've known you for decades. I can't wait to watch you succeed.

A huge shout-out to my beta-reader author friends: **Cassandra Cripps**, for your invaluable Alaska insight and for letting me be part of *Long Flight Home*. I appreciate your willingness to assist a newbie like me and how thorough your beta-reports are. You rock, lady! **Becca L'Amour**, for the Aussie authenticity crash course to ensure Wes doesn't sound like a bloody yobbo. You always make me laugh and I'm happy to know you. One of these days, I'm coming to see you in Australia. Get ready. (Now, finish that damn book!) **Liz Schille**, for your enthusiasm, feedback, and for helping with all my nurse stuff. Keep writing, lady! And to my fellow Aria, **Aria Peyton**, for giving me that final kick in the ass (arse) to actually do this publishing thing. When I come to Australia, we can make a Becca-Aria sandwich. (Flank her with Arias and such.) Much love to you all!

A shout-out to my editors: Thanks for dealing with my needy, self-doubty neurosis. **Silvia Curry**, I can't thank you enough for convincing me to split *True North* into two books. It was the wisest decision I could've possibly made, and I'm thrilled with how *North Star* turned out. Your comments in my manuscript always make me smile. **Eve Arroyo**, your eagle eye is a blessing, and it's a joy to work with you—even when you get super-picky. I adore your ferocity for my heroines and how indignant you get on their behalf. Thanks for the drama dot lesson and for being so accessible, helpful, and encouraging. I'm so happy we connected.

Thank you to my proofreaders: **My Brother's Editor, Virginia Tesi Carey, Marla Selkow Esposito** at Proofingstyle, Inc., and **Amy Briggs**.

To my cover designer **Lori Jackson**: Thank you for bringing my vision to life!

Wander Aguiar, thanks for being a phenomenal photographer and providing the book world with so many drool-worthy pictures. (And for having **Andrey** on your team, who is an absolute joy to deal with.)

Stacey Blake of Champagne Book Design, thank you for making my book innards so darn pretty. You helped me out of a pickle, and I look forward to many future books together.

To **Linda Russell** and team at Foreword PR & Marketing: Thanks for doing the legwork for the bane-of-my-existence necessity that is marketing. Your guidance, encouragement, and virtual handholding has been a Godsend. Thanks for making me feel like a *real* author and getting me on my feet.

To my unwitting muses: **C, J, and J,** keep doing what you're doing and thanks for the inspiration.

Thanks to my husband and children for being supportive of my dream and for letting me spend all those hours at the computer. I love you more than words could ever express.

Finally, to my readers: I appreciate you from the bottom of my heart. Stay tuned because I have a lot more stories to tell!

Much love,